The Picnic Table

CHRISTOPHER CHAPMAN

ISBN:978-0-9976806-1-4

Printed in the United States of America

Chapter One

I met her that summer at camp, 1990, and the summer before my senior year. She was perfect, and I remembered the smell of her hair the most. It was June. June was a good time of year; only May was better, because it was still early enough in the summer that fall and school seemed like a far off hurricane, of no real immediate threat. I was a little older than most of the others, for someone going into their senior year, I mean I was already eighteen. It's a long story, but the short version was a problem with my inner ear, resulting in me sitting out the third grade.

Not to add boredom, and certainly not to deviate from the subject at hand, but that ear infection was bad…really bad. I don't remember doing a lot of swimming, and never really had any problems with my ear, before or since, but something was weird about that ear infection, I mean, more than just the pain. I think it tried to erase my memory of that year, you know, back when I was eight.

But, let's get back to 1990. It was still early enough in the summer so I wasn't concerned with summer reading and back to school shopping which was especially bad, because that was like being sentenced in court to hard time, but not yet wearing the stripes. The summer was there, for the taking, the sleeping, the swimming; the friends although very limited, in my case to my sister, and her occasional non-lame friend, who was "occasional", let alone "single".

We met in the Keys. It was one of those places where I was sent, begging, to get away from the boredom of summer. It was a pretty cool place in that it was on the tip of a peninsula on one of the islands. You show up after a three hour bus ride from the airport, to this outpost of Quonset huts, little sail boats, concrete buildings, scuba gear hanging on racks to dry, sand, and tanned locals. I was getting life guard certified, which was my justification to my friends back in school to not sound immature and presumptively ivy league by going to a summer camp. Sara was there for the same reason. Although her rationale to her friends back home may have been more along the lines of her mother already having paid for it, and she couldn't get a refund.

Either way, it was an escape from siblings, mothers, and sheer boredom. Back when all I would have been doing at home was trying to sleep as late as I could to make the day pass by quicker, blowing off summer reading or hunting for the Cliff Notes, watching the late morning The Price is Right, reading everything I could on submarines, or "escorting" my younger sister to some stupid party where I knew no one and ended up hanging out with some nerd from her school while she played quarters with the varsity football quarterback.

Down in the land of heat, no air-conditioning, tropical waves, and mosquito control DC-3 flyovers to drop diesel fuel on the local dive bar for bloodsuckers; I liked it. I liked it a lot. Going out on a scuba or snorkel trip in the midmorning, returning in time for lunch, then going over to the "swim canal" for lifeguard training. The girls weren't too bad either, not too bad at all. Especially one.

Chapter Two

Who knows how it happened? It's like knowing what your favorite song is, but not remembering how it became your favorite. Was it that you first heard it on the radio, then you thought it was okay, bought the tape, played it over, rewind, over, rewind, over again? I don't remember how it happened. I think it's that she was not merely "hot", or "sexy", or "flawless", I think it's that she was just plain wonderful. No make-up, no tight jeans, no shirt that says "Bad Girl", just a good looking girl in shorts and a t-shirt.

During lifeguard training, Sara was partnered with another girl, and I was partnered up with this dude, who actually turned out to be pretty cool. He liked Sara's friend, thank god - no competition there. When it was time to pair up into fours, we would tactfully position ourselves to where the girls would be right next to us, thus stacking the deck so that they would say, "Hey, you guys want to pair up with us?"

Are you kidding? We thought we were just good at this maneuvering thing, but in reality it came out around the picnic table a little later on, that Kristen actually liked Will.

The partnering with the other two was for some slightly irrelevant purpose like a relay exercise so that the rescue board wouldn't end up at the opposite end of the swim canal, or something else practical, when; however, the gods' motives were more sinister. Getting to see Sara with no primping, any hairspray or defined attractive wear had its advantages, but either way I didn't care, because she was "it" here and now, at least in my mind at the time.

As the application portion of what we learned in the q-hut that morning meandered on, glances were shared more and more frequently. Was she trying to tell me something with her quick stares, or was I looking at her so much that it was inevitable by sheer probability that she would look my direction while I was looking toward her? I would have given anything, at that minute, to have the ability to read minds.

Late afternoon thunderheads, out over the water on the horizon, gave way to an added boost of energy that lent itself to showing off, which led to laughing, which led to more staring. The four of us were in our own little world, or island in the Keys, sporadically interrupted by the lifeguard instructor gently shouting to switch who pulled whom with the cross-chest carry, or who rescued who with the rescue board.

"Okay, good job for today. We'll meet again in the classroom Wednesday morning for more instruction, then back to the canal for the practical exercises. See you at dinner in an hour." That was our cue, to get our gear and hit the dorms. The two girls started back to the q-hut to get their clothes and various sundry, with me looking for a somehow absent excuse to go with them.

"C'mon dude, let's go get changed," Will encouraged as if he knew what my intentions were, yet didn't want me to know that he shared the same. We headed back to our dorm, which was literally a robust stone's throw away from the girls' dorm.

We arrived at our room to find our six bunks pretty much empty, yet somehow complete with the proper regulator or mask on one or two of the beds waiting for its owner to put them in the big duffel under the bunk, not failing to mention the little electric fans clipped, or fastened inventively, to the rail of each bed to act as personal air conditioners, which were notoriously absent from practically all indoor structures.

Carlos yelled that he was about done with the shower, and I told Will he could go next. He thanked me in the selectively non-mature fashion of a "cool" remark instead of the "Thank you kind sir. You are truly a noble and dear soul who gives up your own timeliness of cleanliness so that my humble crown can be made clean with lather of Awapui." He did remind me, however, that there was an outdoor shower downstairs.

Showering outdoors is somewhat of an art, or more like a skill not practiced nearly enough. Not that one should needlessly practice outdoor showering; it's just that you need to understand that there is a "not-so-wrong" way, and a "really wrong" way to do it. Now, all this assumes that the shower is located in public and not in some secluded bunker somewhere in east Africa on some Legionnaire's base.

The "not-so-wrong" way is being sure to bring legitimate soap. Soap that's manly like Safeguard, Dial and not the white Dial, I'm talking about the yellow stuff, or Irish Spring, but whatever you do, do not under any circumstances, whatsoever, use liquid soap.

Also, one must bring a towel. Now, this is very important; do not bring a really fluffy towel, don't bring a colorful striped one, and don't even think of drying off your epidermis with a towel emblazoned with a dolphin or other aquatic life, an old plain one will do just fine. And, if you can find one with a little corner that's tattered, it adds a nice touch. In addition to the soap and towel routine, remember to keep your bathing suit on.

As previously mentioned, there is a "really wrong" way to take an outdoor shower. Two issues come immediately to mind, and I really wish that they wouldn't. Backtracking, one of the problems with taking an outdoor shower, in the public light, is that you can't clean up into all the nooks and crannies of your body. The detail stops here.

One of the main outdoor shower "no no's" involve shampoo. I'm not talking about the woman shampoo that your mother packed for you, or the woman shampoo that your sister "accidentally left in your suitcase", which is creepy in and of itself, because what the hell was your sister doing in your suitcase, or where were you and your sister going where you needed to share a suitcase to begin with? The best response to why you are using woman shampoo is that you forgot your man-poo at home and that this stuff was the only shampoo at the convenience store in the airport.

When we finally made it to the cafeteria we immediately got in line, which is apparently what everyone else was doing. There were a few people already sitting down, mainly counselors, still glowing from their being kissed by the sun, complete with Hawaiian Tropic fragrance. I passed by the baked chicken, to which I'm not a big fan, but hit the lasagna like an Italian boy coming back home to his mama's table, after playing pickup stickball in the late summer afternoon. Seconds later, Will sat down beside me, sporting the baked chicken.

The tables started filling up, but we really weren't paying too much attention because we were too busy eating and talking about what kind of crappy car we drove when we were home, mine being a white Chevy station wagon bejeweled with fake wood paneling.

A couple of minutes later, the lifeguard-counselor-instructor-guy came over to our table and sat down. He had what amounted to a large ass salad on his tray with a Big Gulp mug full of water. Will and I kept eating, being too embarrassed to initiate any conversation with anyone but ourselves. Just then, the lifeguard guy spoke up, "Hey guys. How'd you like today?"

We both looked up and affirmatively nodded our heads somewhat enthusiastically, with Will responding, "It was pretty cool, we liked it."

"Glad you did. It will only get more fun from here," he encouraged, as if he thought we were just being polite. In reality, we were being polite, but we really did like it.

Afterwards, there were a handful of evening outings planned, but optional nonetheless. One was trolling for plankton, one was a night dive, and the other was taking a quick boat ride across the bay to an isolated island to spot night critters. The night dive sounded cool, but we opted out of that because as Will elegantly put it, "Man, screw that! I don't want to clean all that shit twice in one day!" Fine with me. So, we walked over to the sign up board to check the capacity of the other jaunts. It then hit us, why don't we see which trip the girls signed up for? Perfect idea.

Good thing Will solved the night dive dilemma because it was completely full. So full that people wrote their names on ad hoc lines underneath the ruler assisted ones. Under the night critter spotting trip, three lines remained. The name "Kristen" was one of the names printed in that bubble print that high school girls perfect in middle school.

"Okay, sign up for that 'Aquatic Organism Nightime Trek' quick!" Will said as he grabbed a pen from underneath the night dive roster. But, just as he handed me the pen, we noticed, what seemed like to occur at the same time, that there was another "Kristen" signed up for the plankton troll.

"Bro, what's her last name?" I asked Will quickly but in a subdued manner.

"I don't have any idea...crap!" he answered. There was Kristen Phillips and a Kristen Delfaro.

"Well is she white or Italian?"

"Dude, you saw her, I guess she's white, well wait...Italians are white too! What the hell kind of question is that?" he said as he went from being frustrated to laughing.

"Hold up, what's your chick's name?" Will said as he retrieved the pen, like he just discovered the cure for cancer.

"Uhh, I don't think she...I don't remember..." I didn't know it at the time.

"What's wrong with you? You're a fool, you piece of shit!" We were both laughing.

"Okay, does she look more like a Francie Schmitt, or a Patty Clewellen?" He analyzed the important documents.

"Uh, I don't...are those the only choices?" I hoped neither was she, but those were the names listed directly before and after Kristen Phillips on the night time creepy crawly tour.

"Wait. Here...what about...Sara Ellen Wilson?" That's gotta be it, if not, I guess Francie or Patty isn't too bad. Will and I both gave each other the affirmative nod blended with a shrug. He signed both our names on the "plankton troll" sheet.

We headed over to the dock near where the dive boats were waiting empty. The sun was on its way out, but had about an hour left. Sitting on the edge of the dock with our feet dangling over the water, I thought of how much cooler it would be if I was sitting there alone with Sara Ellen Wilson, and not Will. Anyway, the view was amazing nonetheless, especially with the addition of the cliché-esqe sound of the lines tapping against the masts of the anchored sailboats.

People started gathering around various boats awaiting departure to exotic and not too distant ports of call. It was easy to know which boats were not ours, due to the excessive amount of neoprene and flippers on two of them. The other two were a little harder to figure out, until one of the counselors shouted out, "Last call for the isle de mosquito and horse shoe crabs." That left just one boat. So, with confidence we walked over to the remaining 28 foot tri-hulled vessel.

Well, we knew Will had picked the right trip when we saw Kristen, the right Kristen, yet still Italian, sitting next to Sara Ellen Wilson. Jackpot. We were also surprised to find only four other people onboard, and sat down directly across from the two girls. Right then, as if on cue… "Hey, Will!" Kristen noticed right away. The two got up, led slightly by Kristen and sat down on the same row as us. Kristen sat next to Will, and Sara sat on the other side of Kristen. I was kind of hoping that Sara would have sat next to me, but that's wishful thinking especially given the fact that with Will to my left, the only thing to my right was a fuel tank and no more bench. Oh well, maybe I'll plan out where to sit better next time.

The boat exited the harbor and made a wide sweeping turn left, to the south. The sun now had about thirty minutes left in its reign over today, and was bouncing a beautiful red orange glow off the thin clouds toward the west. The sea was calm, but we were still in the somewhat protected waters of a larger bay. The steady drone of the twin Mercury outboards and the slight smell of salt, gas and Coppertone somehow made the perfect backdrop for what, in theory, could be my greatest accomplishment; getting up and going to sit next to Sara. But not yet, I need to give it some time, and about five minutes should be enough for me to either muster the strength or chicken out.

Will and Kristen had now moved on to talking about their favorite television shows, and my five minutes were up, and so as promised, I stood up, walked past Will, Kristen, then Sara. "Hey, where ya goin'?" Sara smiled.

"Right over here." Pointing at the empty seat next to her.

"What were ya waiting for? Kristen to move?" She paused, but was giggling now. "They're in love, don't you know?" Stating as if the whole world knew it, but obviously being sarcastic.

"Yeah, Will, can we come to the wedding?" I added, but neither Kristen nor Will were paying us much attention

"Your name's Sara, right?" I said, but then thought about it after I spoke, that it could backfire, because if she did already tell me her name, then I forgot. However, if she had not told me her name, and now I knew it, she might think that's a little weird.

"Yup, it's actually Sara Ellen, though," she said with a genuine beam, smiling with her blue-green eyes.

"Oh…okay." I've never known anyone with that kind of southern double name thingy. I mean, I have heard of Mary Ann from Gilligan, but haven't actually met anyone like that.

We talked for a good while, mostly feeding off Will and Kristen's conversation, being sporadically interrupted by one of the counselors reeling in the trolling net to see what plankton were caught, lecture about the bio-luminescence and then talk about releasing and resetting the net. As she talked, she had a fascinating southern drawl, which I guess matches her being from Texas. Time was flying though, bummer.

It grew dark, and as we headed back into the bay from the open water, we gazed at the dock and anchor lights off in the distance, with the occasional boat heading past us to another harbor. It was not an unordinary sight, but a sight that I rarely got to see.

"That would be a great view to see every night from a back porch," she said as if she had just read my mind.

"Yeah, it's pretty cool. I wonder what those people are doing that live at all those lights?" I replied as she pulled her dirty blonde hair over to one side so that she could better see me, without stray strands brushing her eyelids. I always liked to imagine where people were going when they loaded up their car, getting gas before heading out of town, or when there was a couple at a restaurant, where they were from, or what they were talking about. Or, more interesting, where their flight was heading, as it left the airport.

"I don't know, but I'd be having a cook-out every night."

"Would you let me come to your cook-out?" I acted like I was playing along with her cook-out idea, but I thought this might be a good opportunity to find out if she actually liked me…like her answer was going to be any indication.

"Depends…"

"On what?"

"On what you were doing that night?"

"What if I wanted to come to your cook-out, but I needed a formal calligraphy handwritten invitation?" I was smiling, and so was she.

"Then I'd write you one, but use mustard to sign my name." She was giggling.

"You'd better use catsup, because if you use mustard, you won't be able to get the yellow from under your fingernails."

"Okay, if I use catsup, will you come to my cookout?" Are you kidding me?

"I just don't know... could I wear a speedo?" I was just being stupid, but she was laughing, so all was good.

"Yeah, as long as you wear clothes over it, and I don't actually have to see the speedo, or even know that you are wearing one!"

"Well, lucky for you I don't have a speedo. And lucky for me I would get to come to your cookout."

"That's right, you will be my special guest!" I liked where it was going.

"What's that mean?"

"You know, you get to stay after the cookout and help me clean up. Then, we'll go out on the dock and look out at all the lights, and remember that we talked about all this on a boat in the Keys." She stopped laughing, but was still smiling. She was pretty cool, I mean, no girl that I've met had been able to go full circle in a story, made up or otherwise.

We talked, and laughed some more. We talked about school, crappy teachers, crappy homework, a little bit about our mothers, not a whole lot about fathers, siblings, pets, and so on. I didn't care at all what it was about, as long as we were talking. She had a younger sister, so did I. She had good grades, I didn't.

The boat began its turn into the harbor. Why did this trip have to end? Well, we had about three more weeks to go. I don't know where this would all end up, but I liked the way it was going. I liked her.

It was time to depart our plankton cruiser, so everyone started gathering his or her belongings, towels, small bags, etc. Sara and I were toward the middle of the boat, and when our turn came, we got up and hopped off.

We were back at the dorms, standing right next to the picnic tables. Will and Kristen started saying their goodnights, while Sara and I briefly stared at each other. "Well, I'll see you tomorrow," I said making sure I added a small decimal point of grief in my voice.

"Okay, see ya tomorrow." She stared at me, while catching the hint that I was dropping.

I thought about her, just a bit, which wasn't a bad thing. She was only in a building thirty yards away, and it was nice knowing that she and Kristen were close. I then hoped I'd dream about something cool, but you know how that goes because when you try to dream about something it ends up being the furthest thing from what you actually dream about.

In my case, as realized early the next morning that instead of dreaming about my intended topics, it was instead about being back in elementary school and trying to decide if I was to give my remaining cupcake, left from my lunchtime birthday party, to Phillip "The Nerd", or eat it myself. I think I actually gave it to him.

Chapter Three

After breakfast, everyone went back to their dorms to get ready for whichever activity was planned for that morning. Will and I didn't have any gear to grab, because this morning was going to be classroom time for the first aid portion of lifeguard training.

We headed toward the Quonset hut, which housed the tables and chairs, and chests full of recessive dummies. As we approached the classroom, Will discreetly mentioned that the girls were behind us.

Instinctively, I looked back to confirm. There they were, about forty yards back, walking not fast enough to catch us before we would enter the q-hut. Should we slow down? Should we be obvious enough so that they know that we spotted them, or that we were indeed in front of them? We'd better play it safe, so we kept with our pace toward the hut.

When we arrived, we picked a table toward the back, with enough room that the two girls could share with us, hopefully. Hopefully, because no one knows what they talked about the night before, after our little cruise. Although it had gone well, there was no telling if they had talked about other potential hunks that they spotted on the way to breakfast. Or that one of them decided that they didn't want to get "tied down" during the first week, or at least didn't want to give the impression to others that they were interested in someone.

Or, could it be, that they didn't want to appear to be a "slut" to the other girls, by becoming somewhat attached to one of the guys? It didn't look promising either way, for Will or me. They were going to walk right into the hut, and go pick a table by themselves, and basically give us the sterile shoulder the rest of the weeks remaining.

"Hey, guys!" Kristen said as she appeared from around the canvas covered "door", her practically black, thick hair getting caught up on part of the canvas. She was genuinely smiling and next to her Sara had her right hand up as if greeting me. They walked over to our table, and sat down.

Once again, I was sitting on the end, with Will to my left. "Not again…" I thought to myself, and with no way to move to her other side, I would have to lean back in my chair to talk to her. And, that's what I did, "Hey, Sara, what's your favorite brand of mustard?"

The class began, and for the next forty-five minutes, or so, the instructor showed us a video on an awkwardly makeshift video screen. I really couldn't pay attention to the class; I was too busy thinking about what to say at the break. I glanced over at Sara, who appeared to be paying attention to the lecture. Too bad. I was hoping she would start passing me notes, or something. No luck there.

Finally, it looked like we were taking a break. "Okay, guys, be back here in ten."

I took another leap. "Hey, Kristen, can I switch seats with you?"

She looked at Sara, and then at Will, then back at me, nodding her head with a confident grin. "Sure, just no hand holding."

I smiled and Sara laughed. Was she laughing because the thought of holding my hand was funny? I hoped not. I hoped she was laughing because she was busted and was now embarrassed. Only she knew, and I would have loved to be able to read her mind again that instant.

The class went on as one would expect from something like that. It wasn't full-fledged school, but almost as boring. For the rest of the lecture, I daydreamed about what would be happening later, either with the four of us, or possibly with Sara and me, you know, later that session.

My mind wandered back to home, and on to what I was going to do after leaving here. I could call Russ, and hang out with him and his girlfriend, or Jordan and his brother Eddie, go to the movies, hit the east coast and surf, or whatever. I really liked it here, though, and the thought of meeting a really cool girl made this place all the more attractive.

My mind continued on and drifted toward my dad and how my mother blamed him for their divorce, my bad grades, and all of my sister's "issues". He wasn't around a whole lot, but it wasn't his fault. His job made him travel, and often to far off places, indicative of a long voice delay when he'd telephone to check in every so often.

My mom said that she was sure he was having an affair, but I wasn't convinced. He would bring me home little things, gifts and stuff, often from Africa, Ukraine, Iran, and other strange locations. My mom and he didn't really talk about it too much, but from what I could gather he flew supplies around for the US government, and it must have paid well because he was able to put my mom through law school and had someone watch my sister and me when we were younger, and clean the house.

One day, when my dad was back in the states, he had to go see a doctor specializing in "exotic" diseases, because he had contracted something while overseas. This, of course, added fuel to the fire in that my mother would then convince herself that he must have picked up some STD from a woman in Thailand. But, in reality, it was due to an exposure he had in '86 to something heavily radioactive.

We followed Kristen and Will through the buffet line watching as Will stocked his tray full of a small sampling of every single container of food available. He was being ridiculous, but it was funny seeing him go to every food item only to scoop out what amounted to a tablespoon of each thing there.

We put our trays down at the table Will selected. Luckily, the four seats were next to each other. Sara sat down to the left of the head, where Kristen had sat. I pulled the chair out for Will as if I were his squire. "Thank you sonny, you are truly a gentile!" He said as I pushed his chair, with him in it, so close to the table that he probably couldn't breathe. "Bad gentile!" He scolded.

I asked Kristen and Sara where they were from. Kristen was from Brooklyn, yet had no accent whatsoever. I then focused on Sara, which is the reason I asked Kristen first. "Fort Worth...where are you from?" She replied.

"Lakeland, Florida, and Will's from Tulsa."

It's funny because when I first saw Will on the long bus ride from the airport, he was sitting about four rows in front of me and to the right. I am really good about prejudging people, highly inaccurately of course. He looked cocky. He had on some surf T-shirt, cargo shorts, with Oakley Frogskin shades on his head. I was thinking to myself, "What a cocky looking wannabe surfer." It wasn't until I met him that I realized that he really did surf, and he was as weird as me. Thanks to the dorm assignments, we hit it off. Yeah, I need to stop doing that prejudgment thing. I am, without fail, always wrong.

We had about fifteen minutes left before the afternoon "in the water" training began, and Kristen needed to get something out of her room, so we headed back toward the dorms. Sara, Will and I sat down at one of the picnic tables, looking down at all the little scribbles and carvings. We started talking again about our hometowns, when Will decided he needed to go get something out of our room. More likely, he had to go take a crap after all that shit he ate at lunch. So, Will got up from the table and headed back to our dorm.

"You come here often?" I said trying to sound like some lounge cat drug dealer hitting on some fifty-something divorcee. It must have worked because Sara started laughing.

"Yeah, when my boyfriend's out of town." Nice reply, I thought.

"Is he a cop?" We laughed.

"My dad was a cop," she softly said as she looked down at the carvings on the table, retracing a "T+M 4 ever" etching with her finger.

"What does he do now?"

"He died four years ago." She was still looking down. I felt like I just stepped in a pile of emotional dog shit. Not that her feelings came out of a dog's ass or anything, it's just that this had been going pretty well.

"Man, that sucks."

"Yeah, he was pretty cool. He died on his way back to his hotel, while doing some undercover thing in Miami." She was looking up again; probably glad to have that issue running its course.

"What happened? Was he shot or something?"

"Na...his surveillance shift was over at midnight and he was driving to the hotel, when he saw this car parked on the shoulder and sticking out into the lane with its door open."

"Uh huh?" I was concentrating.

"He stopped behind the car, and from what the police dispatcher could tell from what he was saying on the radio, there was a Cuban woman crying and mumbling in Spanish," she took a deep breath. "He said he was going to get her calmed down and help her off the interstate. Supposedly she was going crazy."

"Yeah? Did he figure out what her problem was?"

"Something about her only child, a sixteen-year-old daughter, going missing, or dead, or something, over in a desert somewhere."

"That's weird."

"I guess. He then told the dispatcher that he had her in the car, and was now heading to the hospital which was just up the road, you know, to get the woman some help." She paused. "About five minutes later, someone called in from a payphone at a toll plaza to say that they had just passed a really bad accident involving a car that had been rear-ended by a semi truck." She looked down at the carving she was tracing.

"My dad's captain back home, came to our house about 3:00 in the morning to tell us the news."

I didn't know what to say to her at this point. I think my facial expression spoke to my feelings about how sad this was for a really pretty girl to be talking about someone she obviously cared for tremendously.

"Did you get to, I dunno, maybe talk to him one last time on the phone or something?"

"Nope...they said he and the woman died instantly at the crash site."

"Oh."

"When the fire department got there, they said that his car was totally on fire and all crushed up. A week later, his Captain gave us his badge, name tag, and his wedding band to my mom."

"Is that the band there?" I pointed at her neck. I really didn't think about it until now, but dangling from her silver necklace was a tarnished ring.

"Yup, it's kind of beaten up, but it's been through a lot and I never take it off."

"I really don't know what to say, I mean, I can't say that I know how you feel or anything like that. I mean, the closest I have had, was a dog that I had, die." She was smiling again. I hope I never have to see her sad again, I liked her smiling better.

Will appeared from behind, back near the picnic tables. "Is Kristen back yet?"

"You tell us," I said trying to cause him to go on the defensive.

"Huh?"

"Never mind." I joked causing Sara to smile.

"Oh whatever dude!" Will laughed.

Just as I was going to pick on him some more, Kristen came down with her backpack. She had on a white t-shirt, presumably covering her swimsuit, and had the backpack on the "correct" way, as opposed to the "cool" way of only putting one strap on your shoulder. It was pretty interesting because it pulled her shoulders back, and the straps bordered the outside of her chest thus defining her breasts along with a huge increase in magnitude, as a bonus of course.

"Nice backpack." Will looked over at me trying not to bust out in tears of laughter. I knew exactly what he was referring to, and so did Sara, I think.

"You don't like it? What's wrong with it…is it too girly?"

"Noooo, that's not it…" He was trying to contain himself.

"It makes your boobs look really big." Sara was shaking her head, smiling, as if she needed to put the final nail in the coffin. Kristen looked down, and started to blush.

"I think the straps need to be loosened," she said as she began removing the backpack.

"Nice save…" I threw in my two cents worth.

"Why don't you let Will help you with that?" Inferring that Will would have to touch rather close to her breasts to loosen the straps.

"Okay…" She took off the pack. "Here Will," she said and handed the pack to him to carry.

"Ha-ha!" I rubbed it in, while he took hold of her pink, Hawaiian, flowery looking backpack, trying to look manly while he strolled along.

We walked toward the swim canal where the rest of our afternoon would be spent. Will gave up and finally put the backpack on the "cool" way. Sara and I added insults, about every fifteen steps or so, how attractive his backpack looked, alternating with asking him where he got the lovely pack.

The afternoon in the water passed too quickly, but not disappointedly so. Although not directly engaged in flirting with Sara, we were still close enough to act foolish in an attempt to get the other's attention. It was a good afternoon, and still early enough in the session that something really positive could come from all this interaction.

For some reason, yet appreciated nonetheless, I remembered that my uncle would tell me that you could take a mental picture of something if you tried hard enough. He would proffer, "Now, it works pretty well, but you don't have a lot of film."

It worked okay, but if you tried to do it too much you would end up forgetting the first couple of images that you would try to perfectly remember. This advice in mind, I looked over at Kristen sitting on the rescue board trying to balance and laughing, while Will tried to dethrone her. I waited until she looked over at Sara…then snapped the mental picture. If only there was such a camera, or something, that could truly capture not only the image, but the smell and taste of the salt water, sound of the gulls and the distant yet approaching Florida afternoon thunderstorm, the feeling of the warm breeze against my face, and the status of my synapse triggering in response to seeing two hot girls and a new good friend. I guess I'll just have to try.

I needed something as a liaison between what I was remembering and the real world, so I looked down at the only thing that I had on me, and for the foreseeable future, my watch. I paid special concentration to it, specifically the screen…and over to the seconds counting away, which was to be my reference when recalling this instant in time. I looked back at them, to ingrain the image into my cerebral library, which someday I needed to better organize.

The class ended with the instructor-dude summarizing what we learned that day, both in class and in the water. "Remember everyone, to sign up for some of the evening events scheduled for tonight," he pitched. I was just thinking that we would sit around the marina and talk about more things in our lives, to learn more about Sara, Kristen and Will, and to become closer.

"Hey Kyle, let's go look at the sign up lists before all the good stuff is taken." Sara must have had on the "woman mind-reading cap", knowing to do the opposite of what I actually wanted. This reminded me of going to the movies on the first date, where you had to sit there and shut up…then just drive her home, as opposed to finding out what we had in common, if anything.

"Okay, do you know what's up?"

"I think there's more scuba diving, and I think there's a movie on sharks. Oh, and there's that marine aquatic lab." Out of those three, somehow I got the impression that we were going to be playing with sea creatures in the lab.

We passed by the empty picnic tables where Sara and I sat earlier that day; the orange glow from the late afternoon sun being soaked up by the wood of the tables made it seem like time was standing still, waiting for us to come back, but by the same token, recognizing that time was setting on a moment that would never return.

Chapter Four

Will and I departed company from the girls, and headed to our respective dorms. When we got to the room, the shower was empty, and so Will remarked, "Get in that shower, asshole…before I do!"

An hour, or so later, we headed downstairs. Not seeing the girls, and not wanting to look like losers, we headed toward the cafeteria. As we walked, Will and I were swapping questions like what our parents did, and if we were dating anyone back home. Will's dad owned a small house building company, but he lived with his mother and stepfather, who was some rich oilman.

He continued on. He had just broken up with this girl that he had only been casually dating. I, on the other hand, hadn't had a steady girlfriend in over five months, and yes, she broke up with me, for whatever bullshit reason she could come up with, but with the final result of me being very confused about the whole relationship game, and that my overall technique needed an overhaul.

In reality, and come to find out later, she totally had something going on, of course, on the side probably the whole time. My buddy Russ happily reported, "Hey Kyle, bro, she is totally doin' Brad Newsome, and it was only a matter of time before she left you." Yeah, there went my confidence.

My dad, attempting to come to the rescue via the phone line, a-la somewhere deep in Cashmere, pleasantly informed me that he had the perfect girl for me. Apparently, it was someone he gave a ride to in a cargo plane from Kazakhstan to Bella Russia one day early in May, back four years ago. "She's a cutie, and really sweet."

"Dad, that was like four years ago."

"Yeah, I know," he'd pause. "I just figured I'd tell ya."

Will and my conversation inevitably, once again, turned to Kristen and Sara. He stated in some obscure way that he would like to "hit it off" with Kristen. I wasn't really sure what he meant, but I had my guesses. Was it that he desired to build a lasting long-term meaningful relationship with her, or was he trying to imply that he just wanted to have sex with her? I also wasn't sure if he was trying to look a little more masculine by implying that he wanted to merely "love 'em and leave 'em", or if he was being genuine in expressing his feelings in a somewhat amateurish manner. Then, Will laid the question to rest. "Bro, she is really cool, and I could really see myself dating her, but that long distance shit sucks. Man, she is really hot too. I'd really like to give her the ole' HBI."

"Hey Will!" They snuck up on us. In all of Will's ramblings, and me trying to figure out what on earth he was talking about, Kristen and Sara had been stealthily approaching us the whole time. How much had they heard?

"Hey Will, what's HBI mean?" Kristen was asking, or acting. I really couldn't tell either way. Will turned pink as a flamingo, while I started busting out laughing.

"Uh, it stands for...Honey Buns Incorporated." Will was reaching really deep for that shit.

"Oh my god, you are so freakin' stupid!" I could barely get it out, but between breaths I managed. Sara was tearing up, relishing in how busted Will was.

"What the heck does *that* mean?" Kristen was trying to act like she was mad, but wasn't doing a good job with all the laughing.

"You know the people that make those honey buns? They are really good! I just had one at the airport before getting on the bus to come down here." He was trying not to laugh.

"Good save, Will. Good save." Kristen was shaking her head and smirking. She had to know exactly what it meant. "We'll just have to see about the HBI, won't we Will?"

"What!"

"Oh, so you *didn't* have buns on the way down here? You are sooo busted!" Kristen was victorious, again.

"I know what that means, you dumb ass!" She continued, "but I still love you."

Once again, and somehow, Will rose out of his nest of shit like a Phoenix. Next time we'd need to wait a little longer before giving up on the girls, who apparently wanted us to wait for them.

We continued on toward the cafeteria. Kristen playfully grabbed Will's arm, hanging on like a bratty sister. "Hey Will, are you going to eat everything on the buffet this time?"

"Uh, I don't think so…it didn't make sleeping very easy."

I decided to chime in, "I think what Will's trying to say, is that his screwing around gave him the shits."

"Poor baby." Kristen was being sarcastic. "Do you need some Pepto?" She rubbed his stomach. "Does your little belly hurt?"

We were all laughing, again at Will's expense, and continued to pick on him until we got in line. The verbal teasing gave way to Kristen and Sara trying to put peas on his plate, knowing full well that he wanted nothing to do with it. We sat down together, and talked about everything from what type of music we liked, to movies, to brothers and sisters, to high school.

When dinner was over, we headed outside. Will and Kristen were going to wait while the projector and screen were set up back in the cafeteria. Sara and I started walking the hundred feet or so, around to the back of the building where the lab was situated by the water.

It was just us, for now, until the other people who had surely signed up after us arrived. It was a beautiful setting almost designed for a postcard. Our view was of mangroves and small-uninhabited islands. To the west the sun was setting, and the sound of seagulls and diving pelicans filled the air, in addition to the warm salty breeze that would periodically blow Sara's long blonde hair into her face.

I should have brought a camera. The reddish glow of the sunset hitting the water, then reflecting back onto her skin was definitely worthy of another mental camera shot. I hoped I'd remember this picture forever; but I knew that one day I'd forget.

"Are you two here for the sea life lab?" We turned around and nodded to the female counselor holding a signup sheet.

"Okay, then we are just waiting for the other two. You guys aren't afraid to hold little sea creatures, are you?"

"Uh, I don't think so," I said while looking at Sara.

"Not me…I'm not," she announced, looking back at the counselor chick.

"Okay, well if you want to come over here and wash your hands, you can start getting used to some of the animals in these two basins." She pointed over toward a big industrial looking sink. Sara and I went over and turned on the faucet. I let Sara go first. "Hey, we can both share," Sara stated as she moved toward her left, making room for me.

"Thanks lady," I joked.

"Can you hand me some soap?" She pointed with her right index finger toward the liquid soap dispenser. I reached over and put some in my palm, then grabbed her hands and started to lather them up. I then decided to start impersonating some French masseuse. "You are very tense my dear, let me see if I can work out this knot in your thumb." I started kneading her thumb like I knew what I was doing. "Ah yes, you need to come in more often, my dear…you are under much stress….no?" The accent continued.

"Yeah, it hurts when I pick my teeth." She said with a Texas drawl, followed by laughter. I held her hand a few moments longer than required to complete the transfer of soap and to finish the masseuse impersonation. I wondered if I'd be able to hold her hand again, but under the heading of "affection" as opposed to amusement.

During the class, the counselor would pick up a creature, then tell us all about it: what it eats, how it moves, how it procreates, how to identify male from female, if applicable, and so on. After about thirty minutes or so of paying attention to the lecture, we were all encouraged to handle the creatures ourselves. We would pick up some spiny sea urchin or starfish, and then put it down and exchange it for another little critter. Sara picked up some urchin that looked like a fuzzy green apple, while I picked up a sea cucumber.

I held the sea cucumber over near Sara's urchin. "Hey urchin, you come here often?" I said attempting to replicate the not often heard voice of the Lesser Ruddied Sea Cucumber. Sara giggled, while I continued on, "What's the matter, plankton got your tongue?"

"I hang out around these parts from time to time." Her portrayal sounded like some drag queen that had one too many cigarettes.

"So, how do you feel about a cucumber buying you a drink?"

"Well, I like my liquor, like I like my cucumbers, stiff and hard."

I almost choked. I thought she'd been hanging out with Kristen too much. I shed the cucumber voice. "You little hooch!" I laughed while covering the cucumbers "ears."

"Oh whatever, what do you expect the urchin to say when it's getting hit on by a cucumber?" I guess she had a point. In all the screwing around, we didn't notice that the other two girls, and the counselor chick were watching our sea creature puppet show.

"Uh, we were just…I mean a sea cucumber's got to have some fun now and again." I was trying to save it, but then just gave up.

After the little class was over, and Sara and I were alone again, I half-thought about kissing her but the time wasn't right. Of course I "would move too fast" inevitably scaring her away like I did with my ex-girlfriend. Well, at least that's what she told me five months ago when she decided that it would be better to "just be friends." Yeah right, so you can be "friends" with Brad.

"Hey look over there…" Sara motioned toward the south. I could faintly see a thunderstorm way off in the distance, to the south. About every fifteen seconds or so, another flash of light would emanate from the clouds. "I don't know what to think about thunderstorms," Sara spoke softly.

"How come?"

"I dunno…just, well they are really pretty from far away, but…"

"Yeah. But what?"

"Well, when they get closer, you know, it could get bad." She continued to stare out toward the storm.

"I guess, well, depending on where you are. You know, like if you are inside or something, then it's probably okay."

"Well, one thing's for sure, it's beautiful for some, but really bad for others." She laughed, and I was starting to realize how philosophical she was.

The area we were sitting got a little brighter as a result of the cafeteria doors opening. The ambient voices spilling out of the doors and onto the sand and rock walkway reminded me of my alarm clock waking me up from a good dream.

"Let's go find Kristen and Will," she said as she stood up, brushing the sand off her shorts. I got up, and began walking over toward the doors, quickly locating our two friends.

"How was the movie?" Sara asked.

"It was fishy…" Will was trying to laugh like some cheesy comedian who just told some horrible joke. He added, "Damn, I'm funny!" while Kristen shoved him.

"It was good, but not as good as Quint getting eaten by Jaws." Kristen was looking back at Will, "If I was Jaws, I'd find you on some boat and eat you."

"Why?" I think he thought she was being mean.

"I bet you would taste kind of spicy," Kristen continued.

"I bet he would taste sour!" Sara chimed in.

Then I sealed Will's fate by adding, "I bet he would taste like shit!" All were laughing again at Will's expense, of course.

It was time to call it a night, so Will and I headed up to our room, while I asked him if he was trying to get lucky or something with Kristen when we came up to him near the dock. He told me that he had been holding her hand, but wasn't really trying to do anything specifically. He did say that she was "smokin" and that he was hoping that something good would happen in the next couple of weeks. He didn't elaborate on the meaning of "good" but I think I knew what he meant.

Chapter Five

The next morning, Will and I walked to breakfast, catching a glimpse of a big ole DC-3 thundering over us at treetop level, heading out to bomb some mosquito-breeding haven. It shook the ground it was so loud. "I bet that pilot is having a blast," Will said as he motioned toward the plane.

The weather was kind of dicey looking. It was clear right above us, but toward the southwest, it looked ominous. I pointed toward the gigantic cloud height. "That looks like some crazy shit over there." Will nodded while he bit a piece of grass he had placed into his mouth.

We arrived at the cafeteria to find it extra crowded. There was a bunch of older people taking up three of the tables, which left only a couple of seats vacant. Will and I proceeded through the buffet, and then found the only two seats next to each other. We asked one of the girls who Will was sitting next to, what was going on with all the older people. "I think they're scientists or something."

"What are they doing here?" I asked.

"Something to do with weather, I guess," one of the other girls answered.

"Supposedly, it's 'cause there's a bad storm somewhere," some guy piped up.

Will replied, "That's cool." But it really wasn't because we weren't able to sit next to the girls. We did discover, by looking around the room, that it sucked more for them, because they apparently were separated themselves by a counselor and some other chick. I guess we'd have to wait until after breakfast to see them.

Will was going on a SCUBA dive out on one of the coral formations after breakfast, and I was going all of about two hundred feet to another Quonset hut to learn about old sunken crap.

"I think Kristen is doing that nautical archeology thing that you are." Well at least I'd have her in there with me. "What's Sara doing?" he asked.

"Some beach erosion thing." Will gave me the confirming, yet fretfully understanding, nod.

After a little while, people starting getting up and heading outside. We finished eating, and went over to where the girls were sitting. I knew that Sara had sailing with Will and me later, but didn't know what Kristen had going on. "Hey Kristen, what do you have this afternoon?"

"I have this snorkeling trip thing. You guys are all sailing, right?"

"Yeah, if it doesn't get cancelled because of rain or something." Will was dwelling on the clouds that I pointed out earlier.

"You know those creepy scientists probably did a rain dance or something to ruin our shit," he continued.

Although disappointed that Sara nor Will could be there, I was still glad to have Kristen. "You're not going to make me sit by myself are you?" she asked as she and I headed past the marina.

"Uh no. I wouldn't do that to the second hottest girl here, would I?"

"The second hottest? Oh okay, I see." She smiled.

"Hey, what's the deal with Sara?" Speaking of other hot girls.

"She likes you a lot."

"Really?"

"Yep." The only thing though, was that Kristen wasn't completely looking me in the eyes. I wonder if she was trying to save my feelings or something else.

"Okay, I'm going to tell you something. You have to promise that you aren't going to tell Sara I told you this."

"Okay."

"Okay?" She was seeking confirmation.

"Yeah, okay, I won't."

"All right. Well, when we were on the bus on the way down here we were talking about where we were from." She paused.

"Uh huh?" Spit it out Kristen.

"She asked if I had a boyfriend back in New York...." Okay, get to the point.

"I don't. But she said that she did, and they had been dating for about a year."

A whole year! Are you fucking kidding me?

"What?"

"Yeah... I mean, that's what she said."

"Okay?"

"That's what she said...but...I know that she likes you."

"Did she tell you that she likes me?" This had better be good.

"Oh yeah, like every time we are alone."

"You're not just telling me this to make me feel better, are you?"

"No way. You can't tell that she likes you?"

"Well, I don't..." I didn't know what to say.

"She's always talking to you, she always walks really close to you."

"Yeah, but...I mean. Sure, but...is she breaking up with him, or, shit I don't know." Why the hell does she have a boyfriend? I bet he is some freakin' varsity football jock or some baseball pitcher. Fuck that guy! Damn it, this sucks.

"Try not to worry about it, he's probably some overbearing tool." Kristen tried to repair the damage.

"Or some momma's boy," I added.

"Yeah, he probably gets nursed by his mom after they win a game." She added, causing me to laugh.

"Yeah, screw him. That little freak," I concluded. We laughed some more, and Kristen really was helping me see that it really didn't matter if she was dating some stud back home. After all, I was here, with her, and football dude was back holding his dick, or his mom, somewhere in Texas. He was probably glad she was away, so that he could go take Bobby-Jean to the rodeo and "park" afterwards. That guy freakin' sucks.

The "Hot Italian", as Will referred to her, otherwise known as Kristen, and I stepped inside the hut and sat in the back corner. It was easy to see why he was so into her. Dark hair, deep blue eyes, and a great personality, multiplied his attraction toward her, that and her rather large breasts.

The hut was air conditioned, amazing. It had two little window units that made it hard to hear the instructor on the high setting, so some of us in the corners of the room had to suffer a little bit due to the cooling inefficiency. The only good thing about not having any air conditioning, but for this one hut, was that you got so used to no A/C that by the time you got back to civilization after three weeks, you would actually get cold inside, like you were some one-hundred-and-three year old lady. Of course the bad outweighed the good. Mosquitoes, although not bad due to the ever-present sea breeze, were somewhat more annoying inside.

Also, if you've never experienced it, never being able to fully dry off was another interesting side effect. It's not entirely fun, taking a shower, even if cold, then changing into clean, dry clothes, only to get them somewhat soaked again due to 99% humidity. However, oscillating fans were the equivalent of deodorant; your life doesn't depend on it, but it sure does make it a little nicer. I bet if I trafficked in oscillating fans I could make as much as a golf cart repairman in some retirement village.

At our next break, Kristen and I started the conversation up again. I asked her what she had going on that afternoon, after lunch. "I've got snorkeling. Bummer 'cause none of ya'll will be there."

The break ended, and the instructor began agai n. It actually was an interesting subject, unfortunately my mind wandered elsewhere, as it tended to do. Kristen had about the same attention span as I did, displayed by her punching me in the arm every time the instructor said, "and furthermore" a phrase that annoyed us, for some reason.

The class wrapped up early, and we were sure that Sara and Will weren't back from their respective outings, so we decided that we would watch some others getting certified over at the swim canal.

We took up a vantage point near the tip closest to the ocean on the dock, which defined the canal. Kristen took off her flip-flops and dangled her feet off the dock over the water. "What do you do when you aren't in school?" she asked. "Pretty much hangout. Sometimes I'd go see my dad on the rare occasion he's back in the states, we'd shoot rifles and stuff, or I'd hang out with my cousin. She lifeguards at a beach back around Vero."

"That's cool. So, are you seeing anyone back home?" She was probing, but I didn't mind.

"Na. I was seeing this girl a little while ago, but not anymore."

"Why not? What was her deal?"

"I really dunno. I mean, she said that she needed space, whatever that's supposed to mean."

"Yeah, I guess some girls are weird like that," she hypothesized.

"What about you? What's *your* deal?"

"Oh, I hang out with my dad at his office and answer phones and stuff. It's kind of cool, 'cause I really don't have to work real hard and he'll pay me I think, like, $4.50 an hour. According to him, it's just above minimum wage, so I'd better be grateful."

"What, is he trying to teach you a lesson or something?"

"He acts like it, but he always rounds up my time at the end of the day, by like an hour or so. He's cool, but kind of dorky."

"I guess that's parents for ya. You're not dating anyone?" I was fishing for Will, and I'm sure it was obvious.

"Nope. Unless you count the construction workers that work for my dad who hit on me, before they find out that I'm the boss's daughter," she said, grimacing.

"Sweet!" I said, sarcastically.

"Ah, yeah, not really. They are all dirty and sweaty and stuff." She wrinkled her sun-kissed nose.

"Well Will's dirty and sweaty most of the time."

"Yeah, but he's adorable." Her demeanor completely changed any time his name was mentioned.

"I'll let him know that you said he was 'adorable.'" I couldn't wait to rag on him about being so adorable. Maybe I'll start calling him "teddy bear" or something.

"And he's funny too…" she added. I never could really visualize the word "dreamy" until I saw Kristen swooning over Will. It was cute to see it, in a kind of sickening sort of way. Actually, I hoped that someone, somewhere would act the same about me, but I somehow doubted the probability was very high. Maybe that "cute and really sweet" girl my dad met four years ago would dig me the same way, you know, think that I was "dreamy".

We joked some more and casually watched some of the scuba training going on close by. There was one girl that we paid a little extra attention to because it looked like at any minute her bikini top would come off. We couldn't figure if it was the way she was taking on, and off, her buoyancy compensator, or the way she was getting into the water. Kristen had the simplest explanation. "I think she just has big boobs." She was probably right.

The weather was perfect, at least by my standards. It was overcast enough to shield the direct sunlight, breezy, but not enough clouds to look threatening, despite Will and my spotting of the storm clouds earlier that day. We sat for a little longer taking it all in, and then decided to head toward the marina to see if we could spot Sara or Will arriving.

We walked to the marina, found a rickety old railing right near the entrance to the harbor with a grassy patch next to the cafeteria where we could spot the boats as they arrived. We grabbed some rocks that were scattered all around, skipping them and starting a competition of how many times we could skip the rocks, just to pass the time until we spotted Will and Sara.

Kristen was the first to observe one of the scuba boats heading towards the marina. The closer it got, the easier it was to see people, and ultimately who was onboard. It passed by the opening to the small harbor, but we didn't see Will or Sara. So, we kept on skipping rocks.

Getting a little more violent, we decided to put some bark into the water, and then try to see if we could sink it by pelting it with rocks. It's crazy how much fun you can have by throwing shit at other shit in the water.

This one piece of bark wouldn't sink, so Kristen went and got a big rock, about the size of a volleyball, and hurled it into the water, practically falling in herself. It just missed the bark, causing Kristen to get seriously teased by me. "Bark one, Kristen…nothing!" I said to her, and saving the image away to harass her about in front of Will and Sara later on.

Another boat headed past us, but this time we could clearly spot Will. He was standing toward the front of the boat, acting like he was helping the staff dude dock the boat. In actuality, he was probably just looking for Kristen. About a minute later, as the boat entered the harbor, he spotted me and Kristen walking toward the scuba shack and over to the boat's intended mooring spot.

He started posing like he was the topless mermaid on the front of those old ships, or that Rolls Royce lady, putting his arms back behind him and leaning slightly forward. A second later, the driver of the boat probably put the boat in reverse to slow its approach, which caused Will to almost fall into the water. "Eh he!" I loudly teased. Then Kristen added, "Yeah, don't fall in, chowder head!"

We waited until everyone had disembarked before following Will over to the dive shack so that he could clean his gear. Kristen and I were still mildly teasing him about his display in the harbor. "Hey Kyle, where's your girlfriend?" He was trying to change the subject.

I really didn't think of Sara as my girlfriend, but I was flattered by the recommendation. Actually, it would have been okay for others to think that, but it really wasn't accurate.

"I guess she's still on the water."

"Oh, okay lover boy. Like you don't know," Will joked.

"What the hell ever, Romeo!" I responded while looking at Kristen with my eyes really wide opened to display my complete knowledge of Will's lust for her.

"Yeah Will, you are like a whipped puppy dog!" Kristen was playing along.

He smiled with no rebuttal. "I'll just be getting back to cleaning my gear now." He playfully sulked.

We hung around for a little while, then spotted another dive boat approaching the entrance to the harbor. "That's gotta be her," Kristen commented. I wondered if this is what they meant by 'waiting for my ship to come in.' Probably not. Either way, I was glad to see her.

The boat docked and Kristen and I walked over to meet her. They didn't have any gear to unload, so it didn't take long before we were all talking.

After waiting around for Will to stow his gear in the room and change, he finally walked over, clean and smelling like some trucker that couldn't figure out what aftershave to buy with his quarters in the bathroom. "Will, are you trying to pick me up?" Kristen said after catching his attempts at olfactory pleasure.

"For what?"

"Like some fourteen-year-old at prom?" I picked.

"Man…that's this new stuff I got."

"Sure dude, whatever," I said as he put his finger up under his shirt, presumably touching his armpit, then withdrawing his hand.

He then wiped his finger on the side of my shorts, and said, "Here you go so you don't feel left out." That raised the obvious "nasty" and "gross" from the girls, but it was funny nonetheless.

At lunch, we asked Will about his scuba trip, and teased him some more about almost busting his ass into the water. He was telling us about this dude that got seasick on the boat ride out to the dive spot. Will reenacted the way the poor guy was hurling over the rail of the boat, and how that even in the water he was still puking. Will told us how it looked seeing this guy puke through his regulator under water and the fish swarming to take a sample, but Kristen put a quick end to the story.

Throughout these exchanges, I couldn't help looking at Sara. Dirty blonde hair, with her alert, yet calming blue eyes, made me realize why the Miss Texas's always seemed to become Miss Americas. The image of her with her bright red t-shirt and cut off blue jean shorts with her hair occasionally falling into her face, would be the perfect post card to send to some poor sucker up north. "From The Gulf of Mexico, with love."

Kristen left for her room to get changed and grab her gear, and we needed to get over to the sailing area, so we parted ways. As we walked in the opposite direction from Kristen, Will kept turning around to see if Kristen was looking back at him. I let him do it a couple of times before busting him. "Hey Will, did you forget something?"

"Nope, just checking her out. Did you see those shorts she's wearing? Man!" Acting like he was looking at her ass, but in reality his motives were more genuinely affectionate. He did it a fourth time, but this time, Kristen was looking back. She blew him a big kiss, which caused Will to blush. He tried to wave, but was so stunned by her actions and looks that all he could do was stare.

Chapter Six

We rallied up at the sailboat launch area, and received our instructions. Most of the others, including Will, were going solo, but Sara and I decided to team up on a bigger Catamaran. Normally, we would be about to race, or something, but we quickly learned that we'd all be engaging in ship-to-ship combat, only instead of cannons, we'd be armed with big sponges.

A few hours of fun, getting soaked by sponges and capsizing sailboats, and numerous bruises were all good memories of the afternoon. Kristen had joined the fray, making up some story about an earache so that she could join us, and her Will. With her in his boat, Will proved his worth as a sponge launching fool, while Sara took numerous photos. I smiled thinking that things in heaven couldn't have been too much better than this.

A little while later, two of the sailing instructors started motoring around in their Whaler, to the various boats to signal the return to the harbor. Sara and I spotted Will and Kristen's boat, and steered in their direction.

Once we met up, we sailed toward the harbor in a group of three other boats. The wind was picking up, presumably from a cloud formation directly to our south, and the storm way off behind it. As we neared the breaker barrier to the harbor entrance, the sea grew choppy, and the wind brought some colder gusts. I thought to myself that it would have been fun to head back out in this weather, but it also would have been a good way to get struck by lightning.

After de-rigging the Cat, we headed back toward the dorms to get ready for dinner. We all needed to take a shower; Will from some drain plug pulling mission, and Sara and I from capsizing. "Okay we're going to meet right here in fifteen minutes, so don't leave us again!" Kristen teased.

After showering and a successful rendezvous, we headed toward the cafeteria. The clouds were getting darker and more organized. The wind was really picking up, with a cool hint in the air. "I'm not sure about this," Sara commented.

We still had a couple more minutes before they opened the dining room doors, so we walked over to the seawall to sit down and watch the distant storm. I thought that it wouldn't be a bad idea to put my arm around her, but I didn't want any of the other people to see, and you know, I "didn't want to move too fast."

I thought about how pleasant the moment was, and once again wishing it could last for the next couple of weeks. I guess it's better that I didn't have some cool ability to freeze time because inevitably, and usually within the same day, another and even better event comes along that makes me glad that I waited.

My mind wandered to more discouraging thoughts. This heaven was going to end at one point. She was going to go back to Texas and me back home. I would be losing a friend, a potential girlfriend, and who knows where that may have led. She was going back to her high school and back to her boyfriend, then to her college, and on to the rest of her life.

After we leave, our paths would grow steadily farther apart, probably never to pass again. I guess you can't go back to how things were, no matter how hard you try. You can go back to the same place, sit down on the same bench, on the same minute of the same hour, of the same day, of the same month, even with the same weather of the next year, and it will never be the same.

Unlike time, at least I had her next to me right now, and for the next few weeks. If I could move far enough along with her, and have her really start liking me, then maybe our paths would not grow farther apart, and could possibly lead back together.

This was to be a monumental task, and according to my calculations, the odds were pretty remote. Go somewhere for three weeks, away from home. Meet *the* perfect girl. Not only is the girl really pretty, but she is also amazingly wonderful to be around and *truly* cosmic. Then, and this is the unfortunate part, think about the girl all the time.

Now the really difficult part: The girl has to fall in love. The girl must be so enchanted by her love for me that she confesses all of her feelings, and her intense sadness that we are parting ways. She decides that she can't live without me, and tells me that there is only one person for her.

She follows me to the school where I end up, and we immediately and obviously start dating. After dating for a year or so, she decides she wants to marry me, so she asks. I, of course, say "yes", and the date is set for a year later. We finish college together, never get in any arguments, and live happily. We get married, and the rest is history. Yeah, like I said, this was going to be pretty hard.

I decided that I really liked this weather, especially when it would gust in that certain manner that would cause Sara's hair to blow into her face. While I was trying to figure out what kind of perfume she used, she affectionately positioned her foot behind mine. I looked over at her, to catch her profile against the dusky sky. Right as I was turning my head, she looked over at me. "Hi there" she softly greeted. I smiled back, and as if somehow busted in a good way, looked back over the water.

The doors opened to the cafeteria. The methodical flow of people began entering the doorway, which was our indication that we'd better be heading that way too. I got up first, while Sara reached out toward me, to help her to her feet. I grabbed both of her hands and carefully pulled her up. I didn't want to let go of her hands, but I needed to brush the sand off my rear, so priority guided my actions.

"The Hot Italian" and her Will were walking toward the entrance. Apparently, they had sat in something black, thus making their butts look extra soiled. Luckily for Kristen, she was wearing dark blue jean cut offs, but Will had on khaki shorts so he looked like he sat in dog poop. "Did you not wear your diapers?" I teased.

"Huh? What are…" He looked back at his rear. "Eww, what is that?" He started brushing.

"It's just darker sand…here let me…" Kristen started slapping his butt, both trying to assist in the soil removal, and to playfully inflict pain.

"Damn, woman! That hurts!" He was trying not to laugh.

"Well, you wanna look like you just crapped your pants?" Kristen kept at it. After a couple of more good whacks, his butt was about as crap free as it was going to look.

After dinner and twenty minutes or so of talking, we headed back outside. There weren't any night activities going on, whose attendees hadn't already departed before dinner, so we just decided to walk around the shoreline and the docks. It was about 8:00 and the sun was just getting ready to set. We headed over to the smaller seawall on the west side of the tip of land that the cafeteria and some of the labs were on, to watch the last ten minutes of the sun setting. There was cloud cover just enough to shield the last minute or so, but watching anything with them was desirable, maybe even watching mold grow. We walked back around the main docks, and over to the swim canal where we could see about a dozen people both in and out of the water.

When we arrived at the canal, there were a bunch of other guys, and girls, with snorkel gear and flashlights. We sat down about half way up the dock with our feet hanging over to watch the action. After five minutes or so of confusion as to what was going on, we learned that they were trying to raise an old "artificial reef" that was sunk at the bottom of the canal, twenty feet or so down. In reality, it was an old AMC Pacer that was sunk about ten years ago. For some reason, marine life wasn't really attaching itself to the car, and it being a Pacer alone gave Will fodder for hours.

So, they decided to raise it, and put concrete structures in its place which would be a more proven mode of attracting marine organisms. Whatever the reason, it was cool watching dive lights, airbags, and military like activity, where we had "front dock" seats.

"I like the way the lights shimmer through the water like that," Sara pointed out.

"Yeah, it's pretty cool," I replied thinking of how Sara was really good at pointing out objects of subtle beauty that most would take for granted, or never really pay much attention to begin with.

It was great sitting there watching the underwater action, sitting just far enough away as to not be involved. It was interesting, but not so much that we couldn't carry on a conversation. Being with her, Kristen and Will, was wonderful, like eating something so sweet that it made your jaw hurt.

Sara and I continued to talk about what we were going to do after high school, while Will and Kristen tried to kick off the other's flip flops into the water. "So you want to go to A & M?"

"Yeah, I guess. I really don't know. Where do you want to go?"

"If I can get in to University of Hawaii, or Florida, that's where I'd want to go. My grades are kind of dicey, though," I paused, "My third choice is University of Miami, but..."

I wondered if now would be a good time to kiss her, but once again I opted out of an attempt, mostly because of all the people buzzing above and under the water, and the proximity of Will and Kristen. There would be a better time and place, and it had to be just right. I was getting ahead of myself anyway, by assuming that she would respond.

"There's that storm like a hundred miles away, or something, that they think is coming this way," Kristen said, bringing us into the conversation.

"Oh what-the-hell ever." Will chuckled.

"No seriously, I heard about it from that Samantha girl," Sara added.

"Okay, okay, so what does that mean?" Will bit.

"I think the same thing happened last summer, and all they did was cancel some scuba and snorkeling trips for two days. Other than that, it was business as usual," Kristen assured. This was good, because the last thing I wanted was to be evicted from paradise by some storm named "Danica", or something.

That night back in the room, as I drifted off to sleep, for some reason, and as invasive as open-heart surgery, thoughts re-entered my brain of me when I was much younger at the swimming pool. I would go over to the deep end to dive off the diving board. I really didn't want to jump off, but not because I was scared of heights or the water, it was something about jumping into the abyss that didn't sit well. Sometimes, my dad would make his way to the deep end, and hang out in front of the diving board, which brought overwhelming comfort, giving me the courage to dive off the board for the rest of the afternoon.

It wasn't like magnetics either, or that storm, or whatever pulling me towards something there on that Key; it was like a couple of nights ago on the boat, like a kind of navigational buoy out on the out-skirts of that big bay at night. You pass it, but look back as it fades into the darkness, still emitting the red glow. So, you either feel uneasy that you've passed and left it all alone out there, or you remember back minutes earlier to how much better you felt knowing that you found the red channel marker from the open water and how you were on your way back to harbor.

Or, you had confidence in the illusion turned fact, that it was guiding you toward someplace safe. There's something about being between the channel marker with its beacon, and the harbor that is innately comforting; much more so than the lonely feeling of searching for the channel from the open dark sea. However, the dim red glow of the navigational marker would soon begin its pull from the darkness, toward it, but then back out to the open sea, causing my loneliness over again.

I woke up a few hours later, to hit the restroom, quickly realizing that my stress was mostly gone. I was thinking about thunderstorms and deserts for some reason now…and really pretty clouds.

Chapter Seven

At lunch, one of the counselor guys stood up to make a reminder announcement about the afternoon's selection of activities, one of which included a bus to the local movie theater, about an hour away, and that there was a chance that we would be eating dinner somewhere "off campus". The other option was a scavenger hunt that seemed more like a military search and rescue operation, than some lame "Easter egg hunt" game. From what I could gather, certain counselors would go hide in trees, the hulls of boats, in the water, the mud and the like, leaving the others to hunt them down. Sara, again, told us that she really liked that option.

There was also some "red neck" Olympics thing, as one of the female counselors detailed…which actually sounded kind of fun. Really, both sounded cool, but Kristen was sticking to her guns of seeing Pretty Woman, her mind being firmly made up the day before. So, through non-verbal confirmation, Will and I agreed, with a display of sarcastic enthusiasm on Will's part, to appease Kristen by going to the movies.

With almost two hours to spare before the van was set to leave for the local theater, we walked outside and shot the breeze for a little while, trying to figure out what to do for the next few hours. Will and Kristen had their own ideas, and Sara wanted to go over and hang out with the sea urchins and stuff again. So, as obviousness prevailed, I decided to hang out with Sara.

We talked about what cars we drove, siblings, what subjects we liked in school, and other random stuff. We didn't have a whole lot in common, but I didn't think that really mattered. I mean, she was hot, funny, kind of liked me, and a year younger…what wasn't to like?

"Hey, do you wanna go get something to drink?" she asked.

"Sure." We headed around the back of the lab, and over to the other side of the cafeteria, near the marina. There were a couple of vending machines, under a hut next to the fuel dock. I think I remember seeing about five dollars in "ones" in my pocket, which was a good thing, considering that this was our first "date".

We looked at the three vending machines. One had cans of soft drinks awaiting purchase, one was the typical snack machine, and the other was that weirder kind where you could buy frozen foods and stuff.

I looked at that third machine with heightened curiosity, not because I hadn't seen one of these before, but more because I was curious about circumstances in which someone would buy one of the items. I mean, I get why someone would grab a packet of M&Ms, or a Coke, or even a pack of gum, but what would compel someone to get a frozen pimento cheese sandwich out of this revolving tray machine thing? It wasn't that it was expensive or anything, it was just kind of odd in a weird, fleeting, innocent sort of way.

Sara surveyed the goods, first in the classic snack vending machine, her attention wandering toward the other machine. She already motioned that she wanted a Sunkist, but was also deciding on something additional. I watched her, as she looked intently at the items for sale in the "odd" machine. Surprisingly, she appeared to consider each of the different frozen foods awaiting purchase, but lacking a microwave to complete the preparation still confused me as to her motive. At one point, she actually pushed the button that spun the wheel around to reveal what was around the back of the carousel. I continued to watch as she pondered her selection.

"Oh look!" She pointed at the bottom as she released the button. I couldn't see what she was pointing at due to the angle that I was facing.

"Do you want that?" She was excited, as I moved around to view the prize. I was stunned to see an ice cream sandwich, which I silently, and stubbornly submitted was out of the ordinary for a vending machine such as this, yet somehow perfectly wonderful.

"Sure." I reached into my pocket and grabbed a dollar bill. I quickly inserted it into the slot, before Sara had a chance to withdraw whatever she had in her pocket that she was fishing around for.

"Thanks…and it's going to be good!" She said as she did a little bouncy kind of jig while she waited for the funds to process and for the sandwich to be dispensed. As she grabbed the wrapped ice cream, I put in a dollar bill at the other machine and grabbed Sunkist and a Mello Yellow.

We sat down on a bench overlooking the docks of the marina. She looked over at me, and was happy to see that I had already grabbed a drink for her.

We stared out over the marina, and out to the larger bay. The slight smell of fuel filled the air, which undoubtedly added to the experience and the entries into the aforementioned memory logs. The sounds were abundant too, with the pinging of sailboat masts, the gulls, the slight lapping of waves, and an occasional outboard motor revving.

We just sat there, and I couldn't imagine a better place in the world to be, and assumed that the statistical probabilities to be remote. My mind wandered back to when I first arrived there, which was somewhat frightening to think that this could have turned out different. I could have been sitting over at the picnic tables with some other people just talking and laughing, looking over toward the marina to casually glance and catching a view of a guy and girl sitting on a bench sharing an ice cream sandwich, or the girl leaning against him on a lone bench, late into the night. The thought of falling back to that day truly scared me. Surely, the randomness of time would not be so generous the next go around. Either way, I was safe from that happening.

This is just what I needed, too. It was my reward for putting up with all the crap back home, and the lack of things to do there as well. A reward for going to all those stupid outings with my sister, especially going to restaurants to meet up with her friends leaving me to sit to the side wishing I was somewhere else, like off with my dad, or something. I mean, he could introduce me to this "cute and really sweet" girl he told me about, if he could find her again. I laughed at the possibility, but I bet she really was cute.

I mean, it's total bullshit, and yes, that's a legitimate term to describe all the crap I'd had to deal with. Hmmm, let's see, an average summer day would first involve boredom for most of the morning, leading through a nice lunch comprising a big bowl of cereal. Next, my sister would need to be driven to some store, to pick up "art supplies". Oh yeah, and don't even ask why someone who is about to turn 17 can't drive…it's a really long story and one that involves a little trip to the courthouse. Now, these weren't just ordinary art supplies. These were "special" art supplies. Not only were they rather expensive, but they could only be purchased at a certain store where a certain "guy" worked. So, I'd basically sit my unhappy, bored ass in the Chevy while she "reviewed" the art supplies for freakin' hours. I mean, get it over already! I don't give a fuck if you like my sister, and I don't give two shits if she wants to sleep with you. I don't fucking care, just don't involve me as an alibi.

Okay, so that's basically a standard summer afternoon. Well when I'm not thinking, hmmm, well my freaking room is clean, I already scanned, I mean read, my summer reading. I could go to the mall again, by myself, to not buy anything, cause shopping for clothes sucked, check out some of the infrequently hot girls, none of whom would give me the time of day, not that I tried. Or I could try to get to the next level of Duck Hunt. Of course, I could screw around on the piano again, not knowing what the hell I was doing, unless I just tapped around on the black keys, which was okay, in a ridiculous way, sounding like some half-ass Asian musical.

I mean, I was basically a nerd trapped in a skinny surfer dude's body, not that I was that good at surfing or anything, or actually got to do it on a regular basis. Save for the summers, where my cousin from Vero, and I would borrow her dad's little pick-up truck. Now that I think of it, that wasn't all that bad.

Something was kind of off though, I thought as I sat there on the bench with Sara. I mean, I felt like I was missing something and it was rendering itself as a sort of infatuation toward Sara. We hadn't departed yet, and we still had many more days and nights to go, but it felt like there was something bothering me, and when I really thought about it, it wasn't a lust for her…it was something else…something beautifully strange, like that "cute and really sweet" girl sending me telepathic messages or something. I chuckled, eh, it was probably just the storm again.

Watching the marina as a general air of activity increased, a dive boat left for the open water with one on board, and more and more ambient laughter and general chatter could be heard from back toward the dorms. I looked down at my Casio, noting that some time had passed since we left the cafeteria. The laughter grew louder, and more frequent, intermixed with screams of surprise, and yells of miscellaneous energy. Looking back toward the picnic tables, I gathered that teams were being picked for the manhunt game, or some other organization procedure to get the rules out to the masses. From merely the rule and selection process, it looked like the rest of the crew was going to have a good time. I looked back out toward the marina, and settled back into my proximity with Sara.

A little while later we walked back toward the picnic tables, to reunite with our two friends. We found Will, sitting down on one of the benches, facing out, while Kristen sat directly behind him up on the table part. He was leaning against her, which I guess prompted her to begin to massage his shoulders. Sara and I sat next to each other, on the bench, facing out toward the distant marina, where we had been eating ice cream earlier.

Kristen would occasionally karate chop his back, or squeeze his neck too aggressively, yet on purpose, and induce pain resulting in a yelp or two. They were definitely entertainment for Sara and me, and on a whim being able to provide a comedy show for hours.

I spotted the phone booth, unfortunately, because it reminded me that I probably needed to check in with my mom soon. I really wanted to call my dad, so that he could get me fired up again about our trip he planned for next month. I hoped it would be cool, but he did remind me that while in some remote location, he'd have me stay with one of his buddies so that he could do a quick flight, up and back to who knows where.

Chapter Eight

A couple of minutes later, a van arrived practically in front of us. A counselor dude rolled down the driver window, hailing us to see if we were waiting to head to the movie theater. We nodded as we got up and headed over toward the sliding door.

Kristen and Will immediately jumped in the back, while Sara and I sat on the bench seat in front of them. It was just us, for now, but I suspected that we wouldn't be the only ones. The counselor dude turned around, "Hey, we're waiting on one more, then we'll go."

I wonder who that could be. Probably some guy that would attempt to move in on our little group. He'd try to sit with us at the movie, or try to find something in common with Kristen or Sara by saying something like, "So…what type of music do you like?" I mean, come on, what kind of cheesy pick up line is that anyway. Not that it matters, 'cause the girl will probably say what kind of music she really likes, while the stud muffin will inform her that he likes some really "in" music, regardless if he actually likes it, just to sound cool for "listening" to something "current, and with it." Fuck that guy.

Once again, I was wrong. This smoking hot counselor girl jumped in the front passenger seat, and put her seat belt on as the dude put the van in drive. She was maybe two years older than me, at best, and I quickly looked back at Will, in shock, to see his response. He nodded in absolute concurrence with my non-verbal, perfect ten, hot college girl sighting. Lucky for us, Sara and Kristen were engaged in some sort of intellectual discussion about Julia Roberts, and how allegedly it wasn't her body that was used for the poster of Pretty Woman.

Instead of doing that typical, "hey, where are you all from" idle chit chat, the dude just attempted to talk with the hot brunette passenger, who really didn't seem that interested in what he was saying. I wonder what her deal is, I thought to myself. She's probably just stuck up.

Will and Kristen continued to play grab ass in the back seat, while Sara pointed out when she'd spotted a pretty bird. We drove past small houses on waterways, over small bridges, bigger bridges, past quaint little fishing marinas, and little waterside seafood diners. In all, I think Sara and I counted nine of these little diners whose name had "shack" somewhere in the restaurant title. "Shrimp Shack", "Crab Shack", "Lil' Shack", "Shack de Mexico" and even, "Shack's Shack" were sighted as being especially non-original. I decided that one day I wanted to come back and go to one of these little places, hopefully with her, or you know, maybe Miss "cute and really sweet". I laughed to myself, thinking, no big deal, I'd just have to find a way to get her here from the other side of the world, or wherever the hell my dad met her four long years ago. I think going with Sara would have been easier.

As we were passing one of the "shacks" located at the base of one of the causeways, over a small inlet of water, the gorgeous college girl quietly pointed toward it, motioning with her skinny olive-tan arms. It was weird, though, because she wasn't trying to get Dude's attention with the gesture. It was almost like she was pointing for someone in the backseat, or just thinking to herself, "I'd really like to go there one night" and subconsciously motioning with her arm. It's too bad for Dude though, because she was out of this world.

After another thirty minutes or so, we arrived at the movie theater. "Hey, after you get your tickets, let me know what time the movie's supposed to get out," Dude asked.

The four of us went to the ticket window and bought our tickets to, none other than Pretty Woman. Will walked back over to Dude and the hottie to let them know what the deal was, and as Will walked back to us, they walked off toward some small shops down the street.

We made our way into the theater itself, but not without Kristen and Sara stopping by the ladies room for a pit stop, or conversation…probably both. The theater wasn't crowded at all, but we weren't surprised being that it was a weekday afternoon. We found some seats near the middle as Kristen and Sara instinctively sat next to each other, with Will and me flanking them. The previews started, followed by the movie and a brief clap of thunder, muffled by the sound insulation of the theater.

I thought about making an attempt to hold Sara's hand, but I quickly talked myself out of it, for some reason or another. I liked her, but, I dunno, something was telling me not to. I guessed I just didn't need any more disappointment, but, what the hell, I mean two days before I came down here, my sister spotted my ex in some dude's car outside a Dairy Queen, with his hand up her shirt. I'm sure it was just ole Brad what's-his-nuts.

I kept my cool, and didn't worry about the whole hand holding thing with Sara. I would have more chances, so I just sat back and watched the rest of the movie. Sara and Kristen were obviously into it, and I think I even caught Will staring intently at the screen during especially sappy moments…I'd have to remember to harass him about that later.

What seemed like only fifteen minutes, the credits started, and the lights came up. We exited the theater into the orange hue of the later afternoon hours. It was weird coming outside to daylight, because for some reason it always feels like it should be dark when exiting the movie theater. We looked for Dude and Hottie, first straight toward the parking lot, then right, back to the main road, but Kristen spotted them off to the left down the sidewalk in front of the row where a Radio Shack, jewelry store, and Chinese restaurant were located. Dude was walking slightly ahead of Hottie, who held an ice cream cone and a napkin as she attempted to walk and eat ice cream at the same time, at which she was highly unsuccessful, stumbling every five steps or so. Dude nodded at us, then looked back at Hottie and inquired in an annoyed tone, "Damn girl…don't they have ice cream back where you come from?"

"Yes," she innocently replied in broken English. He looked back at us and shrugged his shoulders as if her response had nothing to do with what he actually wanted to know.

"Ya'll ready to roll?" Dude reached in his pocket for his keys, and Will nodded as we walked toward the van.

We piled in the same way we did when we left for the theater, to begin with, a couple of hours earlier. Dude quickly pulled out of the parking lot and onto the main road heading back to the east.

About a minute or so down the main road, Dude said something we couldn't hear, to Hottie, and then turned to us.

"Are you guys in the mood for pizza?"

"Oh yeah," Will and I replied almost simultaneously.

"All right," Dude confirmed as he looked back at the road. He looked down at his watch, and then said something to Hottie that was muffled by the van's air conditioner and the noise from the highway below. She appeared pretty distracted, because she didn't respond to him, or even look in his direction. She merely stared out of her window, and watched as the world passed on by.

We drove over the same bridges as before, but this time slowing down to anticipate a turn off. After signaling, Dude pulled the van into a white crushed shell parking lot in front of a small strip plaza.

It had the typical local gas station on one end, a dry cleaner, a vacuum repair shop, a barbershop, and to the far right, a small pizza restaurant. We parked almost directly in front, and got out of the van to head inside.

Seating was easy. Off to the right side, near a Galaga video game machine and two gumball stands, there was a four top with a small table for two people directly behind it. Will and I sat on one side of the four top with Sara and Kristen across from us. Dude and Hottie were directly behind the girls.

I caught Sara briefly staring out of the window which we were sitting right next to, for just a second longer than a mere glance, as if thinking about something that had happened, or was going to happen. Toward the end of her fifteen-second stare, the right edge of her mouth revealed a slight fretful frown as confirmed in her eyes when she looked back at me.

The waitress, or owner's wife, or co-owner, or owner's mother, or land-lord, or whoever she was came over and placed menus at the edge of the table while asking us what we wanted to drink. I really didn't pay attention to what anyone else was ordering, but Sara ordered a root beer, and I did the same, although I normally forget about root beer as a drink option.

"Did you order something without ice?" Kristen pivoted in her chair and curiously quizzed Hottie.

"Yes."

"Oh...I've never heard of anyone ordering Sprite without ice." Kristen wasn't being accusatory or funny, she was genuinely concerned for Hottie's wellbeing, if you want to call it that. Hottie didn't say anything.

"Does it hurt your teeth or something?" Kristen pressed, compassionately.

"I am not used to it. They do not drink ice where I am from."

Will chimed in, "Why, will you get Montezuma's Revenge?" Sara and I laughed while Kristen glared because he had cut in on her legitimate fact finding session.

"She's not from Mexico, Will!" Kristen quickly replied.

"Huh? Uh...okay whatever. I thought you were."

"Will, just be quiet, sit there and look pretty," Kristen interrupted and smiled thus revealing her perfectly straight teeth, proud of herself for putting him in his place. The rest of the crew snickered while I patted Will on the back.

"Seriously, where are you from?" Kristen asked.

"My mother is Cuban, and father is from Crimea, but claims Russia now." She quickly dropped her head, presumably looking at the menu.

"Oh cool," Kristen said.

"So you live in Cuba, or...what was the other one?" Will honed in.

"I lived with my father, some, then I went to Mazyr."

"Where is that?" Kristen politely inquired.

"It is town, two hundred and fifty kilometers south east of Minsk."

"I have no idea where that is." Will laughed.

"I'm not surprised." Kristen teased. Sara and I were taking in the entertainment, to which Dude was now a party to.

"Well...where is it then, Kristen?" Will sat back and crossed his arms, smirking.

"I'm not...I'm not sure where Minsk is." Kristen looked back at Sara.

"In Turkey?" Will asked, bewildered.

"You're the turkey!" Kristen smiled. Will needed to just hoist the white flag and surrender.

"It is in Soviet Union," Hottie finally admitted, defeated.

"Oh," Kristen responded, at a reduced volume.

We looked back at our menus as Hottie lowered her head, slightly, then looked out toward the parking lot. She looked slightly sad, possibly homesick, or maybe it was that she was ashamed or embarrassed that her dad was from *that* country. She didn't seem so bad. She didn't look like she hated Americans, or wanted to kill all of us for that matter. She didn't look like a demon, just some really hot college girl…albeit with an accent and someone who doesn't like ice.

"What's your name?" Sara broke the uncomfortable silence.

"Patronymic?"

"Um…just your name."

"Isla."

"Isla?"

"Yes."

"Isla like 'Izz-La' or Isla like 'Iss-La'?"

"Isla like 'Iss-La'."

"That's a pretty name," Kristen concluded and Isla politely smiled.

We made idle conversation among the four of us for a couple of minutes before the waitress took our order, and more generic topics like what was going on later in the week, and whether or not Will was going to "break it down" for us at the dance later on in the session.

The pizza came, allowing Will and I to devour our pepperoni and sausage before Sara and Kristen could finish two slices of their cheese and mushroom. We joked around for a while longer before Kristen decided she wanted to go outside and check out some random cat that she spotted earlier while we were all eating. So, she quickly recruited Sara and off they went, first grabbing some pizza crust.

Isla too got up and headed outside. "Hey…that commie chick is hot!" Will said to Dude, who laughed.

"Yeah…*oh yeah*."

"Are you two…you know?" Will asked, while I shook my head. However, it was a good question.

"Well, ya know." He leaned back, proud of himself.

"So, is that a yes?" Will confidently asked.

"Let's just say, we hang out." He smirked.

"Yeah, okay." Will lightly punched me on the thigh, under the table, indicating that he was probably full of shit.

Dude was looking out of the window, just as Kristen handed the cat over to Isla who immediately starting scratching it behind the ears and under the chin. Sara looked back at me and smiled, while Kristen picked up the rest of the pizza crust. We got up and headed outside to meet up and get going.

"Ya'll ready?" Dude asked as he pulled the van's keys out of his pocket. The girls didn't really respond, so we walked up to them to see what the deal with the cat was.

"I think he's a stray," Kristen announced.

"Yeah…me too," Sara added. Isla had the cat over on his back and it was purring loudly and pawing up toward her face and dark brown hair.

"How do you know that?" Will asked.

"I dunno…it just doesn't look real clean." Kristen was rubbing its ears.

"Well, there's nothing we can do. Plus we need to roll," Dude added.

"Yeah…I guess so," Kristen conceded as she retrieved her hand from the soft clutches of the orange and white striped tabby while Isla continued to hold it, very caringly.

"Come on, Isla. We need to get back." Dude said, once again, and slightly rushed.

Isla simply replied, "Yes."

She looked back toward the sidewalk area in front of the pizza place, where there were little benches under the roof outcropping. She walked off while still holding the cat like a newborn.

Placing the cat under one of the benches, she patted it on the head a couple of times while she whispered something we couldn't hear, but was directed toward the cat anyway. She stood back up, and walked into the restaurant just as it started lightly raining. We could see her inside talking to some guy behind the counter, then came back out with a paper cup cut in half.

She leaned over and placed the cup, filled with water, under the bench next to the cat. Kristen handed her the rest of the pizza crust, which Isla put next to the make shift water bowl. Again, Isla placed her fingers on top of the cat's head and held it there for a couple of seconds in silence, just staring.

It was kind of sad, and it was like she knew she was never going to see this cat again, or was telling it something like, "Sorry I can't take you with me, Mister Kitty," or other similar parting words.

She slowly got up and starting walking back to the van, her hair now growing damp from the falling rain. She had probably felt better after outfitting the cat with some sort of ad hoc nest, or showed Mister Kitty that he would be safe under the bench, and at least out of the elements.

Dude started the van and made his way out toward the main road leading back again to the east. Isla looked toward the cat, which had come out of its nest and was quickly walking toward our van. It couldn't keep up, but was intently walking directly at us. Dude couldn't see the cat, but Isla clearly could.

Dude pulled onto the road, while Isla kept her eyes locked on the cat; turning further and further toward the right in her seat to where at one point she couldn't see the cat out of her window any longer. After bumping her head against the window and attempting one last time to see the little cat, which proved unsuccessful, she straightened out in her seat and faced forward, staring out toward the highway.

After a short drive past shell shops and bait stores, we were back "on campus". Dude pulled up to the front of the picnic tables, situated between the two dorms.

We said our "see ya's" and goodnights, and went our respective ways. "That was an interesting day," I said to Will while walking up the stairs to our room.

"It sure was."

Chapter Nine

The next morning the weather had grown worse, and was pretty windy outside. While we were getting ready for breakfast, one of the counselors opened the door and came in with a box full of sandwiches, chips, and sodas. He informed us that we needed to sit tight for at least most of the morning, to wait for one of the storm bands to blow over.

A couple of hours later, I decided to go grab something to drink out of the vending machine, near the docks, where Sara and I had sat the day before.

"You want anything?" I asked Will.

"Yeah, bring me a Coke."

I stepped outside, into the thirty mile per hour wind and rain, and quickly ran over toward the overhang which just barely sheltered the vending machines. I inserted the cash and retrieved a Coke and a Sprite, one by one.

I dropped the two cans into each of my short's pockets and waited a few moments until the rain wasn't blowing as torrential, then rapidly jogged to the next covered spot. As I approached the scuba gear washout area, I quickly noticed a girl standing underneath.

"Hey. You're Isla, right?"

"Yes." She was drenched, her long brown hair saturated and somewhat tangled.

"What are you doing here?" I asked, as she shyly dropped her head and stared at her worn out sneakers.

"I was going to get some-thing to drink," she said in her strange accent.

"What were you going to get?"

"Sprite."

I pulled both cans out of my pockets and handed her the Sprite. Her eyes grew wide with a short surge of happiness like I had magically read her mind.

"Thank you." She smiled, and then gently received the can from my outstretched arm.

"Don't open it just yet, cause I ran with it and it might explode." She remained smiling, me noticing a small scar above her mouth on her upper lip.

"Okay, I will not." She stopped smiling but continued to look into my eyes.

"What?" I wasn't used to such a pretty girl staring at me, and I grew slightly embarrassed and uncomfortable, albeit in a good way.

"I am sorry." She dropped her head again.

"Oh, no…I didn't mean, I just wanted to know if you needed something." She smiled again, "I guess we can open them now." I added.

We slowly opened the cans without incident, and as we stood there and drank, I actually had time to take in the natural beauty of her small frame, thick brown hair, and dark chocolate eyes. I didn't want her to catch me staring, but I dismissed that the possibility was high because she would often nervously look around, then down at her feet.

Her skin was smooth, her fingers slender like her tan legs, and her overall facial features were in near perfect proportion. Maybe it was just that we were alone under this shack in the middle of a thunderstorm, and the static electricity of the far off lightning was having an effect on my brain electrochemistry, but…she was *really* pretty.

Back in the room, I thought about her, a little, especially when Will questioned me about his missing can of Coke. "Sorry man, I guess the machine ate the money."

Later that night, my mind wandered somewhere different as I drifted off to sleep. There was something wonderfully odd happening now, something…uh, it's probably nothing. I had really weird dreams that night too. I guess me and a bunch of aliens in a bar, and thunderclouds looking for navigational buoys would have to do for now.

Chapter Ten

For some reason, I was up really early the next day. So, needless to say, I beat everyone to the "shit, shower, and shave" routine. Except, in my case, shaving always came before showering, albeit once every couple of days, the shaving part that is. It was still early, but the sun had come up, so I got dressed and walked downstairs and out toward the docks.

There were only two or three counselors around the docks performing various tasks and socializing, while a mechanic had his arms deep into one of the outboards on one of the many dive boats in the little marina. I went over to one of the guy counselors and asked if he needed anything.

"Oh no man, we got it. Thanks though." He was genuinely glad I offered.

"Actually, if you want, can you help us load all these tanks onto those two boats?" one of the girls asked. "It will really save the others a bunch of time after breakfast...ya know, if the tanks are already loaded on."

"Yeah...sure thing." I had nothing else to do.

I headed over to the shack where all the tanks were standing at attention to be loaded into the racks on the boats.

"Hey, aren't you Kyle?" the other counselor chick asked.

"Yeah. How come?" I stopped and put down the two tanks.

"Oh no reason. Jimmy just said he met you and your buddies." Who the hell is Jimmy?

"Who?" I hoped he wasn't some young kid or something.

"Jimmy? He's got blonde hair, kind of muscular, and he's like, uh...this tall." She held her hand out to about a foot over her head. She could still tell I had no idea of to whom she was referring.

"You know...he's always hitting on that weird foreign girl?"

"Oh. Isla?" I guessed Jimmy was "Dude's" name.

"Yeah, I guess." She shrugged her shoulders as she placed a scuba mask back in one of the wash-out tanks.

"You have that pretty blonde girl friend, don't you?" she added with a smile. I'm sure she was referring to Sara, and I was happy that the word on the street was that we were together.

"I guess...I mean, sure."

"She's cool too," the chick added.

"Yeah." I picked up the two tanks and walked toward the dive boat, while the counselor girl went back to work on the masks.

I kind of liked mindless work, which allowed my thoughts to wander to random subjects like the storm, submarines, and that trip me and dad were getting ready to take. My daydreaming was quickly interrupted by seeing the two female counselors splashing water from the tank on the guy as he turned around to hang a regulator up on hooks, or the mechanic occasionally revving an outboard motor.

My small, and insignificant, task was complete. I walked the short distance back to where the three were working and started helping out with the masks.

"You want a job here?" The guy asked, causing me to smile.

I headed toward the dorms and the picnic tables where a couple of people started gathering. I didn't recognize any of them, so I walked back toward my dorm and headed up the stairs.

Before I rounded the corner at the top, I looked back toward the tables and noticed someone who resembled Sara in the phone booth on the other side of the wide driveway. Still, I walked around the corner and into my room.

"Did the early bird get the worm?" Will jokingly asked.

"I did see something that resembled your tiny dick out there, but a little sparrow carried it away." He laughed as he exited the bathroom with a towel around his waist.

"How long before you're ready?" I asked.

"Five minutes?" Will walked over to his bunk and opened his suitcase.

"Okay. I'm gonna head back outside."

I walked down the stairs and sat over on the small wall that bordered the tables, trying to figure out who was in the phone booth. The glass wasn't too dirty, but the way the little ledge and phone was placed in the booth, I couldn't make out the occupant. I looked behind me to see the pre-breakfast crowd growing around the tables and wall.

It was already humid out, which really wasn't that bad in that we didn't have air conditioning in the dorm rooms anyway, but, I had the sense that today was going to be extra warm. I looked down at my stained shirt trying to remember when I had spilled mustard, but dismissed it as probably happening months earlier.

The smell of sunscreen and tanning lotion began filling the air, which was always a welcome scent, as mainly girls, applied the stuff to themselves and their associates.

I looked back at the phone booth to see Sara walking toward me about half way between the booth and where I was sitting.

"Hey!" I called.

"Hey." She tried to crack a smile, but was having a hard time.

"What's up?"

"Oh…nothing much."

"Was that your mom?" Right after the words left my mouth I regretted asking for fear that I was being nosy…which I was.

"No…just some friend of mine back home."

"Oh." I looked down at her hands, which were slightly fidgeting around her lower torso, then dropped my gaze to the ground in front of her barely worn-in flip flops.

"Well…today is gonna be really hot." She sat down next to me, but not as close as she had in the past.

"Yeah. I guess it's not as windy as yesterday." I knew that she had been talking to that fuck-wad "boyfriend" of hers back home…or whatever the hell he was.

"Yeah." She sat next to me while we both stared at the ground. This really sucked. I wanted this moment to hurry up and end, yet at the same time I really wanted it to last long enough for us to figure out what exactly was going on.

We sat there in silence for a little while. I thought about how lucky I was to be sitting next to her, and to have experienced being around someone as pleasant as Sara. I mean, even worse case, I basically had a friend who was pretty enough that none of my other friends back at school would believe me. Good thing I had a couple of pictures of her…I'd have to get more, especially with me in them.

"Hey hey!" Hearing a familiar voice, we both turned around to spot Kristen.

"Hey!" I responded as we smiled.

"Where's my boy toy?"

"I think he's still upstairs primping."

"That's good!" She laughed and sat down on the other side of Sara.

"Is it me…or is it really hot out here?" She picked up the back of her thick dark hair off of her neck and held it as she pulled the elastic band off her wrist to form a pony tail.

"Tell me about it." Sara smiled, which was a good thing.

Out of the corner of my left eye I could see Will sneaking up behind Kristen, as she continued to be distracted while sculpting her pony tail.

"Guess who?" He said while holding his hands over Kristen's eyes.

"Uh…Tom Cruise?" She quickly responded.

"No?" Will replied.

"Hmm…Bruce Willis?"

"No."

"Oh…Mel Gibson?"

"No!"

"Tom Hanks?"

"No!"

"Tom Cruise?" She laughed.

"No…you already said that!" He was getting agitated.

"Oh…it must be…it must be, my…Willy bean!" she teased as she turned around and kissed her finger, then touched his lips, causing him to melt. Sara and I both laughed, which is exactly what was needed.

After breakfast, we quickly made our way back to our dorm rooms to change into swim suits and grab what gear we were going to need for the scuba trip that morning. Will and I were back around the tables in less than five minutes, followed by Sara a few minutes after us. Kristen shuffled out in her sandals and cut offs seconds later.

We walked over to the dive boats but first had to grab regulators, weight belts, masks, fins and buoyancy compensators. As we waited for Kristen to find a good mask, two counselors started calling out names of who was going to be on which boat. We were under the impression that we were going to be able to pick which one, so that we could all ride together, but apparently that wasn't the plan.

The counselor, standing in front of the left boat called out the following names, "Matt R, Carlos, Kristen D, Mark, Jen, Sara, Suiza, William B, Debbie, Katie C, Ian, and Natasha."

What the fuck! There were only four other people left that weren't counselors and basically an empty boat on the right. I walked up to the counselor-guy that was reading the names, and asked if my name was on that list.

"Let's see, Kyle A...Kyle A. Nope. You must be on the other boat. Go check with Cindy over there and ask if you're on her boat." I looked over at Will, Kristen and Sara who appeared to be as shocked as I was.

"Hey Kyle, I'll just switch with someone on your boat so that we can ride together," Sara confidently added as she walked over to Cindy to check, while I stood around with Will and Kristen.

A few moments later, Sara reported, "Okay, for some reason, they want the boats divided up like this." Sara resigned.

"Man, this sucks." I fretted.

"Well, don't worry about it too much...we'll just meet back at lunch." Kristen's attempted cheer fell on deaf ears with Sara, but I did feel a little better.

"Yeah, okay. See you guys later," I said while looking at Sara.

"See ya," she responded, while genuinely wanting us to be together on the same boat.

I walked toward Cindy, and asked if I was on her boat, and what I had done to be so lucky as to be separated from my friends.

"Oh, Kyle...is it?" she happily asked.

"Yeah."

"Jill wanted you to go with us." She motioned over toward one of the counselors that I was helping earlier, to which Jill must have caught the tail end of the conversation.

"Hey there Kyle! I thought you'd be able to help us out on our boat," Jill pleasantly added, brushing her strawberry blonde hair out of her tan, lightly freckled face.

"Uh…okay, I guess. Why?"

"Well, you are a better swimmer, and, well diver for that matter, you know, than the others. You know, and a little older." She smiled.

"Okay…I guess I can do whatever…"

"Yeah, don't worry, it will be cool," Jill added.

"Well, all his friends are on the other boat," Cindy softly responded.

"I know. But, we need you over here, to help and stuff," Jill responded.

"With what?" I sat down.

"We need to take some scientists out past the Pourtales Escarpment." Those freaking asshole scientist-clowns at it again. Whatever.

"Oh." I had no idea what she was talking about.

I helped move some stuff around on the boat, and eyed all the scuba tanks that I had loaded a couple of hours earlier. However, now we had about twice as many tanks.

The guy from earlier, who I was helping wash masks, was behind the helm, and checking fuel levels in the red tanks that were added moments earlier. He must have seen me looking at him and what he was working on, so he motioned me over.

"Can you move this over there?" He pointed at one of the fuel tanks.

I picked it up, full of fuel, and carefully placed it behind a stack of waterproof hard plastic cases. I wondered what was in the cases as I stepped past them, while Jill and Cindy were apparently inventorying something in plastic bins toward the front of the boat.

Five individuals approached the boat from the edge of the dock, appearing to know exactly what they were doing. My guess was that these people were the illustrious scientists that I so loathed. Actually, and on second glance, they didn't appear that bad.

Two girls and a guy in their mid-twenties with the two other guys much older…like in their forties or something. They had some of their dive gear with them, and one had a big duffle bag that looked like it had been to the moon and back, embroidered with worn out "U.S. Navy" stitching.

The "better" boat was departing the harbor. I could see Will flanking Kristen to her left, with Sara at the farthest seat aft on the other side. Good thinking, Will. Kristen had her arms stretched out behind the both of them, making me smile for some reason, which was typical Kristen. The wake of the left outboard arrowed right to where they were sitting, the boat now turning to maneuver out of the marina.

"Hey Kyle," Cindy called out.

"Huh?"

"Can you help me put anti-fog on these masks?"

"Yeah…sure." I walked aft to where a little water-filled well was located, with the masks, and Cindy leaning over with her t-shirt billowing out around her neck, her light brown hair tucked into the collar so that it wouldn't blow in the wind.

As I snaked my way around the gear, I was surprised to find Isla, trying on fins presumably to find the right size. She looked up and revealed a brief, slight smile, then focused back on the fins.

I really couldn't estimate her age, not that it really mattered, but she was probably only a couple of years older than me. I think it was difficult because she was Cuban, or Crimean, or Russian, or wherever the hell she was from. But, regardless, there was something very strange about her, yet not uncomfortable. If ever someone deserved the title "exotic" it was she. On one hand, she could be Miss Universe, but at the same time, a professor with a white lab coat, her slightly tangled hair pulled back into a bun, with her eyes shielded by the glare of horned rimmed glasses. Fortunately, there was no lab coat, just dark blue shorts and a snuggly fit, light yellow t-shirt.

Jill and I were signaled into untying the lines that held the vessel in place, as one of the male scientists, Doug, engaged the throttles into reverse. We slowly backed out of the slip, and made a shallow right, then left turn to depart the marina.

The two older male scientists, Doug and this cat named Terry, stood at the helm, while Doug continued to pilot our boat. They would look down at some charts, check the compass, then talk among themselves, every once in a while saying something to one of the younger assistants.

Cindy was trying to get the attention of the younger male assistant, for whatever flirtatious reasoning, covered by a "work" related task. As for Isla, she simply stared out over the water.

Occasionally, I could see the other boat about a half of a mile or so in the distance. However, it wasn't long before it made the predicted southeasterly turn. We continued south, then eventually southwest.

After about an hour of steady motoring, we slowed down, then stopped. Terry and the male assistant tossed out two anchors, which required the addition of rope. I couldn't see the ocean floor, which indicated, along with the additional rope, that this was going to be a deeper dive than the usual forty to fifty feet. The water was a much darker blue and the wind was coming out of the south, probably from where the storm was churning.

All but Cindy started gearing up. I informed her and Jill that I would stay on the boat, but for some reason, Doug, overhearing, said that he had a job for me. Jill handed me a buoyancy compensator and a regulator, which was much newer than what I was used to. Terry handed me a writing tablet with a pencil attached, and a big ass Citizen dive watch. Terry too, was somewhat interesting, but in a completely different manner from Isla. He was cut…muscular but not bulky. He had a short buzz cut in salt and pepper color, angular eyebrows, a stern jawline, and a permanent "five-o'clock shadow". Basically, his face defined the word "chiseled."

"This is what I need you to do." He pushed the mode button on the watch, and set it to "timer".

"Yeah?" I moved my Casio to my right wrist, and strapped the Citizen on my left.

"This has a depth gauge on it, so you can use it as a backup."

"Okay, cool."

He explained to me what he wanted me to do in some detail, then handed me a dive knife. He seemed pretty relaxed, yet calculating, and wanted to make sure I took some roll in this little operation.

After a couple of minutes, the team started jumping in the water, after selecting their "buddies". I was last, except for Isla, which by default left us as buddies.

As we bobbed on the surface, waiting for the command to submerge by Doug, Isla had trouble getting water to stay out of her mask.

"I think mask broke," she said in her weird accent.

"Do you want me to get another one?" I offered.

"No. I have it." She swam back over to the boat where she tossed the mask back on the deck. Cindy must have known exactly what throwing the mask on the boat meant, and retrieved a different one.

"Thank you," Isla said as Cindy tossed the mask toward her. She pulled her hair out of her face and clumsily fitted the mask.

I turned my attention to the other divers, but they had already submerged. I looked at Isla who was grabbing her regulator, appearing oblivious to the others' departure.

"Hey...they left," I said as I readied my regulator.

"Yes." She didn't appear concerned.

"Well, which way did they go?" I quietly remarked, trying to trace the bubbles.

"I do not know." Isla looked back at me.

"Hey Cindy!" I yelled.

"Yeah?"

"Can you tell which way they went?"

"Uh...oh I think I...yeah. They went that way!" She pointed toward the south.

"Are you ready?" I asked Isla.

"Yes." We began to deflate our buoyancy compensators, sinking into the dark blue ocean.

Underwater, we had a hard time making out the intended heading of the team. I looked down at my compass and tried to maintain a southerly heading.

I looked over to my right at Isla, who was a little behind me but off my waist about three feet away, looking straight ahead. I looked back at my compass, trying my best not to get us lost.

I glanced over at Isla again, and waved my hand in front of her so that she would look at me. I put my palms up to signal that I really didn't know what I was doing or where we were supposed to be heading. She looked at me and slowly took the lead and put about four feet of distance between her flippers and my face.

For about thirty seconds, or so, we continued on. She glanced back, then stopped. I approached, and as I swam to within feet of her, she pointed off ahead, presumably indicating that she had spotted the rest of the crew, but in the process had accidently knocked my mask off my head.

As I repositioned my mask, I struggled just to maintain site of her, as she swam in the direction, where she had earlier pointed. Right before I lost sight of her, she stopped and waited, allowing me to catch up.

Locating our crew, the dive continued. I performed my mundane tasks, while Isla took in the undersea sights. The rest of the group did their jobs, me thinking that this would have been much cooler had we been diving on a shipwreck or something.

We followed and ascended, slowly, back toward the north, but not without me having to get Isla's attention so that she wouldn't be left behind, most likely distracted by the fish and coral.

I was glad to be heading back to the surface, because I was getting a little cold down below. I didn't have a decompression chart with me, because this wasn't my normal gear, but I figured I was probably the least experienced diver here, so I wasn't too worried about the decompression stop that we probably needed to make.

Sure enough, we arrived back at the anchor line; where there were eight air tanks suspended around fifteen feet. We grabbed the new regulators, hanging from the spare air tanks, and started our decompression stop.

It felt like forever, but I really didn't care, because my job was over. I looked around at the others, checking their gear and each other for whatever reason. Isla was still right next to me, but only occasionally looked over. She was gazing back in the direction of the team's earlier activity on the ocean floor.

I couldn't read her. She was very pretty, naturally tan, skinny, and, for some reason I couldn't figure her out…not even a hint. It was like looking into a dimly lit room where I could barely see anything, but knew that there were tables, couches and chairs and other stuff scattered about, and a flickering television off in the distance. Oh well.

We completed our stop, and got back on the surface and onto the boat. We took our gear off, and stowed our tanks.

"We've got another spot we have to hit," Terry announced. "About ten minutes south west of here." He pointed in the general direction.

Doug fired up the engines, and put the boat in gear. I sat down next to Isla, my partner for this little trip.

"So, where are you from again?" I leaned back on the bench resting against my gear bag.

"Mazyr." She had a strange accent, but somehow pretty cool.

"Where is that?"

"It is near Minsk."

"Oh, that's right. Where's that?"

"In Soviet Union."

"I mean…is it a city or a small town, or something?"

"Yes."

"Oh." I wasn't really getting anywhere…apparently she doesn't like to talk.

"Do you go to college, or something?"

"I attend university."

"Where?"

"Leningrad." She looked out over the water.

"Where is that?"

"North west Russia."

"Uh…okay." She was short with me, but I persisted.

"So, uh…what are you studying?"

"What you mean?"

"You know, what do you, uh…like to learn about?"

"Cel-es-tial mecha-nics and astronomy."

"Huh? What is that?" I politely asked.

"Specifically, orbital com-puta-tional physics and, um…how do you say, sub?"

"Sub?" I had no idea what she was trying to say.

"Sub, uh…you know, um, after?"

"Huh?"

"Like simul…but after. I do not know how to," she grimaced in frustration.

"Oh, like simultaneous?"

"Da. I mean, yes. But after."

"I really have no…oh. Subsequent?"

"Yes." she smiled, "sub-se-quent interaction with wave versus pho-tonic mechanisms," she immediately continued while looking out toward the horizon.

"I really don't…I mean, I know what an orbit is." This girl is *deep* and I uh, well, I'm starting to think she's pretty groovy.

"Also, you know? Di-men-sion-al strain on galactic under-currents? And learn ring systems, reference frames, mathematical anomaly asso-cia-ted with nano-particle cancel-lation?" She looked down at her hands, fidgeting with her already short fingernails.

"Uh…what about, escape velocity?" I pulled that out of my ass, but it sounded good…at least to me.

"Depends on mass, density, comp-osition, rotation, vi-sco-sity of atmosphere, elemental, oh, um yes, propulsion mode and reactionary vec-tors." Again, I had no idea what she was talking about.

"What about reaching apogee after pre-orbit burn?" I think I heard apogee somewhere before, and I remembered what a pre-orbit burn was from some TV show I watched about a week before I arrived. I barely understood one word of what she was talking about, and it wasn't her accent that was the barrier. However, I was glad that she was finally talking.

"You meaning nuclear pro-pul-sion engine or chemical?" She pulled up her leg and retied her discolored, old white, right sneaker. Then she looked back at me, probably sensing my total confusion, but hopefully not sensing my growing intrigue.

"If referring to stan-dard, oh uh, no. How do you, eh, I don't remember how to say."

"What don't you know?" I asked as she looked into my eyes, breaking a slight smile causing my heart to beat just a little bit faster.

"Word for Earth."

"Globe?"

"Nyet, I mean, no."

"Sphere?"

"No. Sorry." She looked down at her knees.

"Land?"

"No. Like terra, ter-rast."

"Oh, you mean terrestrial?" She grinned, showing her pretty teeth.

"Yes!" She paused, taking in a breath, "Ter-restrial based propellants, than capacity needed to obtain escape velocity and achieve ap-og-eal transfer, one must…well, you want to know formula? Here I write." She took my tablet, and on the back wrote a bunch of crap in some foreign language scattered about with numbers, algebraic signs, and other weird stuff, which I have feared that college math would attempt to reveal.

"You see, pro-pel-lant mixtures required to obtain escape velocity of say, lunar body orbit-ing this planet, primarily depend on chemical energy contained within in-di-vi-du-al molecular composition of combined oxi-dizer and, eh, how do you say…um, com-bust-ible."

"Uh huh." I was basically out of anything remotely intelligent to add.

"It is achievable on other celestial body to obtain escape velocity with liquid or solid pro-pel-lants, however in…efficient."

"Oh."

"Why are you interested in this?"

"Uh…I dunno."

"It is okay to be concerned with sit…uations like this." She looked briefly at the empty air tanks, then back at me.

"Like what?"

"Like *our* pos-i-tion in this universe."

As if on cue, and inconveniently interrupted by Doug, we arrived at our destination and dropped anchor. The brooding storm off in the distance was generating a disproportionately higher wind speed than the team expected.

"Man…that's gotta be a brisk twenty knot wind," Doug exclaimed.

"Yeah, but it'll be smooth underneath," Terry calmly added.

The team started getting ready, including me. We still had a bunch of full air tanks, and the way the assistants were organizing them, I figured we were in for a longer dive. Doug grabbed some device he called a rebreather, out of his duffel bag, and starting doing some sort of diagnostic bullshit on it.

Isla merely sat still, taking in all the activity, presumably tired from her physics lecture. In fact, she put her shorts back on, over her swimsuit, and grabbed her shirt. I guess I'd have to find a new dive partner.

Doug briefed us on what we would be doing, and that we had some different mixture in our air tanks than the standard percentages. This was way outside my level of comfort, but these people knew allegedly what they were doing so I figured that I'd be just fine. I was a little disappointed that Isla wasn't joining us, but I guess she'd had enough.

We gathered toward the front of the boat in preparation to hit the water. The wind grew substantially stronger and knocked over some half-full cans of Coke and a bottle of sunscreen.

"How much wind was that?" Terry asked Doug, who was looking at some sort of portable wind meter.

"Twenty-five knots."

"Oh well, let's get ready to dive." The wind picked up even more. It was now getting hard to stand up, so Jill and I quickly planted ourselves on the deck.

"Thirty knots," Doug yelled over the wind, while he stumbled.

The boat was pitching back, away from the wind, barely held by the two anchor lines. The wind gusted more.

"God damn, that's a lot." Doug signaled to Cindy and Jill to retrieve the anchors.

"We're getting outta here." Doug stumbled back to the helm while taking off his gear. Jill and Cindy were having a difficult time with the lines.

"Cut 'em," Doug yelled, while Terry pulled out a knife and sliced through the anchor lines, allowing them to disappear beneath the sea.

Doug fired up the engines and made a one hundred and eighty degree turn back to the northeast. The wind quickly died down, but was sustaining a good twenty knots, which seemed like a lot on the water. I took my gear off and sat back down, next to Isla.

"What the hell was that?" I rhetorically muttered.

"I am not ex-pert on ther-mal con-vey-an-ces or cy-clonic forces." She looked toward the churning blue-grey sky off to the south, while sucking and gently chewing on her lower lip and fidgeting with her fingernails.

She was now completely dry, as were basically all of us, and fully clothed, with a faded purple towel flecked with old bleach stains, wrapped over her thighs. She was very serious, but for her brief and refreshing smiles. In a way, I kind of felt bad for her yet was slightly envious at her displayed knowledge of space. Add in her accent, her adorable attempts at pronouncing big words, and her true physical perfection, despite the small scar just above her mouth, and beauty took on a whole new meaning.

I looked toward the water then back at Isla, and down toward her towel, where she was gently twisting one of the corners with her left hand, while she continued to look back toward the storm, occasionally sucking on her puffy lower lip, which caused me to smile, for some odd reason.

We proceeded on course for about an hour before catching sight of land. The wind had almost completely subsided, but for our typical headwind as a result of our speed over the water.

Isla was gazing out, but only about twenty feet to the side of the boat, down at the water, her shadowy brown hair blowing, sweeping across her chest, occasionally revealing a fretful demeanor.

"What's wrong?" I asked, yet received no response.

"Isla…what's wrong?"

"Oh…sorry." She looked down at her towel.

"What's going on?" I looked out to where she had been staring.

"Sorry?" She glanced up, but then dropped her mystical dark brown eyes back down, and started twisting the worn edge of her towel with her skinny tan fingers.

"What are you thinking?"

"I believe intra-species com-mu-ni-ca-tion of Delph-inus Cap-en-sis more com-plex than human." She looked out toward the ocean with her eyes watering, probably just a result of the drying effect of the wind.

"What are you talking…I mean…what do you mean by that?" She was breathing a little heavier.

"The to-nal range, in-flec-tion, ca-dence, volume, wave-length, oscil-la-tion, frequency var-i-a-tion, and broad-cast prop-a-ga-tion, is applied at much greater effi-ciency than human." She shifted her fretful eyes back toward mine.

"Do you like animals?" I attempted to distract her, because for some reason, this was making her slightly emotional.

"Yes." She looked back down.

"Like what?"

"All of them."

"Me too." I looked down at her olive toned hands.

"What is fav-orite?" She was still looking down, but able to engage.

"My grandmother had this German Shepard dog a long time ago. He was my best friend."

"Where is dog?"

"He died." She was nervously fiddling with the tattered corner of her towel again.

"What caused death?"

"I don't...I don't remember. I think he had a heart attack or something."

"Was it im-pro-per, eh, how do you say heart?"

"Uh, I guess pump?"

"No, not that." She looked down at my hands, smiling at my attempts to help find the word she was looking for.

"Cardiac?"

Yes, car-diac." She smiled again, "car-diac sync, non con-for-ming pal-pi-tation, dil-ation, fatigue, ext-ernal stressor, foreign body ingestion, allergic reaction, in-ap-pro-pri-ate immune response?"

"Uh...I don't...I think it was just old age."

"I see."

"What about you?"

"I made convenient acqua-in-tance with minor carn-ivorous mammal, felis catus."

"Huh?" I grinned.

"Cat."

"So, do you have a cat?"

"I do not have cat." Her eyes dropped again, obviously saddened.

"Why not?"

She paused for a moment, and bit her thumbnail. "I do not know."

"Well, where...what do you like about cats?" I tried to cheer her up.

She paused, again.

"Cat is efficient hunter. Utilizes effective cam-ou-flage, adap-table, audit-orially superior, engages in play for honing of stalking, dex-terity and combative ability, can release oh, um, how do you, oh se-ro-to-nin and mela-tonin on intern-alized command. Cat can mobilize off-spring rapidly, effect-tuate pronounced adrenal response, and for mass, is apex pred-a-tor." She was looking back at Jill who had just dropped her regulator, which she was stowing.

"I really never thought of it like that."

"Yes. And cat is capable of display affect-tion without ability to hide emo-tion-al and social oh no, um, this one is, I do not, ah okay, hi-er-archical functioning. Which is ad-van-ta-geous as trustworthy companion."

"Oh, okay." For some reason, I really felt sorry for her again. Somehow, in her ramblings, it felt as if she was off by herself on some distant moon, or island, or something, and that I was the only visitor she'd had in years.

"I would like to be-friend cat." Her mouth formed a slight distraught frown.

"Didn't we see a nice cat at that pizza joint?"

"Yes." She barely got the volume loud enough for me to hear.

"Well?"

"Well." She looked up and toward me.

"Can't you go get that cat?"

"What you mean, 'get'?"

"I think he was a stray, so why can't you…"

"I attempt-ted to locate cat two days ago."

"And?"

"I was not suc-cess-ful." She glanced away.

"Can you try again?"

"Yes." She nodded and looked down at her torn thumbnail. After picking it to the point of drawing blood, she gathered the small amount of gear that was presumably hers and neatly folded her towel into a perfect square, and repositioned it on her lap.

Back into the harbor, and over toward the slip, we had arrived. The crew efficiently gathered the gear, and then formed an ad hoc line to remove the air tanks from the boat. Isla was still sitting in her seat, looking down at her folded towel.

It only took us a couple of minutes to unload all of the gear. I walked a short distance over to Terry, who was washing out his gear in the fresh water bin.

"Hey…here's your watch back." I extended my hand so he could see what I was holding. He took the watch.

"Oh, and here's the knife." I unfastened it from the buoyancy compensator. He smiled.

"You keep it." He handed the watch back to me.

"Huh?" I was shocked.

"Yeah…you did a good job back there." He took his hand away after I retrieved the watch, going back to his cleaning.

"And the knife too…it's yours."

"What? No…I can't." I *did* want to keep them.

"No. They're yours. Besides, they issued me a new watch, and I have another knife just like that one." He winked again at me.

"Seriously? Are you sure?"

"I sure am, kid. They're yours now."

"Man! Thanks!" I buckled the watch back on my left wrist, while my Casio hung to my right.

"You did a very nice job. You deserve it." With that, he stored his gear back in the worn duffel bag and walked toward his team and Doug. What a cool watch, and a cool dude, after all.

Isla was coming off the boat, and I wanted to double check that I didn't leave anything on the boat so I walked back toward it.

"Hey Isla."

"Yes?" I didn't really know what I wanted to say.

"See you around" was all I could come up with.

"Okay." She headed back toward the little dive shack, and past it to the left down the driveway and out of view. It was 11:30, and had indeed been a strange morning.

Chapter Eleven

It was lunchtime and I headed back to the cafeteria, but solo this time because Will and the girls were still out on their dive trip. As I egressed from the line, I saw the three graduate assistants from the earlier dive trip sitting at one end of one of the twelve person tables. I determined that at least they would not be total losers about letting me sit next to them. As I got closer, I saw Isla sitting near the other end of the same table, with three seats between her and the closest assistant. I sat down across from her, while getting a "what's up" nod from the dude at the other end of the table.

"Hey Isla."

"Hello." She briefly looked up and smiled, probably glad she had someone to sit with.

"What's shakin?" I put some baked beans on my spoon and into my mouth.

"Eating." She took a sip of one of the three small chocolate milk cartons arranged in a semi-circle in front of her plate.

"Oh." I picked up a corncob.

"Hey Isla?"

"Yes?" She looked up again.

"Do you like it here?" I asked, causing her to glance at me, then immediately dropped her somewhat blank stare back down toward the only thing she had put on her plate, peas.

"Yes."

"Oh…me too," I cheerfully replied.

"It is a nice place," she added while skewering two peas with the small metal fork, and gently placing them into her mouth.

"Yeah, I'm gonna miss it." I took another bite of corn.

"I do not want to leave, but eventually, we will all leave here." She slowly stabbed two more peas and ate them.

"I guess so."

One of the female assistants called from the other end of the table, "Hey Isla! I saw your name on top of one of the sign-up sheets outside."

"Yes," she responded in a low, yet audible volume.

"What's that for?" the girl pressed.

"Looking at stars." Isla seemed embarrassed.

"Hmm. That sounds neat. Do you know a lot about that stuff?" The other girl added.

"Not as much as I want." Isla finished her second chocolate milk.

"I bet you are a real hit back home," the first girl called out. I really couldn't figure out if they were teasing her, or if they were just being funny or nice, but I think it made Isla very uncomfortable. She buried her gaze back toward her peas.

"That's really cool. When is it?" I consoled, but was actually really interested.

"Tonight." She placed two more peas on her fork.

"Oh...then I want to sign up for it."

"You'd most likely be the only one." She glanced up, so that I knew she had received my support.

"No, 'cause my pals would do it too." She smiled then returned to her pea stabbing.

"Where are they?" She didn't look up.

"On that other dive boat."

"What other dive boat?"

"The one that left right before we did, this morning."

"I did not see."

"Oh. Well, they aren't back yet."

"I under-stand."

A few moments of silence passed, but I really wanted to know more about my new friend. "Isla?"

"Yes?" She looked up.

"What else do you, you know, know a lot about?"

"What you mean?" She looked slightly confused.

"Well, you are an expert on astronomy and all."

"I am not expert." She smiled, flattered that I stated the obvious.

"Okay, well, I think you are."

"Thank you, but I am not." She stopped eating and stared at me, still slightly smiling.

"So, do you like cars?"

"No."

"Airplanes?"

"Airplanes are good, but I do not know anything about them." She giggled.

"Guns?" I laughed.

"Guns. What you mean?" Her accent was as thick as her pretty hair.

"You know, like machine guns, cannons, and stuff?" She looked confused.

"Oh, like Kalashnikov?" Her eyes widened presumably because she knew something about a subject she figured I liked.

"Uh, what's that?"

"It is as-sault rifle. I can shoot." She made a gesture with her hands like she was shooting whatever gun she was talking about, and then looked at me for approval.

"Oh, that's cool." I smiled and so did she.

I heard a familiar voice behind me.

"Yo Isla!" It was Dude...otherwise known as Jimmy. I turned around.

"What have ya'll been up too?" He looked at me like I was moving in on his lady, but rumor had it that they were definitely *not* together.

"Not much. Isla and I went on some crazy dive this morning."

"Oh really." I wasn't sure if he was jealous that we went on some adventure or if it was because I was hanging out with Isla.

"How ya doin', Isla?" he asked.

"Fine." Dropping her smile, she calmly stabbed the last two peas and ate them.

"Cool, cool." He looked over at me.

"So...tell me about your little dive." He pulled out a chair at the head of the table, right next to us, and began his interrogation.

"It wasn't a big deal," I responded.

"Yeah?" He looked quickly over at Isla, then back at me.

"Yeah bro...there was just this crazy wind and stuff, and we had to do this surveying at like a hundred feet."

"Hmm." He looked back at Isla, who was looking down, once again, appearing evasive, and most likely because this was not the first time he tried to talk to her and she refused.

"Did your boy, Will, and those cuties go too?"

"Na…we got separated." I glanced over at Isla, him catching me.

"Isn't one of them your little girlfriend?" He tilted back his cup filled with lemonade, gulping practically half of it.

"Uh, I'm not sure who you're talking about," I added, looking at him, not wanting to add fuel to the fire.

"Well whatever," he stared at me for a second, silently attempting to assert his dominance. He then stood up and walked off, but not before leering at Isla one last time.

"I am sorry." Isla said, quietly, as she raised her head back up.

"For what? Oh, him? Whatever." He was definitely bigger than me, and I really didn't feel like pissing him off, but he made her uncomfortable, and I don't owe him anything.

"He thinks that I like him," she lowered her fork back to the plate and concentrated on my face with her big, dark brown eyes.

"Do you?" I hoped that she didn't and, for some reason, actually dreaded the answer.

"I do not like him, at all." She slowly spoke, in her broken accent, so that I would fully understand that they weren't an item. I was relieved.

"Okay." I broke a slight smile.

Isla briefly smiled too, then stood up, took her tray and walked over to the trash receptacle, and out the door.

I sat there, for a little while longer, while I quickly finished the rest of my meal then emptied my tray where Isla did moments earlier, and headed outside to sign our four names to her activity. "Stargazing with Nikki and Isla" was the title, and I was sure that she wasn't the one that came up with the "catchy" phrase.

I walked toward the docks to give one last look for Will and the girls, before returning to my room. As I rounded the corner of the science lab, I spotted the other dive boat, and the crew disembarking.

"Hey!" I happily yelled as I walked closer. They didn't hear me.

"Will!" I was a little closer, and now in earshot.

"Hey man!" Will reported.

"Hey Kyle!" Kristen added while Sara looked up and smiled.

"Hey guys! Did you have fun?" I asked.

"Yeah...until we had to tow some fisherman in." Kristen shook her head.

"Uh huh! This dude was waving frantically at our boat as we pulled up the anchors and got going," Sara said.

"And we were like, 'oh boy, this is how horror movies start!'" Kristen continued.

"Yeah...and Kristen was like, 'hold me Will! You are such a big stud!'" Will laughed. Sara shook her head, smiling.

"I dunno about that part," I replied glancing at Sara.

We had another class starting in twenty minutes, so we quickly grabbed all the gear and washed the masks and stuff in the bins. The girls ran back to their room, while Will and I hung out at one of the picnic tables. "Hey! Where did you get that watch?"

"Oh yeah! This scientist dude gave it to me. Can you believe it?"

"No way!" He looked down at the watch.

"That thing is really cool." He nodded his head with genuine approval.

"Oh hey, how was your dive? That sucked that you couldn't go with us."

"Yeah...it was weird."

"What'd you mean?"

"I dunno...it was just strange. Oh but...hey, I signed us up for a star telescope thingy tonight."

"What's that all about?"

"Isla is doing it."

"Who?"

"You know...that cute foreign girl." He thought about it.

"Oh right. She's kind of weird."

"I guess so."

"Did you talk to her?" He was perplexed.

"Yeah, a little."

"What's her deal, anyways?" Before I could answer, the girls arrived back from their room.

"Hello there!" Kristen announced while they both did the standard cute girl wave. Will and I stood up and the four of us proceeded toward the Quonset hut where the lifeguarding class was held.

"I signed us all up for this star gazing thing tonight." I wanted to make sure it wasn't going to be a surprise later. Kristen didn't look convinced.

"Aren't they showing scary movies in the dining hall?" She was trying to hint toward her real desire.

"I think so," Will chivalrously responded.

"Don't you think that'd be cool?" She looked at both Will and me.

"I guess…well, but I told Isla that we'd go tonight."

"Who?" Kristen apparently didn't remember.

"That girl that we ate pizza with, you know, Will thought she was from Turkey, or Mars, or something?"

"Oh yeah…she was okay, well, weird too." Sara didn't seem to care what we did, but I got the impression that a movie was more to her liking.

"So?" I hung the topic out there.

"Doesn't matter to me," Will abstained.

"Okay, well, that might be fun." Kristen grimaced and rolled her eyes, ever so slightly.

"Whatever Kristen! You know you want to find out what planet Will is actually from," I added.

"Okay…okay! Astronomy one-oh-one it is!" Kristen was a good sport.

We headed on to the classroom for more lifeguard instruction. War stories mixed with cheesy videos occupied most of the class time, along with me thinking of "Stargazing with Isla" later on that night.

It was six o'clock, and time to head back to the dorms to get ready for dinner, which was going to be a little later than usual, due to one of the groups not getting back from Key West in a normal fashion. As a result, and after I hung out with Will in the room, while he showered the salt water away and changed, we ran back downstairs.

Back downstairs, girl-less, he told me about how annoying it was to tow in the old fisherman guy, which was now the obvious reason that they were late arriving earlier that afternoon.

"Bro...that fucking guy was a total retard." Will laughed while looking down at the sand underneath the picnic table, and back at all the carvings. It was funny the way he had said it. "Why? What'd he do?" I provoked.

"Oh man. This whack job, was like lit, or somethin'."

"He was drunk?"

"Like my Irish uncle!"

"I didn't know you were Irish?"

"I'm not! But this clown was so freaking drunk that we could smell his ass from over on our boat!"

"Are you serious?"

"Oh yeah! He was like, 'blah blah marlin blah wahoo, blah blah. Ugh!" I was tearing up because it was funny seeing Will's impersonation and genuine frustration.

"Man! I was like, fuck! Bro, I had my freaking arm all up around Kristen, and she was leaning all over me and ya know." He was acting out what Kristen was allegedly doing at the time.

"Yeah?"

"Oh yeah! And this drunk mother fucker sinks my mojo with his whisky swigging ass!"

"Oh, and check this out! His wasted butt decides to take up chain smoking while moving his gas tanks all around. Not to mention guzzling one-fifty-one."

"That's crazy!" I was still laughing.

"I was like, 'Die asshole! I hope you blow yourself up!'" Will played out what it would have looked like as the guy lit up a cigarette, then exploded.

"Yeah, well, except you would have guts and blood all over the place." I tried to foil Will's plan.

"Nah! Maybe a shit load of fish guts, but that fucko was so wasted that his shit was pickled." Will even found humor in his rant, and couldn't contain a smile.

"And he even got pissed off the way that we tied his crap-vessel up to ours!" Will continued, "He was like, 'You need to tie it this way…up to this cleat! Ya hear? You are going to rip my goddamn shit off!'" I could barely catch a breath I was laughing so hard. "What were the girls doing?" I asked.

"Not much! Kristen was like, 'What is that guy's problem…? I mean, we're towing him in.'"

"What about Sara?"

"Oh Sara? She was all, 'He better not fall off cause he doesn't have a life vest on.' Then I was like, 'I hope that Uncle Jesse lookin' motherfucker *does* fall off and gets eaten by fucking Jaws and shit!' Fuck his sorry drunk disgruntled ass! I mean, god damn! I was hungry and we were missing fried chicken for this old retard and he had the nerve to bitch up a storm cause we tied the rope to the wrong fucking cleat!"

"That's unbelievable!" I was still laughing.

The girls emerged from their dorm, but he wanted to finish his story.

"I was foaming at the mouth, I wanted to pick up a dive weight and shot put it right there on his freakin' forehead!" Will acted out how he would pick up a weight and fire it at the old man. Will too, was laughing, and ended with a simple, yet complete, "Eh…whatever!"

"Hey guys!" Kristen announced.

"Hey! I heard about your little sea rescue." I looked at Sara who looked a little confused.

"That drunk fisherman guy?" Kristen inquired.

"Yeah, that dude."

"Oh yeah…Will's buddy!" She got it.

"Shit…he ain't my buddy. I wanna kick his ass," Will defended.

"Oh Will, he was a nice old man. Probably a lot like your granddad!" Kristen added.

"Why is Will so pissed at him?" I goaded.

"I dunno." Kristen continued, "He claimed that he was checking out my boobs, when I was bending over to fix the rope that had gotten caught on something." "Oh…I see." I punched him on the shoulder for not telling me the whole story.

"Well…I guess. But I really was hungry for chicken." He shrugged. Kristen looked down at her watch, "Well Will, you're in luck, it's time for dinner."

As Kristen consoled Will, we were "treated" to a low level pass of another rumbling DC-3 mosquito bomber flying right overhead. "Bad ass!" Will and I both said almost simultaneously. We stood up and walked toward the cafeteria.

Chapter Twelve

Later that evening, we arrived at our star gazing location. There was some new pale, green eyed, redhead who I had only seen once or twice before, and who someone referred to as a graduate student in business management, or some crap, at University of South Florida or UF or something. The other was Isla, who was cleaning the lens of the binoculars with her thin t-shirt. There were three others too, whom I'd only seen in passing.

The redhead, Nicole, or "Nikki" as she was sometimes called, started in with the basics of what we were looking for in the sky. The three telescopes were pointed in slightly different directions, and she directed those who weren't using a telescope to look through the binoculars.

"Okay, the telescope over there is pointed at Saturn." She motioned, with a red flashlight so that we could see which telescope she had pointed at Saturn.

"This one is pointed at Venus, and this one here, is pointed at the moon." She walked over toward the one that was pointed at the moon and adjusted one of the knobs. Sara looked at Venus, and then gave me a turn, while she walked to Kristen and Will, who were hogging the one pointed at Saturn. Venus...just another planet, I thought.

"Those rings are really cool. It looks fake," Kristen commented as she stepped back from the telescope to give Sara a chance.

"Totally!" Sara agreed. I didn't really care that much about Saturn either, and I imagined what would be basically a small version of a photograph from a larger telescope depicted in textbooks everywhere.

It was okay regardless, because the girls were actually not wanting to go back inside to see a movie, which I figured was rare.

Will, providing the slightly needed comic relief, would look over at me occasionally, and only when Kristen was bending over to look through the telescope, so that I would see him motion like he was smacking her on the rear.

Isla was sitting on a piece of concrete block, staring up without the aid of anything, concentrating between two different parts of the sky. She was totally quiet, and it almost seemed like she didn't realize we were there, which seemed to be the status quo for her.

I looked through the telescope pointing at the moon, which was slightly more interesting than the other two. At least here, one could see the big craters, and it took up much more than the field of view. It was almost eerie because I felt like I was just hovering over it in some sort of space ship, or airplane. Pretty cool, I thought to myself, but I think I like stars better.

"Okay gang, Isla is going to show us some other stuff," Nikki directed like she was a physics professor at Cambridge in her spare time.

"Isla?" Nikki looked over at her.

"Hey, Isla." She tried to get her attention. Isla was still staring skyward, oblivious.

"Isla!" Nikki walked over to her and waved her hand in front of her face.

"Oh." Isla snapped out of her daze and stood up.

"Do you want to show us some star clusters, or other things that you study?"

"Yes." She went over and re-aimed and adjusted the telescopes one by one, without looking through them, which was kind of strange. Nikki picked up a pair of binoculars and started scanning the sky where Isla had pointed the telescopes.

"Look," Isla hastily offered to the rest of us. I checked out the one that had been previously pointed toward the moon, while Will and Sara looked through the others. Thousands of stars filled the viewfinder feeling like I was looking at glitter thrown up into the dark sky…beautiful.

"What are we looking at?" Will asked.

"Yeah, I really don't see anything," Sara added. Nikki walked over to the telescope Sara had stepped back from, and looked for herself. She adjusted some of the knobs and peered through the aiming device.

"Hey Isla, what are we looking at here?" Nikki inquired.

"This is called HR four nine seven one."

"Okay?" Sara, Kristen and Nikki looked at each other, perplexed.

We stood in silence, looking back through our respective telescopes.

"What's that flashing thing?" some girl asked.

"Where?" Nikki tried to see what the girl was referring to.

"Right there." The girl came over to Nikki and handed her the binoculars.

"Oh that?" The girl nodded at Nikki.

"That's a weather blimp," Nikki confidently reported. I picked up a set of binoculars and could clearly tell that it was a blimp, of some sort.

"Do you have those in Russia, or Cuba, or wherever?" Nikki had a surprisingly sarcastic tone, but Isla didn't hear, or wasn't paying attention. Nikki looked over at Isla, to see if she had received the sarcasm.

"Hey Isla." Nikki called.

"Yes?" Isla innocently and respectfully turned toward Nikki.

"What do you think that is, right there?" Nikki handed her the binoculars, and pointed her finger at the blimp. I was a bit confused, because Nikki obviously knew what it was, and had already answered the kid's question.

"That is teth-ered aero-stat radar system." Isla lowered the binoculars causing Nikki to shake her head in disbelief. Isla continued, "Most TARS balloons, pro-vide radar data on attempt-ted drug inter-dictions. This one also broad-casts television and shortwave radio trans-missions toward Cuba."

"Come on, Isla." Nikki took the binoculars back, outwardly disappointed in her answer. "Do you honestly think we believe that mumbo jumbo?"

"It is true." Isla looked down at the base of the telescope where Kristen was planted. "It is also believed that number station operates from location."

"Okay, okay." Nikki's tone was one of total disbelief. "Can we get on with our astronomy lesson, please?"

"Yes." Isla cautiously walked over toward the next telescope, which was probably a good thing since she tripped over one of the legs holding up the first telescope thus throwing off its alignment with its intended subject.

"This one," she said, pointing at the one Will was looking through, "is M fifty-one."

"All I see is a star," he called.

"It is very nice galaxy." She walked over toward the telescope I was peering through.

"Hmm, what about that one?" Nikki pointed toward me.

"This is astro-metric binary system, called Alpha Tucanae A." She stood next to me.

"Okay." Nikki looked at me with bewildered regard, rolling her eyes.

"It is located in the constel-lation Tucana approx-imately two hundred light years from this place, plus or minus five light years." Her accent sounded thicker as her explanation grew more complex.

"Really." Nikki displayed false interest, and possible disbelief.

"Yes. It has an observed mag-ni-tude of plus two point eight, relative from Earth. It shares in spec-tral class K, three-triple-I."

"Could you please explain to us what an astrometric binary is?" Nikki was trying a little to either compete, or shut Isla down completely.

"It is two celestial bodies orbiting one another." Nikki had no response.

"If we had special telescope we could observe accretion ring around de-duced body, which is most beautiful." She looked down at her feet, and me thinking how much better this would have been had no one else been around.

"It is also one of the few bodies which sometimes in-dicates as blueshift from non-ter-res-trial based stations," she continued.

"If you follow down, relative to our position, when system is at apastron, you will notice Cephied Var-ia-ble star which displays four terre-strial month cycles."

"Where did you go to school?" Nikki sternly, yet civilly asked.

"If you can observe at proper moment, circum-stellar disk is revealed which was resulted from impact with planet AT seven seven alpha three, only fourteen thou-sand years ago," Isla mumbled on.

"That's really not that long ago," Nikki piped in, probably in an attempt to sound superior to Isla.

"Impact debris also revealed event horizon of dark body in binary system, in which eccen-tricity orbit decays at a rate of four degrees, point zero zero zero two three astro-nomical units, using Earth distance from Sol as re-fer-ence and we cannot yet determine mass, size, density, evolution, rotational speed, surface content or chemical and physical makeup, nor molec-ular and atomic properties of atmosphere."

"I see." Nikki looked up with binoculars.

"And, if you take non-metric common ruler and hold it two feet, plus or minus two to three inches, in front of you, with the tip of the ruler on the position of Alpha Tucanae A, and look vert-ically below approx-imately one and one half inches, you will see small point of light."

"All of these little stars look the same," Kristen announced, somewhat frustrated.

"This small point of light is GMC seven omega." Isla's voice revealed some sort of importance to whatever she was referring.

"What is seven-whatever?" Will joked.

"It is stellar nursery."

"What is that?" Will engaged.

"It is where stars are born."

"Oh." He looked back into his telescope. Nikki walked to where Isla and I were standing.

"That's about it...only a couple more minutes, then we'll have to start packing up." Nikki grabbed the star chart, which Isla never looked at.

"One more thing." Isla added, "If you look three inches down, and to the right, you will see three small stars forming a tri-angle, relative to our position." She moved Will's, and the second telescope, without looking through them.

"The star on left has three bodies orbiting."

"I can't see them," Sara whispered.

"The body the farthest from this star has four-teen moons, two of which are in geo-sync-hronous orbit. And the farthest of the two is at helio-pause." She looked over at Sara and me.

"This irregular satellite possesses retro-grade orbit, but when it reaches certain velocity on perceived decay, some believe that it re-pulses and re-achieves stable orbit. This would disprove Kepler's third law of orbital mechanics. And, I would imagine the views from this large moon would be im-pres-sive, and, well, beautiful." She cracked a slight smile.

"Hey Isla?" Kristen chimed in, somewhat startling Isla from her entranced narratives.

"Yes?"

"Do you believe in UFOs?" Will laughed at the question, followed by a punch on the shoulder from Kristen.

"Do you refer to unident-ified flying objects, that have possible terre-strial origin, or do you mean life not beginning here on Earth?"

"Uh...I guess life from somewhere else?" I don't think Kristen realized there was a difference.

"Single cell, mi-crobial, carbon based, or intelligent?"

"Intelligent?" Will interjected.

"Scientists have not yet detected intelligent life." She looked down at a small stain on her shirt, and picked at it.

"I wonder if we'll ever get to see aliens." One of the other guys piped for the first time, which was not a good thing because he looked like an obnoxious nerd, who needed to keep quiet.

"I wonder where they would want to land and say 'Hi'?" Kristen probed.

"Probably L.A. or New York City or something," Will said.

"Maybe London or Paris, or Rio," Nikki added with a confident pseudo-sophisticated tone.

"About one half mile south east of Nagla Devjit is where, I think, something wonderful will first be detected," Isla unconfidently announced while rubbing her elbow with her left hand.

"Come again?" Nikki contested.

"Near river bank." Isla lowered her eyes with embarrassed reflection.

"Oh really." Nikki was verbally going after her.

"Yes."

"Are you serious?"

"Yes."

"Do you actually believe that?" Nikki was releasing some pent up anger that she and some of the other college students apparently shared toward Isla.

"It should be there, near Agra on bank of Yamuna." Her voice was a mutter, completely void of confidence and it was difficult to hear what she was saying.

"Again, what *are* you talking about?" Nikki's voice displayed near total hostility.

"India." Isla sat down on the cement block and started picking at her fingers.

"India?" Nikki laughed.

The rest of us were silent as we watched the exchange, but I really wanted to interfere. Isla was merely stating what she believed to be true with me thinking that it was downright beautiful, but Nikki wasn't having any of it.

"Yes." Her finger picking was causing her left thumbnail to bleed.

"How? What does India have to do with it?" Nikki was laying into her.

It became very obvious that there was indeed animosity toward Isla that had been brewing long before I met her, or arrived here for that matter. I looked over at Sara who really didn't seem to care that much about it, and Kristen who was still looking through the telescope trying to decipher the astronomy lesson, or argument, that was presented moments earlier. Will was taking it all in, hoping that they would fight, or kiss, or something. I, on the other hand, just wished Nikki would leave her alone.

"Hey Nikki…where do you want me to put this?" I picked up one of the telescopes and acted like I was having trouble holding it.

"And listen here, Isss-la, I'm sick of you going around with that shy ass attitude! You aren't fooling anybody!" Nikki was pointing at her like she was scolding a bad dog, and Isla was looking down probably hoping all of us would disappear.

"Hey Nikki?" I pestered. "I'm about to drop…"

"Oh, okay. Here, put it…Will, help him carry it over there." My distraction paid off, and I briefly hoped that Isla could have some relief as I fumbled with the telescope and she fumbled with her shirt. I was starting to get pretty stressed out, for Isla, and I wished that everyone would just leave her, and me, alone together so that she could continue her astronomy lesson with someone who actually cared.

Nikki, in an attempt to calm down, started grabbing binoculars, a flash light, and with Will and me in tow, walked over to an older pick-up truck to place the gear in the bed. Nikki was having a hard time settling down, and I wanted to ask what her problem was, but I didn't want to antagonize her anymore.

"Hey Nikki…what's up with you and Isla?" Will read my mind.

"She's a little bitch!"

"Why…what did she do?" I think Will enjoyed their little exchange.

"Don't worry about it." She slammed the tailgate shut.

"Seriously, you looked like you wanted to slit her throat."

"Okay, well every guy is like, 'Look at that hot foreign chick' and, 'I'm gonna ask her out' and shit!" She cut her eyes back toward where the gear had been, and Sara and Kristen were still sitting, about thirty feet away from Isla who was now alone.

"I mean…she is playing all hard to get, and all these guys think she's a challenge, but she's a total retard! And, she mumbles on about this and that, and no one knows what the hell she is talking about, but for some reason, she's still here! She brings nothing to the table!"

"Really?" I added, "She seems, nice…"

"She doesn't teach anything, she goes to movies by herself, eats a crap load of McDonalds, hates ice, tears up at the drop of a hat, doesn't want to hang out, cowers when anyone talks to her, and chews her fingernails to a bloody pulp! That bitch is autistic or something, I'm telling ya!" This was a strong reaction from an otherwise reserved graduate student.

"Plus, she's a freaking commie! I mean…what the hell is she doing here?" I sensed some jealousy, or something, but this was over the top. She pulled the truck keys out of her pocket and climbed in behind the steering wheel.

"I'd stay away from her, if I were you guys." She fired up the truck and slowly drove off. Will and I turned around and walked back toward the girls, interested to hear Isla's side of the story.

"What was that all about?" Kristen asked Will and me.

"I dunno, she was pissed at something." I tried to downplay the lopsided assault.

"Yeah Isla, what was her problem?" Will antagonized. Isla just sat there, looking down at the dirt and small rocks beneath her worn-out sneakers, where one of them had become untied.

"Let's just leave her alone." I cautiously responded, not wanting to piss off my buddy, but also not wanting to upset Isla further.

"Yeah." Kristen took Will's hand and started toward the dorms, with Sara right behind motioning me to come with her, while extending her hand.

Isla muttered something I couldn't hear, so I walked a little closer, while the others slowly walked further away.

"Isla?" I cautiously whispered. No response.

"Isla?" Nothing.

"You did not get to see Ursa Minor," she faintly whispered.

"Sorry? What is…?"

"It needs to be watched." She shyly looked up from her drooped head. I stared down at her, trying to figure out what she was talking about, or what exactly I could do to put a mental bandage on my new acquaintance's psyche.

"Isla? Are you okay?" She shifted her feet, turning the tips of her shoes in toward one another, burying her forehead down into her palms.

"No," she shakily responded.

Just then, Sara made a "psst!" noise which caught my attention. She waved me over, so that I would leave Isla alone. I quietly walked away toward Sara, Kristen and Will, but as I got about fifteen feet away, I heard Isla faintly sob, "Don't." But, I kept walking, which was unfortunately something that I would get to be good at.

That night, for the first time since I arrived well over a week ago, I didn't obsess over Sara, and I wasn't happy about it.

Chapter Thirteen

The next day was going to suck. No dives, classes, or anything with Will, Sara or Kristen. For some stupid reason, I woke early, again, showered, and walked downstairs to see if anybody was out doing anything even remotely interesting.

In the cafeteria, Jimmy and Cindy were sitting at a table, in the otherwise empty room, plotting out the details of the dance. Cindy was cool, but I wasn't a big fan of Jimmy. Cindy quickly hailed me, so I walked over and pulled up a chair. While Jimmy rolled his eyes, Cindy went on about how they needed to drive multiple places, which was going to take essentially all day, to pick up some lights and a DJ sound system, or something, and were pissed that they were tasked with the job.

"So Kyle. Do you wanna go with us today?" Cindy asked.

"Uh..."

"I mean, it will really help us out, and I could get you out of whatever else you had scheduled today." She said, while Jimmy looked up at the clock, agitated that Cindy was trying to involve me.

"Yeah, that's sounds good, I guess." She smiled at my acceptance.

"Great! Okay, we'll grab one more, and be underway after breakfast."

"Sounds good." I didn't have anything better to do, but really didn't feel like hanging with Jimmy. I guess I'd just stay in the back seat.

I ate with my gang, luckily sitting at the same table. Sara and Will had something going on in Key West, while Kristen was heading to some sculpting class thing. Regardless, today was going to be pretty boring.

Jimmy and Cindy pulled up in one of the vans. I hopped in behind, and slid across the seat toward the opposite window.

"Thanks again," Cindy added. We weren't moving, probably waiting for one more.

A few minutes passed, causing Cindy to look down at her watch.

"Where is she?"

"You've got me," Jimmy replied.

"Okay, well, let's drive." She paused. "Wait. That's her." It was Isla, slowly walking toward our van.

"Just get in the back, with Kyle." Cindy motioned for Isla to open the side door and jump in.

She quickly fumbled with the door, and thinking it was locked, stopped and waited for Cindy or Jimmy to unlock the door.

"It's open!" Jimmy shouted, prompting Isla to try again, and this time successfully opening the door. She climbed in, glanced at me, and cautiously slid onto the bench that I was seated on.

Jimmy pulled the van onto the twisty street, and out to the main road. We headed right, and out toward the east, leaving the dirt and gravel behind.

"Okay, so first stop is Sammy's Systems, in Marathon." Cindy pointed at an address, and dropped the piece of paper containing it on Jimmy's lap.

We continued on, over a really long bridge and ultimately making only one right turn from the main highway, finally arriving at our first stop. Jimmy checked the address again, and after looking quickly over at Cindy, pulled into a recently paved parking lot.

"Okay, you guys stay here for a second, while I go in and find out what we are supposed to do." He hopped out, but left the van running so that we could still listen to the radio. He disappeared inside.

"Hey, Kyle?" Cindy turned around in her seat.

"Yeah?"

"Where are you from?"

"Lakeland. Uh, Florida."

"Isn't that near Plant City?" That was a shock.

"Yeah, how do you know Plant City?" I chuckled.

"Oh, well, I have a friend of mine from there."

"Cool."

Jimmy walked back toward us, and got in. "We gotta go around back." He placed the van in gear, and slowly drove around to the backside of the one story structure. We hopped out, me after Isla, and followed Jimmy inside.

Basically, "Sammy" instructed us on what to grab, how, and the best way to put the speakers, and the various components of the sound system into the van, so that it didn't get damaged during the drive. It was rental equipment, but was in decent shape, nonetheless.

It wasn't too difficult, moving large awkward speakers, with Cindy being the door holder for the store and the van, occasionally following up with a small component herself. As I placed the various items into the back of the van, Jimmy would climb in and carefully organize the gear so that we had enough room for the lights and so that we still had a place to sit.

Isla was having trouble, and couldn't carry any part of something that had a cord or wire without clumsily tripping over it. If my hands were free from a return trip from the van, I would hurry over and retrieve the part, out of her arms, and get back to the van and hand it to Jimmy.

"Where's Isla?" Jimmy asked on one of my trips.

"Oh, she's a, well, she's helping me inside," I defended.

"I knew she'd be basically useless." He shook his head, grabbing a roll of cable that I handed him. I quickly jogged back inside, so as to not get Isla any deeper in disregard than she already was.

Cindy, who had propped the door open with a rock, went back around and into the retail portion of the store, to call our next destination and get better directions than merely an address. Isla was trying to untangle some wires, one of which had wrapped around her ankle.

"Here, let me." I knelt down next to her feet, while she cautiously held one of the record players, and attempted to unwrap the cord.

"Sorry." She looked down at me, breaking a slight smile so that I would know she really meant it.

"It's okay." After successfully untangling the cord, I took the record player from her, and proceeded outside to drop it off with Jimmy.

She and I performed our little tasks, of her retrieving the component from the rental counter, walking about five feet, and in just enough time for me to come back and retrieve the item before she could re-tangle a wire, or bump into another piece of equipment, or something. It wasn't that she had problems performing anything that required dexterity, well not that I could really tell anyway; it was just that she was off in her own little world, leaving only distraction behind in this one.

Upon the final trip indoors, I retrieved Isla, and walked into the retail section to find Cindy. She was talking to some guy, who looked to be attempting to schedule a date, or something. Isla and I stood there, for a moment, waiting for their exchange to finish.

Back outside, we hopped in the van, and off we went. This time, we needed to go all the way back to the mainland, which was about thirty minutes south of Miami. I sank back into my seat, resting my knees on the back of Jimmy's seatback, and gazed out of the window.

Cindy and Jimmy carried on between themselves, occasionally pointing at something outside, and changing the radio stations as soon as an advertisement or radio announcer broke in. Isla was staring out her own window, to her right.

I wanted to talk to Isla, but didn't want to embarrass her with stupid questions, or anything which would involve Cindy or Jimmy listening in. While thinking of her, I looked over to my right, and stared at her for a brief moment, watching her look out of the window.

In the reflection, I could see her eyes dancing left to right as she watched the scenery pass from Cindy's to her window, and back behind. It was eerily relaxing, however I quickly looked back to the left, out my window, realizing that the steady movement of the van was the most likely cause of the mild tranquilizing effect.

The road trip continued, as did Jimmy and Cindy's conversations. I didn't pay too much attention, mostly because I couldn't fully hear them over the radio, but also because I really didn't care too much. I glanced over at Isla, mainly to make sure she was still there, spotting her eyes once or twice, attempting to catch me in her periphery.

Upon reaching the mainland, we took an exit down to a side road, where we headed for another five, or so, minutes. Eventually, and finally, reaching our destination.

We jumped out, Cindy stretched, and she and Jimmy walked inside, leaving Isla and me to hang out by the van.

"Hey." I gently kicked a rock in Isla's direction.

"Hi." She looked down at the rock that had stopped rolling about an inch from her dirty old sneakers.

"How long have you been here, you know, this summer?" I leaned against the van with Isla standing about ten feet in front of me.

"Um, a month?" She replied.

"What, sorry. I mean, when do you leave?"

"Two and a half more." She lightly pushed the small rock with her foot.

"Oh. Hey, are you having fun down here?" I watched as she leaned against the van with her back.

"Yes, now. What about you?"

"Oh yeah. I like it, a lot." I smiled, and hoped my comment would cause her to do the same. Instead she looked at my eyes, just a bit longer. Jimmy and Cindy reappeared, and motioned us to come in with them.

We walked inside, and toward the rear of the party supply shop, which is where we were going to retrieve the lighting, that was to be leased to add some ambience to the big dance. It was somewhat disorganized, allegedly due to "inventory" being taken, at least that's what the manager told Cindy. We stepped around, and avoided knocking over all sorts of party crap, which was scattered about, and "temporarily" placed on makeshift shelving.

As Isla and I weaved our way around the pawnshop look-a-like, a tied up hound decided to test Isla's nerve by barking at her incessantly. It lunged, and almost made contact, but she was just out of range, stumbling as she attempted to catch herself against a shelf. I positioned myself between it and Isla, which may have appeared heroic, but actually it had no interest in harassing anyone but her.

Jimmy, not really paying attention to the small distraction, directed, "Isla. You and Kyle get all the lighting, while Cindy and I sign the contract, and pay the bill." He then quickly walked around the corner to some side office.

Isla looked over at me, and then proceeded toward the spot on the floor where the manager had pointed out all of the equipment that we were supposed to load up into the van. There was a lot of shit.

She picked up a black metal stand; I grabbed another, following her back outside. I propped mine against the van, and opened the side door so that she could deposit hers inside. She slid the stand on to the front bench seat, where we had recently been sitting, while I laid mine next to it, and shut the door.

We performed our mundane job without talking too much, which was probably better because it was somewhat challenging navigating the cluttered store, especially with big metal rods, stands, and delicate lights.

On one trip, Isla knocked over a fake bronze statue of some Greek god, or hero, or something, causing a loud clang, and a nasty glare from one of the employees. The front two benches in the van were getting full, leaving only the bench in the rear of the van for her and me to later sit.

During our last trip inside, to retrieve the last three lights, I hit the restroom. "I'll be right back," I informed Isla, so that she didn't think that I was sticking her with the task of loading the final lights into the van by herself.

As I dried my hands, and unlocked the door, I heard the sound of glass breaking. I quickly opened the door and rounded the corner, to find Isla kneeling on the ground and leaning over, trying to pick up something off of the floor.

"What the hell is wrong with you?" The manager arrived from a side room, with Cindy and Jimmy close behind. Isla didn't talk, frantically collecting shards of glass from one of the final three lights.

"That's a four hundred dollar lamp, with a one hundred dollar filter!" he ranted, turning toward Jimmy after barking at Isla. "You are out a lamp for your little party, and five hundred dollars!" He pointed at Jimmy, while snarling over the broken glass.

"I need to make a phone call." Jimmy passed me, bitching about Isla to Cindy.

I dodged some of the "inventory" and knelt down beside Isla, helping her.

"It's okay," I quietly assured, while I picked up the broken glass.

Her hands were shaking, as an obvious result from dropping the light, but also from the shouting of the manager. I tried to pick up the pieces faster, so that she could hopefully begin to calm down.

"It's okay. Don't worry," I reassured, and adding, "that guy is a dick." As she grabbed smaller and smaller pieces, she looked up and over at me, shaking her head in self-disappointment, her loosely tangled hair covering half of her face.

"Why did you drop it?" Jimmy approached, visibly agitated.

"I, uh...I am sorry." She kept to her task of picking up the remaining pieces.

"Well, you just cost the administration five hundred dollars." He stood over us, pissed that he had to make the call, or that he was ultimately the one responsible for the whole excursion.

"I can't believe this shit." He turned around and walked back toward Cindy.

"She didn't mean it," I defended, but most likely falling on deaf ears.

"What was that?" he quickly turned around, angry.

"I'm just saying, she didn't do it on purpose." I continued to pick up the glass while kneeling next to Isla.

"Look guy, everyone has tried," he shook his head, smirking.

"What's that supposed to mean?" I looked up.

"Oh nothing."

"Huh?"

"Everyone has tried to get a piece of that," he nodded toward Isla.

"Come on bro. Cut it out, I'm just trying to help her clean up this stuff." I picked up a few more shards of glass.

"I'm just sayin', stud," he shook his head and walked off, finally.

Isla and I cleaned up the remaining glass, and we had two remaining lights to transport to the van, so I handed her one, having trust that she wouldn't drop another, while I grabbed the last.

After our completion of the final load-up, Isla and I climbed all the way into the back of the van, while Jimmy slammed the door, shaking his head. We pulled out, and ultimately made it back to the main highway, which would take us all the way back to campus.

After a little while, Cindy informed us that we'd be stopping for lunch. Jimmy pulled the van into a McDonalds, shut off the engine and slid open our door.

"We're at your place, Isla," Jimmy said sarcastically, causing Isla to look down at her shoes, embarrassed. I didn't see what the big fuss was about, I mean, I loved McDonalds.

We walked inside, Cindy and Jimmy ordered, he paid and then the two abandoned us in line.

"May I take your order?" The woman asked from behind the register, causing Isla to look back at me.

"Do you want something?" I gently asked.

"Um, I don't think so." She looked down at the counter, then back up at the menu.

"Are you sure?" I moved closer to her.

"Okay." She looked back toward the cash register, "Can I please have a hamburger and French fries?"

"Do you want the meal?" The woman asked, while Isla stared at the register.

"No thank you." She looked back at me, and then again toward the register. "I'd like a Sprite too, but…but with no ice."

"So, you don't want to make it a meal?" The woman looked at me, then back at Isla.

"Oh, um, yes. A meal." She reached into her left pocket and pulled out some crumpled up cash, and placed it on the counter. The woman who took the order, with the tips of her fingers, untangled some "ones" like they were infected. She handed her back some change, followed by Isla stuffing the wadded up cash back into her pocket.

I ordered, paid, and stood next to Isla so that she could select a seat, knowing that it wouldn't be with Jimmy and Cindy. She looked up from her tray, and broke a slight smile.

"Where do you want to…?"

"Where you want," she quickly responded before I could finish. So I led, and she followed me into a corner booth near the drive-through exit.

I ate, while watching her delicately place individual fries into her mouth, taking small bites of the hamburger, and sipping her Sprite with no ice. She was very pretty, yet still being difficult to pinpoint her exact age, most likely due to her ethnicity.

"I really liked your astronomy lesson," I said while taking the final French fries out of the carton.

"Oh, I am glad," she smiled.

"How did you, you know, learn so much?"

"I just really like it, so I read a lot." She gently dipped one fry into the little pile of catsup.

"Well, I really like it too, but you blow me out of the water." She giggled.

"I can teach you. If you want," she said while looking down slightly embarrassed.

"Really? That would be awesome."

"Yes. You are good, I mean, smart person so you will be good at learning," she smiled again, showing off her understated yet puffy lips and surprisingly white teeth.

She walked up to the counter and grabbed a pen and the back of the paper covering the tray. It was the first in what I hoped would be many astronomy lessons.

As she gently spoke and sketched, every once in a while glancing up, probably to make sure that I wasn't getting bored with her, or some other innocent concern. I collected all the empty wrappers, leaned my elbows onto the table, and watched her as she slowly, and carefully, drew out whatever area of the cosmos she was concentrating on. She must have had a spell book somewhere in her back pocket, because through her uniquely subdued and docile eating habits, conversation and ad hoc astronomy class, something emotionally mysterious was happening.

Back in the van, we left the parking lot, and drove back down the long single lane highway. She and I were all alone in the back of the van, and knowing that no one could hear us, I decided to strike up another relatively innocuous conversation before reigniting the next astronomy lesson.

"So, what are you going to do, you know, next session?" As soon as the words left my mouth, I realized that it was a completely stupid question.

"I will help with activities, dives, and things," she attentively responded.

"Cool."

"What will you do?"

"When?"

"When you leave." She looked down at the space on the seat between us.

"Uh, let's see. Probably sleep a lot, hang out with my sister, and be really bored." She smiled.

"Why not stay here?"

"Oh, well, I guess…that's a good question." I always figured it was obvious. But, she awaited a further response, while she repositioned her hair, which had fallen down in front of her eyes.

"Um, I'm only paid through this session."

"Oh, I see." She revealed a fretful smile, but possibly not fully grasping the overall concept.

I scooted deeper into the bench seat, and propped my knees onto the seat back in front of me, with her shifting in her seat, facing her body toward me.

"Thank you," she said, as I turned my head to face her.

"For what?"

"Things."

"What…what are you talkin' about?" I smiled.

"Helping me with the glass."

"Oh that? Hey, try not to think about it." It was obviously still upsetting her.

"Okay." She leaned the side of her head onto the back of the seat, looking at me, and still bothered by the previous events. A couple minutes of silence passed, as she cutely tucked her hands behind her knees.

"Isla?"

"Yes."

"It's really not a big deal."

"Okay."

The journey continued, another wonderful trip through the universe commenced with Isla as my guide, and after a few hours, we arrived back on campus, albeit way too soon. We unloaded the gear, while Jimmy "allowed" Isla to simply hold the door.

After finishing, Jimmy snickered, and he and Cindy left Isla and me standing near the front door of the cafeteria.

"Are you gonna be at dinner?" It was starting soon, and I wanted to distract her from Jimmy's bullshit.

"I do not think so." She dropped her eyes, then looked back up at me.

"How come?"

"I just, I'm going to go back to my room," she quietly voiced, as the wind picked up.

"Okay, well, I guess I'll see you around." I smiled, attempting to comfort her again, but also genuinely wanting to talk to her some more.

"Okay." She stared at me for a quick second, then turned around and walked back toward the marina, suddenly stopping.

"Kyle?" She turned around.

"Yeah?" Me glad she stopped.

"Do you want to, I do not know, may-be sit for a while?" She looked down at her shoes, both laces now untied.

"Yeah." I guessed she was a mind reader too.

We walked over toward the marina and sat down on one of the docks, my legs dangling over the water and hers crossed Indian style.

"So, what else do you like? You know, besides animals, stars, and Kalashni…"

"Kalashnikov?" She smiled.

"Yeah, Ka-lash-ni-kov," I laughed, and so did she.

"Um, let me see. Oh, I like the beach," she looked at me for acceptance.

"Well, the beach is pretty cool."

"Yes. I like walking alone on the beach."

"Yeah?"

"Yes. Well, you can come too." She looked over at my right hand which was to my side.

"Huh?"

"Yes. If you want." She quickly looked back toward the water, somewhat embarrassed.

"Oh, yeah. I see what you…oh, I would," she looked back at me and smiled.

"Yes?"

"Definitely." We sat and stared at the ripples bunching up against the pylons under the dock.

"So, do you like flowers?" I broke the silence, and smiled.

"I think, but I do not know that much about them," she appeared a little confused by my question.

"What about sail boats?"

"They are okay, I think." She smiled, still trying to figure out if I was merely hoping that she'd like them, "I like ships."

"Ships?" Her response threw me.

"Yes."

"Like what?"

"Submarines." I almost lost my flip-flop I was so stunned by her response.

"What? Really?"

"Yes. Is that bad?"

"Oh. No it's not bad. It's, well, really cool." I smiled, bewildered.

"Yes?" She was happy we made another connection.

"Oh man. You really like subs?"

"Not like sandwich, like big vessel that dives underwater." She hesitated.

"Oh no, I totally hear you, I just can't believe it."

"Why not believe?"

"Uh, I dunno, it's just. Man, you're something else." I grinned.

"Is that good?"

"Oh yeah. It's awesome." She smiled too.

I couldn't believe it. But, I guess, why not? I mean she was Russian, or Cuban, or whatever. I mean there's no telling what they teach kids in school over there, and I guess the likely hood of submarines was not out of the question.

"What's your favorite submarine?" I figured she's just say something normal like, "any kind", or "all of them", or that she merely thinks they are neat, or whatever.

"I like, what American calls our Oscar class, well and Kilo class too." I was speechless. "I would sometimes watch them from Sevastopol or Odessa," she added.

"I think that your Los Angeles class and Ohio is good, but favorite is Russian Typhoon?"

"Typhoon!" I was dumfounded, and not because I didn't know what she was talking about.

"You know, twenty ballistic missiles each with ten multiple in-de-pendant-ly target-able reentry vehicle?" She paused, "It has multiple hull design, powered by two O.K. six-fifty nuclear reactors, conning tower aft of launch tubes, and very quiet." Will you marry me? Jokingly thinking to myself.

"Really! Where are you from?" Heaven, I gathered, while I sat there in total shock.

"Mazyr. Why?"

"Uh oh, no reason." The question was rhetorical anyway.

"And you have good new submarine coming soon."

"Huh?"

"Yes. It is Seawolf class."

"What?"

"Yes. It is attack submarine. It is for locating and stalking Typhoon. It is very fast and quiet, has eight torpedo tubes and fifty cruise missiles on board," she paused to catch her breath. "And it has test depth past six hundred meters."

"How do you know this?" To say that I was stunned was an understatement.

"I like to read about submarines." She smiled.

"So, they teach that in school?"

"No. I have books." She smiled.

"Wow. I uh, I don't know what to say."

"What do you mean?"

"You're incredible." I laughed, and so did she.

That night, at dinner, Sara and Will told Kristen and me all about their excursion into Key West and how many M&Ms Will could stuff into his mouth, followed by Kristen reporting how her sculpting class had gone. After dinner, we played volleyball into the evening, and finishing with thirty minutes of laughing by the picnic tables.

After Will telling me how groovy Kristen was, I slowly drifted off to sleep. I don't really remember what I dreamed about, but Will happily reported the next morning, that I had briefly talked in my sleep. When I jokingly confronted him the next morning about trying to get into my bunk the night before, he told me what I had said. It was a name, and it wasn't Sara.

Chapter Fourteen

"Are you ready for more sailing today? I'm bringing my camera again!" Sara cheerfully grinned, as we headed toward breakfast.

"Oh yeah, sure am!" I smiled.

We walked toward the cafeteria, with the breeze picking up again as we came around the bend.

"It's gonna be a good day for sailing." Will looked back at Sara and me.

"Man! I wanna go bad!" Kristen pouted.

"Well, I guess tracking minnows are more important than us," Will teased, causing Kristen to quickly slap him on the back.

"I know, but I need to be there and I already missed one, and I would like to apply this toward school credit, ya know." She looked back at Sara and me for support.

"Don't look at me," I said.

"Yeah, why don't you just talk to your lover boy?" Sara teased. Kristen latched on to Will.

"Oh Will…you'll forgive me, won't you?" She glanced back at us, smirking.

"I dunno…what's in it for me?" Will asked.

"Hmmm…what did you have in mind?" Sara laughed as Kristen buttered him up.

"*You* know." Will glanced at me, as he slowly started lowering his hand over her ass.

"How about…?" Kristen looked up, thinking.

"What?" Will was confident.

"How about, I don't tell them what you told me yesterday?" Kristen was good.

"Huh?" He stopped.

"You know, Willy." She looked again at Sara and me.

"Oh man." He shifted back toward Kristen, his otherwise confident shoulders, now slightly slouched.

"Yeah…that's right Willy."

"Come on Kristen…you said…"

"Don't worry, your little secret is safe." She giggled.

"What is she talking about?" I whispered to Sara.

"She already told me." Sara quietly laughed.

"What?"

"Will said that she was the most beautiful girl he has ever seen." She softly leaned into my ear.

"Aww…that's really sweet." I was half serious, half kidding.

"Yeah. She has him totally wrapped around her pinky toe." Kristen, one - Macho Will, zero.

We rapidly progressed through the buffet line, and found some seats. It wasn't as crowded as the day before, so we basically occupied a whole table by ourselves. As usual, comfortably so, Will and Kristen picked at each other, while Sara told me about this time she had to play goalie because both the starting and back up goal tender were injured. She said her favorite position was full back, but that she really liked running, so mid field was probably what she'd try to play in college, if she could make the team. I really couldn't see her playing soccer in college because she just didn't look the part…maybe cheerleader was more fitting, at least in my mind anyway.

After breakfast we parted ways with Kristen, and walked out toward the sail and rigging storage building. It was a little weird, because a few nights earlier, we were looking at the stars from where that little sailboat hull was still turned upside down. I thought about Isla, feeling…I dunno, like I needed to be, ah hell, I mean I guess I just really like astronomy.

It was a good day for sailing. The wind was steady out of the south around fifteen knots; that weird storm again. It actually was somewhat of a blessing, because although we had to tack to get out into the southern part of the bay out toward the ocean, coming back was a piece of cake.

Sara had her camera, which was luckily waterproof, because the little Sidewinders loved to fill up with a small layer of water near the drain plug. Will and I would try to haul ass right by her, showing off for the camera, and trying to upstage one another while she took some pictures.

On one pass, she waved me over, and handed me her camera so that I could take a picture of her. Good idea, I thought, as I snapped off only two, trying to conserve film.

After much more horseplay between Will and me, the group sailed the ten minutes, or so, back to the marina, with the Whaler taking up the rear. We beached our boats, and unrigged them. Sara ran over to me. "That was hilarious! I think I got you trying to push Will overboard!" She was very excited.

"Yeah…did you get him flipping me off too?" Will fake sulked, but was smiling as he lowered his sail. Sara said something about him being upset because his little sweetie was somewhere else, and I added in that he was totally whipped. He just grinned, as if he was silently plotting his next move against me, but was probably just thinking of Kristen.

We took our time putting everything away, which was somewhat of an exercise for me because I was so used to rushing my way through stuff, that I usually didn't get to sit back and enjoy it. I placed my gear neatly under the spot where Sara had just deposited hers. Will basically shoved his stuff into a cubby hole in the corner, which elicited a "that doesn't go there…" from some pale skinned girl with small round sun glasses.

We hung around on the small dock near the sail hut, and tried to skip rocks like Kristen and I were doing many days earlier. Will was really good, which was not surprising given his football-throwing arm.

A short time later, we met up with Kristen at one of the docks at the marina. She had a towel around her hair, and was skipping over to us to report in on her morning.

She chattered away to Will about these cute fish that she helped catch, photograph, measure, document, and release. She made sure, of course, to tell him often that she had fun, but really missed her Will. Will told her that he won the sailing race, which she didn't believe. Especially with Sara calling Will the worst pirate she'd ever seen.

Kristen leaned her towel crowned head up against him and put her left hand on his waist. "Oh Will, were they being mean to you?" She consoled.

Lunch was basically the same as breakfast, but a bit more crowded. Conversations were equally as normal, and Will's recount of his morning exploits was cause for sustained laughter.

"Can I have your attention, please?" one of the older, head counselors' announced.

"We aren't gonna be in here for dinner, because we are going to be setting up for the dance," he continued, "so, we are ordering pizza, which will be delivered to each of your dorm rooms around six o'clock tonight."

"Can I get one with anchovies?" some smart ass called out.

"How about you get only anchovies, Michael." He pointed back, smiling.

The ambient background conversations rose in volume again. I looked over at Sara imagining what she would be wearing. Half hoping for some sexy cocktail dress or something, which wasn't realistic.

"Are you gonna dance with me, Will?" Kristen glanced over at Sara and me, and then looked back at him.

"Depends," he replied. "On how good you look tonight." He leaned back in his chair, cocky.

"Don't sass me, William!" She pointed her bony little finger at him.

"Oh...play rough with me, that is a sure way to light my fire." He smirked, and briefly glanced toward me.

"I'll stomp your fire!" Kristen parried.

"Oh...you little..." Will hesitated.

"What?" She smiled.

"Nothing."

"That's what I thought." She crossed her arms as he handed her an unopened carton of grape juice as his peace offering.

"Hey, Kristen, isn't your fiftieth wedding anniversary coming up this weekend?" Sara jabbed.

"Hmm. Will would only be so lucky to make it that long." She winced her eyes at him and opened the grape juice, triumphantly taking a sip.

We took our time, joking around, then realized that it was time to go get changed for the water portion of our lifeguard training. We briskly walked back toward the dorms, changed, and met back at the swim canal.

The breeze was getting stronger, and a couple of grey clouds were heading our way from the east, while the ominous big storm churned way off to the south, over the horizon. It was still pretty warm, but it was nice to get a slight cooling effect from the wind.

After practicing the designated life saving techniques, the instructor came over to observe. "Hey, what's your first name again?" Kristen asked, while he waited for Will to reattempt a rescue.

"Me? Anthony." He was glad to be asked.

"Cool...I'm Kristen."

"Yeah...I know." He laughed.

"Yeah, dummy, he has the roll!" Will fired at her.

"Shut up Willy!" she lovingly snapped back.

"Where are you from?" Kristen asked politely.

"Oh...uh, Georgia originally." He started splashing for Will, to make it more realistic.

"Cool...are you in college?" she pleasantly queried.

"Oh no...that was a long while back." He smiled.

"Hmm...how old are you?"

"Uh...thirty-seven." He seemed embarrassed.

"What?" She was shocked.

"Yeah." He looked back at Will.

"No...I mean, you look like twenty-five or something."

"Oh, thanks!" He moved his wet, dirty blonde hair, from his face.

"Yeah...seriously, you don't look thirty-seven at all!"

"Well, that's cool!" He was pleased with the interaction.

Kristen had "an ability", as Sara phrased it earlier in the week. Sara surmised that a few special people had this ability, "Words can make magic, you just have to know what to say." I figured it was just called "the gift of gab."

Kristen continued, "What do you do, you know…when you aren't here."

"Uh…I'm a rescue firefighter and paramedic over in Marathon." No wonder he knew this first-aid shit so well.

"Cool!" Kristen looked back at Sara and me.

"Yeah, I use to work as a commodities broker, but that wasn't for me."

"That sounds boring," I added.

"The money was good, but, you know, things change." He looked over at me.

"Yeah." Kristen glanced at Will, smiling.

"What changed?" Sara examined.

"Oh. Well, I was married, and was doing really well."

"Yeah?"

"I got sick, well, sort of, and got a divorce and stuff."

"Oh," I added.

"Yeah. It kind of sucked." He looked up at one of the clouds.

"I bet your job is better now, right?" Kristen fortified.

"Yeah…I guess. I was doing really well before. Had an apartment on the upper east side, near Central Park."

"Really?" Kristen knew exactly what he was talking about.

"Yep." He wiped the seawater out of his eyes.

"Oh man…that's big time." She added.

"Yeah. It's okay, I really like my schedule now. Plus, I wouldn't get to hangout down here with cool cats like you!" He looked back at Will and splashed him.

We watched Anthony and Will practice some techniques which Will was having some trouble with, for a while longer, while me and the girls would try to see who could swim the width of the canal underwater on one breath. Sara was pretty good, with Kristen being lousy, but it didn't matter much, and I didn't think Kristen was trying very hard.

Another darker cloud band passed uneventfully overhead, and with it, any chance of rain that afternoon. The wind was still blowing, and the sun peaked its way through the broken thin cloud layer way up high. The afternoon was coming to an end, and I really didn't need to look at the ole Casio to know what time it was, mostly because I didn't care.

We climbed up the ladder, and onto the dock where we toweled off. After a parting announcement, Anthony came back over and asked if we liked the class so far, and if we had any questions. My guess was that he felt somehow loosely connected to our little group. Kristen seemed to have that effect on people.

"See you guys later. Oh, don't forget to put alcohol in your ears. Okay?" He waved as we walked toward the dorms while he sat back down on the dock, alone, untying a knot on some of the ropes. He was a good guy, and I would have liked helping him put the gear up, but it seemed like he enjoyed doing it, and didn't seem to mind being alone, or was already used to it.

Chapter Fifteen

Will and I were all showered and changed, and about thirty minutes before the dance officially started we proceeded downstairs to the tables. One of the guys brought down a Frisbee, so we formed a loose square and started the informal passing. I really liked this feeling, the anticipation, or the calm before the storm, or something, but it was somehow very comforting.

Some of the girls started coming down from their respective structures, but no Kristen or Sara. The girls integrated into the larger group of guys, with one of the chicks invading our "square" of Frisbee tossing, to join in the act; some British girl named "Tully", or something. She wasn't very good at throwing, but had a cool accent, so we didn't mind.

The wind picked up a little more, hearing the rumble of thunder off in the distance. "It's gonna storm tonight," this one dude opined. Our Frisbee group gazed to the south; while Carlos held off his next throw to wait for the wind to die down.

"Yeah." Will shrugged his shoulders then motioned for Carlos to pass him the Frisbee.

More girls trickled from their dorm, with Sara and Kristen part of the group. Will and I both left the Frisbee gang, and headed directly for the girls. As we closed the distance between us, Will remarked how amazing they looked.

"Wow!" Will was impressed with Kristen's primped appeal.

"You look great," I added toward Sara.

"Thanks." She affectionately grinned.

"Don't get any ideas Will!" Kristen warned while Will checked out her short dress, which perfectly matched her penetrating blue eyes.

"I've got a lot of ideas," Will teased.

Sara's outfit was much more conservative, just tight jeans and a button down shirt, whereas Will and I looked like we rolled off the set of Magnum, P.I., but with longer shorts, and no mustache. Well, and less chest hair too.

"You are a hot little…" Will caught himself.

"A hot little what?" Kristen smirked.

"Uh…person?" He looked over at me.

"Nice one Will." She walked over to him and gave him a slap on the shoulder. Sara sat down on the wall, with me next to her, while Kristen posed for Will as he stood back and took in the modeling.

Arriving at the surprising "upscale" dining hall, we poured in and made our way over to the far side of the large room where a long row of chairs were arranged. Kristen immediately sat down and fixed the strap on her sandal. Will broke instantly into a moonwalk, which was totally non-aligned with the song being played. Kristen then popped back up and grabbed Will's hands and started to sway to the rhythm. Sara and I watched Kristen's attempts to tame Will while we moved with the typical Top 40s track.

I really hated dancing, but began to take cue from Will. He'd grab Kristen, ballroom style, and "waltz" her around, jokingly, and basically making a mockery of anyone who was seriously attempting to showboat their way onto American Bandstand. He was actually pretty smart, despite his star quarterback façade.

Will grabbed Sara in an attempt to convince her that his dancing "technique" was superior to the other dudes, and so that Sara could, "see for herself" that Will could turn on the charm of a Spanish tango dancer. And, as I "danced" with Kristen, I spotted Jimmy and Anthony talking near the soda fountain with Jill, Jimmy pausing and glaring at me to make sure that I knew "he was on to me".

A couple of seconds later, Anthony and Jimmy walked over.

"Did you get tired of Will?" Anthony joked, as Jimmy shook his head, still pissed off at something.

"Na…he just wanted to show Sara the correct way to do the foxtrot." We laughed. "What a show off!" Kristen yelled over the music, shaking her head, but secretly lusting for Will's return.

Kristen spotted Jill, Nikki, and Cindy sitting near the "D.J." stand and pointed so that Anthony could see what she was looking at. I wasn't really sure what she was doing, but I suspected she was playing some sort of matchmaker from a safe distance.

Sara and Will came back to where Kristen and I were standing, now near the soda fountain, so that she could refill her cup. "Hey, I gotta go change my shoes," Sara shouted into Kristen's ear, attempting to overpower the music.

Kristen approached Will, as Sara maneuvered around toward the door. I yelled at Kristen, "I thought you were going with her?" She shook her head.

I quickly hurried toward Sara who was almost at the door. "Sara!" I yelled, but she kept walking. "Sara!" I tried again, but the only people to hear me were some other kids that I was passing.

I finally caught up to her as I exited the swinging door. "Sara." I lowered my voice, because we were now outside in the calm.

"Oh hey!" She stopped and walked back toward me.

"I wanted to make sure you had someone to walk with."

"Well thanks! But I'm sure I can manage." The wind picked up, blowing her hair.

"Oh, well, I can…"

"I *want* you to walk with me, silly!" she teased.

"Okay cool." She had me confused, there, for a second.

We walked, slowly, toward the dorms with the wind steadily blowing, rustling the palm trees.

"I wonder if it's gonna rain tonight," she softly said.

"I dunno." We continued slowly toward the dorms, passing an opening in the mangroves where we could see the ocean off to the south, the water lapping just feet away.

"It's really pretty here, at night." She said.

"Yeah." I thought, but it was pretty here all the time.

"I'll be right back." She shuffled toward her dorm.

As I sat on the bench, I spotted someone who appeared to be Isla walking by, about half way between the tables and the scuba shack. She was holding something on her shoulder, and was attempting to be cautious.

She disappeared into the duskiness off toward the cafeteria. I thought about her for a minute, and decided to make sure that I was going to say "hi" later that night, so that she knew I still thought she was cool, plus it would probably make her smile.

"Okay." Sara arrived next to me, in her usual tennis shoes which replaced the sandals. She grabbed my hand, and we headed back over the shell and gravel driveway to the cafeteria, where we could hear the music leaking.

We passed by the cut in the mangroves, revealing the ocean.

"Hey, Sara?" I turned toward her.

"Yeah?" Some of her hair blew into her face.

"Uh…" I briefly thought about kissing her, but for some reason, things were missing.

"What?" she gently prodded.

"What if I…" I swallowed.

"Huh."

"I, uh…" Something told me not to.

"What's wrong?" She smiled.

"Oh, nothing." I brushed the hair out of her face.

"Then?" she calmly added. I took one deep breath, swallowed again, smoothly grabbed both of her hands, and…I couldn't do it. This wasn't going to work. "You look great," was all I had in me.

"Uh…thanks!" She laughed.

"Yeah!" I laughed too.

This was much, much better, for some weird reason. It may have been better if I had kissed her, but, well, I guess that's how it goes.

She locked her blue-green eyes on me, flickering in the light of an otherwise unromantic buzzing streetlight. "Come on…let's get back inside. You have to dance with me!"

We looked at each other in silence for a few seconds before gradually making our way toward the music of the cafeteria.

As we approached the front of the structure, I caught sight of Isla again, on a bench a short distance away. She was holding a small cat, like an infant, wrapped up in her tattered purple towel.

We walked over, and stood for a second, watching the tenderness which Isla was exhibiting toward the lanky cat. "He's really sweet," Sara whispered.

"Is that pizza cat?" I asked while straining in the dim light to see if it had the orange and white stripes.

"Yes," she said, while looking down at her little friend.

"Oh…he's really cute." Sara reached down and pet its little head. The wind picked up again, which caused the reaction in Isla to gently cover the cat's belly with the edge of the towel, while neglecting her dark brown hair that was blown back into her face.

"Does he have a name?" Sara unobtrusively inquired as the little cat narrowed its eyes in total contentment.

"Ernie," she said in her thick accent, which sounded more like "Ear-nee" than the common "ur-ne".

"That's a cute name…did you name him that?" Sara kindly asked.

"No," Isla whispered, while tenderly rubbing Ernie's ears.

I didn't spot a collar, and he looked kind of ragged, so I'd guess that she picked up the "Ernie" name from the people at the pizza place. The tip of his tail was gently waving back and forth, and we could hear his loud purr, if we got close enough.

"You are good, Ernie," she whispered while shifting in her chair, so that he could stretch out more on her lap.

Sara and I watched for another minute or two, before walking inside, part of me wanting to go back and sit on the bench with Isla and Ernie. People were still going strong, which wasn't surprising since the Mello Yellow was flowing like water.

We located Kristen and Will as we squeezed by Nikki who was looking at her watch and walking toward the door from which we had just entered. Kristen looked over at Sara as if she knew, or more accurately, *thought* she knew, exactly what had happened outside minutes earlier, by the mangroves.

Moments later, some UB40 track was playing which was a knock off of some Sonny and Cher song. As if loosely rehearsed, and clumsily performed, Will and Kristen started serenading each other during the corresponding parts of the song. Sara and I laughed, and couldn't figure out what was more humorous, the horrible singing, or the overacting. Sara and I sat down, still watching, as she fumbled with a half full cup of soda.

Finally, more slow songs arrived, which was good, because I could simply hold Sara closely, and didn't have to display my total lack of rhythm. Plus, it gave me the chance to try to log another wonderful memory into my mental film bank. During one rotation, I spotted Isla following Cindy and Nikki through the door, and into the main hall. Isla was looking down, scolded, and mentally limped her way over toward the row of chairs near us and sat down.

"Did you see Isla?" Sara whispered in my ear, as we slowly spun.

"Yeah."

"You should go talk to her," Sara calmly encouraged.

"All right." I thought I really just wanted to stay with Sara, or so I told myself. I walked over to Isla who was looking down at her shoes, which were turned in toward each other.

"Hey Isla." I sat down next to her.

"Hi." She was still looking down, her elbows on her knees and face now buried into her hands. I sat there for a minute, with no one seated anywhere near us.

"Um…do you want to dance?" It was all I could come up with. She remained in her little protected position.

"Isla?" I leaned over to try to get level with her ears.

"Isla?" I gently touched her back, which was slowly heaving from sadness. I held my hand there, and looked up at Sara who had glanced over. She turned back around and continued dancing with Kristen and Will. I gently rubbed Isla's back, through her thin peach colored t-shirt, while she attempted to calm her breathing. She took a couple of shaky sighs, and removed her head from her hands, but stayed leaned over and was still looking down. I didn't say anything.

Nikki walked by and didn't even see us, which was a good thing, not that Isla would have noticed, but I was relieved nonetheless. Another slow song came on again. "Hey Isla?"

"Yes?" Her voice was weak and it felt like it took all her strength to answer.

"Do you wanna dance?" Once again, I didn't like dancing so this was a huge deal. Isla sat there, not responding.

"Isla?" A brief moment passed.

"Yes?" She looked over at me, and pulled her hair out of her tear-streaked face.

"Do you want to dance? It's a slow song," I encouraged while she stared at me for a moment.

"Okay." She sniffled. We slowly stood up, and stayed close to the side of the room, near the dark unoccupied hallway, and mostly away from the others. She pulled her hair away from her face in preparation for our brief encounter.

I slowly, and cautiously, placed my hands and arms behind, and around her waist. She was stiff, like an unoiled robot, and positioned her arms around my neck. She looked off to the side, avoiding eye contact. This was not going to win us any awards for being graceful.

She unevenly took some deep sighs, presumably to calm down and accept whatever situation Nikki, fate, or whatever threw her into. And, after another minute or so, she relaxed her arms, and stabilized her breathing. The song was winding down, and so was she.

After another thirty seconds or so, the song ended, but Isla continued her gentle, uneasy embrace around my neck. Not wanting to upset her further, I kept my arms around her waist, and waited for the next song to start, which would most likely be a faster song, prompting me to release and go back over to Sara.

Another slow song. Isla rubbed her nose again, still sniffling, which wasn't very romantic, but I didn't care because that wasn't my mission. She was beautiful, exotic, and sweet, but odd, and otherworldly, to say the least...and my task was purely rehabilitative, at least that's what I told myself.

The song continued, and Isla tightened her grip, while resting her cheek against my upper chest. I really felt bad for her, but that may have only been my excuse, and it seemed like she was getting comfortable at last, so I was starting to feel successful about the little project.

This was something different, and I had no real way to organize the feelings into thoughts. She had a gentle and inwardly kindheartedness way about her, which somehow reinforced in her now secure embrace. Her body temperature felt like it was being transmitted into my core, and when she raised her hand to rub her nose, shifting her torso slightly away from mine, I felt a slight chill and a general sense of reservation all around me from the air in the room. She was probably simply fighting off some sort of fever, or something else brought on by her self-induced stress, because her small frame was warmer than what I would have assumed to be normal for a girl.

The song continued, and I wished, even though I hated dancing, that it wouldn't end soon. Her breathing was now completely under control, and for a second, I got the impression that she had fallen asleep, which I quickly dismissed because she was still standing. She really wasn't moving, and didn't rub her nose anymore, so I felt more at ease in my success in tempering her trauma.

She re-positioned her arms to a more comfortable angle, for me, around my neck, which drew her in even closer. She had her forehead now completely buried into the side of my neck, with her soft hair brushing into my arms and chest. She was pinned into me now, and it must have looked, to everyone else but Sara, that we were separated soul mates and I had just come back from years at sea. She gently stopped our slight rotation, and our technical "dance" had now turned into an intense, unwavering, long, wonderful hug. I smiled, comprehending that I was really happy the song continued.

I realized that I wasn't looking around at the other people in the room, and that my eyes were shut with my head tilted down into hers, her hair signaling my sinuses with the faint smell of coconuts. The somehow magical warmth of her arms around my neck, her soft exhale on my chest, the steady cadence of her expanding and contracting breathing, and gently brushing of her hair around my arms was unconditionally hypnotic.

I moved my right arm slightly up her back, so that she knew I was comfortable with her innocent affection. I could feel her delicate ribs under her thin t-shirt, which were methodically yet faintly moving in and out as her lungs provided oxygen to her blood. I accidently nudged the slightly, yet unintentionally, exposed skin above her right hip; it felt like I was merely touching air. It was so incredibly soft that I almost didn't know I had even contacted it, realizing my otherwise sensitive nerve endings on my fingers were practically useless.

The only external signal I received that the song had ended, was the loud thumping of the next fast dance mix. With annoying percussion pounding in the background, I gently loosened my arms from around her waist, followed by her unlocking her arms from my neck. We slowly pulled apart, her entangling her big brown eyes with mine. We stood there for a couple of seconds, not knowing what to say, but hoping that the other had been sufficiently comforted in the subtle and undisclosed fact that we were part of something different…whatever it may be. She slowly turned back toward the dark hallway leading to some administrative offices, and disappeared into the blackness.

"That wasn't so bad." Sara cheerfully jumped me from behind.

"Yeah…not so bad," I lightly responded, leaning back into her, while shivering for a split second from the absence of Isla's remarkable thermal energy.

We sat down and watched Will and Kristen having fun and making fools of themselves. Will was breaking out everything in his dance arsenal while Kristen grooved, laughing at him, of course. This kept us entertained for the next three or four songs.

"Kyle?" Sara leaned into me.

"Yeah?"

"Can you get me some more Dr. Pepper?" Handing me her cup.

"Sure." I walked over toward the soda dispenser, near the corner of the room just past the dark hallway, and filled her cup. Walking back, I glanced down the dimly lit hallway, and spotted what appeared to be Isla, about twenty feet down the hall, sitting on the floor. I stopped for a second, straining my eyes, and made out her silhouette on the floor against the wall; her knees pulled up to her chest with her arms wrapped around them resembling a sitting fetal position. I stared for a couple of seconds longer, then proceeded back toward Sara.

"Thanks!" she shouted over the music, as I handed her the drink. I smiled, and settled back in to watching Will and Kristen.

At that moment, a wave of compulsion overtook me, coming out of nowhere. As Sara turned around to see what Kristen was doing, I quickly made my way back toward the dimly lit hallway where I had just spotted her. But, I was too late…she was already gone.

After a few more songs, the event started to wind down. Most of the people were spilling out of the main swinging door, but we stayed as long as our two strange friends continued to entertain, or we were kicked out.

Before we realized, we were the last non-staff or counselors left in the room. The music stopped after an annoyingly melancholy song, and Sara handing Kristen her cup so that she could get one final refill. Will was exhausted from his entertaining, and hung on my shoulder, probably in a humorous attempt to make me stumble.

We too filed out of the swinging door and back to the ambient light of the buzzing streetlight and thin crescent moon, which would step out from behind the thick passing clouds. We slowly walked back toward the picnic tables and dorms, attempting to take as long as possible.

Kristen re-directed us toward the vending machines on the edge of the harbor near the bench which I had become pretty familiar with.

"I'm hungry, Will." She snuggled against him.

"What do you want?" He reached into his pocket and pulled out a couple of dollar bills.

"Uh…those powdery donuts." She released her right hand from her grasp on Will and pointed.

"Okay." He fed the bill in, and pressed the "K" then "3" keys.

"Thanks, sweet cakes," Kristen affectionately voiced.

Sara then spotted Isla again, sitting on our bench, holding the little kitten from the pizza place.

"Let's go see little Ernie." She grabbed my hand and led me over.

As we got closer, Sara lightly called, "Hi, Ernie." Isla looked up at her, and then spotted me. She didn't say anything, briefly glanced at only me, and continued to hold the tiny cat, endearingly staring at it while smiling.

Sara leaned down, and patted him on the head and behind the ears. I merely watched the exchange, and scanned Isla's responses. She had apparently calmed down, but now more obvious as a result of her little cat friend's purring than anything I lent earlier inside.

She sat there, looking affectionately down at Ernie in silence with her arms cradling him with the ragged purple towel. Ernie was loving all the attention, but surely more content to be lounging in Isla's protection.

He reached up and playfully batted his paw at her dangling hair. She softly whispered something, touching his little paw, causing him to purr even louder and leaned his head up to nuzzle her nose. It was a delightful experience to see the usually worried Isla now happy and normal. She had finally befriended a cat.

We stood by for a couple of minutes longer, watching the caring interaction, and while waiting for the lovebirds to finish their donut dessert. With the playful cue of Kristen wiping her now powdery white hands on Will's shirt, we formed back up and walked toward the dorms, leaving Isla and Ernie with the quiet harbor and distant stars.

Arriving back at the dorms, we each walked our separate ways and I logged this night permanently in the memory banks.

Gold colored chairs, dip-a-stick's, and anteaters playing Frisbee occupied my nightly snooze...weird.

Chapter Sixteen

Days passed, as did the early summer session. Sara and I had a good bit of time together, but something wasn't there. Maybe it was all the other people around, or maybe it was just the fate of the end of this session approaching. But Isla, and her hidden yet immeasurable depth and our continued astronomy lessons and shared liking of submarines, she was something different, something…incredible.

I mean, her personality would corral me in ways that I could have never foreseen. She would sometimes obsess on certain points out in the visible universe, causing a little stress in her voice, but in the same spoken paragraph would describe nebulae or star clusters with a level of beauty that could never be rivaled.

Her humor was something amazing too. Her favorite would be to attempt other accents while speaking in English. She was especially fond of the British and Irish accents, and something about a gorgeous girl with a heavy eastern European accent attempting to sound like a member of the British Secret Service was pretty funny, to say the least. But the true reward, however latent, was the effect of having her smile and opening her mouth just wide enough to expose her beautiful front two teeth.

The more I was around her, the more I wanted to know her, and the thoughts of merely sharing the same room with her grew as intense as her obsession with astronomy. These feelings were something new to me entirely, and I was absolutely, positively, and certainly not going to do anything to rock this potentially and infinitely wonderful emotional boat.

One early evening after dinner, Sara and Kristen decided that studying for the lifeguarding test was more important than hanging out with Will and me. This had the result in pushing Will and me toward walking aimlessly around looking for something to do, since studying was definitely not on our agenda.

After some time of rock skipping and football passing, a storm cell decided to make its way in our direction. As one last attempt at freedom before committing to the forsaken act of lifeguarding test preparation back in our room, we made our way to the vending machines near the old bench on the docks.

Will made his drink selection, as did I, and as he popped open his can of Coke and motioned to some big tarpon or something, I noticed something else.

"Hey, Isla." I waved toward her, standing underneath the outcropping on the back of the cafeteria. Will looked up.

"Hi." She slowly walked toward us, her foreign accent ever present no matter how basic the spoken word.

"Hey man, I'm gonna head…" Will was going back to the dorm, presumably to "study" which I assumed, in his opinion, was more interesting than listening to another astronomy lesson from Isla.

"So, what are you up to?" I looked down at the can of Sprite that I had grabbed from the vending machine.

"Oh, uh…not much." She glanced down toward my hands.

"Do you want…?" I held up the can.

"Okay." She smiled. I opened the top and handed it to her.

"Do you want to go…" I pointed toward the bench.

"Or we could…" She motioned to the small gravel area facing out to the bay, behind the cafeteria near where Kristen and I had skipped rocks.

"Okay."

We slowly walked around the small bend, to our lower vantage point out over the bay. I wasn't sure if the sun had set, probably because it was completely covered by the approaching clouds. We stood there, for a second, staring out over the water.

"Oh…how's Ernie?" I asked.

"I fed him, and gave him new water." She faced me, smiling.

"What do you think he's doing?"

"Sleeping." She nodded, still innocently smiling.

"He's really good, isn't he?"

"Yes. Smart too."

The light rain approached closer and closer, until it gently fell on the water immediately in front of us.

"Do you want to leave?" I asked, and turned slightly toward her.

"What do you want?" She continued to stare out toward the water.

"Um…I don't really know, whatever you want." I was surprised that she didn't want to immediately head back to our respective dorms. Another minute or so passed, and we were about to get wet.

"Do you want to go inside?" She slowly spun toward me, once again smiling.

"I do." I said.

"Okay," she softly spoke as she took a couple of steps backward, then waited for me to turn around, like she was disappearing into some fog or something in the back of my mind.

I followed her, a few paces, not exactly sure where we were heading, but as we passed the door leading toward the rear office and conference room, she intently swung the door open and entered.

We made our way into the conference room, which had been the venue of a movie or two, and sat down, with one chair between the two of us.

Isla took another sip of Sprite, before fretfully saying, "Oh…I drink all your…I'm sorry." She put the can down staring at it, wishing it was completely full again, so that she would not feel like she had been any negative impact on my life, or the world, whatsoever.

"It's okay…seriously, don't worry about it." I smiled.

"I'm really sorry." She looked up, her head still held low.

"Isla, it's really okay…really." I leaned in and playfully flicked the can at her.

"Okay." She broke a slight smile out of the corner of her mouth, as she looked down at the empty green can.

It was comfortable, sitting in the empty conference room, well…empty building, for that matter. The rain lightly tapping the shelly driveway outside and the leaves of a small tree batting the side of the building and window, causing a sense of security, for we had no real reason to exit the dryness anytime soon.

"Isla?"

"Yes?" She looked up, again, while keeping one hand in her lap, and the other on the table in front of her.

"What's the coolest place you've been?"

"What do you...I do not understand." She looked confused.

"Oh, I dunno." I didn't want to frustrate her.

"You mean, here on earth?" I briefly laughed so that she would know I received her perceived attempt at being humorous.

"Or anywhere," I added, as she placed her other hand on the table, causing her to fiddle with her fingernails as she thought.

"Other than here?" She intently looked up, like she was attempting to answer a question a professor just asked.

"Yeah...'cause this place is really cool."

"Oh, well..." She glanced up at me, then back toward her fingers. "I think, um...Miami?"

"Miami?" I was kind of shocked, both because it was not *that* great, and that I was sure that there were better places...somewhere. Also, Miami was kind of close to here, almost like twin sisters, where Miami is the uglier of the two. Actually, forget it...not like twin sisters, maybe second cousins.

"How...I mean, what, or...uh, why were you there?"

"I was there twice."

"You visited it twice? Where did you go, South Beach?"

"Sorry?" She was confused.

"You know, like, the beach?"

"I was there with my mother, the first time."

"Where?"

"Miami." I laughed inside at the answer, but I didn't want to upset her. "I mean, did you live there?"

"Yes."

"Where in Miami? I mean, I was there too, for a couple of years."

"When?" She perked up.

"Oh, uh...I dunno, maybe...I think maybe like ten years ago."

"I don't know how old I was, when I was there." She looked back at her hands.

"That's okay. What were you doing there?"

"I was with my mother." She smiled, presumably causing a flash of a fond memory with her mom.

"Me too." I chuckled, somewhat sarcastically.

"Why were you there?" Isla asked and quickly looked back up.

"I'm not really sure, I think its 'cause that's where my dad and mom used to live before, you know, they broke up."

"Oh," she responded, with pure understanding.

"What about you?"

"My mother and I lived together." She smiled.

"Yeah?"

"Yes." She was looking down at her cracked fingernails, but obviously fondly remembering her mother.

"Where did you all live...I mean, I know in Miami, but do you remember where?"

"In apartment." She nodded.

"No, I mean...oh, okay." I paused. "Did you like it?"

"It was good, but some of our neighbors were some-times noisy." Her accent growing slightly thicker the harder she thought.

"Where did you go to school?"

"I did not go, to...school there."

"Oh."

"I was with my mother." She looked back toward me, slightly saddened.

"That's really nice," I consoled.

"Yes. She was...I...she..." She put her hands up to her face to cover the wave of memories tugging at her conscience.

I sat there, silent for a moment, trying to figure out what to do to bring a slight smile back to her face.

"Isla?" She dropped her hands down from her eyes, but continued to cover her nose and mouth.

"I went every-where with her." She sniffled. "It was only a very small apartment, but I was glad because I did not want to even be in a dif-ferent room." She wiped her nose with her t-shirt sleeve. I didn't say anything.

"And, she would take me to her work and I would sit near her in waiting room." She brushed her hair from her face and looked at me, trying to crack a smile, but unable.

"Where did she work? In a doctor's office or something?"

"She cut hair."

"Oh."

"Yes."

"That's good...right?"

"Yes. She said that I needed to be quiet and polite because there were very wealthy women who came to the place to have their hair cut." She glanced to her right, and behind toward the window where some leaves were brushing against it. I quickly hid a smile, because her description of the salon sounded like the type of place where my mother would frequently go.

"Did you like it there?" I tried to get her to smile again.

"Only...I did when my mother got breaks...well and, these other times." She tucked some of her deep, coffee colored hair, behind her right ear, now intently hanging on every question I asked.

"Did she get breaks a lot?"

"Sometimes."

"Oh."

"Be-tween customers, and if someone can-celled we would go get something to eat, or she would bring us food from home." She wrinkled her nose, hopefully holding back a sneeze, but I suspected she was missing her mother again.

"She was very pretty." She made a loose fist with her right hand, and tucked it under her chin, her elbow resting on the arm of her chair. There wasn't any doubt, in my mind, that she wasn't beautiful, and if she just barely resembled Isla, she would have had no problem winning the Miss Cuba or Miami contest.

"What did you do when she was working?" Crap...I think I already asked that.

"I would sit in the waiting room," she responded, genuinely.

"Was anyone else, I dunno...you know, like, nice to you?" She started brushing her dark eyebrows with the last two fingers of her right hand, most likely out of nervousness. I regretted the question, and tried to retrieve the words as they made their way to her ears, but...well, you know how that goes.

"Oh. I don't think...um...I don't really know." She looked down, slightly embarrassed.

"Sorry, I mean, I didn't want to..."

A few moments passed, while she briefly looked around the room, then settled her eyes back onto mine.

"There was one," she said, while perking up; straitening up in her chair.

"Huh?"

"There was one."

"One what?" I had no idea what she was talking about.

"Somebody who was nice. He was my friend."

"Who?"

"This boy…at my mother's work."

"Yeah?" I was getting a little jealous, well, not really jealous, more defensive…as I tended to do, not wanting anyone to take advantage of her, especially when she was younger.

"I think his mother worked there too."

"Uh, okay."

"Yes."

"We would read magazines together, on the couch in the waiting room." She smiled. "I really couldn't read English, so he would try to show me words and things."

"What kind of magazines?"

"Bazaar, Cosmo-pol-itan, Vogue, People…American magazines." She had a good memory, or at least a firm understanding of boring, woman magazines.

"Did you two play together too, you know, when you weren't at the salon?"

"No. We only saw each other when his mother would bring him." I could tell she was trying to remember this boy, which was good, because at least she wasn't thinking about her mother, and the inevitable tears that would follow.

"He was very nice to me." She smiled, looking at me, trying to draw some remote similarity between him and me.

"Did you two keep in touch?"

"He never touched me."

"No…no…I mean," crap, that didn't go as planned.

"He was very nice."

"I know, I guess I mean, how long did you stay friends?" She furrowed her eyebrows and forehead, trying to recall more of the details.

"Only that spring."

"That kind of sucks."

"Yes." She grimaced, trying to hold back a ripple of sadness for her forgotten childhood friend. Silence filled the room, for what seemed like minutes, as she most likely replayed his memory in her head.

I pushed my chair back, with her now looking down at her hands on the table, picking at her fingernails again, and removed the chair which was between us and rolled a couple of feet closer to her.

"Kyle?" She continued to work at her fingernails.

"Yeah?"

"Did you like Miami?" She sniffled.

"Uh…yeah. I think I did."

"Good." She sighed, buffering her emotions.

A few more moments passed, "Isla?"

"Yes?"

"When was the second time you were there?"

"My mother's work?" She looked up, preparing to talk about her mother again.

"Oh, no. I mean Miami."

"A few months ago."

"Did you go visit your mother?" She sank into her chair.

"She was gone."

"Where did she go?"

"I do not know." She moved her left hand up to her forehead and rubbed it slowly, trying to push back the feelings. She paused for a second, and then continued, "I looked for her. I found her old work, and…" I didn't say anything.

"And…I looked around for her apartment." Her eyes were starting to water.

"And." Her lower lip started to quiver, tears fully forming in her soulful eyes. "I could not find her anywhere. I don't know where…where she went." She covered her face with her palms, her shoulders heaving up and down, confirming what was happening behind her thin fingers.

I sat there, staring, for a moment, trying once again to figure out what to do to calm her down. She was so wonderfully strange, and so amazingly sweet that being near her was like a window left open on a cool, clear, starry night. I moved my chair closer.

"Isla?" She didn't hear me, and continued to silently weep.

"Isla?" I touched my fingers onto the back of her head, and slowly brushed her slightly tangled hair. She was whispering something, but it was too muffled by her hands for me to hear.

"Isla?" I whispered, and her voice grew slightly more audible.

"I came back for her." She removed her hands from her face, which caused a large lump in my throat. Her eyelashes were stuck together from the obvious, and clear mucous was lightly strung between her hands and her nose. I wish I knew where her mother was.

We sat next to each other, for a while. I wasn't going to leave her…not upset like this. Besides, everyone else was studying, back in their rooms.

I really wasn't sure if it was productive, but I really cared about her little story, and somehow it was my mission to make her feel better. I struggled with what to ask, balancing out trying to find out more about her, with not upsetting her further.

"How did you get down here?"

"Where?" She rubbed her nose with the collar of her faded blue t-shirt.

"Here, in the Keys."

"Oh." She paused. "I was at University of Miami."

"What…why where you there?"

"I saved up for two years."

"Sorry?" I wasn't sure what she was getting at.

"Yes." She paused. "As soon as I went back to school, two years ago."

"Where, in Leningrad?"

"Yes." She pulled her hair around to her right.

"Where, I mean, what did you do to save up?"

"Worked." She attempted to force a smile.

"Oh, okay. That's cool."

"I really wanted to get back to Miami. My memories were all happy there." She attempted to roll her chair a little farther from the table, but one of the wheels was jammed. She leaned over to her left, and looked down toward the wheel, causing her long hair to fall into her face with her gently brushing it aside so that she could again see.

She continued, while attempting to free the jammed wheel. "I wanted to get there, very bad."

"Yeah." I reached down and freed the wheel, so that she could push her chair away from the table.

"Thanks." She smiled, picking her feet up into the chair. "I did not like my job." She hugged her knees. "It was very hard."

"Why? What was it?"

"It was, I'm not sure how…I think man-u-fac-turing? I had to put two metal pieces together." She held her hands in front of her, and made a slight twisting motion, presumably depicting some sort of manual assembly.

"Yeah?"

"Yes. At first it was okay, but then after a couple of weeks I would get in trouble a lot." She rubbed her eyebrows again, with her fingers.

"How come?"

"I would be late sometimes, because the bus did not run all the time, so I would have to sometimes walk really far. Especially in winter."

"That sucks." She nodded her head, but me not fully sure she grasped the slang.

"And I would drop metal parts, and sometimes not put them together correctly." She paused looking back toward the window again, "The super-visor said that I could transfer and go work in the office with him, but…" She looked down at her knees, then up toward me. "One of the other women told me not to. So, I did not, and I had saved just enough, and later took a bus to airport, and went to University of Miami"

"I'm glad, you know, that you made it here." My comment caused her to reveal a full smile and an enjoyably nervous shrug of her shoulders. We stared at each other for a few moments, me just barely hearing her slightly congested breathing over the light tapping of the rain outside.

"So, what did you want to do, you know, when you finally made it to the University?"

"I was going to take a class, or look for a job, or maybe both." I wouldn't go so far as to say she was cheering up, but she was growing more removed from the fretful memories she revealed earlier. "I then saw a job notice for this place."

As she reached her hand up, toward the side of her face to brush aside some stray hair, the door opened, and in stepped Anthony.

"Hey….hey there!" The surprise was mutual. Isla quickly pushed her chair back away from mine, a foot or so, and Anthony's eyes grew wide, shocked that someone would be in the conference room this late.

"Hey!" I stood up, raising my hand, "We were just…"

"Oh, it's okay…I'm just heading through to that back office, for a file." He pointed.

"Oh, well, we were just getting out of the rain," I explained.

"Yeah…it's not raining anymore." He then quickly added, "But it was, for a while, wasn't it?" He smiled, trying not to look like he cared that we were in there, which he was honestly as surprised as we were. Isla shyly sat quiet, allowing Anthony and my friendly exchange.

"Yeah…me and Isla were just getting ready to head back." I pointed toward the door with my thumb.

"Oh, no problem. See you later!" He exited with a smile, opened the other door, and passed down the hallway.

Isla stood up. "I should probably go check on Ernie," she worriedly added, but not as a result of any proximity of danger or concern for Ernie's safety. She looked down at the chair where she had been sitting, and the table, like she wanted to reignite our conversation. I guessed that she simply didn't want to leave the conference room. But, as my amateurish sensory ability tended to prove, I didn't fully receive the message until I thought about it much later on.

"Yeah, I guess we should be getting back." I was glad to have made her feel better, but still there was much of her beautiful conscience which remained for me to discover.

We exited the room, and the building, and into the darkness and damp shelly driveway. We slowly continued on, and unfortunately, much too quickly arrived in front of my dorm.

"Good night, Isla." I stopped and turned toward her.

"Kyle?"

"Yeah?" The sea breeze picked up some of her hair and blew it into her face.

"Oh…oh nothing." She glanced down at her broken lace on her right shoe.

"I'll see you late…I mean…I'll see you soon." I smiled, reaching up to move her hair from her face, she beating me to it.

"Okay." She smiled, as I turned around and headed back up to my room. As I rounded the corner of the stairwell, I caught one final glimpse of her disappearing down the dirt pathway, leading back to her room, which caused my breathing to hasten, just a little.

Chapter Seventeen

This was one of those crappy mornings, where I was separated from the gang. No dive or snorkel gear were required for this morning's jaunt, but we were told that we may get a little wet. Great. Few things are more frustrating than wearing normal shorts and a t shirt, getting wet, then sitting around with a soggy ass. I guess it was too late to go back and grab a bathing suit, not that it really mattered, because I would have no place to change back into dry clothes.

Our new friend Anthony, Jill, and Isla were our "guides". Isla sat aft, near Jill, while Anthony piloted us out of the harbor and into the bay.

We motored along for about fifteen minutes, before beaching on a small island. We disembarked, and gathered around in a semi-circle while Jill gave a talk about what we would be doing. We were divided into three groups, with Jill, Anthony and Isla each "in charge" of a group.

There was something really genuine about Anthony, I thought, as he started calling out names for the groupings. He seemed very happy to be here, but at the same time, was somehow forcing himself to be happy. It wasn't one of those fake happy faces that sales people put on when you walk in the store; it was more like he was convincing himself that he *should* be happy. Throughout my time there, he put forth the most effort and definitely took his job seriously. However, every once in a while I would catch him, when no one was looking, trying to forget the situation that he was in, had fallen into, or how successful he was a few years earlier. He was unsure of himself, and it was hard to imagine that he had once been a successful commodities broker.

I was assigned to Isla's group, with me and two other dudes, both of whom appeared annoying…how wonderful. The tasks at hand were to locate different kinds of plants and animals, each group being assigned certain species to find. Obviously, I didn't pay much attention to the list.

The groups split up, with ours heading south, down the shoreline. One of the guys in our group was a total nerd, while the other cared less than I did. The nerdo wouldn't stop running his mouth. He would ask me and the other guy, who called himself "Daps", all sorts of shit anywhere from the standard, "So guys, where are you from?" to the "Can I hang out with you two after dinner and we can check out the ladies?" And even, "Hey, my mom thinks I'm going to Brown…wouldn't it be cool if we all went together?" Mister Daps - I have no clue why this dork called himself Daps - would yawn with each question from Captain Nerdo, so somehow I was targeted and left to fend for myself.

"Hey, you're Kyle aren't you?" Nerdo squawked.

"Yeah."

"Nice to meet you." He extended his hand, which I reluctantly shook.

"Same here." I was trying not to be too much of an asshole.

"Man…we have that hot counselor chick all to ourselves." He eyed Isla as she walked about thirty feet in front of us.

"Ohh yeahh," Daps chimed in.

"Man, ya'll need to keep it down," I insisted.

"Whatever, I would totally tag that!" Daps continued.

"Oh certainly!" Nerdo piped.

"Ya'll need to stop," I loudly whispered.

"Look at those thighs and that ass! And that skinny waist!" Daps knew that he was pissing me off.

"Seriously bro, cut it out."

"What? Are you tapping that?" Daps added, as Nerdo nodded his head while looking at Isla gently brushing a small branch aside as we continued to follow her.

"No." I tried to drop back further, so that I could be sure that Isla was far enough away that she couldn't hear.

"Come on! You've gotta be!" Daps looked up ahead.

"I'm telling you that I'm not."

"Yeah, well, that's not what I heard." He raised his eyebrows while lowering his cheesy sunglasses, smirking at me.

"What are you talking about?" I was concerned.

"Oh nothing."

"No, cut the shit. What are you talking about?" I stopped and grabbed Daps' elbow.

"You two are totally doing it," he confidently added.

"No, we aren't."

"Dude, everyone knows." He started walking again, leaving me a couple of paces behind him.

"What do you mean...come on, seriously, I'm not freaking playin'." Nerdo was walking next to him.

"And everybody thinks it's real cute that you like a retarded girl," he persisted.

"She's not retarded. She's foreign, from Cuba or something." I shook my head, with a raised voice.

"That's not it. She ain't the sharpest knife in the drawer...just admit it."

"She's way smarter than your stupid ass." I laughed, hoping he was joking.

"No dude! She has no idea what she's doing."

"She's very...yes she does!" I was getting more defensive.

"Well...you love a retarded girl. That's all there is to it."

"No I don't!" I needed to calm down, but this asshole was relentless, "And she's not retarded. Stop fucking saying that shit! She's..."

Daps turned around. "Bro, you can totally tell. I mean, look it, why else would you be getting so pissed?"

"Bro, leave her alone, I'm serious. Plus, I'm with that Sara chick," I confidently shouted back at him.

"That blonde? Whatever! You totally want to nail that piece right there." He pointed up the shoreline about fifty feet where Isla was kneeling down to look at something. I didn't really know how to take his banter...I wasn't sure if he was insulting, complementing, harassing, or displacing his own sexual fantasies onto me. Whatever the reason, I was downright mad, and slightly confused.

I slowly jogged away from the two dumbasses and headed quickly for Isla.

"Hey, Isla."

"Hi." She was looking down at something in the sand, about ten feet from the beach.

"What are you doin'?" I knelt down next to her and was glad to get away from the other guys, if only for a minute.

"Looking for something." She pulled her hair back, which had fallen into her face.

"Oh."

The two dorks were now standing over us. "Hey girl…whatchu up too?" Nerdo was trying to sound cool. Isla didn't respond.

Daps picked up some short sticks and started chucking them into the water, obviously bored. Nerdo just stood there, behind Isla.

"Hey, what are you two looking at?" Nerdo asked. I didn't say anything, nor did Isla.

"Hey!" Daps called again, and started walking over.

"What are we doing here?" He was getting a little agitated. Isla was concentrating on the sand.

"We're trying to find a sea turtle egg," I responded, having no real idea if that was actually what we were looking for.

"Hmm." Daps looked toward Nerdo, who motioned something.

"Can we go back with one of the other groups?" Nerdo squeeked. Isla was still looking down at the sand, gently poking around with her index finger.

"Hey…counselor chick! Can we go find the others?" Nerdo wailed out again. I looked up at him, but no response came from Isla.

"Hello. Can. We. Go. To. The. Other. Group?" Daps said as if he was deaf or had a speech impediment, trying to be insulting toward Isla, and somehow thinking he was funny at the same time. Nerdo thought it entertaining, and was lucky I didn't kick him in the head.

"Yes," she said while continuing to analyze whatever was in the sand. The two dorks gave each other a standard "high five" and walked off, triumphant.

She stopped looking down, and rested back, sitting on her heels; her knees turned in toward each other.

"So…" I tried to fill the awkward silence created by the two dorks.

"Yes?" She looked up from the sand.

"Uh…so, those guys…"

"Yes?" She was concentrating on what I was about to say.

"Sorry about that."

"What?"

"Those guys."

"Oh." She looked down, drew a small arrow pointing toward me in the sand, and then looked back up.

"Yeah…sorry." I looked down at the arrow.

"It is okay." She broke a slight smile, and lightly tugged on the side of her t-shirt where it had risen up just barely, exposing her waist.

"Okay." I stared at her mocha colored eyes to see if I could tell if she was really okay, or sense that she was somehow covering up some other distress.

"They are being ty-pical guys." She looked back down and doodled a small star at the tip of the arrow.

"Yeah."

She looked up again. "Thank you for defending me."

"Huh?" I didn't think she heard my exchange with Daps and Nerdo.

"Yes." The sunlight touched her eyes but was quickly absorbed into their darkness, with just a slight broken image reflecting back toward me.

"Uh…I didn't really…" I looked at her hand as she re-positioned her shirt.

"You are a very nice person, Kyle," she softly spoke in her innocent expressing accent.

"Oh, okay…thanks." I looked down, the both of us pausing for a moment.

"Do you think I'm…" she softly spoke then too, looked down. The wind was picking up which coincided with the weird feeling that I was having deep in my chest.

"What?" I moved some sand around with my fingertips.

"I don't know." She looked out toward the water, off in the distance, and toward the ever-present ominous weather to the south. Her hair gently blew across the left side of her face.

A couple of minutes passed, and I could sense that her feeling of anxiety and uneasiness returned. I thought of something comforting to say, or ask, but I didn't want to send the wrong message to her, or cause her any additional stress.

"Isla?"

"Yes?" She pulled the hair out of her eyes. I paused.

"I think you are awesome." She managed a smile then looked down toward the little drawing and sketched some fletching on the arrow.

"I hope it will all be okay, in the end," she added while touching the back of my hand with her skinny tan fingers.

"What will?" I gazed back into her eyes.

"I...I am not really sure." She then quickly looked down, as if thinking of something much more deep and troubling. I was starting to worry a little more about her at that moment, more than I had over the past week. She definitely had some emotional issues, not suicidal or anything remotely similar, but certainly some hopelessness, or something, somewhere inside her.

"Hey," I softly tried to get her attention.

"Isla?" I asked again, but she was looking down at her little arrow; the wind still blowing hair around her face.

"Hey, there," I whispered.

"Huh?" She looked toward me.

"What are you worried about?" A pelican dove into the water, catching our attention.

"I don't know." She looked toward the blowing palms, opposite the beach, then back at me. "Just things, I guess."

She then dropped her eyes toward her thumb, which she started picking with her middle finger. A couple more moments passed, while the waves beat against the narrow shoreline.

"Kyle?"

"Yeah?"

"Do you think that...?"

"Do I think?" I verbally nudged.

"That I am nice?" She quickly shifted her eyes quickly back toward the water and moved so that she was sitting on the sand; her knees tucked to her side.

"You are." I stared out at the ocean.

"Are you sure?"

"Totally." I looked into her eyes, while she drew a border around the arrow and star.

"Thank you." She smiled, but I somehow got the feeling that she wasn't fully satisfied. I really didn't know what she was looking for, which was not surprising being that I wasn't exactly an expert on women.

A boat passed by, causing the waves to crash against the beach with a slightly higher intensity. It was still breezy and the sun dodged from behind the clouds, mixing for a comfortable temperature contrasting the otherwise immobilizing heat and humidity of central Florida, back home.

"Isla?"

"Yes?" She glanced over.

"If I tell you something, will you promise not to take it the wrong way?" My voice was a little shaky, because I wasn't convinced this was a good idea.

"Yes."

"Promise?" She cracked a slight smile as I attempted to look through her eyes and deep into her conscience.

"Yes. Promise."

"Okay." I hastened while she continued to stare at me with her usual entranced contemplation.

"You are very different from everyone else," I attempted.

She dropped her eyes to the sand again. "I am sorry."

"No, not like that." I screwed up.

"It is okay. I know." Her voice grew unsteady and softer.

"No. Not like that. Like…I dunno…"

"It is okay," she repeated.

"Isla…" I touched her on the arm causing her to cautiously look over toward me, which I really shouldn't have done because I noticed a tear fall onto the arrow, absorbing into the sand. She didn't speak, just stared blankly, her eyes glazed in tears and me hoping that the floodgates didn't open.

"You are very…*very* pretty," I added, while she continued to stare. "You really are." I looked down, then back up to see her reaction. Another couple of tears slowly streamed down her smooth cheeks, then dropping to the beach. It was like slow motion; the tears like a departing friend driving off into the distance, never to be seen again, as they absorb into the sand. I felt my nose starting to run.

"I don't know what it is, but…" I continued. She wiped her left cheek as her right one released another tear into the sand. My emotions were being tested, for sure.

"You are really special. And I'm sorry that the others pick on you, and…" She softly sniffled and wiped her eyes with her knuckles so as to not get sand in them.

"I wish I could sit on this beach with you forever." I quickly looked out toward the brewing storm so that I didn't give myself some sort of aneurism. We didn't talk and I continued to stare out toward the water. I could feel her looking at me, trying to figure out exactly what I was getting at, or how to respond.

I quickly began worrying that I may have offended her, me being slightly younger than her and obviously so far out of her league, whatever that may be, that the mere odds that we were sitting on an isolated beach together was so improbable that I probably could have won the lottery that day, had I played.

As I looked toward the ocean I heard her shift or move in the sand and I could sense that she stood up, or something. I didn't look over, which would add to my temporary emotional instability, so I concentrated on the distant storm, while for a moment, thinking that she was standing up to leave me there alone.

Seconds later, I felt the brush of her soft, yet thick hair as the wind blew over my neck and face. She had sat down right next to me, placed her arm cautiously on mine, and situated herself to where our hips and shoulders were touching. Her hair gently whipped around the back of my neck and around my ears with the smell of salt air and coconuts drifting by my nose. I wanted to say something, but decided that she was content and so I kept my gaze seaward.

As the wind briefly subsided, I could hear her mild breathing through her congested nose. For a moment, I thought that the best thing for her would be for us to stay on this beach forever, away from other people, and free to not talk about anything. I quickly dispatched the idea as highly unrealistic, but still, for a moment, the thought crossed my mind of somehow remaining here with Isla, watching storms, stars, seagulls, drawing in the sand, listening to the waves, her soft breathing, and with my pure sensitivity toward her anomalous existence here on this beach.

An hour or so passed, marked somehow by the dipping afternoon sun. The little island was just big enough to not see or hear the others, which the lack of, seemed to temper her quiet and congested breathing. She didn't say anything, nor move closer than she already was, nor did she flirt, or send any signals that would indicate physical attraction; she just sat there staring out at the ocean and turbulent sky.

"Kyle?" she cautiously whispered while still gazing out toward the horizon.

"Yeah?"

"What is time?" I wasn't quite sure if she was asking a philosophical question or merely the time of day, her accent still adding to the mystery and confusion.

"Uh, what do you mean?" I whispered back.

"We need to meet back at five," she said, still entranced on the orange and grey clouds.

"Oh." I looked down at the Casio. "It's four fifty."

"Okay." She sighed which to me felt like she didn't want to leave.

Normally, I would have stood up and started the fifteen-minute hike back to the boat, but this wasn't "normally".

Another five minutes of silence passed, and my impulses were to tell her that we needed to get going, for I really didn't like being late. The urge was tugging at me, but I figured that she had a reason for sitting here and I didn't want to somehow disturb the balance, plus I really liked it.

Some time passed, with Isla still sitting next to me. It was peaceful, and sharing the silence with her was entrancing, not to mention that it would have probably made another perfect post card. I briefly thought that most guys would kill to be sitting next to someone of this level of beauty, on this beach, but also most guys would be tortured by Isla's nonstandard interactions. I guess it really didn't bother me much, because I just took her for what she was, embraced her mysterious intelligence, and tried not to challenge or conquer her circumstance...whatever it may be.

"We should probably…" I looked down at my watch; we were already late.

"Yes." She pleasantly smiled.

We stood up, and brushed the sand off. As we walked toward the path leading through the brush and back to the boat, she momentarily stopped and looked back at the spot where we were sitting. It caught me off guard because for a second I thought she may have lost something, but I realized that she was intently concentrating on the spot there on the beach. She only looked for a couple of seconds longer, then turned around and followed me back to the boat.

After a short ten to fifteen minute walk, we arrived on the other side of the island and back at the boat where the others were waiting. Everyone was onboard but Anthony, who was in the water checking something with one of the engines.

"Hey guys!" Anthony cheerfully called, while walking toward us, his lower half soaked.

"Hey Anthony," I greeted. He inoffensively looked over toward Isla, then back at me.

"You guys ready?" he happily asked.

"Oh yeah. Sorry about that." Me referencing our tardiness.

"Oh, no problem." He was genuine and continued to smile while walking back toward the front of the beached vessel.

Isla climbed up first, with me boarding right before Anthony. Isla and I sat down at the rear of the boat, while Anthony pushed us off the beach, then jumped aboard and fired up the engines.

Nerdo and Daps had apparently become fast friends and were laughing at something or another. I really didn't know any of the others, nor did I really care to, other than someone like Anthony, and I guess, maybe Jill.

After the short trip, we steered into the harbor and docked. Everyone quickly disembarked, leaving me, Jill, Isla and Anthony, who immediately started cleaning up the deck of the boat.

Jill grabbed a hose from the dock, and started rinsing the deck, while Isla organized the nets, plastic containers, and other miscellaneous gear into perfect little piles. Anthony disconnected the two portable red gas tanks, and walked toward the front of the boat, where I was standing.

"Can I help, or something?" I asked Anthony.

"Oh…no thanks. I got it." He smiled, but was probably glad that I offered.

"Are you sure…I don't mind." I really wanted to help, or just stick around the three of them for a little while longer. My gang wasn't going to be back until right before dinner at 6:30, Anthony and Jill were very nice, and it was either that or I could be hanging out in my room, so the choice was an easy one.

"Okay cool…do you want to walk with me to fill these up with gas?" He handed me one of the empty tanks.

"Yeah…sure." I looked back at Isla who was sitting next to the little piles of gear, while Anthony and I walked toward the maintenance building.

"She's really sweet, isn't she?" I wasn't sure if he was referring to Isla.

"Who?"

"Oh…Jill."

"Uh huh…she's really cool," I replied.

"Yeah." He looked down at the tank he was carrying and smiled. We continued on toward the concrete block shed.

"Hey….what do you think about Isla?" I couldn't resist attempting to shed light on her situation.

"Oh her? She's…well, I don't really know her that much." We walked behind the white building where a gas pump was located.

"Oh…okay."

"I mean, I know that most of the other girls don't like her, and the other guys don't talk to her anymore." We put the tanks onto a small ledge.

"Anymore?"

"Yeah. At first, like a month or so ago, when most of us first got here, you know." He grabbed the nozzle and started filling up the first tank.

"Okay…why?"

"Well, I think every guy thought that she was this hot foreign chick, and they were either intrigued by her, or she was a challenge, or something, but basically wanted to hook up with her. It was like a game, or something."

"What about you?" I asked as he curiously looked up from what he was doing.

"Huh?"

"You know...I mean, did you...you know, try to make a move?"

"Oh no...not me. I really like Jill." He smiled.

"Cool." I was relieved, for some reason.

"Yeah, Isla is a special one, for sure." He shook his head.

"How come?"

"Well she basically gave all the guys the complete cold shoulder." He chuckled.

"Oh yeah?"

"Yeah...it was pretty funny. They would all get shot down one by one. Like planes taking off one at a time, only to get blown out of the sky by the Red Baron, or something." He made motions with his hands like he was machine gunning into the air. We laughed.

"It's got to be a kind of joke. Where one by one, each dude here would try to take a crack at her, or something." He looked down at the tank he was filling.

"That's lame," I added.

"That's what I thought. She's very innocent, or something, so I had a pit in my stomach every time some other guy would mention his attempted conquest." He continued to fill the tank, the smell of gas now filling the air.

"So...did anyone...you know?" I dreaded the answer, but had to ask.

"Do it with her?"

"Yeah." I winced.

"Oh, no." I released the air from my lungs, relieved.

"How do you know?"

"It wasn't a mystery. It was like a total game...some of the girls were keeping score."

"Huh?"

"Yeah, like one point for getting her to respond to something they said. Five points for sitting at the table with her throughout a whole meal. Minus two, if she got up before the guy was done eating..." He was smiling.

"And…let's see. Oh yeah, and ten points if she asks you a question before you say something to her. Fifty points if you are alone with her for more than ten minutes, without her leaving. One hundred points if you make it into her room. Oh, and I think you can get like twenty five points if you can carry on a conversation with her for more than five minutes." He swapped out the tanks, and began filling the one that I had held.

"That's crazy." I smiled, still curious.

"And that didn't even count the other stuff, that obviously never happened. Like one thousand points if she hugs you, five thousand if she kissed you, and fifty thousand if you and she hook up." He shook his head again, laughing at the perceptively immature actions of his fellow male counselors, and the astronomical points that could be hypothetically obtained.

"That's really kind of mean…you know, if you think about it." I felt bad for Isla for the mere existence of such a game.

"Yeah…Jill and I think so. I mean, the highest anyone ever got to was like a whopping four points…and it was Jimmy!" He paused, "man, he thinks he's such a stud, and he's always trying to prevent any guy from talking to her. What a douche." He laughed.

"Were they seeing each other, or something?" I grew worried.

"Hell no!" Anthony laughed, "look, it's a well-known fact that not only has she not done anything with anyone here, she doesn't want to have *anything* to do with *any* of 'em."

"That's good." I smiled, now completely confident in Isla's decision making ability.

"So are you and Jill, you know…like dating or something?" I needed to change the subject.

"Oh…no, not really." He looked down at the tank that he was filling.

"Okay, well…okay." It felt like a touchy subject.

"I think I am too old for her…she is like twenty eight, ya know." He kept adding fuel.

"Well…I don't really know how much that matters. She seems really cool," I attempted to comfort.

"Yeah." He didn't look up.

"You guys get along really well, right?"

"Oh yeah…we are really good friends and all. But…"

"I get it." I said while he put the cap back on, so we grabbed the tanks and started heading back to the docks. Something was still bothering him.

"I mean…I lost my good job and all."

"Huh?"

"You know…I mean, I really don't make that much to take care of someone, you know, like that." He nodded toward the harbor where Jill presumably was still hanging around.

"Oh." I really didn't understand that much about whatever complicated money matters he was referring to, other than my mother incessantly reminding me how important it was to finish school and go to college, and how that was the only way to get a decent job. "You want to be able to support a family, don't you?" She would always lecture, "you have to finish high school, no matter what. Then a good college."

"Yeah…I wish. Ah, fuck it." He smiled while shaking his head, somehow defeated. I kind of knew how he felt.

We arrived back at the docks where Jill was still hosing off the boat, and Isla was messing with something in one of the big sinks.

"We filled up the tanks." Anthony looked for a smile or response from Jill.

"Awesome! Thanks!" She jogged over toward him and me, as I put my tank down next to Anthony.

"Thanks Anthony." She brushed a fly off his shirt, causing him to grin. They boarded the boat and rearranged some of the gear, to make room for the tanks, with him trying to take care of all of her small requests.

I walked down the dock toward Isla, who was washing something in the sink, her old purple towel draped over the side.

"What do ya got there?" I stood next to her looking down in the sink.

"A shell." She was scrubbing something small, pausing to sweep the hair from her face.

"Cool. Can I see it?"

"Okay." She picked up one of the frayed corners of her towel, and wiped the object in her hand. She held out the shell, as I opened my palm, she neatly placed the shell in my hand, which was one of many things I knew nothing about. It was beautifully glossy, tan with darker brown stripes wrapping around its cylindrical shape, and reddish hollow circles spotting the shiny surface.

"What is it?" It was pretty cool...for a shell.

"It is Lyncina Argus Con-tas-triata." She stared at it in my hand.

"Wow, it is really pretty." I gently rotated it.

"Yes." I carefully handed it back to her.

"Where did you find that?"

"American gave it to me, about four years ago."

"When you were in Miami?"

"Kazakhstan." She paused, "and he gave me an old stuffed animal. A stuffed kitten, he said his little boy gave to him many years ago, but that he wanted me to have it." She dropped her eyes down to the shell, furrowing her eyebrows, presumably attempting to recall more of the details.

"That was sweet of him."

"Yes. But, I lost kitten." This made her sad, and I realized the significance of the shell and, well the kitten, and why she had a special connection to Ernie.

Jill's laughing distracted me for a second, turning around to see her joking around with Anthony on the boat.

"I need to..." Isla placed the shell back in the right front pocket of her shorts, and tugged on her dull blue t-shirt.

"Huh?" I asked, her brain working away at something.

"Oh...uh." She paused.

"What's up?" I tried to temper her slightly elevated stress level.

"I need to go to my room." She looked down, and then quickly back toward me.

"Okay. Uh...see you later?" I responded as she dropped her eyes again and looked at her worn sneakers where a lace was again completely untied.

"Yes." She kept her head low while she walked off toward the staff housing area. I turned around and watched her for a minute, until she turned a corner and disappeared beyond the maintenance building. I headed back to the dorms, and up to the room. Kazakhstan.

Chapter Eighteen

"Yo!" Will beckoned while dropping his gear and shoving it under his bed with his foot.

"Hey stud!" He caught me up on what he did that afternoon, and added that he had to kick some guy's ass for hitting on Sara, later admitting that he made the whole thing up. I didn't really believe him to begin with.

A short time later, we met up with the girls and walked to the cafeteria and did our normal routine. I didn't see Isla at dinner, and hoped that she was merely hanging out with Ernie back in her room.

We finished eating, and walked outside. There wasn't anything scheduled for Will and me, that is, but unfortunately Sara and Kristen were going to some lame art exhibit back in Marathon, that was planned early on before we all knew each other.

After the girls jumped in the van and departed, a couple of guys we knew decided to pick up a game of touch football between the dorms and the harbor, where we were playing Frisbee two nights earlier.

Will and I were on opposite sides, which gave me many chances to rush him as the quarterback. He really had an incredible arm, and we all made it our eventual mission to bring him down, which never proved successful.

After a half hour of heavy playing, and with indefinite amount of time remaining, I took a break and let someone sub in for me. I walked toward the harbor to get a drink from the vending machine.

As I passed the scuba shack, for lack of a better description, I immediately noticed the tattered purple towel draped over the edge of the sink where Isla was cleaning her shell hours earlier. I quickly grabbed it and walked out toward the others, trying to figure out how I was going to get the towel back to her. I carefully carried the towel, which I was now a custodian of, and sat down at one of the picnic tables, looking around for a counselor or someone who would know how to get it back to Isla.

After a few moments of contemplation, I decided to return it myself, and got up and walked toward the maintenance building, looking for the staff housing dorms. I walked past where Anthony and I had filled up the tanks, and continued to head down a gravel pathway past a couple of bikes propped against a palm tree. I spotted Terry.

"Hey, kid." Terry took a puff of his cigarette.

"Hey."

"What's goin' on?" He stood up, from leaning against a palm tree and rubbed his free hand over his buzzed cut hair.

"Do you know where Isla stays?" I asked.

"Who?" He smiled. "Oh, you mean…your little friend?"

"I need to…well, this is her towel." I looked down.

"Oh, I see." He took another puff, not really caring.

"Do you know where she is?"

"Probably in her room." He laughed. "I'm just playin', her room is back down over there." He pointed away to the direction, which I had come, and motioned over toward a different dirt pathway.

"Thanks."

"Hey, kid?"

"Yeah?"

"How's that watch treatin' you?" I smoothly covered my left wrist with the towel, so that he wouldn't get offended that I was safely storing the watch back in my room.

"Good! It's really cool."

"Oh yeah…me and it go way back." He smiled again, then flicked the cigarette on the gravel pathway and mashed it with his foot.

"Okay kid…see ya around."

"Yeah…see ya." I turned around and headed down the path toward the other one.

I approached a two-story concrete block building at the end of the dirt path, which looked like a very small, old rundown motel. Bicycles, plastic furniture, and an old grill, bordered the lower slab where the rooms were immediately located. There were two levels, and I had no way of knowing which room was hers. I could rule out a couple, based on funny welcome mats or an odd ornament on a door, but other than that, I was lost. Not seeing anyone, I climbed the steps to the upper level.

Walking past the row of doors to the left, and the railing to the right, I tried to listen for any voices I might recognize. One of them opened up ahead and some guy who appeared to be Jimmy, egressed and started walking down the opposite set of stairs away from me.

"Hey, man," I cautiously called out as his head disappeared down the first flight of stairs.

"Huh?" He poked his head back up, it *was* Jimmy, great.

"Hey, man." I walked closer.

"What." He stood on the landing between flights, looking up and smirking.

"Do you know which room is Isla's?" I felt weird, and very out of place, plus this guy totally wanted to kick my ass.

"Why do you want to know that?" He confronted.

"Oh, well, I need to talk to her." I draped the towel over my neck.

"Why?"

"Because I do. Come on, man, just tell me." I didn't want to agitate him more, being that he outweighed me by probably thirty pounds of muscle, but somehow I don't think that was avoidable.

"No." He walked back up the stairs, toward me.

"All right, I'll just," I backed up. I didn't need this shit and I could just ask someone else.

"Where are you going?" His voice grew hostile.

"Uh, back downstairs."

"Do you know how they decided to give her that room?" He laughed as he stepped to within arm's length of me.

"No." I took another step back.

"Because the highest she can count is three. One-two-three." And with that he connected his fist with my stomach, causing me to exhale and buckle to my knees.

"Don't fuck with her." He grunted as he passed by, nudging me while I attempted to rise back to my feet. I needed to puke, but first I needed to finish something.

"Hey, Jimmy." I stood up, and turned around, facing his back.

"What!" He spun around, and stepped back toward me, squaring off, as I approached. I quickly cocked my right arm, my hand clenching into a tight fist, and rifled my knuckles directly into his throat and deeply impacting his trachea. My dad would have been proud.

He immediately dropped to the concrete like a rippling wet sack of potatoes, grabbing his throat with both of his hands. As I continued to nurse my stomach, I turned around and headed back down the stairs, not real proud of myself, but, well, I guess I just really wanted her room number.

I continued down stairs, and made my way to number three and knocked. No answer, so I knocked again. I waited about half a minute and trained my ear on the door to hear if she was inside and watching TV or something. I knocked again, louder, but no answer.

Jimmy's dumb ass came stumbling down, looked at me, then like a scolded dog, made his way back to who knows where for moral support, or a beer. I really shouldn't have punched him, especially in the throat, but then again, I didn't want to let down my dad, or fail in my quest to return Isla's towel.

I tried to see if she had maybe left the door unlocked, and was hopefully inside and just didn't hear my knocks, as I imagined was possible. Strangely, the door was unlocked, so I cautiously pushed the door open and quietly entered.

"Isla?" I called out, while glancing around the room.

"Isla? Are you there?" No response.

The room was very small, and laid out like a sterile motel room. Immediately to the left was the single narrow bed, pushed up against the wall. A chair was about two feet past the end of the bed, closer to the slender entrance to the bathroom. No TV, but a single lamp on a thin table behind the chair, up against the wall. A small old transistor radio was on the table, and her bed was semi-neatly made.

Near the entrance to bathroom were two Styrofoam bowls from the cafeteria with water and a bit of cat food, sitting on a paper towel underneath acting as a place mat. It was kind of gloomy feeling, and I continued to feel, inexplicably, increasingly more interested in and protective of her as I sat at the foot of the bed, staring at the chair and makeshift cat bowls.

It was growing darker outside, and the room turned an even colder hue. The louvers on the door were closed, even though it was the only means of fresh air, and there was a protective screen in place, but she probably had her reasons.

I stood up, nudging something that was peeking out from under the corner of the bed. I raised the sheet to reveal an old green backpack, which looked like the kind you'd find in the back of an Army/Navy store. I had no desire to cause stress for Isla, and didn't want to snoop further, so I dropped the sheet the way I had found it.

I suddenly realized that I needed to leave her towel, and I quickly figured that she would have discovered that someone had gained access to her room. I looked around for a piece of paper and pen so that she would know that it was I, and not freak out, but I found nothing. So, I quickly and neatly folded the towel over the back of the chair, and exited the room.

I arrived at the football game without incident, and stood on the makeshift sidelines. "Where did you go?" Will yelled before he received the snapped football.

"I had to go give, uh…something." I didn't want to say her name and certainly didn't want to bring attention to my melee with Jimmy. Will took the ball and fired it downrange.

"Man you suck!" He joked with Tom, who didn't catch his pass.

"I'm done!" Will laughed while walking off the field and over to me.

"Let's go get a drink," I said.

"Cool." We headed toward the vending machines.

"Okay, now what were you doing?" He wiped the sweat off his face with the collar of his t-shirt.

"Man, Isla left her towel over there and I wanted to get it back to her." I pointed toward the sink, which we were passing, causing Will to inquisitively gaze at me.

"Why?"

"Well…she left it and was probably looking for it."

"Oh, okay." He simply left it at that, which was a relief.

We grabbed some drinks then sat down on the wood planks of the docks. We talked and joked for a while, Will now laying down on his back staring up into the sky.

"I really like Kristen." He continued his gaze skyward, shaking his head. We sat in silence for a while, followed by more random conversation.

An hour, or so, later, we heard the van arrive so we jumped up and headed over to greet the girls.

Will and I got an earful of how cool and pretty all the paintings were and the sculptures of who the hell knows, but we really didn't care other than simply to be talking with the "ladies". We carried on for a bit, before it was time to call it a night. As I dozed off, a deep pit entered my stomach as I realized that time was starting to quickly run out for me and…eh, maybe it was just the blunt force trauma rendered by Jimmy.

Chapter Nineteen

We spent the entire day together, Will and the girls, plus two counselors, Nikki and Anthony, and one other girl. But, time was still slipping on by, and I was growing more conscious of it, for some reason.

The afternoon waned, while the wind reminded us that there remained a weird storm still brewing off to the south. Speaking of storms, I don't think the scientists actually ever figured anything out. Terry was cool and all, but I tried to understand what poking around on the seafloor had to do with anything. Whatever.

Another day was winding down. We all passed our test, even Will, the practical portion, leaving only the written test tonight after dinner. We slowly walked back to the dorms, Will, Kristen and Sara sensing the impending departure three days later. Sara was more quiet than usual, me chalking it up to the unavoidable trip to the airport.

Dinner was cool. Kristen barraged Will with practice questions for the test after dinner, realizing that he didn't study.

"Will. You need to pay attention." Kristen humorously scolded.

"Yeah, Will." I laughed.

"Oh man...Kristen? Sweet cakes?" She smirked, knowing what was coming.

"What?" She crossed her arms across her chest.

Will twiddled his fork, "You're gonna let me...you know."

"No, I don't." She was serious, holding her glass just below her mouth.

"Come on, Kristen?" He whimpered.

"What?" She leaned back in her chair, tapping the fingers of her right hand on the table like a parent waiting for a child to fess up to taking "a sample" of a recently baked cake.

"You're gonna let me, you know, look at your test. Right?"

"No." She crossed her arms again.

"Kristen!" He looked bewildered.

"No, Will. You should have studied." She glanced toward Sara and broke a smile.

"Come on, baby?" he was laying it on thick.

"Oh Willybean, you are a *sad* sight." She chuckled.

"Yeah, Will, you really suck." I added, for good measure.

"Thanks, Kyle, now shut up." He briefly laughed, then went back to business, "Kristen? You know you love me, and need me, and all."

"So?" She teased.

"Well, I mean, you gotta let me."

"We'll just have to see how things are going." She parented.

"See what?" He was concerned.

"About your behavior." She raised her eyebrows and picked up a forkful of mash potatoes. Sara smiled, and so did I.

The rest of the room was finishing their meals, so Anthony walked around to various tables to inform us to stick around after dinner for the big test. Will, who was visibly nervous, worked Anthony and attempted to gain whatever inside information he could spare.

As the rest of the room was emptying, leaving a dozen or so others, I spotted Isla entering and proceeding through the buffet. She had her purple towel draped over her arm, while she cautiously placed a few items on her tray.

After the tables were cleared by all but the test takers, we were told to put a seat in between each of us at the table, to discourage cheating, but also because we had a lot of extra room. One of the other kids passed out the pencils and scrap paper while Anthony prepared to hand out the tests. I sat back in my chair, glancing over at Sara who was taking off her watch and placing it in front of her on the table as she probably did all the time, back at her high school, immediately before an important test.

I looked for Isla, and quickly located her sitting at a table in the corner by herself. She essentially had her back toward most of the room, but the way I was sitting, I could see her side profile. She had a couple of small cartons of milk, and what appeared to be a bowl of cereal. Her head held low, her left arm in her lap with her shoulders turned in, while she slowly ate.

I wanted to get the test started, and didn't want to have my interest and empathy elevated by looking at Isla, but Anthony apparently had not made enough copies of some section of the test, nor had he brought enough test booklets.

Sara was busy concentrating on memory recall, so I looked back toward Isla. She had her three milk cartons neatly positioned as some sort of barrier around her bowl, and was tightly holding one napkin in her lap with her left hand, while another napkin was immediately to the left of her bowl. Her purple towel placed carefully on the table, off to the side, but within sight and reach so to not be left behind.

The way she was eating was cutely awkward, and I dug all of it. It appeared as though she would fall over into the cereal bowl had she cowered much further. Her faded orange t-shirt with short sleeves revealed her skinny, naturally tan arms, and boney little elbows. She was a little scrawny, but at the same time had a great body. My guess was that she just didn't eat that much or that her parents where handsome and it was genetics which took hold. It was really quite strange, because if you never heard her talk or observe her quirky mannerisms, you would swear that she was just another really hot Latin girl…albeit with a funny accent, and I wouldn't change a thing.

My judgment was surely being tested in this whole situation with Isla. It was hard to look past the physical attraction, her love of stars and submarines, and even harder to look past her extreme peculiarity. But then, and only then, could one discover the true eccentric beauty and perfection of her sensitive little soul.

She stopped eating, and merely stared at the table. Thoughts of sitting with her in the conference room and beach invaded my consciousness, as I continued to watch her. She didn't look around the room, just gently gazed at the table, a foot or so, in front of her bowl. I wondered what she was thinking, or worrying about, analyzing, calculating orbital decays, or something requiring three milks and a bowl of cereal. As I became more concentrated on her small, isolated world, I began, for the first time in my life, to attempt to release her perceived emotional pain and pull it over to me in which to handle.

I didn't fully understand my own thoughts or really grasped the consequences, but I deeply wanted to take the agony she felt inside, away from her. Displaying some absurdly juvenile desire, I concentrated like I've never concentrated before and forced the visualization of an ethereal manifestation of distress passing out of, and away from her body and into thin air.

Serendipitously, but more accurately by sheer coincidence, she stood up and took her tray toward the trashcan. More due to the obvious fact that she was simply done eating, as opposed to telepathy or ghostly emancipation, she slowly deposited the refuse and set the tray down next to the trashcan.

Isla walked toward the swinging door, and paused. She shyly looked back, around the room, and spotted me looking at her. She moved the towel to her left hand, then raised her right hand and faced her palm outward toward me, gently and slightly waving her fingers. I smiled, and so did she, but before I could raise my hand to wave back, she was already gone.

Anthony was back, handing out the test booklets, followed by some basic instructions. It was the standard test thingy, but different because it was for something a little more practical, and with better company.

I looked over at Will, who was visibly frustrated. Kristen, feeling his pain, would occasionally reach across the table and gently touch the top of his outstretched hand for reassurance and comfort. Despite her tough, funny shell, I actually believed that she would kill for him. As I raised my hand for some simple, probably self-explanatory question, I continued to study Kristen's underlying adoration for him. She too, could hear his elevated breathing, and the concern was firmly displayed on her face. She would actually stop reading and look up at him, making sure he was going to be okay before she looked back down at her test, making sure he never actually saw her doing it.

The test wrapped up for Sara, who, after turning in her papers, sat down at a table near the exit, away from the rest of us. I smiled as I watched her point at me, laughing like she beat me in some race; giving me added motivation to hurry with the last three questions.

I too turned in my stuff, and headed directly for Sara. She leaned over, grabbing a deck of cards, and quietly started shuffling.

We only played about three rounds of black jack before Kristen was finished, and joined. She sat immediately next to me, so that she could have a clear view of Will, probably wishing that she had stalled on completing her test, so that she could continue to loan him emotional support.

We played another couple of games, while most of the others finished, turned in their tests, and left the room. This ultimately left Will as the only one still taking the test.

Sensing Will's hesitation, lack of studious motivation, or whatever, Anthony pulled up a chair next to him. Being that it was just the five of us left in the room, Anthony and Will started discussing the subject matter on the test out loud, in an attempt to assist Will in any way possible.

A half hour passed, and Anthony was still at it with Will. He obviously cared about his job, or thought Will was worthy of extra attention, but regardless he guided Will through basically the last half of the test, even going so far as to reviewing the first part before the real-time tutoring began.

Finally, Will had finished, but was still stressed out. We felt bad for him, and were kind of shocked that Mister badass football quarterback folded under academic pressure. Anthony, in another compassionate gesture, graded his test on the spot.

"Nice work, Will." Was all it took, from Anthony, to restore Will's trampled spirit.

"Do you want me to grade yours too?" He offered to us, which we agreed. He sat back down in front of the stack of papers, and sorted out our tests.

He sat there, for about fifteen minutes, grading. Sara, I was sure passed, as well as Kristen. I wasn't that worried, but I never had a strong love for the testing sort of thing.

"Okay...you all passed. Good stuff!" Anthony beamed.

"Thanks Anthony!" Kristen approached.

"Yeah...you didn't have to stay late for us. But, thank you!" Sara added, as the both of them hugged Anthony, which embarrassed him slightly.

"Well, no problem! You guys are fun." Will helped him pick up the rest of the tests, paper and pens, and we all walked outside.

"See you guys later!" Anthony took hold of the organized stack of papers as we neared the dorms. We said "goodbye" and sat down at the picnic table where only a few others were remaining.

We carried on for a little while, with Sara and Will visibly tired. Sara gave me a really good hug, while saying "goodnight" and playfully batting her eyes.

The girls walked off and Will motioned toward our dorm, and the steps leading up to our room.

"I'll meet you up in a bit. I gotta get something to drink." I said while he smiled and headed up to our room.

I left the ambient light of the dorms, and made my way over the gravel driveway toward the docks and vending machines, the crushed shells crunching beneath my feet. I passed by the wash racks, and the big sinks, and past the dive boats that delivered us to and from the reefs and distant ocean.

Approaching the flickering dim light of the vending machines, I caught sight of someone sitting on the isolated bench where Sara and I had shared the ice cream sandwich. It was Isla.

I quietly walked up to her, her back toward me, but made enough noise so that she wouldn't think someone was sneaking up on her.

"Hey, Isla," I calmly announced, while coming along side of her, seated at the bench.

"Hello." She looked up.

"What's up?"

"I'm not sure." She looked down at her towel draped over her lap, covering her thighs.

"Are you okay?"

"I guess…" She paused. "I do not know." She twirled one of the ragged corners of the towel with her fingers.

"Those stars look really cool." I motioned toward the sky.

"Yes." Her response confirmed that something really was bothering her, because normally she would have broken into more deep conversations about the universe, usually until someone or something interrupted us.

"Hey, what's wrong?" I sat down beside her, but giving room so she would have enough space for whatever she may need it for. She then repositioned her towel next to her, between us, and picked up her legs and pulled her knees into her chest, wrapping her arms around her legs. Something painful was eating at her.

"Kyle," she softly voiced, holding back a deluge of pent up sadness. She rested her chin on her knees, while she tightened her grip with her arms around her legs.

"Isla?" She didn't immediately respond, but I could hear her breathing intensify.

"It was bad, Kyle." She turned, looking dead at me.

"What was?"

"It was bad."

"What was bad?"

"What they did."

"Who?" My eyes grew wide.

"I got out of there, very fast." Her breathing grew more unsteady.

"What? Who? Got out of where?"

"That place where…that island," she sniffled and wiped her eyes.

"What? In the Keys?"

"In desert, in Aral Sea."

"What desert, where is the Aral Sea?"

"Where my father worked."

"Huh?"

"I took a boat to shore, then walked far, to a small sea port." I couldn't respond. I mean, I really wasn't sure why she was spontaneously telling me this, but it must have been really bothering her and she figured I was the only one who cared enough to listen.

"Then, I hitch-hike for two days to nearest hospital, near Aralsk. When I final-ly made it to hospital," she paused. "I had bad burns from sun and had to stay for de-hydra-tion." She continued to wipe tears from her cheeks.

"Oh my god." I couldn't believe my ears.

"I had bad sun burns and blood was sep-tic. But I could only stay very short time because they would come. I had to leave, and hid on cargo train and arrived at re-mote airfield." And with that, the floodgates were released. Her sniffling turned into a quiet sob. I turned toward her, catching sight of tears glistening from the light of the vending machines as they ran down her face.

The somewhat restrained sob turned into an all out weep. The lump in my throat felt like it lodged itself into my chest, and it took all I had to not add to the saline dripping onto the dock. She continued crying, burying her head into her raised knees.

I moved closer, not knowing what else to do given this slight glimpse of something so intensely disturbing. She attempted wiping her eyes and cheeks with her hands but couldn't keep up with the torrent. I probably shouldn't have, but I couldn't help but looking over at her again. The crying grew worse and clear mucus from the bottom of her nose was uniting with the top of her knees.

I put my arm around her back and shoulders, and pulled her into me. I really didn't know what I was doing, because I had never been in a situation like this, and briefly hoped that this sort of thing would never happen again.

I picked up her towel and covered her knees, letting the rest drape over her legs and shins and down to her discolored old sneakers. She was leaning into me and now had her nose and face buried into my chest, still heavily sobbing.

Gently brushing her hair with my right hand, I leaned down and placed my chin, nose and face onto the top of her head and into her hair, her heavy breathing causing her head to nod slowly up and down. I pulled her tighter into me.

"I'm really sorry," I softly spoke, not effectively containing two tears that escaped my eyes. Although I didn't actually do anything wrong to sadden her, I somehow felt responsible for the world's behavior toward this blameless, beautifully wonderful person.

"It's gonna be okay," I faintly whispered, and now wrapped my left arm around her shins and knees, my right arm still around her back and shoulders, encapsulating her, while she dug her head in tighter. I had no idea what else to do. I was helpless and she was revealing something deep inside of her, releasing, or pulling me in so that she wouldn't be alone with it anymore, and probably also knowing that I wasn't going to ever see her again after this Saturday.

She was trying to tell, or show me something. Mentally adding me to this struggle as her ally, in some sort of fight that I was losing innocence too. I really didn't get it, but I was trying. I had this compulsion to do something, maybe because of inexperience and immaturity, but the force pulling me wouldn't let go.

"I can…" I barely got the words out, attempting to regain composure. Her sobbing continued. I wanted to know more, but figured this was something so disturbing that she'd tell me when she was ready. I needed to say something, and she had to know that I was there, for her.

"I feel…" Again, I had no idea what I was doing, and probably was going to say the wrong thing, and dive her deeper into a spiral to complete and absolute depression.

"I think…I can feel your soul." My voice ending in a shaky murmur. I had said it, and at least it was something. The weird combination of words I spoke now some faint echo somewhere, however, her weeping and heaving breaths remained.

We sat there, me holding her as tight as I could, so that she knew that I was not going to leave her that night until she was okay. I buried my head into her hair again, and took slow deep breaths to hopefully temper hers. I wouldn't let go.

I had no idea how long it had been, but knowing full well that I hadn't dozed off. Eventually, and somehow so slowly that it was like watching flowers bloom, but infinitely more beautiful and rewarding, Isla was now breathing normally, and wasn't crying any longer. Still, I didn't let go.

I totally lost track of time, which was starting to prove the norm around Isla. From the moment I walked over toward the vending machine, before spotting her on the bench, I never checked my watch. It was probably late in the night, or early the next morning before I walked her to her room, my arm around her waist the whole way back to room number three.

She fumbled for her key, and handed it over. I unlocked the door even though the mechanism was not functional, and quietly pushed it open. She reached for the light switch, turned it on, and both of us walked in. She sat down on her bed, where Ernie was curled up on her pillow, and rubbed his head causing him to purr.

I watched her and Ernie for a brief moment, while she took off her shoes and picked her legs and feet up onto the bed. Ernie stood up, stretched, and repositioned himself at the foot of the bed, where she had placed her towel. I really wanted to know what had happened, there on that island, and thought about asking, but she was calm and I again figured she'd tell me when she was ready.

She curled up on her side, facing out toward me, on the narrow bed, with her back to the wall. She pulled the thin beige sheet, with little flower print, up and over her shoulder. I leaned down, and gently placed my fingers on the top of her head. She released a trembling sigh and closed her eyes, while I turned off the light, and left her room making sure the door firmly shut behind me.

I slowly walked down the dirt path, back to my dorm, and fell asleep as soon as my head hit the pillow.

Chapter Twenty

I was tired the next morning, and slept through breakfast. I was glad that the rest of the guys in my room had let me sleep, most likely loosely directed by Will, who probably figured that there was a good reason for me to be so tired. I needed the extra hour and a half.

A kayaking trip was in order for the morning, followed by the final dive trip that afternoon. Luckily, the kayaking was something where I was able to switch into it from some other classroom stuff. No Will or Kristen, but Sara was the only medicine I thought I needed that morning.

About fourteen of us, each in our own kayaks formed a loose line and paddled into the mangroves of one of the nearby islands. Sara and I were side by side, other than when the mangrove roots were so dense that we had to proceed single file. Birds, insects and frogs were all chirping away adding to the experience of the dense canopy and muddy water trails.

The morning grew shorter and as we made it back to the open, calm bay, she and I paddled immediately next to each other, which was actually pretty difficult due to only being able to paddle on one side of the kayak. It didn't matter to her.

"Kyle?"

"Yeah?"

"We only have one more full day."

"Don't remind me." I looked over, and into her eyes.

"This actually sucks." She frowned.

"Tell me about it." No one realized that later, more than me.

"We're gonna keep in touch, right?" She said, but I was actually concerned that she asked. I mean, she was a cool chick and I always assumed that we would stay in contact, so for her to ask the way she did, made it seem like she knew that there was a really good chance we were never going to see one another again, or anyone else for that matter.

"I'm gonna write you, you know…a lot." She held my kayak so that we wouldn't drift apart.

"Me too. And I can call you."

"Okay, that would be really good." She smiled.

We drifted, our kayaks connected for a little while longer, before it was time to paddle back to our beaching point, near the sailboat launch area. My shoulders were a little sore, presumably from paddling, but some small part was most likely stress related from only having one more full day.

We ditched the kayaks and gear, and walked back to the picnic tables, before lunchtime began a short time later. She talked about her high school classes, and how she was going to apply to three or four colleges later that year. Although she didn't come right out and say it, I was starting to realize that she had straight A's, all from honors classes, not to mention a job, and all her soccer stuff. She wasn't going to have any problems, for sure.

After lunch the four of us approached the moored dive boats, where once again, I was "selected" to accompany Terry and gang. I'm not quite sure what I did to deserve this honor, but unless it was going to somehow involve Isla, I'm sure a swift protest was in order.

I looked at the girls and Will, who were outwardly disappointed in the crew selection of each boat. Sara reached up and briefly grabbed my hand. "It's okay…we'll see you tonight on the cruise," she comforted.

I walked over and climbed aboard the other boat, just as the first one started the engines and idled out of the harbor.

"You've got your watch, right?" Terry patted me on the shoulder. I quickly covered my left wrist, so I didn't offend him for wearing my old watch instead of the one he gave me. Doug and he jumped off our boat, and walked over toward the shack, leaving Jill and me with the three graduate students.

"Hey, Kyle!" Jill walked over and sat down.

"Hey."

"You got separated too, I see." She smiled.

"Yeah."

"Me too." She adjusted the strap on the mask she was holding.

"Huh?"

"You know…from Anthony." She looked up and smiled.

"He's cool."

"Uh huh. He's very sweet." She looked down, embarrassed at her affection.

"He's our favorite," I confirmed.

"He's really smart. Do you know he's a fireman and a rescue paramedic?" She bubbled.

"Oh yeah…that's right."

"Yeah…he's awesome! And he thinks I care about his past problems, but I just really like him the way he is, especially here and now," she continued to smile.

"Yeah, he said something about New York, or something."

"He used to make a lot of money, I mean, a whole lot. But, I guess fate had different plans," she grinned.

"I guess that happens."

"His ex really stressed him out, and his job was real hectic I guess his nerves finally gave out one day," she glanced off in the direction of Anthony's departing dive boat. "I mean, he thinks I don't really know, but late one night after, I guess, one too many beers he opened up."

"What happened to him?"

"He, uh, I guess he basically had some sort of breakdown. Ya know, he didn't do anything bad, or anything, but he just couldn't handle that life any longer."

"Oh."

"Yeah, he said that he had horrible sleep, would wake up in the middle of the night for hours, and then after he shut down on the trading floor, you know for commodities?"

"I remember him saying something about lumber, or steel or something."

"Well, after he had enough, he checked into a hotel and didn't come out for like two weeks. I think he said he slept the whole time."

"Jeez. Poor guy."

"Yeah, then I guess he had enough. Broke up with 'that bitch' and got away. Lucky for me, cause he's here now," she smiled again.

"He's really cool."

"I think he's supposed to take me out Saturday night." Saturday was going to suck for me…well, at least not for Anthony.

"Oh cool! Where are you going?" She looked down at her mask, thinking.

"I'm not sure. He said whatever I wanted, but I want to go where he wants." She warmly grinned. I felt really good for Anthony, and it seemed like Jill wanted to be more than just a friend to him.

"I bet you'll have fun. I know that we always love being around him." I tried to boost Anthony's image, but apparently she was already sold.

"I wish I had got to go with him." She looked out over the harbor where the ripples from the departing boat remained.

I glanced toward the harbor, then back around to where Terry and Doug were talking. At that moment, I spotted Isla coming from around the bend, to the left of the shack, and was walking toward our boat. I was relieved, and smiled.

"Well…I'd better be getting back to work." Jill motioned aft.

I watched as Isla cautiously walked across the wooden planks of the dock, making her way past the shack, boarding the boat, and catching her first sight of me. She raised her hand to wave, but was distracted by one of the assistants moving some gear. She climbed over and around the scattered equipment, finding a place next to me.

"Hi there." I said as she cautiously slid her old green bag under the seat.

"Hi." She looked back at me, and broke a slight smile, while she nervously tugged on the front of her beige t-shirt.

Terry and Doug jumped on board, and walked aft to where the console and some captain's chairs were located. "You all ready?" Doug called out, and immediately started the engines while one of the others untied us from the dock.

We motored out of the harbor, and out into the bay, before turning south. It was pretty calm out, and not too windy, but the same old "interesting" storm was churning way off in the distance to the south. My guess was that's where we were heading.

I looked over at Isla again. She was seated between the bow, and me looking out toward the water. She had taken off her shoes and neatly stowed them under her bag, and had positioned one foot on top of the other with her hands tucked underneath her thighs. She had on short burgundy colored shorts, exposing her tan legs, and was now putting her long, chocolate dark brown hair into a loose ponytail.

"Hi." She caught me smiling, and looking at her.

"Hey," I replied. "Do you know where we're going this time?" I continued.

"No." She pulled her hands out from underneath her thighs and began picking at the skin around her right thumbnail. She looked down at her feet.

"Hey…Isla?" I wanted to make sure there wasn't anything bothering her.

"Is everything…well, are you, you know…doing okay?"

"I think, yes, now." She looked up from her feet, toward me.

"Hey…how's Ernie?" I figured that'd help, and later I'd switch to submarines or astronomy for good measure.

"He is probably eating right now, then he will clean, then he will go to sleep for a couple of hours."

"Oh okay. So, is he your first pet?"

"What do you mean?"

"You know, like a pet. Pet rabbit, or pet hamster, or something?"

"He is first cat." She smiled.

"What about any other, you know, animals?"

"I do not know." She was visibly confused, furrowing her otherwise flawlessly smooth forehead.

"Didn't your parents ever get you a puppy, or fish?"

"No, I do not…" She was trying to remember. "My father had a lot of animals at his work."

"Why?" I paused. "Was he a zoo keeper, or something?"

"I do not think so. He was animal doctor." She was growing a little troubled.

"Oh. Where?" I didn't want to push her.

"On island."

"Cuba?"

"Vozrozhdeniye." Never heard of it, and I was starting to wonder if this was the island she was referring to where she escaped out into the desert. My compulsion threw me toward asking but I figured she wouldn't want to talk about it with the others around, and I really didn't want this trip to start off too traumatic for her.

"I bet that was fun…you know with all the animals?"

"It was not fun and I only got to see the animals, but not play, and I wanted to pet and feed horses there too, but they would not let me," she paused. "I got mad because I just turned sixteen so I was not little girl anymore. But," she brushed the hair out of her face, and looked back toward the water.

"But what?"

"They were sick." She looked down, ashamed of something, or trying to forget.

"Oh, okay."

"I really wanted to play with other animals too." She was staring at me, obviously distraught.

"What where they?"

"Rhe-sus Macaque, African Green, and small Ca-pu-chin."

"What are those…dogs?"

"Monkeys." Her lower lip quivered.

"I'm sure he just didn't want you to get hurt. Right?" I was running out of things to say about the subject, but I didn't want to stop her from releasing whatever she was concerned about.

"I do not think so." Her voice trembled, a little more. She briefly looked around, concerned that others could hear, but reassured that her voice would not carry over the sounds of the two outboards. I didn't say anything, and I was starting to wish I hadn't inquired about the whole animal thing. She was getting more and more stressed out, but was trying to keep her composure around the rest of the group.

A few moments passed, as she grew more agitated. She was fidgeting more, and kept glancing over at me with a very troubled look on her face. There was some internal battle happening before me, and there was nothing I could do about it. In fact, I felt like I had caused it, and now it was a runaway chain reaction waiting to explode. She took a couple of deep breaths, trying to relax, but it didn't seem to help. She was picking even firmer at her thumbnail, triggering it to release some blood from the wound that she had re-opened.

Her eyes were starting to water as she blankly stared at me. "I was part of experiment."

"What?" I couldn't believe my ears.

"They used me." She cupped the sides of her head with her palms, trying to somehow add some pain relief to her memories.

"How? What! I mean, what are you talking about?"

"I can't…" She shook her head.

"It's okay." I looked around to the other people on the boat, who were completely oblivious to our conversation, perhaps distracted by the drone of the engines or the wind, or something.

"It was real-ly bad." She buried her face into her hands, as she propped her elbows on top of her legs.

I moved closer to her, "hey, what happened," I softly asked.

She took a few seconds to collect her thoughts and compose her breathing, "I would go to that place with my father sometimes, while he worked, on that island."

"Yeah?"

"I found out he was involved in testing, and things."

"Testing of what?"

"Infectious weapons," she picked at her left thumbnail.

"What do you mean?"

"It was bio-logic-al weapons research station."

"Huh? Why were…what the hell?"

"My father was research doctor there, for mili-tary. He would use monkeys for tests. Inject monkeys with bad viruses," she sniffled.

"Oh man." This was insane.

"Monkeys would sometimes go to sleep, some would bleed from mouth, nose and eyes, and some would go wild. But, but most would die." She paused to steady her breathing, "the doctors said that they were doing it for Soviet Union, but some did not like their job."

"What about your dad?"

"He said he did not like it, but, I think he did," she was ashamed.

"Then, one day," she stopped and looked down at my hands, then grabbed my right hand with both of hers and squeezed.

"I only went sometimes, but, one day soldiers took me and put me in room, with glass walls."

"Where was your father?"

"At first I did not know, but then he was with military and doctors on other side of glass. And, they then…"

"What? What did they do?" This was obviously very disturbing and the way Isla was softly speaking, I figured I was probably the only one to have ever heard it.

"They released Macaque into room. Its mouth was foaming and gums were bleeding," she continued to stare at my hand. "Macaque was infected and they wanted to see if it would con-taminate me."

"What the fuck!" I couldn't believe my ears.

"Macaque was very aggres-sive and tried biting me. I hid behind gurney and some oxygen bottles. But, Macaque was stronger than I thought, because of infection," She wiped the tears slowly streaking down her face.

"Oh my god." I shook my head.

"It broke window on the door with reg-u-lator from oxygen bottle," she paused. "And soldiers and doctors ran away."

"Did the monkey leave?"

"No. It came after me."

"What, what happened?"

"I looked around, and did not know what to do so I pulled towel off bed," she made a wringing motion with her hands, like she was winding up a towel into some sort of thick rope.

"Yeah?"

"Then, while Macaque got its arm caught in gurney and scratched me with paw on my mouth. I jumped around and put towel around its neck."

I just sat there, staring at her mouth, and the scar, as she slowly spoke.

"I twisted towel around its neck and squeezed hard. I was very scared and my eyes were so blurry I could not see," she looked up and into my eyes. "I broke neck of the Macaque."

"I don't know what to…" I was speechless.

"I cut my arm on glass but got the door open, and ran fast. Soldiers and doctors ran away from me, they thought I was infected. But, when I got outside some tried to shoot me."

"Oh my god."

"I made it to boat, and you know, I already told you the rest."

"Yeah. Yeah, you did."

"I promise, I am not infected," she trembled as if I was concerned for my safety. I was stunned, and couldn't speak for a few moments. She stared at me, her mouth quivering due to the account of the trauma, but also because she thought I was somehow worried and wanted to now stay away from her.

"Is that the purple towel that you," I nodded toward her tattered towel.

"Yes," she handed it to me.

"I have no idea, I mean, I don't know what…jeez, I'm sorry."

"It is over now. It happened four years ago."

"You, you are…something." I shook my head.

I was dumbfounded, to say the absolute least. I felt worse for her than I ever had for anyone or anything, and never could have imagined that something so sinister, evil, retched and monstrous could actually be happening somewhere on this earth. I guess it partially explained her love of the cosmos and strong longing for an escape to the heavens, I mean, shit, after what happened to her, it was truly miraculous that she was not dead either from infection, rifle bullet, or her own doing.

I handed her towel back to her, while she took hold and pulled it up into her chest, under her chin and held it tight, while she attempted to calm her breathing. I moved closer to her in an attempt to shield her from the potential stares of the others.

A few minutes of silence passed and she was exhausted. "You didn't sleep last night, did you?"

"I do not think so. At first I did, but then I kept waking up." She stared at the deck, a couple of feet in front of her.

"Do you…why don't you lay down? I bet no one will care." She didn't move.

"It's okay…it's cool," I encouraged, while scooting away a little to give her some room, and moved back toward the rail. She was sitting near the bow, and it was basically only the two of us on this side of the boat, so she had plenty of room to stretch out. She leaned up, and folded her towel on her lap. She then looked around at the others, then back at me.

"No one will care." In fact, I doubted anyone was even paying any attention to her, or me. She put her towel over my knees, and laid her head down on the towel, facing away from me. She pulled her legs up onto the bench, and put one hand between her knees, her other hand curled, touching her face.

I gently placed my fingers on top of her head, so she would know that I was cool with her using me as a pillow, although catching me off guard a little. Either way, she was settling down.

After a short while, and with the wind picking up, I figured she might be getting cold, so I cautiously leaned over and found a bit of tarp and draped it over her legs, as best as I could. She didn't react, which made me think that she had probably fallen asleep.

I was shocked at her situation. My breathing was still somewhat erratic, now that I had time to process what she had told me. I didn't consider myself to be especially violent, but if I could call on death himself, or a really accurate hunting rifle, there wouldn't be enough gunpowder in China to support the onslaught my conscience would reign.

I realized that this was bold thinking and slightly immature on my part, but shit like this cannot go unpunished. Maybe the Marines need one more good man, well eighteen year old, but you get the picture. I mean, I only have one more year of high school, so what the hell. Fucking Russians.

Our boat bobbed and cut through the waves and wind for another thirty minutes, or so, while my boldness waned. The others were taking in the relaxing ride out to wherever we were going. Jill looked over and smiled, presumably for letting Isla sleep on me.

The engines slowed, and finally were cut back to idle. One of the assistants stepped around the gear, toward the bow, and dropped the anchor.

"Okay, guys. Listen up for a minute." Doug directed our attention aft, where he was standing while he gave us the briefing.

Isla was still asleep. "Hey," I whispered in an attempt to gently wake her.

"Hey, Isla," I whispered again.

"Isla?" I rubbed her head, causing her to stir.

"Hey, there," I lightly spoke. She rolled over onto her back, and slowly opened her eyes.

"Do you wanna get up? We're here." She smiled, hopefully because I was the first thing she saw.

"Okay." She closed her eyes again, for a second or two, still with a content smile, and then slowly sat up.

She put her towel in her bag, and started fumbling around with her assigned dive gear. I did the same, but didn't want to move faster than her so that she wouldn't get stressed out and needlessly rush.

I took off my shirt and squeezed into the wetsuit. Everyone else was basically ready, but was still working on final preparations. Isla slowly took off her t-shirt, exposing her smooth olive skin and light blue bikini top. She did the same with her shorts, which drew unwanted stares from the others on the boat, revealing her lack of color coordination with the yellow bikini bottoms. She then climbed into a slightly, too large wetsuit, and glanced at me to see how I was progressing.

"Hey, Isla," Susan called out.

"Yes?"

"Where did you learn to dive?"

"Black Sea." Susan shook her head at Isla's response, either in disbelief, or total lack of geographical understanding.

We were all set. Doug and Terry jumped in first, followed by Eddie and Sue. We were last, which was cool, since we had really nothing to add; I was still confused as to why I was even there because simply logging times and shit was pretty simple.

"Okay…here you go." Doug swam over and handed me the tablet. The rest of the crew was laden with various measuring stuff, cameras and a large grid. I looked over at Isla who was fiddling with her mask.

A minute later, everyone let the air out of their BCs and started the descent through the choppy water. Terry and Doug swam off while the rest of us closely followed, making our way toward the ocean floor.

It grew colder, the deeper we progressed, and the light shifted toward the blue end of the spectrum. All I could really hear was the sound of my breathing through the regulator, the bubbles rising around my head, and the crackling of Parrotfish as they munched on coral. Isla was just to my right, and back a little bit; she and I bringing up the rear of the group, which felt rather strange and isolating. However, I felt much more comforted when I reminded myself that Isla was next to me.

As we reached the floor, Terry took hold of the grid and placed it precisely over a spot on the sand. I didn't understand the significance of this location on the sandy floor, but it was apparently serious business for the rest of the crew. I looked over at Isla, who was visually taking in the activity around us, and most likely as clueless.

I looked at the time and rough location on the tablet, but I wasn't really sure what I was supposed to be doing. I mean, he gave no instructions to me before hand, and my prior task of recording intervals and headings seemed wholly irrelevant this time. Whatever…I guess I'm just along for the ride.

Sue took some photos, while Eddie sketched something on a tablet that he was holding. Doug and Terry then pulled out a tape measure, did something, and reeled it back in, followed by more photos.

We started our swim back, and Isla and I were about twenty feet behind the others, when she tugged on my right fin. I turned around, and made eye contact with her, while the others disappeared in the direction of the boat.

She then slowly swam closer and reached her hand up, and gently touched my face, holding her hand there for a few moments. Thoughts swam around my head, as she continued to merely stare. She smiled, at least that's what it looked like with the regulator in her mouth, and moved in a little closer, picking up my hand.

Her hair was eerily stunning, the way it swept back and forth with the current and waves above. She moved her hand down toward my regulator, from my face, and lightly grabbed on. She did the same to hers and just held them in place for a moment. I had no idea what she was doing, but whatever it was, felt unearthly. It was like a spell, not that I had much experience with that sort of thing, and more likely wanted to kiss me underwater. I kind of laughed inside, at the remote possibility, but I wagered that she didn't want anyone to see us on our first one, if in fact, the remote chance proved accurate. She then released and lowered both of her hands, yet still stared through the blue-green water, and into my eyes.

We hovered there for a moment before slowly swimming in the direction of the boat. I figured I would just say, "I didn't want to leave my buddy" if anyone questioned why we weren't back, and I also started concocting a believable story like her mask fogging up, she lost a flipper, dropped a weight off her belt, or something else that required my assistance and could easily explain our delay.

After a few minutes of progress, I made out the silhouettes of the rest of the team hanging on the anchor line. We got closer, and grabbed the regulators attached to the two additional spare air tanks. No one seemed to care that we were late, or simply that there was nothing they could say because we were obviously still underwater.

Our decompression stop was completed, and on command of Doug, we all surfaced. The members of our crew started tossing fins on deck and handing gear to Jill and Carla, while Isla and I climbed up the ladder, dropping our gear onto the deck.

Doug and Terry checked their measuring devices and stowed them back into big plastic crates. The rest of us secured the empty air tanks, and the remainder of our gear, before peeling off the wetsuits and toweling dry.

I put my t-shirt back on, and wrapped a towel over my, now quasi-dry, board shorts. Isla quickly, either through modesty or just because she was cold, pulled her shorts back on, donned her shirt, and sat down in the same spot that she had occupied earlier. As I watched her, I was starting to figure something out, analyzing her place and mine, there on the dive boat...I mean, I think I was falling for her. After all, *she* was perfect.

Doug fired up the outboards, and spun us around in the direction of land. The wind wasn't that bad, but the storm still remained to the south, yet getting much closer. To me, it was just some standard Florida thunderstorm, albeit lingering for much longer than normal, but to these "scientists" it was some anomaly that needed to be solved in the name of "research" or what the hell ever.

Isla sat back, held her towel on her lap, and retied her ponytail.

"What time?" She looked over at me.

"It's four thirteen." She nodded her head, silently confirming.

We motored on for a while, while my shorts and Isla's hair slowly dried. I only had one more day, and I felt lonely whenever I looked around the boat and away from her.

Isla, on the other hand, being part of the staff or counselors, or whatever, would carry on down here for two months longer, with Ernie, but without an ally, and…well I guess just me. I thought there might be some chance I could drive the seven or so hours down here, and visit for a day. Perhaps take her to lunch at McDonalds or something, or to get ice cream. But, as fate usually checks my imagination at the door, this time was probably not going to be any different.

Of course, there was always the very remote chance, that I could convince my mother that I needed another dive certification, or some bullshit, so that I could make it back down here for another couple of weeks to see her. Maybe I'd just have to try, and it would probably make Isla very happy, and that, alone, *would* be worth it. Sadly, I could already smell September.

I looked over at Isla, my heart growing heavy knowing that this wonderfully sweet person, would lose my discrete, and usually weak support, but also I would be losing something that I was actually starting to fully grasp. I guess she was the first person that I ever knew; that I could honestly say was truly something special, awesome, wonderful, or whatever, and I wasn't going to be helping by leaving. I wasn't going to help myself by leaving.

"Hey, Isla?"

"Yes?" She tucked her hands under her thighs, and looked over at me.

"Where are you going, you know, afterwards?"

"What do you mean?"

"You know, after you leave here."

"I am not sure." That was the answer I was afraid of.

"Oh." I needed to change the subject, because I was going to fail in regaining a smile from her, which was starting to be inexplicably linked to my own emotional state.

"One day, we need to go watch submarines." I said, in an accidently despondent tone.

"Yes." She dropped her head, probably realizing the remoteness of my suggestion.

She *was* in a slightly better mood, after the dive, but most likely after her short nap on the way out, and the distractions of the dive. She untied her ponytail and faced the bow, and into the wind. Her slightly damp hair whipped up and brushed my face. Again, coconuts...maybe it was just the sunscreen.

"Isla?"

"Yes?" She looked over her shoulder while picking her hair up into her hands to help speed the drying time.

"Oh. Uh...nothing." My mouth was working faster than my brain, as usual.

"It is okay." She put her hair back into a ponytail, and faced me. I was confused at her response, but was comfortable that her general worry was in remission, even if temporary. I wanted to keep talking with her, in the hopes of diving deeper into her infinitely unique universe and to feel much closer than I already was, before time ran out.

"What's your favorite movie?" I know, lame question.

"American?"

"Well, I guess." I didn't think there was another kind.

"Casablanca."

"Oh." I heard of it, but I figured it was a movie that only old people saw.

"I saw it last month," she added.

"On tape?"

"What is tape?"

"You know, like video tape?" She had no idea what I was talking about, and I somehow doubted that even in Cuba, Minsk or Mazyr, or wherever she was from, that they didn't have videotapes.

"Oh, yes."

"Did you rent it?"

"It was in the-ater." I watched her, very closely, her beautiful facial features engraving themselves deep into my sub-conscience, her slight smile opening up some vortex into a place where only dreams could attempt to explain.

"What was it about?"

"This man who owned bar. He was in love with woman who came to bar after being apart from this man." She looked to see if I was paying attention.

"And, woman and the man wanted to leave the country and go to America because they wanted to be together."

"Yeah?" She wasn't going to win any awards for being a movie critic.

"And then she convinced man to get tickets so that they could leave." She nodded like it was a good idea, whatever this man and woman were doing.

"But this man did not want to leave, so he put her on plane for America by herself." I was confused, but it was really cute the way she described the events in the movie.

"And then man and his policeman friend said that they would always be friends." Her account was so bad, for lack of a better word that I laughed out loud.

"What is funny?" She smiled, but looked like she had missed out on a good joke and wanted to know what it was. I noticed again, her really white teeth, with her two front teeth slightly larger than the rest. I'm sure that she got teased in grammar school, being called 'little rabbit' or that she was bucked toothed or something. To me, they were wonderfully perfect, contributing to her smile, which I had grown very addicted to.

"Uh...I dunno. It's just funny the way you said it." I stopped laughing but was still smiling.

"Hmm. Well, I try to remember what happened. Maybe I forgot something." She actually laughed for a quick second, which caused a feeling to come over me like being warmed by the sun on a really cold day.

"Why do you like that movie so much?" We had stopped laughing, but even she was still smiling.

"Because. Uh...oh, woman is very beautiful," she paused, "and man is un-sat-isfied with her and likes to drink a lot in his bar." She smiled and giggled again, her eyes sparkling in the sun, for the first time.

"I need to rent that movie when I get home."

"You should see it in the-ater."

"Oh...uh...okay, I will." I didn't think that they even showed old movies like that anymore, but maybe they still did somewhere in Cuba or Russia.

"I want to see another movie." She leaned back and wringed her hands.

"You should."

"Maybe we can go?" She turned toward me and anxiously awaited my response.

"When?" We only had one day left, Friday.

"Saturday night, maybe?" She lightly bit her bottom lip in anticipation.

"Oh. Well, you know, we go home Saturday morning." She blankly stared at my mouth, while a wave of sadness overtook me. She didn't know, or had completely forgotten.

"We could go eat pizza again, afterwards?" she tried.

"I can't...I mean; I have to go home." I felt like I was denying presents to a kid on Christmas. More accurately, telling your best friend that you were dying, well, that you were indeed leaving someone who really needed you. Well, I kind of needed her. I'm not good at this, and that trip with my dad, which would probably be our last, and that "finish school no matter the cost" crap, was really biting at me. Oh man, this freaking sucks.

"Umm...when?" She started picking at her fingers, again.

"I think my flight leaves at 11:00 am or so, you know, Saturday." She nodded, slightly, before looking down at her fingers.

"Oh," she said, completely drained of the previous happiness she displayed moments earlier.

She moved closer, and shifted her body so that she was directly facing me, then grabbed her towel, and tucked it tight onto her lap.

"Please?" Her voice was shaky.

"I can't." Crap.

"You can't go." She dropped her head and looked at my hands, while picking at hers.

"But, Isla...I can't." The lump was forming in my throat again; this really was bad. I could stay, but shit, I had been brainwashed by all the "intelligent adults" in my life. They suck.

"I do not want you to," She softly tried again.

"I know, but..."

"I do not know, what to do." Her eyes were watering up.

"Oh Isla..." I was having problems speaking.

"Please?" she lightly begged, her voice breaking.

"Isla." I shook my head.

"No." She sniffled; tears were forming in the corner of her eyes.

"No...please, no." Her voice was barely audible.

"Please." She pulled herself closer, the tears now rolling down her cheeks.

"I'm sorry," I whispered, while mentally kicking the shit out of those "responsible" model citizens who made all those "stay in school" public service announcements, and those stupid-ass after school specials where the kids would drop out, get pregnant, get on welfare, and do drugs and shit.

"Please." She stared deep into my soul, trying to snatch it out so that she could stuff it into her backpack, with her towel and shell, and hold onto it forever.

"I really wish I could."

"But, please?"

I couldn't talk.

"You can't...please don't." She pulled herself in tighter, and buried her head into my chest, which was probably better so that I didn't have to see her cry and saving me from a similar fate, which, unfortunately, was already beginning. I put my arm around her back, and held on.

I felt completely helpless. I wanted to stay...here...and I imagined that Sara's more normal personality kept her from expressing similar emotions. However, I then fully realized what was infinitely better, in the now, the long run, and forever, and I was also sure which internal motivation was more pure. It was Isla, and a deep meaningful desire to truly care for someone with whose gravitational pull, between us, was growing stronger than anything known to science. Not to mention the, now proven, internal fact that I was falling for her like a million lead bricks. It had only one simple answer, and fate agreed.

The steady drone of the outboard motors, drowned out the deep breaths and sobs that she was emitting. I knew it was happening; her heaving underneath my arm was confirmation enough, and her tight grip and teardrops on my arm boxed in any doubt of her unwavering emotional attachment, which was growing much more mutual with every passing minute. I continued to hold her, and had no intention of letting go.

The boat ride continued on. The real clouds were now moving in, with the storm this time, from the south, hiding the sun and adding a bit of wind, which threw the smell of fuel and neoprene in our direction. Isla slowly calmed down, succumbing for the most part, but her grip remained tight and she kept her head and shoulder lodged deep into my chest and ribs.

We cleared the outer channel marker, and were rounding a small island inhabited by some tropical resort, on our way into the bay and onto the harbor. Everyone onboard was physically tired, from the long boat ride out and back, not to mention the demanding dive and gear hauling.

It was around 5:00, or so, as someone asked the time of someone else, and I think I remember hearing the double monotone beep of my watch as we pulled into our slip near the dive shack. Everyone else calmly collected their gear and slowly began the somewhat tedious task of rinsing the salt water off of the equipment, hanging the regulators and BCs and lugging the empty air tanks into the shack.

"We're here," I whispered to Isla as I released my arm that was around her shoulder. She remained, for a moment, before reluctantly letting go of her grasp and sitting up. She looked around, then back at me.

I reached underneath the seat for her bag and shoes, to make her life just a little bit easier, and handed them to her. She cautiously took hold of her old sneakers and picked up one foot at a time onto the seat, and tied a standard bow. The left sneaker, missing a couple of inches of shoestring, proved slightly more difficult for her to tie, but had probably been like that for some time.

She picked up her worn green backpack, and neatly placed her now folded towel inside. I collected what little amount of gear I had, and stood up, staring down at her, still sitting, trying to mentally bury her in whatever comfort I had available, and giving her a few more moments, hopefully not to have her worry more, but maybe, I don't know, smile again.

"Are you ready?" I softly comforted.

"I do not want this to end." She looked around the cleared deck, and then reluctantly stood up. Me neither, I thought to myself.

We climbed off the boat, and onto the dock. She and I walked the short distance to the shack, which was now growing abandoned; most of the others finished with their cleanup and now trying to get away from the approaching rain. She reached deep into her pocket, pulled out the shell that she had showed me a couple of days earlier, briefly looked at it, and then quickly lodged it back.

"What time?" she asked, softly.

"Five nineteen."

I wasn't quite sure why she cared so much about the time, but I didn't try to think about it too much. She pulled her backpack securely over her shoulders and turned toward me, attempting to compose herself from the earlier events.

"Sorry." She looked directly into my eyes.

"For what?"

"Being sad and telling you my bad past," she said, and then deeply swallowed.

"It's okay. Really."

"No…it is not." She looked down at her shoes, then back up.

"*I'm* sorry," I replied, placing my bag onto the shelly ground.

"What are you sorry for?" She stared, and placed her backpack next to mine.

"For everything bad that ever happened to you and that I can't be here. You know…with you."

"Oh." She slowly blinked then formed a slight frown.

"You are happy with your friends and Sara, and you will have a good life," she glanced around the dock, then back to me, "and I take away from that."

"No, you don't."

"Yes."

"*No*…you don't." I smiled, slightly, and so did she.

We looked at each other for a moment, while her brain processed our situation. Her smile changed back into a solemn manifestation of the reminder that I was actually leaving on Saturday. As she stared deep into my pupils, I felt like something different was happening, causing the world to spin just a tad bit slower.

She reached forward, and lightly grabbed my left hand, and cautiously pulled me in to her. She was still staring into my eyes, like she was attempting to fall into them. As she pulled me in, closer and closer, her eyes slowly shut, and reached up with her other hand and placed it around my neck. She was breathing slower and deeper now, like she was trying to meditate her body into mine. She stepped into me, released my left hand, and replaced her arm around and over my shoulder, and behind my neck, rising up onto her toes.

As she pulled closer, she raised her head and tilted it back, so that our noses were now inches apart. She took one more deep, calm, breath. She was going to kiss me, and in certain anticipation, lightly bit her lower lip.

My heart beat faster, pounding in my ears, as she moved her nose even closer, and slowly and barely, pushed her tongue out, just slightly noticeable, to moisten her lips in preparation, touching the little scar above. It was going to happen, and there was absolutely nothing I was going to do to stop it. As inches turned into millimeters, she breathed in through her nose, and tilted her head.

She gradually raised her eyelids one last time, checking her alignment, softly closed them again, and moved her mouth intently toward mine. As she gently pressed her warm body into me, I could feel her windblown hair dancing around my upper arms and neck. The wind picked up one last time, as the distance closed to where only a few air molecules stood between her lips and mine.

She stopped her advance, for one last moment, and then gently pressed her slightly open mouth onto mine. All the sounds of the harbor, and clanging masts of the sailboats drifted into silence, the buzzing of the generators ceased, the windy palms and the whole world vanished, and all that remained was the slow, constant softness of her breathing. At that moment, absolutely nothing in the history of the world mattered, nor did life itself have anything to trade which would be even close to equaling one second of this alignment of every atom in the known universe.

I had no perception of how long it lasted, but from that moment, my life was altered. I wasn't sure if it was internal cliché, or merely elevated endorphin levels, but whatever it was, I knew that things were different, and I guess I should have known from the moment I laid eyes on her. Maybe all the fish and birds were watching, or the DC-3s simply shut down their giant engines, or just maybe, there was some astronomical anomaly, which formed moments ago, in some distant part of some remote galaxy somewhere, which pulsated its strange energy earthward.

One of her hands was pulling on my upper back, firmly attaching her body to mine, with her other pressed on the back of my head, her fingers weaving my hair between them. I could feel the gentle movement of her eyelids against the side of my cheek, and the softness of her lips pressed deeper into mine. Our bodies were meshed so closely together that her warmth penetrated deep to the air in my lungs.

I didn't know what Isla was thinking that moment, but then again, I was never completely sure. Still, her embrace was perfectly genuine with a sort of delightful ghostliness I had never felt before in anyone, ever. She continued to weave her fingers through my hair, and moved her head to where her nose and mouth nudged as much of the skin on my cheek and neck as she could. The temperature of her body was so comforting that it felt like I was submerged into a hot tub, outside in the middle of a snowy winter. Even the tropical wind, when it picked up, felt like some Siberian blast on my arms compared to Isla's radiating warmth.

As we held on, I wondered if anyone else was looking, not that I really cared much, but to anyone else, especially some other guy, Jimmy, or that "Daps" clown, this was a curious situation. She stayed deeply rooted around me, pulling her head slightly back one more time to multiply the swapping of some beautiful cosmic magic from her lips to mine.

Some immeasurable amount of time had passed, but her locked embrace remained strong. She repositioned her head, slightly and leaned up toward my ear, whispering, "Please don't leave." I wished she hadn't said it, but with that, the spell was gently cast.

The wind grew stronger and stronger causing her hair to whip up and swirl around my head again, softly contacting my ears and neck. A crack of thunder broke in the distance, and the smells of rain blew in off the water. She moved her mouth and nose down from my ear, and back deep into my neck, which she held in place with her smooth, warm hand. The rain rolled in, and started falling on us.

We remained in our situation, probably hoping the rain would stop. But, it grew more intense, and the thunder sounded like it was getting closer. A few more moments, and her hair was now beat down with water. My back was getting cold and saturated with rain, and water was starting to run into my face and eyes. I wasn't going to move, until she did; it was the least Isla deserved, and…and I was falling in love with her.

The wind grew stronger, driving the rain into the side of my face and forehead. A bolt of lightning struck just past the harbor, signaling to us that the storm wasn't going away anytime soon. The rain grew more intense, completely drenching us.

Isla rapidly released from our attachment, yet cautiously so that I wouldn't think she was completely finished with me. She stepped back, holding just the tips of my fingers with hers, and stared deep into my conscience. For a moment, it felt like the rain had stopped, but I soon realized that it was her content gaze that had caused my distraction. Well, that, or the fact that I was so soaked that I couldn't feel the individual rain pellets striking me anymore.

She let go of my hand, picked up her backpack, and began walking backwards toward the pathway leading to her room, still facing me. I briefly smiled, because I felt like I had caused a wave of confidence in her, which would hopefully last long after I departed on Saturday, and fully confident that I had also finally found…perfection.

She smiled back, and reached out her hand toward me, wanting me to come forward, toward her. She kept her arm extended with her palm facing up, willing me to grab hold of her hand once more.

I stepped closer and reached out my hand, and grabbed on to hers firmly. She started walking backwards toward the direction of the building where she was staying. She smiled again, and pulled me along side of her, while she turned around. With me in tow, she picked up her walk and started a light jog down the pathway.

We quickly meandered through the now muddy path, and found our way back to the off-white concrete building where her room was located. The rain was a steady downpour now and the white noise that it was generating made our footsteps inaudible. We reached her room as she fumbled in her pocket, pulled out the key, and placed it in my hand

I quickly opened the door to her room, allowing her to enter first. She spun around, and pulled me into the room, while I flung the door shut behind me. She reached past me and fastened the chain lock.

The room was dim, but she kept the lights off. I could easily make out her features and the rest of the room; spotting Ernie curled up in the chair at the foot of the bed. She ran to the bathroom and grabbed two white towels and handed one to me, while she laid hers out on the floor, and dropped her backpack in the corner. I did the same, now standing on my towel, and staring at each other.

She smiled again, and slowly sat down on the floor, on the towel, and faced me. I sat down, the both of us still completely soaked. I crossed my legs, too, while she moved closer toward me. The rain beat loudly against the screen and louvered door, which covered up any other sounds normally coming from the outside.

She grabbed hold of both of my hands, with hers, and continued to stare intently at me. Her content smile with sopping clothes and drenched hair was a beautifully spectacular image, sitting alone with her, and all I could do was gaze back into her big, deep brown eyes.

At that moment, I wasn't totally confused anymore as to my place and existence. Something was wonderfully celestial about it, as though lying on my back on an abandoned beach staring up at the stars on the darkest, clearest night ever and the heavens were revealing a cosmic mystery never before seen by human eyes.

She sat there, holding my cold, wet hands, mysteriously weaving the fingers of her mind around the folds in my brain. I was helpless yet had never felt less worry toward anything, nor less anxious, stressed, tired, or emotional strain as I did that moment with her. It felt like someone had shot me with a tranquilizer dart, or drugged me with some serotonin-releasing super drug, which if I could traffic would make me a billionaire. Amazing was an understatement, not only, but a new word, phase, sentence, paragraph, page, or complete encyclopedia couldn't even come close to describing the overwhelming feeling of absolute and total satisfaction with my situation with her in this galactic binary.

She was a witch, sorceress, cunning hypnotist, or angel, or perfect goddess, but whatever it was, gave enchantment a new meaning. I think I even stopped breathing for a moment, or my heart had ceased pumping…actually I was convinced of it. The human body was not designed for this sort of entrancement; her disheveled, soaked image completely stole the very nature of space and time from the room. I was captured, in orbit around her, and no amount of thrust was going to provide the adequate escape velocity.

She pulled in closer to me, and again, with an absolute drive, grabbed the back of my head and guided our mouths together. I had never imagined, through my limited experience, a more definitive emotional transfer from one person to the next. It felt like she was actually reaching in and pulling my soul out of the core of my body, and intertwining it with hers to where it was unrecognizable as two separate entities.

Her sweet, perfect lips continued to touch mine, while her steady breathing caused mine to fall into sync. The rain continued to pound away at the door and concrete slab outside; I couldn't imagine a more perfect place.

As was now the norm, I had no idea how much time had passed, other than how many microseconds I recalled where our mouths were not in contact. But like all things, we released and sat there infatuated by the other's wonder.

Another inexplicable amount of time passed, but only noted by the rate in which we were now completely dry.

"Are you hungry?" I carefully asked, not wanting to upset the mystical balance, feeling like this was the first words I have spoken in years. I wanted to make sure she had everything her little body and mind needed, and my compulsion drove me to ask.

"Yes." Her smile blanketed me in euphoria.

"I don't want to go...you know, to the..."

"I know." She confidently responded, knowing exactly what I was going to say.

"What do you want to do?" I gently asked.

"Be with you."

"I know." I smiled. "I'm not going anywhere."

"Please do not leave me, at least for tonight."

"I won't." I didn't care about anything else.

I stood up and grabbed her hand, pulling her up.

"Where do you want...?"

"I can get keys to van." She smiled.

"Okay," I whispered.

"Stay here." She picked up the white towel she was sitting on, and walked toward the door. She pulled it over her head, opened the door, and jogged out into the downpour.

I sat on the corner of the bed, looking at the floor where we were sitting. Ernie got up from his nap, stretched, and hopped over onto the bed, and started to rub against my arm. I responded by scratching him on the ears causing him to roll over on his back. I looked down at my watch, 5:59…the others and Kristen, Will and Sara were most likely making their way to the cafeteria. I didn't give it a second thought, and would have died if someone suggested I trade locations.

I counted the seconds on my watch, which turned the minute counter to double zero, moving the hour to six, and being marked by the double monotone beep. Once more, while affixed on the seconds, 6:01 rolled into the now. I wanted her back more than anything, and watched the seconds turn into thirty.

The door flung open, rattling the louvers and banging the doorstop; with Isla rushing in while removing the white towel from atop her head, and triumphantly displaying a car key.

She smiled and grabbed my hand. I snatched up the other towel, placed it over my head, and followed her outside. The rain was beating the gravel and mud, while we jogged through it, coming around a short bend.

Isla was tightly holding my hand, with the car key in the other. I glanced over to see her mind-blowing smile and eyes focused on the van that was now coming into view. I couldn't quite place the feeling, but it reminded me of playing hooky from a Thursday afternoon of middle school math class, except that was all small preparation for this instant, and no one could have predicted *this*.

We approached the van while Isla followed me toward the front passenger side door and reached out her hand to open it, me wondering why she didn't just head toward the driver's side instead. I jumped inside, and onto the seat, thinking that she was going to run around to enter on the other side. She quickly hopped up, onto my lap, and slammed the door shut. She threw her towel onto the driver seat, exposing her head, hair, and content expression. She positioned her body so that her knees faced the driver's position, while grabbing hold and locking onto me. She ripped the towel off of my head, and grabbed the side of my face with her free hand, firmly planting a long, wonderful kiss.

The rain was pounding away at the windshield and steel roof, rising to a deafening level. She pulled back, smiled, and carefully sat down in the driver's seat, and started the engine. She gazed into my eyes one last time, before putting the car in gear and turning on the wipers.

She drove us out of the complex, and onto the small side street, passing by modest yet comfortable houses, which wove back and forth before yielding into the larger main road.

We took a left, heading west. Although not driving especially fast, she was on a mission to escape and steal me away with her, to who knows where. She gripped the steering wheel with both of her hands and would occasionally glance over at me and smile.

The rain continued, and we passed only a few other head lights. We drove over a few smaller bridges, while her eyes now stayed fixed dead ahead, negotiating the road and weather.

After a few more bridges, we reached a cluster of stores, a gas station and a Mexican restaurant.

"Do you want?" She looked at me, indicating the Mexican restaurant.

"I want whatever you want." We both smiled, while she pulled into the deserted parking lot.

She turned off the car and pocketed the key, and for a moment contemplated her next move, while she stared down at her lap. She looked up and over at me, unbuckled her seatbelt, climbed back across and straddled her legs over my lap and waist. She dove her lips onto mine, taking one more deep breath, indicating complete satisfaction with her capture of every emotion I have ever felt.

She leaned back, yet still consciously locked telepathically to me.

"We don't have to…" She motioned toward the restaurant with her head.

"I know…but you should," I said, knowing that she was probably hungry and me wanting her to never go without something she needed.

"Okay." She smiled, and leaned toward the door handle.

I grabbed, and handed her one of the towels, which we placed over our head as we exited the van, and dashed through the downpour and into the restaurant.

We found an isolated table next to one of the big windows, and after sitting down across from each other, she buried her hands into mine. We were the only people in the restaurant, which was not entirely surprising given the monsoon outside.

The waiter walked over and placed two menus on the table and filled our glasses with water. She now had, what seemed like, a completely elated smile etched onto her face. We stared, un-distracted, into each other's soul at our table next to the window.

Sometime later, "Can I take your order?" the waiter said with a Hispanic accent. We hadn't looked at the menus.

Isla continued her gaze and asked, "Do you want to share?" I nodded.

"Dos enchiladas con queso," she softly spoke, while not taking her eyes off of mine.

The waiter left us, while our hands and brains grew more welded. I couldn't look at anything else, nor any other part of her beautiful hair and face, in which I wouldn't change a thing. I fell deeper and deeper into her dark brown, mocha irises. She had put a tender, yet colossal spell on me that drew all of my thoughts into the singularity of her dilated pupils. I was incapable of independent thought, and if I had a heart attack right there, then at least I knew that I'd finally reached heaven.

Our food came some time later, placed off to the side opposite the large window. I couldn't eat, or drink, or simply didn't want to release from her smooth firm grasp. Again, I wasn't going to move.

The food grew cold and untouched, and the water level in the glasses remained. I had no way of telling her the emotional spoken equivalent and I probably didn't need to say anything, but even on other worlds, my compulsion remained intact, however abated.

"Isla."

She had it, she had everything I wanted. Her mind was beautiful, much more beautiful than thunderstorms, the sunset, the moon, the stars, the entire cosmos put together. It was like a brilliant chemist, somewhere, sat down, locked away in some deep basement for eons, and mixed every bit of sand from the most untouched beach, every bit of sunlight, happiness, emotion, conscience thought, and energy from every corner of existence to brew a goddess. And, I'm certainly not overlooking the fact that her quirky clumsiness, funny accent, strong yet delicate soul, and aurora of origin far beyond this world, just barely overshadows her cute sense of humor, stellar knowledge, and physical flawlessness.

"Yeah?" she softly whispered, waiting.

"You are perfect." This caused her to smile the most amazing smile anyone has ever witnessed. At that moment, and as intense as our first kiss, all of my blood left my body then immediately rushed back in, a prickling feeling overwhelming my skin. She didn't verbally reply, but formed a small tear in the corner where her eye meets the bridge of her nose, which then trickled down the side of her face.

I let go of her right hand, and reached across the table with my left. I didn't want another part of her to become abandoned away from us, or outside of her, so I extended my fingers, and gently touched her cheek where the teardrop was falling, and captured it.

Somehow, she knew exactly my reason for saving part of her. I rejoined my hand with hers, and breathed in deeply. Her smile remained.

Time had escaped us, completely. The waiter had long since removed the food and no check had been left. For a second, I felt like we were invisible, or shadowed to the rest of the world, where the rain had now stopped.

"Let's go back to room," she quietly spoke, and I simply nodded.

We rose from the table, her continuing to hold on to my hand. We walked by the cash register, where the manager was counting money and receipts.

"Do I owe?" He interrupted me with a simple headshake and a smile.

I opened the door for Isla, and we slowly walked back to the van. I placed her in the driver's seat and planted a kiss, before jogging around the back of the van and into the passenger seat.

We drove back to our Key, over the bridges, and hit a stoplight.

"What time?" She turned toward me.

"Nine fourteen."

"Less than thirty three hours." She fretted.

We continued on, and down the winding street. She pulled back in to the same location where we had removed the van, and jumped out meeting me behind it. She latched on to me with all of her strength, while we slowly walked back to her room.

We sat down on the bed, while Ernie ate some of his food from the bowl near the bathroom. She repositioned herself so that we were facing, and for a moment, simply stared at me again with her cavernous pupils.

Like a strike from a cobra, she jolted forward into me and pressed her lips deep into mine, grabbing the sides of my neck with her warm hands. We fell back, from her intentionally unbalancing my position, onto the bed with my head on her pillow. She buried her tongue into my mouth, roping it around mine; with a level of passion I had no capability of imagining.

She rolled to the side, and pulled me on top of her, while not releasing her mouth from my own. Our teeth occasionally touched, but not forcefully, and the taste of her lips was unfathomable. My world was totally complete.

She sighed and breathed with completely innocent intoxication while she whispered affectionately, "I am yours." And that was all it took to send my brain chemicals into unobtainable overload.

The smell of her hair, taste of her lips, sounds of her happiness, and touch of her soft hands all over my face and neck became so rooted in my sub consciousness that not another person, lobotomy, mental torture, alien abduction, or religious experience could unseat the piece of heaven that had carved out a space somewhere deep in my personality.

Our inseparability continued for some time, however, due to the fact that it was now very late and we were growing tired, she smiled and rolled over on her side, and pulled my arms over her, while she wedged her body back into mine. A few moments later, she sighed one last pleasant sigh, closed her eyes and fell asleep.

Chapter Twenty-One

I wasn't sure at what point I had drifted off, but because all of my dreams were invaded and occupied completely by Isla, I had no way of keeping track.

The distant calling of seagulls was my first real indication that morning had arrived, further confirmed by sunlight slowly brightening the room. Isla was still asleep, exactly where she had been some hours earlier.

I laid my head back down, taking in the final scents of the back of her smooth neck and hair, while the room grew brighter.

She stirred a couple of times, before rolling over to bury her head and hands into my chest. She leaned her head back, on the pillow, and slowly opened her eyes.

"*You* are perfect," she whispered, while blinking the last bit of drowsiness from her eyes, taking away any doubt whatsoever that our emotional attachment was not still fully intact.

I took tremendous comfort knowing now that through my intense love for astronomy, fascination with submarines, and me telling her how fun, smart and beautiful she is, was certainly the reason for her thinking fondly of me. Also, I gathered that the addition of the way I laughed at all her strange and sometimes funny jokes, the way I listened to her past, wanted revenge on all the people who have ever done her wrong, and how I hung on every last word she spoke multiplied exponentially my status in her conscience.

She gently leaned in again, and kissed me, passionately so as to know that this was definitely more than a simple morning kiss. We stared at each other, only inches away, while the sunlight cascaded into her room. We didn't move, other than to breathe.

A little while later, we heard voices from outside, indicating the routine morning activity, as the rest of the world got ready for breakfast in the cafeteria. After slowly succumbing to the realization that the previous night had elapsed into a distant eternity, we rose out of the sheets, and sat on the side of the bed.

"I guess we should...oh man." I looked down at my feet and shook my head in disbelief that in less than twenty-four hours I was never going to see her again. She wrapped her arm around my shoulder and pressed her face and head into my chest.

"No," she lightly whispered.

"I guess I need to be getting back." I brushed her hair with my hand.

"I...do not, please?" She faintly spoke, so quietly that I wasn't sure if it was she, or just in my head.

I leaned down, collected my shoes, and tied them on. Isla, didn't move, but kept her hand touching my shoulder and back. I slowly stood up.

I just looked at her, sitting all alone on the side of the bed, the sheets disheveled around her. It was both beautiful and horribly tragic all at the same time, which pulled the life out of my chest and caused it to sink. I was abandoning her, and I had no choice.

I unlatched the door, opened it and stepped outside. I took in one last stare of her beautiful face, cocked down a little, and to the side with a fretful smile. She blinked her lids one last time over her wonderfully supernatural eyes, before I shut the door between us.

It was 8:10, and breakfast had already started. I made my way to the cafeteria so as to not get Isla in trouble, because certainly now, the rumors were probably quickly brewing. I really didn't remember the walk, but I knew that I must have gotten there somehow.

I shuffled through the line, only grabbing some cereal and a carton of milk, located Will, Kristen and Sara, and sat down.

"Hey there!" Kristen called, surprised.

"Hey."

"What happened?" Sara was concerned.

"Oh...I didn't feel too good."

"Yeah...I figured since you missed the boat ride and dinner last night." Will was silent, because he knew that I wasn't in the room last night, at all.

"Yeah." I looked down at the bowl and took a bite.

"What's going on today?" Will faithfully interrupted.

"Uh…I think Sara and me have this quick visit to that art gallery this morning, so that we can get that credit." Kristen looked over at Sara.

"Yeah…kind of sucks," Sara said, while looking at me.

"Uh huh." Will looked toward me, while I tried to eat my cereal without emotionally shutting down.

Kristen and Sara carried on, laughing and being generally funny. Will somehow felt some small portion of what I was feeling, and basically distracted anytime a question was directed toward me.

We walked outside, and into the warm morning breeze. Sara glanced over at me and smiled, before she and Kristen walked off toward their rallying point, leaving Will and me.

He and I walked past the vending machines, and lone bench, and onto one of the docks that overlooked the bay.

"How are ya?" Will was concerned.

"I don't know."

"Oh." He knew I hadn't been sick. We stared out over the water for a couple of minutes.

"You wanna go throw the football?" He motioned a toss with his arm.

"Na."

"Okay." A few seconds passed.

"Man…can you believe that rain last night?" He shook his head in disbelief.

"Yeah…it was intense."

"Oh yeah. I thought we were gonna fucking drown!" He grinned while his eyes grew wide. I broke a slight smile.

"Hey, Kyle?"

"Yeah."

"Are you okay man?"

"You got me." I looked down at my shoes and shook my head.

"Bro…what happened?" He patted me on the back.

"I don't know."

"Oh." He pulled his hand away. A couple more seconds passed.

"Hey, Kyle?"

"Yeah?"

"We're gonna stay in touch, right?" He turned toward me.

"Yeah." I smiled.

"For sure?"

"For sure." He grinned again.

"Cool." We sat there for a few moments, staring out over the water.

"Will?"

"Yeah?"

"Let's go throw the football."

We walked over to the picnic tables, where he left me while he ran up to our room to retrieve the football.

"Head's up!" He tossed the ball at me, causing me to flinch while he laughed. He and I walked to where the two gravel paths split, the right one leading back toward Isla's room.

We walked a distance apart and started throwing the football. Will broke into some lame made up song, which made me laugh.

"Kyle is a total momma's boy," he crooned.

"And I am her studly man toy."

"Some times when Kyle goes to sleep."

"I creep in and stick it in deep." He smirked.

"That's totally sick, you fuck!" I yelled, while smiling.

"Do you even know what my mom looks like?" I chuckled.

"No. But I bet she looks annoying like you!" He fired the football toward me, and put his finger in the air like he had just scored a touchdown.

Our banter continued on for a while longer. I was hoping to catch sight of Isla, but never did that morning. Will and I walked back to the docks, and grabbed a Coke from the vending machine, before heading toward the rocky beach where Kristen and I had skipped rocks weeks earlier.

We joked around, but he never tried again to find out what was bothering me. We raided the vending machine one more time, and split a candy bar and chips. It was good stuff, but would have been much better had this been a simple sharing of time with a good buddy, with many more unlimited moments to come, occurring after wonderful nights, and infinitely more destined, with Isla in room three.

Another hour or so passed, and lunch was fast approaching. The girls weren't going to be back for the meal, so Will and I made our way over, and sat alone.

While chowing down, he told me what he was going to be doing for the rest of the summer, and how he and Kristen were going to meet up again, three weeks later, when he and his family travel to New York for some play his sister was in.

He asked what time my plane was leaving in the morning, 10:30, with his leaving at 5:05 in the afternoon. The inevitability struck home with Will, as he looked down at a beaded necklace Kristen had made him many days earlier. There was nothing good about the situation we shared.

An emotional wave blasted over me, quickly causing me to shiver. I *had* to see her. "Hey, I'm gonna head back to the room for a second."

"Okay." He probably figured where I was going.

"Meet you back at the tables."

"Sounds good." He dove back into his sandwich.

I dumped my tray, and quickly exited the room. My walk turned into a jog as emotions took hold of my feet.

I was running now, past a couple of counselors, and other random people, while I blew past the picnic tables and dive shack. I needed to see her, and there was nothing that was going to prevent me from kissing her, probably for the last time.

I rounded the corner of the damp dirt path, and arrived at the door leading to her room. I knocked firmly, so that there was no doubt that someone was at her door. Nothing.

I knocked again, and again. No sounds at all. My breathing grew faster and faster, and I tried the door handle, which moved allowing the faulty latch to disengage.

I opened the door, and stepped inside. All the lights were off, and the bed was neatly made. I noticed Ernie batting around a piece of lint on the floor, off toward a corner, but no Isla. I poked my head around the bathroom wall, and called out for her. The room was empty.

I quickly leaned down and patted Ernie on the head, and left the room, securely pulling the door shut behind me. I ran back down the path, and up the other toward the additional staff dorm. Nothing.

Back down the path and out to the large drive where the tables and shack were. I jogged over to the shack, hoping that she would be cleaning something, but only Anthony was there.

"Hey, Kyle." He waived.

"Hey," I panted.

"What's up?"

"Have you seen Isla?"

"Um…well about an hour ago, she was going to the administrative offices for…." He looked down trying to avoid eye contact.

"What's up?" I was concerned.

"Uh, well, I think she's in trouble for something."

"What?"

"Kyle, you know the deal. We're not supposed to be…"

"Yeah" I knew what he was talking about, and most likely this was Nikki's, or any of the seven or so other female counselors' way of getting rid of her. That, or Jimmy was well in revenge mode. "Well, where are the offices?"

"They're off campus, about three miles up the road."

"Crap," I murmured.

"What are you trying to do?"

"I don't know."

Will and I hung around the tables while my mind raced far beyond the speed of light. I couldn't organize my thoughts; I couldn't think about her without causing my brain to swell with incredible attachment. I looked out toward the scuba shack where it had first happened, and tried not to think about it for emotional stability purposes, but her image replayed over and over and over again. It was especially bad when I closed my eyes, seeing her wet tangled hair, a little wavy near the ends, and intoxicating smile as she reached her hand out toward me.

Will knew something was happening to his friend, and didn't speak, which was probably pretty hard for him. He and I sat on the table, with our feet on the bench, in silence. I dropped my eyes, away from the harbor and stared at some of the old carvings, which people over the years had etched. I had seen all these before, most of them being pointed out by Kristen, Will, or Sara.

As I repositioned my right hand down at my side, planting in on the old wood, I felt what seemed to be a recent scratching. I glanced down, and then looked up toward the harbor again. Something was different, I thought, and I focused my eyes back toward the wood next to my hand.

I strained my eyes, but as the late morning sun peeked around a cloud, the etching became clearer. I stopped my breathing, and concentrated on the image. A small arrow pointing toward a heart was freshly carved out of the wood. I confirmed, in my head, that it had to have been done recently because all the rain last night surely would have weathered a carving before this morning, turning it into a darker grey hue.

The image looked vaguely familiar, and I deeply focused on the meaning it represented, trying to decipher the artist's intent.

I thought a little more about it, but in the end, left it for another to interpret; my mind not very capable of complex thought at that point.

Will and I sat for some time longer, him probably soaking in the inevitability of his separation from his Kristen, while random activity picked up around us, causing our melancholy brooding to become increasingly difficult.

Sara and Kristen had finally arrived; a pleasant distraction was what I was half hoping for.

"Hey, guys!" Kristen called out, while the two walked over toward us.

They carried on about some more paintings of who knows what. They were outwardly happy, which I thought rather inappropriate for our final day. I assumed that most would be glad to get back home, to their family, friends, and life, and Sara probably to her boyfriend.

Kristen had other motives, for sure. She knew for a solid fact that she had successfully corralled Will in to her cute little Italian web, and that only weeks later, they would be hanging out in her home town, with nothing to do but kill time through some mutually benefiting means.

About that time, Anthony walked over to tell the larger group that we needed to meet back in the cafeteria for an announcement.

"Hey, Anthony!" Kristen and Sara said almost simultaneously, after he was finished with his direction, causing him to turn toward us. "You were awesome! Thanks!" Kristen added.

"No problem." He sincerely smiled. "I really enjoyed you guys."

He continued to joke around with us, asking us about our potential college selection, and what we were doing for the rest of the summer. I didn't want to think about it.

As we filed into the dining hall, one of the head instructor dudes, called the room's attention toward the podium.

"All right." The room quieted.

"Okay. Thank you all for attending this session. I hope you had a wonderful, and informative time down here," he paused. "Some of you are now seniors, so some of your courses can apply toward your high school credit, and the level three marine biology classes will go toward your freshman year at college."

Kristen turned around in her chair, and smiled at Will. The speech continued, "We have two buses leaving tomorrow for Miami International, each with a van to haul the extra baggage. The first bus leaves at six thirty, in the morning." That was the one I was going to be on.

"The second bus leaves immediately after an early lunch, because for some reason, a couple of you knuckleheads have much later flights." He laughed, while Kristen pointed at Will and smirked.

"So, this afternoon you all are on your own, but I suggest you start packing, because tonight we have a cook out and a big bon fire." He finished with, "Okay…that's it!"

We headed outside, detoured through the docks, and made our way back to the picnic tables. The line for the payphone was about ten deep, with people presumably calling home to confirm rides and times.

Sara cued up with Will, while Kristen needed to meet up with Jill so that she could drive her to the off-campus administrative offices for some course credit issue that she was having.

"See ya." She waved as she hopped up into the front passenger seat of the van, and off they drove.

I was all alone, and thought that surely enough time had passed to where Isla had returned to her room. My compulsion told me to sprint, but I didn't want anyone to know what I was doing, so I casually strolled beyond the girls' dorm, and past the maintenance building.

As I cleared the last structure before the pathways split, I picked up my pace to a jog, my brain racing and obsessively reminding me that I needed an address for Isla and something more than just a first name. I rounded the bend past whatever the hell kind of bushes lined the slightly damp dirt pathway, and then quickly made it to the off-white building and Isla's door.

This time I didn't knock, because I solidly knew that she wouldn't care. There was absolutely no doubt that her desire to see me, for the last time couldn't be dampened, so I twisted the knob and pushed the door open.

"Isla?" Silence. "Isla!"

Ernie stood up on the neatly made bed, and was now stretching.

"Where is she?" I whispered to Ernie, hoping that he was some form of exotic, English speaking marvel, but knew that my efforts were completely futile. He started to purr.

I sat down on the bed, and began to pet the lanky tabby. He swarmed around, through my arms, and hopped into my lap. I rubbed his little ears and chin, but all I could think about was back to twenty-four hours ago when she showed up for our last boat ride together. I dropped my head, in total defeat, while Ernie licked his arm while sitting on my lap. At least Ernie's happy, I thought to myself.

I sat still for a while, waiting for Isla to return, looking down at my watch, the same way I did the night before while she retrieved the key to a van. I wanted a "do-over" but I didn't want to change a thing. I wanted to completely, and slowly, relive those rapidly vanishing hours, over and over again. Here, in her room, I could just barely feel her memory, as I closed my eyes tight and tried to drown out the ambient noise from the other side of her door, breathing in deeply to try to catch a faint smell of her coconut scented hair.

An hour, or so passed, and Ernie was fast asleep. I didn't want to wake him, and thought that perhaps he was trying to tell me something by snoozing on me so that I wouldn't leave before Isla returned. I decided to wait.

I looked for her backpack, hopefully indicating an inevitable return, but didn't see it. I carefully leaned down, trying not to unsettle Ernie, and looked under the bed. Nothing. It was like she was never there.

Ernie, tightly curled up on my lap, gave me some confidence. There was only a little bit of food in his bowl, and surely he would need more water at one point. She was coming back, I was confident.

My breaths became easier, and a fraction of my short-term worry subsided. She was going to have to come back, at one point.

Or does she? My heartbeat picked up again, and breathing intensified. She absolutely could have left, I told myself. She could have someone else feeding Ernie. She could be spending the night in Key West, or Miami or something for some good reason or another. She could have gotten roped into any number of things that would prevent her return that night. This sucked, really bad.

Ernie sensed it, causing him to rise from his nap, stretch, and slowly stride over toward the food bowl. I sat still for one last moment, and decided to count to one hundred, and if she wasn't back by then, I would surrender and exit her room.

I slowly counted, and eventually made it to five hundred and ninety-three, before solemnly saying my sincere good-byes to Ernie. I slowly opened the door, and took one last long look into her room, and of the bed. I caught a fleeting glimpse of Isla lying there, but it quickly vanished as I confirmed the illusory mental trick.

I don't remember the walk back to the picnic table. I know I made it to my room, somehow, and shut the bathroom door, while I buried my head deep into my hands.

After a short while, and after packing, we reunited with Sara and Kristen, and began the walk toward the sandy volleyball court, where the cookout, bonfire, and music had already begun.

The overall experience, I thought, was probably really cool. Will reported to me, that he had located numerous, dark, "make-out" spots, if I cared to partake with Sara…but he knew the deal.

Kristen and Sara were giggling, mingling in hugs, as they faithfully promised to stay in contact while Will, always hungry, required my escort so that his voluminous visits back to the grills didn't become unwelcome. He and I sat on one of the logs, facing in toward the bonfire. Kristen sat down toward Will's left, while Sara positioned herself to my right.

"I'm really going to miss you," she said while we stared into the fire.

"Me too."

"We're gonna stay in touch, right?" She leaned onto my arm.

"Yep." I felt like I was cheating on Isla, causing a tear to streak down my face.

Sara looked over at me, noticing. "Oh, Kyle, it's okay," she consoled; surely thinking I was regretting *our* unavoidable departure.

"Okay."

"I'll send you copies of all the pics I took." She attempted to cheer me up.

"That sounds good." I hastily smiled, while she leaned her head back on my shoulder.

A short time later, the cookout came to an end. We walked back to our dorms; Will and I received genuinely affectionate hugs from the girls, as we unwillingly closed the last night.

For a while, I fought sleep, but eventually fell prey to the still, outdoor air. I had this recurring dream…that I was 37 years old, and had just lost everything.

Chapter Twenty-Two

The annoying, neurotic alert of the alarm clock coldly woke me up. I fumbled out of bed, and was the first one into the bathroom and under the shower. I hurried, in the dark, so that I could steal ten minutes and try to find Isla, one last time, before the bus departed.

After a lukewarm shower, I quickly brushed my teeth, threw on the t-shirt and shorts that I had already laid out, and darted out the door with my big black duffle bag on my shoulders.

I dumped the bag at the base of the wall near the picnic tables, and ran toward the winding dirt pathway. It was six o'clock on the nose, so I knew that I would find the chain on the inside of the door latched, with her inside peacefully sleeping on the narrow bed.

I blew past the maintenance building, and buzzed through the bushes lining the pathway, catching the first sight of the cement block structure.

I took one final breath, and twisted the knob praying for resistance as the door slightly opened.

The door flung open…and all I saw was a startled Ernie, with prickled tail and bristled back, standing guard on the bed.

It couldn't be true, so I rushed past the bed to my left, and bolted back into the bathroom. Nothing, except for the pounding in my ears of blood firmly pumping through my head.

I sank, into the bed, and curled up into a fetal position. I winced my eyes shut and muttered, in a unsteady voice, *please, you're all I want* over and over again, thinking that if I just said it enough, and concentrated with every cell in my brain, I could bring her back into her room, and curl up behind me, holding on with all her strength.

I finally got up, and walked to the bathroom and took a piece of toilet paper to wipe my eyes and nose. It was over; I petted Ernie, for the last time, and pulled the door shut behind me. I never got her address.

We boarded the bus; Will catching the late one, while Kristen and Sara shared the seat directly in front of me. Our windows faced the picnic table, but I wished, that it faced the scuba shack and docks where Isla first firmly captured my entire existence.

I waved, along with Kristen and Sara, back toward Will, as we drove down the driveway back to the curvy side street. All I wanted was for time to be set back thirty-six hours ago. I didn't know if that would put me and Isla in her room together, on the towels on the floor, or leaving in the van that she commandeered. I didn't care; I just *needed* it to happen.

We neared the main road, and turned right, where Isla and I had, in now what felt like a completely different timeline, turned left. I twisted in my seat, so that I could absorb the final glimpse of the winding side street leading back to paradise, bumping my head on the glass.

All I could do was stare out of the window, on our way to the Miami airport. Kristen and Sara had dozed off, in attempts to combat our early morning departure.

Old diners and gas stations passed my window, as we drove over numerous bridges. I tried to remember precisely where she and I had stopped, to pick up the stuff for the dance, but in what became obvious to me, that I was simply distracted by her magic. I really never paid much attention to anything other than her sitting next to me in the back of the van.

Chapter Twenty-Three

We had arrived. All of us exited the bus and picked out our bags, which were neatly aligned next to one of the white vans, which escorted us here. The rain was coming, so we hurried inside each toward a handful of ticket counters.

Sara and Kristen, knowing that they were already on the same flight to Atlanta for their connecting flights, were standing in line in front of an airline check-in counter, one down from my check-in for my short flight to Orlando.

We rallied back near a central hub, which spun off different metal detector lines going to different terminals. My flight was leaving in one hour.

"Okay, Kyle…now you stay in touch with poor Will. I don't want him to get too depressed without me," Kristen teased in his absence, knowing that she would see him in only a few weeks. "And you've got Sara's and my phone number and addresses, right?" I nodded.

I then looked over at Sara, paused for a second, before she reached toward me for a meaningful long hug. She simply whispered, "It'll be okay." We stepped back and briefly looked at each other.

Sara and Kristen walked away, and disappeared into a security line; their plane boarding in seven minutes. I stared at the metal detectors, in an attempt to catch one last sight of them, but was never able to.

I took a deep breath, and turned around and faced the security line leading to the terminal where my plane would board in thirty minutes. I couldn't do it.

I quickly spotted a café and threw the bag over my shoulder, and made my way inside to a small table. I rested my bag on the floor next to me, and opened the zipper to make sure I had all of their contact information, knowing that it wasn't going to be complete due to no address or phone number, or even a last name for Isla.

I carefully tucked the piece of paper back in and closed the bag. I then slowly placed my elbows on the table, burying my face into my open palms, trying to recall every memory of her.

A short time later and after looking down at my watch, I was reminded that it was time for me to head for my gate. I reluctantly passed through security, and cleared the final return points leading back to the main concourse. It was over.

I slowly moped past the first few gates, while blankly staring toward the distant end of the terminal. I passed by, without paying much attention, the various shoe shine places and magazine racks, past numerous restrooms, and past the small coffee shops. I had reached the end.

Through complete distraction, I had walked past my gate at some point. I turned around, in the end of the terminal, and walked over toward a television screen, which had departing and arriving gate information, in front of a gate that was essentially vacant.

I dropped my bag and knelt down to retrieve my ticket. I slowly stood back up, looking down to find the flight number. 5193…how the hell do they come up with these flight numbers?

I looked up at the screen and strained to connect the flight number with the correct gate. The screen was old, and decided to become unreadable at the exact moment that I was visually tracing the line to my gate. Stupid thing.

I peered to my left then back in front, over in the corner near an unused boarding turn-style, quickly locating a different screen. I grabbed my bag and walked over, then flung it down on a row of chairs that had dual views, where one side faced the window out to the planes, and the other side was facing me and toward the terminal.

I checked the screen and located my gate, ironically right next to me, then leaned down and heaved my bag back over my shoulder. I slowly spun around, my eyes catching sight of a surprisingly familiar profile, facing out toward the airplanes.

My walk turned into a jog, as I grew closer.

"Isla!" I yelled, praying that the profile matched, causing her to turn toward me.

It was her. "Isla!" I yelled again, to confirm that she wasn't going to vanish somehow.

"Kyle?" She jumped up out of her seat, and quickly climbed over the chair-row to the side I was on, stumbling as her feet cleared the last armrest.

I had barely dropped my bag to the floor before she lunged her body into me and plunged her lips deep into mine. "Kyle," she whispered, and then quickly reconnected her mouth, passionately locking on.

She had returned my soul, and we settled down onto the seats, without releasing from our locked arms. This is what I asked for, I thought, while I smiled deep inside.

The embrace didn't release. Her hair, tangled around my head and face, and her hands interwoven around my neck recharged my depleted endorphins. The noise of the announcements, and voices of the passengers faded into silence, leaving her breathing with no other goal than to re-capture my comprehensive emotional attachment.

What felt like a few microseconds, was actually a half hour, denoted by the annoying distraction of my flight's final boarding announcement. She could sense my dismay. "Is that your flight?"

"Yeah." She curled her head into my chest, wrapped her arms around my neck, and picked her legs up and draped them over my lap.

"Please don't leave me again," she lightly pleaded, then buried her head back into my arms and chest, adding, "You owe me a movie." My eyes watered up, while I tried to maintain my composure.

"Remember?" she whispered, her voice barely audible due to her obvious dismay. My mind raced, as the synapsis kicked into overdrive. I wasn't going to get on that fucking plane.

"I'll catch a later one," I whispered, as she contently sighed and dug her head back into my chest; her hair emitting the beautiful, familiar scent that I already missed.

I held her for way over an hour…of course feeling like mere minutes. We watched planes arrive and depart, imagining where we would be going, if only toward the same destination. Our breathing was in sync and thoughts obviously intertwined and indistinguishable.

"What is time?" She softly raised her head.

"Eleven forty-five." She settled back down into my arms and chest.

I stretched my arms across her side and unbuckled my watch, releasing it from my wrist, and moving down into her view.

"Here," I softly offered. She responded by un-tucking her hand and gently held the watch.

"This is yours...you need to keep it," she whispered.

"No. You take it. I *need* you to have it." I reached back around, and buckled it to her left wrist, while she analyzed my insistence.

"Okay." She ran her unkempt index finger across the watch face, and then re-tucked her hand back between her chest and mine.

"My plane leaves in two hours," she whispered. "But I am not going on it."

I was a little confused. "I thought you weren't leaving the Keys for another couple of months?"

"There's nothing for me there, and...I needed to see you." She smiled.

Some time later, the once vacant gate where we were sitting, began to fill. There was no need to remain, and it made more sense to re-locate to another isolated nook somewhere in the busy terminal. We apprehensively released our arms and gathered our bags. All she had was her green backpack, which was now stuffed full.

We began our search for seclusion, finding nothing, then slowly walked back toward the main concourse; our hands latched firmly to one another.

"I need to..." She pointed with her free hand toward a restroom, waiting for me to release the other.

"Okay."

She repositioned her backpack, and slowly walked toward the restroom opening. She spun completely around, facing me, and waved her fingers while smiling, then disappeared around the corner.

Not wanting to be apart for any longer than necessary, and heeding the advice of my granddad, "Don't ever pass up a meal or bathroom in an airport", I expeditiously entered the men's room, not taking any longer than absolutely necessary.

Coming back out, and no Isla. I quickly assured myself that this was completely normal for a girl, and that there was nothing to worry about. I leaned up against the wall and dropped the bag at my feet.

Minutes passed, and still no Isla. Passengers rushed, while some pleasantly promenaded through the terminal hallway in front of me. Announcements blared, babies cried, and recently re-united couples held hands presumably walking back to the parking lot and on with their lives, which I was growing envious of.

Additional minutes elapsed, and I grew concerned, but I wasn't leaving. I walked across the width of the terminal corridor, and sat in a row of chairs facing the restrooms under a flight information screen. I looked down at my watch-less wrist and smiled.

"Hi." Familiar dull old white sneakers stood in front of me, with half tied laces. I quickly looked up, and instantly noticed a change.

"Do you like?" She had donned some light makeup, and was innocently smiling, waiting with maximum anticipation my response.

I grinned. "That's a hard question."

"What do you mean?" Her smile erased, biting her lip.

"You were perfect before, and now you are perfect with make-up." I stood up. Her smile returned, as she snared her arms around my neck, leaning in and kissing me.

"Let's go find a better place," I added, while she re-attached her hand to mine.

We slowly walked through the terminal, passing the small coffee shops and magazine racks, eventually reaching the exit back to the main concourse.

"Do you wanna?" I nodded toward the direction of the terminal exit.

"Yes," she immediately confirmed.

We entered the main concourse where Kristen, Sara and I had stood earlier, me desperately wishing for Isla. We continued on, past an entrance to an airport hotel, its hallway leading off to the registration lobby. If only I had enough cash, we'd stay here forever, I thought to myself, but the worry of how to make money above all else was something my mother subtly drilled into my head, even though she did just fine.

We finally found an isolated corner, behind an abandoned check-in counter turned into temporary storage for old computer screens. An unoccupied row of chairs made the perfect barrier between it and a large window overlooking a parking lot. We dropped our bags to the floor and leaned our backs up against the chairs, facing out toward the window and an approaching thunderstorm.

She leaned her head into me, grabbing my arm with her hands.

"Isla?" I loved her name, and merely saying it warmed me.

"Yes?"

"I didn't want...I didn't want to leave without seeing you."

"I know," she whispered.

"I mean...I went to your room and all. I couldn't stand leaving." She listened.

"I felt, I dunno...really alone, in your room."

"It is okay." She softly touched my face.

"I'll never get that memory out of my head."

"It is okay."

"It's gonna haunt me for the rest of my life...you know." My breathing grew slightly erratic.

"I am sorry." She leaned up and nuzzled her nose and face into my neck.

"Please...I don't want to ever see that again."

"I know." She put her hand around the opposite side of my neck, her face still buried. I settled my breathing.

"How's Ernie?" I had to change the subject and realized the ridiculousness of my question, but I wondered what her plans were for him.

"Oh, Jill said that she and Anthony would watch him." She removed her hand and starting playing with my fingers.

"Cool. For how long?" I asked, but already knew the answer, and based on her comment I was convinced that she would never return. She was silent thus confirming my conclusion.

I briefly paused to process my growing worry, "where are you going?" I softly spoke.

"I don't know."

I paused again, "where was that plane going to take you?" She gripped my hand.

"To JFK airport, then back to school, I guess." She sighed.

"Oh. In Leningrad?"

"Yes."

"That's far away."

"Yes."

I wrapped my arm tighter around her back, pulling her in closer. I silently prayed that time would stop, while I gazed out the window at the dark grey clouds of the large approaching storm.

"Hey, Isla?"

"Yes?" She leaned in closer.

"How come you came to the airport?" I continued most likely knowing the answer, "I mean, I know you said that there was nothing, you know, left there for you, but…" There was a brief pause.

"I needed to be with you," she whispered, reconfirming her earlier expressed intent.

We remained there, all alone, looking through the big window at the brewing wind and dark sky.

"Isla?"

"Yes?" She leaned up, to face me so that I knew she didn't want to miss out on anything I had to say.

"What's your last name?" I realized how frightened I was that I never got her name or address, but every time I was around her all I wanted to do was fall deeper into her world, and a concern for technicalities never crossed my mind, most likely as a direct result of her cosmic distraction. I always figured I'd get to say good-bye.

"Debrova." I smiled.

"That's a pretty name. Isla Debrova."

"Thank you, but it is just a name."

"Well, it fits you, perfectly." She smiled, showing her pretty teeth.

We sat still for a few moments longer. I could feel her worry grow again that we would be leaving each other soon.

It then dawned on me, "hey."

"Yes?"

"I need your address, and uh, phone number."

"Oh. I do not know where I will be, when I get back," she fretfully looked down at my hands as I took out a piece of paper and dug for a pen. "I give you name of my school," I thought to myself again at how much I loved her accent, as she reached her hand out to retrieve the pen. She immediately scribbled some weird kind of address in a format which I was completely unfamiliar with, and handed the paper back to me.

"Can I have?" she innocently replied.

"Oh yeah. Of course, sorry, I should have given you mine first." She smiled while she carefully watched as I wrote, starting with my name and phone number.

"I will try to write, but mail is not reliable, and going to America is even less. Oh, but maybe instead, I can call?" Her smile faded as she processed our departure. I left the address out, figuring that her calling would be way better, and being that the Soviet/American relations weren't exactly "peachy" the likelihood of her mail reaching me was pretty low. Also, I'd hate for her to write letter after letter, only for them to never reach me, and having no way to respond, further upsetting her. Plus, hearing her voice would make me realize that everything was going to be okay. Yeah, phone calls would be much, *much* better.

"Please. You *have* to call me."

"Yes. Yes I will call. I will call for sure." She smiled again, but once again, it quickly faded as more moments quickly passed.

"Isla?"

"Yes?"

"I'm glad you made it out of there okay. You know, that island."

"Yes."

"Did they ever, you know, find you? The soldiers, or, your dad?" I had to know the rest of it, but I wasn't going to press any harder than I already did. However, it was going to drive me crazy forever had I not known the ending.

"They did, but it was too late, I was already more than two thousand kilometers away, in Mazyr. I moved in with my friend I had as child, Anisya, and her family."

"Well, that's good."

"Yes. Her father was local head of police, so he would not let anything bad happen to Anisya or me." She smiled, recalling fond memories. She leaned back down, into my shoulder, and contently sighed.

"Hey," something was still missing.

"Yes?" She leaned back up, happy that I cared so much to ask.

"How did you get there?"

"Where?"

"Mazyr."

"I took a plane." She looked puzzled as if there was no other way to traverse the large expanse.

"Oh. Like commercial? I mean they weren't looking for you at airports?"

"I did not fly commercial. And left from small dirt airfield."

"Really? Did you sneak on board, or something?"

"No," she paused. "There was a cargo plane taking on supplies. So, I ran up and asked pilot."

"Jeez. You weren't scared, I mean he could have kidnapped you, or worse." Man, she was a brave girl, but I guess given what she went through, it shouldn't have surprised me.

"He was kind and not from area."

"What do you mean?"

"He was American. He was many years older and had not shaved in a while. He smelled of gasoline from airplane." She gently touched the side of my neck with her right hand.

"He said he would take me, but first he needed pick up someone near Pripyat, you know?"

"Where is that?"

"It was where nuclear plant exploded. But it was on way to Mazyr."

"Was it scary, you know, flying in some cargo plane?"

"It was bumpy, bad weather, and we mostly flew very low to ground," she took a breath, and smiled. "He was a good pilot, and wanted to get to Pripyat very badly." She paused, thinking back.

"He gave me this, to make me feel better," she pulled the shell out of her pocket she had showed me many days earlier. "He said it was for someone else, but wanted me to have it. He said I could make a pretty necklace for myself with it."

"I guess he really was nice."

"Yes. Then he dug deep in his bag and handed me an old stuffed kitten."

"Yeah, I remember you saying something about that."

"He said it always made him feel better, and now wanted me to have it." She smiled, "he wanted to make sure I was okay. Then, I sat in back, with cargo and two goats." She giggled.

"That's really funny. You're crazy." I laughed too, at her really cute depiction of the events, and as she described them, they were so detailed that I felt like I knew this man.

"It was long flight, and I was glad to land near Pripyat. But, uh," she looked down briefly, and then glanced back up. "He wouldn't let me off of plane."

"Oh, god. You're kidding. He was gonna,"

"No. He said it was dangerous outside, and for me to hide and stay in plane because there had been a bad accident. He then jumped out and was gone for almost a whole hour."

"Really? Where did he go?"

"I do not know. I hid in plane, behind crates, and I could hear many helicopters and sirens off in the distance."

"So you don't know why he was there?"

"I do not know, but he came back with a woman."

"A woman? She must have been someone important."

"She was very beautiful, and spoke to him in Ukrainian." Isla looked at me, finding some similarity between this guy and the woman, and me and her.

"She sat in front with him, and we left for Mazyr. I could sometimes hear her thanking him for coming for her and," she paused, and sniffled like she was remembering something troubling again.

"What did she say?"

"She said that she was in love with him, and that she wanted to be with him, forever." She looked down at the watch, and then stared back into my eyes.

"We landed in Mazyr, and after that, I never saw them again." She looked at me for a few seconds, smiled, and then laid her head back onto my shoulder, while I processed the experience she had shared.

Chapter Twenty-Four

We stayed there, all alone, watching the dark grey clouds, me concentrating on every moment so that I would never forget the feeling of her smooth skin on my neck, the sound of her breathing, smell of her hair and beauty of her soft voice.

"Kyle?" She leaned up, and grabbed her backpack, slowly unlatching the buckle.

"Yeah?"

She removed her old purple towel, which was neatly folded on top of the rest of her stuff.

"Here." She looked down, while she gently placed it in my hands, like it was a sacred flag being offered to a widow.

"No. No way." I shook my head.

"But,"

"No, I'm not…"

"Kyle. I want you to."

"No, Isla…I can't, no way." It was her prized possession, most likely the only thing that ever brought comfort, not to mention the emotions it soaked up and was a witness to. I mean, it was her weapon, what saved her, and it had her memory imprinted into its worn out fibers, strands of her hair, and cells from her skin contained deep within the dyed cotton.

I couldn't accept it, no matter what. It was part of her, and I wasn't going to let anything else slip away, lost while she soldiered on. And the addition, and as important, of being placed in charge of its security, would require me to convince Fort Knox that it was more worthy of protection than all the gold contained therein.

She gathered it back in to her chest, held it for a brief moment, and returned it to her backpack, which she pulled in closer between my bag and where we were sitting, curling back up into my chest and arms.

"What about pretty shell? Here, I give you," she reached into her front pocket.

"Nope. No way." I gently grabbed hold of her hand, and kept it closed with my hands around her little fist.

"Okay," she leaned in and kissed me on the cheek, while another hour slipped on by.

"Kyle?" She looked up, staring at me.

"Huh?"

"Are you hungry?"

"Yeah. But..."

"I know. But we'll be together." She leaned into me, and softly nudged her nose into my ear.

"Okay...but are we actually going to eat?" She paused for a second, and then lightly giggled.

We slowly got up, and collected our bags. My body was groggy from sitting still with Isla in my arms, as we shuffled back toward the population and collection of restaurants.

We passed the check-in counter where I had received my boarding pass, earlier, and the café where I had silently wished for Isla, passing along various posters depicting far away destinations and me wishing that we were about to board a flight there...not caring at all which one.

"What are you in the mood for?" We passed a food court.

"Pizza?"

I smiled. "Perfect."

We made our way to some of the tables, letting Isla pick out one by another window. We dropped our bags. "You sit down, and I'll get you, you know...whatever you want."

"Okay." She smiled, still standing.

"Uh...can I get..." She smiled, while I fell again, deep into her eyes.

"Mushrooms, olive, jalapenos...uh...oh, and green pepper?" I hated olives, but it was something I could soon like.

"Okay, sure thing. What about to drink?"

"Sprite?" She gently pleaded as if there was some chance I wasn't going to comply.

"Cool." I smiled, and walked over to the counter, not wanting to turn my back away from her, but with no other way to navigate, I had to.

I was the second person in line, and knowing exactly what I needed and it wasn't pizza. I turned around and looked back toward Isla. She was staring out of the window, hopefully imagining something wonderful, like some immediate departure to Hawaii or something, weeks alone with her, with time to spare.

"What'll you have?" The male voice called out from behind the counter.

"Uh...two slices with mushroom, jalapenos, green pepper, and olive."

"Well...that may take me a bit...but, if you don't mind waiting."

"Okay, and a Sprite with no ice." He walked over to the cash register.

"That'll be four seventy-nine." I retrieved five dollars and handed it to him.

"I'll bring it out to you." He handed me the change.

I sat back down across the small table from Isla.

"What were you thinking?" I pointed at the window.

"Oh...you." She smiled, and grabbed onto both of my hands with hers, reaching across the table.

"That's good, 'cause I can't stop thinking about you." She looked down at our hands.

"I wish we were going somewhere." She softly seduced my emotions.

"Me too." I looked through the window at distant views of airplanes being loaded and unloaded with baggage. I added, "Where would we go?"

"Anywhere." She turned her head back from the window, toward me, her smile fading.

The pizza guy came and skidded the paper plates across the table. She looked down at her piece and over at mine. "You got the same thing."

"Yep." I nodded.

"Why?" She lightly bit her lower lip.

"I dunno, it just...it just made sense."

"You are mine, right?" She stepped on the last part of my response.

"Oh yeah. You have no idea."

"You are sure?" She pulled her plate in closer.

"Definitely."

I was indeed hungry, but felt like it wasn't worth wasting time eating. However, she wanted pizza, and this was probably the last good meal she was going to have before her long journey back to her university, half way around the world.

"Thank you." She looked up from her plate.

"For what?" She paused, deeply diving into my eyes, connecting directly with my brain.

"The pizza."

We finished, me leaving some crust, and her leaving the odd loose olive. I tossed the plates and empty cup in the trash, while we got up and looked for another quiet spot in a futile attempt to delay time.

It then dawned on me. "We need to go change our tickets."

"How come?" Her voice elevated with certain anticipation, perhaps thinking we were going to both divert to some distance oasis together.

"You know...'cause we missed our flights."

"Oh." Her volume lowered, somewhat defeated.

We walked back toward the ticket counters. "I'm gonna get the last possible one tonight," I said, thinking that was the correct decision, and that I was somehow rebelling against the world to spend another couple of hours together.

We had the same airline, which made it easier to stand in line. I went first. "I missed my flight," I calmly said, handing the agent my ticket.

"Okay, let's see." She typed away.

"You're heading to Orlando?" She scrutinized the small computer screen.

"Yeah."

"Well, it doesn't look good." She tapped a couple of keys.

"How come?"

"Most of the flights are cancelled this evening. Cause of some really bad weather that's coming in." My mood was elevating.

"All I can do, is put you on the last flight there tonight, which is at…" She tapped some more. "Eleven thirty-five."

"Okay." I contained my excitement.

"Sorry about that."

"Oh no…it's totally cool." I stepped to the side so that Isla could get closer to the podium and agent. She reached in and retrieved the ticket from her backpack and cautiously placed it on the counter.

"Why don't we just put you two on the same flight?" The agent smiled and retrieved the ticket, without looking at it. Isla looked down at her worn out sneakers, then back up at me.

"Oh. I see." The agent looked up at us, and then to her screen, realizing that we weren't going to the same place.

"Well…your situation is a little harder." She pulled out a piece of paper, and typed some more. Isla helplessly looked into my eyes, and grabbed hold of my left hand.

"You have three choices." The printer buzzed away, spooling out something. She tore the printout from the reel, and showed it to Isla.

"You can either leave at five ten, which boards in about fifty minutes," she paused, "giving you an hour layover in JFK, then to Paris for one hour and ten, then on to Leningrad." Isla gripped my hand tighter, sensing inevitability.

"Or, you can leave at eleven o'clock, connect in Frankfurt for one hour, then direct to Leningrad." Isla started to nod, because this choice gave her the most time with me.

"Well, you probably don't want this other option." The agent directed her attention to another line on the printout.

"Depart at eleven fifty seven tonight, to JFK with a five hour layover, then onto London, on the ground for two and a half hours, to Helsinki for an overnight, then the next morning to Leningrad."

"That one." Isla touched her finger on the third option.

The agent inquisitively looked at Isla for a moment, but then reprinted and handed her the new ticket, we gathered our bags, and headed away back toward the food court.

Chapter Twenty-Five

As we walked, I repositioned my bag over my shoulder, and held her tighter around the waist. We passed the pizza shop, triggering my memory, "I owe you a movie." We halted and turned toward each other.

"I thought you had forgotten." She smiled.

"I need to find…" I started looking around for options.

There were various television screens around one of the lobbies, but nothing on but news and weather stuff.

"We don't have to," she fretted, realizing the difficulty of her request.

"Maybe if we sit over there, we can convince one of the airport agents to change the channel." She smiled at my determination.

We parked our gear on the floor in front of our feet, and sat in front of one of the TVs hanging from the ceiling, and out of reach. More random news, and weather alerts.

We sat there, for about thirty minutes, hoping for someone to walk by who had some ability to change the channel, but it never happened. She was curled up again, with her legs draped over my lap, and her head tucked deep into the side of my neck, holding on firmly with her arms and hands.

"It's okay," she whispered.

Another ten minutes or so passed while I formulated my plan. There had to be a way, and I was going to find it.

"Hey Isla?"

"Yes?"

"I think I know where we can find a movie."

"You do?" She leaned up, raising her eyebrows and eyes wide.

"Yeah…let's go." She let go of her grip and we picked up our bags. She was doing a good job of keeping up, as I quickly walked down the concourse.

"Where's one of those airline clubs?" I leaned into a conversation that two agents were having.

"What airline are you on?" I handed over my ticket.

"Go back to your terminal and it's about half way down on the left."

"Thanks." I folded the ticket and stuffed it back into my pocket.

We turned around and briskly walked toward security, clearing it smoothly due to the greatly reduced foot traffic as a result of all the flight cancellations.

I checked behind me to make sure Isla was still there. "I am here." She smiled. We located the private airline club and pushed open the thick, dark wooden door.

"Can I help you?" A female attendant called from behind the green marble counter.

"Uh...yeah."

"Can I see your ticket and membership card?" She reached out her hand.

"Well, uh...I don't have it, but..."

"Sir, you can't come in, if you don't have a membership card." She pleasantly remarked.

"Well, my mom is a member, but I don't have her card."

"Unfortunately, that doesn't count." She looked over at Isla.

"Please? You gotta let me use her membership," I begged.

"I'm not supposed to."

"You've got...I mean, can you please just check?"

She glanced around. "How do you spell her name?" She looked again, around the room to see if anyone was going to realize her capitulation, then discreetly handed me a piece of paper and pen.

"Here you go." I handed it back to her. She typed on her keyboard, "Okay, got it."

Isla, behind me, wove her hand around my waist and stomach, latching onto me.

"You know, I'm not supposed to do this, but..." she looked around, "since we're basically empty...just don't say anything to anyone. Okay?"

"Okay." I slung my bag over my shoulder and grabbed hold of Isla's hand. We walked past the counter, and through a room with an untended bar, various cocktail tables, a few people, and six or seven big lounge chairs gathered in front of a large projection screen TV.

"There we go." I pointed toward the TV.

Isla stopped for a second, while I walked toward the lounge chairs. Realizing that she was not immediately behind me, I looked back.

"What's wrong?" I walked over to her.

"What is there?" She motioned toward a staircase, in the opposite corner of the room.

"I dunno." I passed by Isla, who was now holding her backpack with both hands in front of her.

I walked up a couple of stairs, not hearing anything, and stepped back toward Isla.

"You wanna..." she nodded before I could finish.

I closely followed her up the stairs, coming to a brief landing overlooking a giant picture window, revealing a blackish blue-grey sky and catching a quick flash of lightning. We turned the corner, and climbed the remaining stairs.

We came to a large dimly lit room, a couple of rows of overstuffed chairs facing each other, with a dark hallway leading off into what appeared to be extra restrooms which was in addition to the ones located downstairs.

I felt the suspicion that we were not supposed to be up there, but the staircase wasn't roped off, and the check-in clerk didn't relay a warning, so I dismissed any worry. We were alone, which was good, and Isla quickly spotted a flickering television off in one of the dark corners.

I followed her, swerving around the chairs and tables, to a big couch, which was directly facing the TV. She stopped, looked at the couch, then back at me and smiled.

We lowered our bags, and settled on to the couch. She slipped off her sneakers, curled her legs up on the couch, and leaned into me. I bent forward and picked up the remote from the coffee table.

"Let's see what we can find." I started flipping through the channels.

"Thank you." She snuggly moved her head deeper into my chest.

"I just hope we find something."

"Not for that," she whispered.

"Huh?"

"For trying so hard." She wrapped her arm around my waist.

"What do you mean?"

"For trying so hard to make me happy." Her breathing shuddered. I pulled her in closer to me, and continued to scroll through the channels. News, sports, telethon, game show…more sports, weather, old show…and, The Little Mermaid.

"What about this?" I asked.

"Uh huh…this is perfect." She nodded, her head still leaning into my chest.

We settled in to the movie that had probably started a couple of minutes earlier, at five o' clock.

"Can you hear okay?" The volume was still low.

"Yes. Can you?" she softly asked.

"Yep." I didn't want to drown out the sound of her slightly congested breathing, which always caused my heart to melt.

We sat there, perfectly still, for a few minutes anyway. She had to be downright exhausted, and curled up on the thick leather couch probably didn't help her alertness. Still, she began one final astronomy lesson.

"There is one more thing I need to tell you about stars," she softly spoke, while turning to face me.

"There's a lot I still don't know…a whole lot." I smiled.

"But this is more important."

"Okay."

"Do you know Ursa Minor?"

"Yeah, isn't that the little dipper, or little bear?"

"Yes. But this is different from other things I told you."

"Okay."

"You see, there is a goddess," she paused, while I looked at her thinking that she looked in a mirror and finally realized that it is she who was the goddess.

"Yeah?"

"And she guards Ursa Minor from the doomsday hound, Simargl."

"Like mythology?"

"Yes, ancient things, but important because if the hound escapes from the chain, it will destroy Ursa Minor and entire universe."

"Oh."

"You see, astronomy is more than just mech-anics, physics, and chemistry. It is, much more...fateful."

"Yeah, it sure is."

We stared at each other as my emotional attachment to her was completely embedded and reaffirmed, while she made sure to tell me of other beautiful things that were at work somewhere deep in the cosmos. Something that professors who wrote text books could never understand.

The credits rolled, finished, and it was time for a newsbreak and weather. We stared at the screen, hoping that it was the beginning of the movie all over again, but more importantly hoping that it would reset time back by an hour and a half.

The watch around her wrist alerted us to the top of the hour, with the faint monotone double beep, causing her to lean up from me and stretch.

"I go to the restroom." She stood up, kissed me, and walked behind the couch over toward the hallway. I didn't want to be away from her, but I guess nature had different plans.

I watched the weather; a big front was passing, from the south, causing the brewing thunderstorms. "Good job," I said, thanking the front for the resulting cancellations and delays of departing flights.

A few moments later Isla reappeared. She had brushed her hair, or something, causing her hotness factor to jump clear off the scale. It was probably only the few minutes of her absence that caused the reaction, but nevertheless, she was perfect.

"Kyle?" She stood in front of me.

"Uh huh?"

"What are we going to do?"

"Hopefully stay on this couch, if you're okay..."

She interrupted, "No, I mean...about us."

"Oh," I replied while she stepped closer so that her stomach was equal with my face, and looked down, staring deep into me. We silently processed our inevitable separation.

"Kyle?" She cautiously spoke.

"Yeah?" I grabbed her waist and pulled her into me, encircling her mid-section in my arms.

"I don't want to go." Her voice broke down.

"I know, I don't either." I deeply swallowed, trying to quash the lump that was forming in my throat.

"Please, Kyle," she murmured, grasping both of her hands around the back of my neck and shoulders.

I couldn't talk. My throat was swollen shut, and any attempt would surly end in a complete emotional breakdown on my part. I held her as tight as I could, while a few teardrops fell onto my forehead, causing me to look up. Her mouth was twitching, sucking on her lips, her eyes completely flooded.

I buried my head into her stomach, with her pulling me in, securing us together. I couldn't ward off the tears any longer, and finally gave in.

Her abdominal muscles were twitching, revealing her quiet sobs. The only thing I could do was hold on so tight that nothing in that moment could wrench us apart. I submitted, that if all I could remember was her thin frame between my arms, I would be okay…out and on with my life. But, my wish called for absolute memory perfection, and I knew that this desire was incapable of being fulfilled.

More tears fell onto my head and neck, as I lightly soaked the front of her clean brown t-shirt with my own, which somehow had captured all the wonderful scents of the past three weeks into one thin piece of fabric.

She suddenly released her grip from my neck, and gently stepped back a couple of inches. She put her hand underneath my chin and pulled my stare upwards.

She paused for a moment, and then leaned back into me, straddling her tan legs over and around my waist. She grabbed around the sides of my face, and plunged her mouth onto mine causing our tears to smash together between our noses and face.

Isla, breathing harder now, was releasing whatever reservations she had ever had, and was passionately kissing all over my face, and neck. She leaned up, sucked and bit on my lower lip, then reattached her mouth firmly to mine, wrapping her tongue deep inside.

After a few perceptively short moments, she climbed back off of me, repositioned her footing, firmly placed her palms on my chest, and shoved me down causing me to fall back first onto the couch. She straddled my waist, and reunited her lips to mine.

Her hair draping over my face, while her hands groped my chest and tugged at my shirt. Hopefully we were well enough hidden behind the high back of the couch, in the dimly lit room that spared us from anyone else's eyes. But, I really didn't care.

Thankfully this went on for a while, with the only real break to catch my breath. She would occasionally lean up, sit back on my waist, gently bite her lips, sweep the hair from her face, and pounce back into action. I couldn't imagine anything being any better.

Every moment was like the first kiss on the dock near the boat and dive shack, like the one on the floor in her room, like the one back on her bed, like the one right after I spotted her at the gate, this one was just as electrifying, if not multiple times better.

I never imagined, three short weeks ago, that I would discover her. As her mouth moved intensely into mine, I remembered the first time I spotted her, in the van on the way to the movie theater. I would give anything to start that session over, so that I could walk up to her, day one, and tell her how unbelievable she is. We would have had three whole weeks.

Her breathing grew stronger, hard to believe, given the rate at which we were heading. All at once she stopped. She pushed herself off, up from me, and sat back on my shins. Her stare penetrated deep into my body and mind, while her widely dilated pupils snared my soul back into her.

Minutes passed, while she continued to stare, slowing her breathing. She didn't speak. A smile passed across her face, and was gone as soon as it arrived.

"Kyle?"

"Huh?" My eyes attempting to focus, blurred from her hypnotism.

"I have not..." She paused. "I..." she couldn't finish.

"What's wrong?" I reached up and touched her face.

She didn't say anything, just bit her lower lip, and held my hand to her face. We gazed at each other for a while longer.

She slowly climbed off of me, and onto the edge of the couch, looking down at her socks. "What's wrong?" She was silent.

She then reached down, and moved her shoes closer, slowly placing each foot into them and tying the broken laces. I sat up, not knowing what brought on the departure from moments ago.

She stood up, tugged the side of her shirt down over her exposed hip, and picked up her bag. I was baffled.

"What's wrong?" I reached out my hand.

"Let's go," she softly responded. My face grew cold, sensing the inevitable end of our short, beautiful relationship.

I slowly rose up, and slung my duffle bag over my shoulder. I had completely lost track of time, but figured that it was getting late, and she had probably realized that our boarding calls were fast approaching.

We stepped around the couch, and twisted our way through the dimly lit room, arriving in the corner near the restroom. She looked over at me, and walked down the dark hall and toward the ladies' room.

She stopped at the door, turned around and stared at me. I stood there, waiting for her to either speak, or to disappear through the door on her last trip to the restroom before our flights.

Her mouth formed a smile, while reaching out her hand. I stood for a second, confused. She kept her hand out, beckoning me, so I slowly walked toward her, down the dark hallway.

She grasped my hand, and firmly tugged me with her into the ladies' room. She swung the door inward, pulled me inside, and then locked the door. She touched my lips with her finger, indicating that I should remain quiet, and then grabbed my hand leading me around some stalls and down to another dark hallway, deep within the restroom.

"I found something," she softly whispered; as she pressed up against another door, and swung it open.

We passed into the pitch-black room, while she fumbled to lock the door. She grabbed my hand and guided me around another corner, where a dim light was flickering.

"Where are we?" I whispered.

"I found showers." We cleared a wall, and arrived at six shower stalls. I was confused.

"Okay." I quietly responded. She walked backward and opened the furthest stall door to the right, leading to a small private changing area, with a curtain on the other side, leading back to the individual shower stall.

We stepped in, and she latched the stall door behind us, with only the curtain left to open. I placed my bag on the floor in front of the stall door, to get it out of the way, followed by her resting her backpack securely on top of it.

She pushed the curtain to the side, and reached in and turned on the shower.

"Kyle?" She turned around.

"Yeah?"

"This is my first time." She innocently whispered while I tried to prevent my heart from going nuclear.

"Mine too," I replied, as she took hold of my hands, and smiled while our eyes locked.

She leaned in to hug me one last time, pausing to remember the brief moment before everything was about to change forever.

"Kyle?" She pulled back.

"Huh?"

"You are mine."

"I know."

"This means more than it would to others."

"What do you mean?" I replied.

"It will only be us, forever. Okay?"

"Yes."

"No one else will ever matter again. Do you understand?"

"I do."

"There can be *no one* else, ever." She softly said.

"I know."

"Once this happens."

"Yeah," I whispered.

"Our thoughts will never leave orbit from each other."

I was silent.

"You can never go back."

I paused for a second. "I know."

"Are you *really* sure?" she whispered, as she slowly blinked.

"Yes."

"You have to be abso-lutely sure." She stared deep into me.

"I'm sure." I buried the lump into my throat.

"It's happening, Kyle."

"I'm ready."

"It's happening." I was silent. *"Our souls are connecting."*

She sniffled one last time, and closed her eyes, the steam now filling the air.

She slowly reached out and took hold of the bottom of my shirt, raising it up over my head. I slid my arms through, and then helped her.

After removing the only things preventing our skin from touching, the air was all that remained between. She pulled me into the shower and drew the curtain shut.

Her moans and intense breathing were felt as much as they were heard. The steady spray from the showerhead, attempted with all of its energy to muffle her deep sighs, but was wholly inadequate.

I had never imagined anything like this. You can keep your heaven, bliss, nirvana, paradise, or whatever…I'll take these few moments with her, over whatever anyone, or any god has to offer.

Her watch must have beeped a couple of times, but we never heard it. Her towel provided just enough drying for the both of us, as we re-clothed, pausing to intently kiss so that the other was still absolutely sure they were the only one, for the rest of history. Something *had* changed.

She quietly placed the damp, purple towel into her backpack, and unlatched the door.

I don't remember the walk out of the club area, my mind removed from time's lineal progression, reliving only the downpour and steam of the shower.

Our eyes took a minute to adjust to the brighter lights of the terminal, like coming out of a dark movie theater into daylight. Our hands and fingers so tightly woven, that I was sure I had lost all circulation, but didn't care.

"I do not want to go back to school," she softly spoke.

"Huh?" I knew she couldn't come with me, and wanted to know what she was talking about.

"I'm switching my ticket to that other flight."

"Which one, I thought…"

"There is one more," she quietly added.

"To where?"

"India." She leaned in closer, to where we were practically stumbling over one another.

There were only a few people hanging around a couple of gates near the end of the terminal corridor. We passed by the same screen displaying flight information, which had flickered many short hours earlier, causing me to relocate to another one, and finally causing me to find Isla.

I didn't want to look up, but had to. It was 11:20, and my gate was fifty feet away. All we had was fifteen minutes. "Which one is your gate?" I asked.

"The one next to yours," she softly spoke, and then took a long deep breath.

I kept hold of her hand, while we closed the short distance to a support column that could lend some privacy. We dropped our bags at our feet, and stared at each other for another moment. She softly sucked on her lips, and leaned in to kiss me. My flight was boarding.

She wrapped her arms around me and pulled her torso so close that it caused every last air molecule to displace. She reached up on her toes, and buried her smooth face into my neck, and returned to re-connect her mouth with mine. It was over.

What seemed like seconds later, the final boarding announcement came over the loudspeaker, which caused her breathing and pulse to temporarily stop. We didn't move.

The last boarding call was announced, and it was just me left to board. The gate was empty, but for the one agent, who was now obviously waiting for me.

Isla leaned back into my ear. "Please." She had barely any breath remaining with which to beg.

"Kyle." She whispered, "No." Her sobbing somewhat contained, but nose and eyes watering.

"Kyle...please." She was stopping my heart, and yanking the lump in my throat to the back of my mouth.

"Sir?" The agent called.

"No...please no," Isla whispered.

"Sir? The plane is leaving."

"Kyle..." Isla's sobbing grew stronger.

"You have to board now, sir!" The agent shouted from the jet-way entrance.

I thought about it, again, but I had no choice, I mean, crap! I needed to finish school, I mean that's what everyone always drilled into my fucking head. "Just finish school," my mother would always say. "How are you going to make a living," she would argue. "You won't be anyone unless you go to college." And, "no one will want to marry you if you don't have a good job." Yeah, I fucking got it. Loud and clear. I guess I could hurry up and finish and come back here, well, there really won't be a "here" anymore.

And my dad. He wasn't in the U.S. as much as he used to be, and this was probably going to be our final trip, I mean, he wasn't getting any healthier. Other than Isla, he was the only person I could ever really talk to, and that was really rare, at best.

I guess if my dad was better, or around all the time I could stay, I mean, god damn it! Fuck! She's perfect. I'd totally stay, I could get a job at McDonalds. I mean, Isla loves McDonalds. Or a movie theater. That ain't gonna work. How would I provide for her, I mean, I want to be her hero, not some poor guy who can barely take care of himself. The shit is so drilled in my psyche that I don't even think I could be half ass for her even if I forced myself to. Plus, she needed to get her degree, and become some brilliant astronomer. I certainly am not going to be the guy to hold her up.

Sure, she'd say, "It is okay, I love you more than that," but I would never be able to live with myself. I would *need* to provide for her. I'm sure I could do anything and she'd love me all the same, you know, sweeping floors afterhours at some laundrymat, and obviously I'd love her as much also, but some things will get the better of me, in the end. I need to think like a "responsible adult", not some lonesome, love-struck teenager. Fuck.

I let go from behind her back, causing her body to shake. She reluctantly released, and took hold of my hands, locking her distressed eyes deeply on to mine.

"I'm sorry, Isla." My eyes swollen, causing her image to blur.

I leaned down and retrieved my bag, slinging it over my shoulder, my eyes not leaving hers.

"I'm sorry, Isla," I whispered again, as I reached out with my right hand to touch her face for the last time.

"No." Her voice trembled. "Please, no."

I walked slowly past her, and headed directly toward the jet-way, and awaiting agent, turning one last time as I handed the ticket.

She was standing, all alone, the way the stars and fate had predestined. It was over, and there weren't enough resources in the world capable of reversing time for the few hours we needed.

I raised my right hand attempting somehow to wave, transferring the last image of perfect beauty into my memory, and then turned around and stepped toward the jet-way.

"Kyle!" she cried out.

"Kyle!" I stopped and turned around.

"Please, Kyle!" Her voice trembling, "Don't leave me! It was not sup-posed to end this way! This wasn't supposed to happen!"

"I love you, Kyle!" She yelled, sobbing. "We were sup-posed to be together!"

"I love you!" She stomped her feet and made tight fists with her hands, throwing them down to her sides.

"I'm sorry," was all I could mouth and a quiet, "I love you."

"I love you!" She yelled again, throwing her hands again to her side, and tensing every muscle in her body.

"Oh my god!" She screamed out in a panicked fear, "Kyle!"

"*I love you!*" She fell to the floor, collapsing in total defeat, her voice just recognizable over her intense weeping.

Chapter Twenty-Six

I don't remember the walk down to the plane, or much of the flight, other than sitting all alone. I didn't look out the window, back at the terminal, like I internally promised I would. I couldn't believe I left her. I should have run back up the jet-way, into her arms, the both of us running toward the concourse and out to the parking lots.

I wished that the plane would develop some minor mechanical problems, forcing us to return to Miami International and giving me a few more hours with her. But, by the time we reached the gate, her plane would have already left for who knows where.

Of course, the plane landed uneventfully in Orlando. As I waited for the few other passengers to disembark, I reached into my bag, for the first time since earlier that morning, and retrieved the Citizen dive watch that Terry had given me, and buckled it to my wrist.

I exited the plane, in a complete trance, not knowing what the hell I was really doing. I made my way down the empty terminal, but for the few passengers that were on the flight.

I located a pay phone, and dialed my number.

"Mom?"

"Yeah baby?" She was tired.

"I'm here."

"Okay…see you in a little while, by baggage claim."

I didn't want to go to fucking baggage claim. I located a flight information screen in some ridiculously futile attempt to find a plane back to Miami, quickly realizing that she was well on her way to JFK, or was it somewhere in India.

There were no more flights. Not that it mattered because all I had was thirty five dollars and that wasn't even going to buy me a bus ticket, which would have taken too long anyway. I would have given anything for a plane ticket back to her, if only just to see her for a few more moments.

I moped down the terminal nearing the exit and roped off security area. As I rounded the corner, three men stood up, two in some sort of business suits, from a row of seats for people who were meeting arriving passengers.

"Mister Allendale?" one of them called out.

"Yeah?"

"Kyle Allendale?"

"Yeah."

"Come with us, please." I was tired, and probably dreaming.

I followed the man who had called my name, while the other two escorted.

"Hey, am I in trouble?" I asked the man in front, who was probably in charge.

"No."

"Well...then what, I mean, where are we going?"

"We just have a couple of questions," he finished, while one of the other guys took hold of my duffle bag.

"Who the hell *are* you guys?" Silence.

We entered a side door off the main concourse.

"Sit here." The main guy pointed at a chair on one side of a metal table.

"Where's...what? Where's my bag?" I looked around.

"We'll get it back to you shortly."

"Come on...what am I doing here? What do you want?" I was confused.

"Well let's just say you are traveling a known drug route, and it's your unlucky day."

"Man! Come on." I pushed my chair back from the table, something I normally wouldn't do under the circumstances, but I was really in no mood for any of it.

"Stay right here." They left me alone in the room. What energy I had left, was now devoted to figuring out what I was doing here. A couple of minutes passed.

The door swung open. "Hey there, Kyle." It was Terry.

"Terry! What the hell...I mean, what are you doing here? What's going on!"

"I'll explain everything." He leaned up against the table, in front of me and reached out his hand. "The watch...can I have it?"

"I thought you gave it to me?" I unbuckled the latch.

"I did. I'm going to give it back...I just need it for a second." He took the watch, and stepped outside of the room for a moment, then quickly returned.

"Kyle." He pulled up the chair to the table, opposite me.

"Yeah?"

"Do you know this man?" He flung a photo across the table, of some old guy in a white lab coat.

"No."

"Are you sure?"

"Yeah, I'm sure."

"Take another look." I analyzed the photograph.

"I have no idea who he is."

"Hmm."

"Who the hell is he?"

"His name is Ossolo Youssef Debrova." Debrova? What the hell.

"Who?"

"He's a scientist."

"So?"

"So." Terry leaned back and folded his arms.

"What's so important about him?"

"Are you telling me you don't know this man?"

"No. I have no earthly idea who he is." The door swung open, a man tossed the watch toward Terry while shaking his head. Terry nodded back toward the closing door, confirming he got the non-verbal message.

"Okay, okay." Terry slid the watch back toward me, across the table.

"What's his deal?"

"He's a scientist."

"Okay, you said that."

"He is employed at a biological weapons research station deep inside the Soviet Union." I furrowed my eyebrows, trying to understand why this applied to me.

"I still don't know..." I shook my head, but I did.

"I believe you know his daughter."

"Yeah, I think so."

"Yep, you sure do."

"Zorya Ossolovich Debrova." He leaned back in his chair, crossing his arms again.

"Wait, what?" I was confused.

"You know her."

"Zorya?"

"The weird girl from the Keys."

"Isla?"

"That's her."

"I thought her name was Isla?"

"Not technically, it's actually Zorya, but apparently she changed it to Isla on her way down there."

"What the hell do you want with her?" I was confused.

"Nothing with her, but we need to find Youssef."

"I don't know, I mean, we barely talked about her dad." I looked down at the watch, and attached it back to my wrist.

"Well, what did she say?"

"Not much, that he worked with animals, or something."

"Yeah, well, I'm not sure you are telling me the whole truth, and we have reason to believe you and her were at Miami International together."

"Yeah…so?"

"Do you know where she was heading?"

"No…I have no idea."

"She's not in trouble, in fact we think she is incapable of anything other than eating, sleeping, and wiping her ass." He leaned back into his chair again, laughing at his own obnoxious comment.

"What's that supposed to mean?" I clenched my teeth.

"Oh…did that bother you?"

"Man…when my mother finds out about this shit, you guys are screwed." Shit, I bet all I had to do was tell my dad, and this guy would be toast.

"Threatening me won't help."

"Whatever." I leaned back in my chair.

"Can you help us, or not?"

"I mean, you were there, why didn't you ask her yourself?"

"We made a tactical decision."

"Huh?"

"We didn't want to spook her, plus, we knew that you and she were an item."

"Oh come on, we were just friends." I pulled my chair up to the table.

"Look kid, it was pretty obvious how she felt about you, so, we figured she'd open up to you."

"Well maybe it wasn't important enough, to her, to tell me the freaking latitude and longitude of his goddamn outhouse."

"Don't be a smart ass." He adjusted his chair.

"I just don't want any trouble, and all she wants is to be left alone."

"So…you have no idea where she is going."

"No."

"Interesting." He folded his arms. "It doesn't matter anyway, because we are intercepting her on the ground at JFK in two hours."

I was getting pissed. "I thought you said she wasn't in trouble?"

"She's not."

"Well then what do you want with her?"

"The same thing we want from you."

"Well goddamn! What the hell is that?"

"To know the location of Youssef."

"Bro, if I knew where he was I'd tell you."

"Don't call me bro."

"Okay then, *Terry*, I don't know where he is."

We sat, facing off quietly, until he realized that questioning me was like squeezing grape juice from a raisin.

"All right. Here's my number…if you come into contact with anyone who knows the location of Doctor Debrova, call me immediately." He slid a business card across the table, and I put it in my pocket, "and I'll be in touch, and uh, I wouldn't talk about this to anyone," he added.

"Can I have my bag back?"

"Sure. But first I need a phone number where we can contact you, you know, in case we have any more questions." He stood up, and escorted me back through the door and out into the hallway, "allowing" me to first write my home phone number down on the back of my airline ticket.

I slowly made my way down the escalator to baggage claim, not needing to stop, because I only had the one big duffle bag. I walked outside, through the automatic doors, and onto the curb.

A few taxis loaded up the remaining passengers; groggy from the late night flight. I dropped to the curb, and buried my face into my hands.

The light traffic had all but disappeared with cars full of baggage and tired tourists, happily heading the next day to beaches, theme parks, or family. A half hour, or so later, a familiar horn quickly honked.

"Hey, baby." My mom rolled down the window of her black 911, as she popped the front storage compartment. I stuffed my soft duffle in, and climbed down into the passenger seat.

"How was it?" She smiled, glad that I was home.

"It was okay."

She released the clutch and smoothly sped out of the passenger pick-up area.

The ride home was quick, due to her lead foot and the turbocharged horses with nothing in front of them but dark open interstate. I stared out the window, at the flickering streetlights and reflectors on the road, which blurred by. I wasn't fully used to being in air conditioning again, which caused me to shiver.

While on the dark open interstate between Orlando and Lakeland, I stared up toward the sky. I tried to locate some of the stars, which Isla had liked to talk about, but the reflection of the car window prevented it. For a second, I caught a glimpse of the lights from a commercial airliner flying way overhead from south to north. I wonder if that's her, I thought to myself.

We arrived home, to the house on the quiet lake. I yanked my bag out of the front of the car, and shuffled upstairs to my room. I didn't want to unpack, and I didn't want to change out of the clothes that still had Isla's scent merged deep into the fibers. When I finally closed my eyes, a day that I could never return to was officially over. Why was I trying to be so mature, why was I ignoring my heart and the only thing that really ever mattered to me? I shouldn't have gotten on that plane...I shouldn't be here.

Chapter Twenty-Seven

A couple of days later, while waiting around the house for the phone to ring. I received a call, but it wasn't who I was hoping, it was however, the next best thing.

"Hello?" There was a slight delay.

"Hey, Bud!"

"Hey, Dad!" Another long pause, he was definitely somewhere far away.

"What's up?"

"Not much."

"How was camp?" A rush of emotion overtook me. It was him. *He* was that American. It was him…I mean, it had to be. And Isla was the cute and really sweet girl. Fuck! I shouldn't have gotten on that plane. What was I thinking, I mean, that information was pretty god damn important! Why didn't my dad describe her better in a way I would have been able to tell? Shit, maybe he did. Maybe I was too busy to listen and he knew way before that she was the one. Why didn't some freaking angel fly down to the Miami airport to let me know this? I mean, that probably would have helped! Well, I guess an angel did tell me, and now she was somewhere in India.

"Hey, Dad?" I deeply swallowed.

"Yeah?"

"Remember that girl?"

"What girl? Oh, Kyle, is your Mom bothering you again about me, or something?"

"Huh?"

"Nothing. What girl?"

"That one you used to tell me about, from Russia?"

"What girl from Russia?" Come on Dad, just tell me.

"Come on Dad. You know the one. From four years ago?"

"How do you…oh. Oh I see."

"So you know, you said she was cute and really sweet?" He was quiet on the other end for more than the simple delay in transmission, confirming my realization.

"Hey, Kyle?"

"Yeah? You remember?" I held my breath.

"Can we talk about this later?"

"Dad!"

"Kyle, now's not a good time, and we're gonna have all that time together next week. I'll tell you about her then."

"Come on, Dad! Just tell me."

"Kyle. I can't now. You have to trust me, I really can't." My guess is he was somewhere where someone was listening, "Look, I'll call you Monday afternoon. You'd better get packing."

"Okay. Talk to you then."

"Yep, talk to you then. Love you Bud."

"Love you too."

He was really nervous, and as soon as I hung up the phone I realized that he probably thought I had somehow "busted" him about that beautiful Ukrainian passenger he picked up in Pripyat. I should have made it more clear, but I'd be sure to tell him I didn't care about that part when I see him next week.

The following Monday came and went, but no phone call from him, or *her*, for that matter. But, he'd sometimes say he would call, or come pick me up, only to be left holding my suitcase on the front porch and later having to unpack the clean, folded clothes. He was *my* bud...but I always figured that one day he'd be gone.

As the summer progressed, my suitcase stayed packed, although recently repacked after my return from the Keys, in preparation for my trip to somewhere far away with him. Something had happened, probably something expected, at least that's what my mom said when she'd lamely attempt to console me. I never heard from him again.

Chapter Twenty-Eight

June was coming to an end, and the boredom of summer lay in front of me. Game shows, going to the mall, outlet stores, watching my sister's summer cheerleading practice, and juvenile parties with her and her jock friends flooded the rest of July. Occasionally, I would call Will, or Sara, to check in so as to not let completely go...of summer.

I would often mail out letters to Isla, at the address she gave, and most of the time having them returned, stamped over with all sorts of notices from whatever Russian mail service employee received them and sent them back. As the number approached thirty, I would then just merely put a single piece of paper inside, mailed out with my phone number and address, and saying to simply call me and that I loved her.

Occasionally, the phone would ring and there'd be nothing but static on the other end. I hoped it was Isla, or maybe my dad trying to call me from who knows where, and merely got disconnected. The uncertainty drove me practically crazy, to the point that I would run to the phone every time it rang.

"Hello?"

"Kyle?" It was Will.

"Hey Will."

"What's up man? Long time no hear!" Actually we talked every week or so.

"Same ole, same ole," I replied.

"Yeah." He already knew about my father, and deep longing for Isla, and I could sense his compassion over the phone line.

"What's up with you?"

"Football crap, watching my baby brother, and other bullshit."

"Have you talked to Kristen lately?"

"Every other day." He laughed.

"How's she doing?"

"Crazy as usual." We chuckled.

"That's cool."

"Yeah...I saw her in New York two weeks ago."

"Oh yeah? How was that?"

"Well, all I can say is that I'm going there for college." He laughed again, indicating certain obvious attraction.

"You totally should...she's a fox."

"That's what I'm sayin'!"

He didn't ask about Sara...or Isla, but he knew the deal.

August was quickly approaching, and so was the school year. As the weeks passed on by, I obviously still thought about Isla, but my memories of her perfect face, eyes, nose, and wonderful body faded, along with the phone calls covered in static. I had no photos of her, no real address, no phone number, no tattered purple towel, no nothing, but the ever present waves of emotion I couldn't banish, every time my head hit the pillow, or I simply closed my eyes for more than a second.

Sometimes, when I would dream, I would see her slowly walking toward me, on some isolated beach somewhere right after sunset. As she stepped closer, the wind would toss her hair about, and she would begin to smile. As she stood in front of me, she would then lean up and in, to kiss me. Of course, I would always wake up, right before she connected.

One late afternoon, during a typical summer thunderstorm, I decided to check on Anthony down in the Keys. I rifled through my mother's desk, looking for the paperwork and phone number of the place, finding it, and sitting down in front of the phone in her home office.

"I'd like to speak with Anthony, please?" There was a pause.

"Anthony Kilpatrick?" Crap. I had completely forgotten his last name.

"Uh...yeah."

"Who is this?"

"Kyle Allendale."

"And what is this regarding?" Shit.

I paused for a moment. "Uh...well. I'm his cousin, and we had a family issue."

"Okay. Let me see if I can locate him, he may be out on a trip." That was close.

A couple of minutes passed, "all right, he's on his way."

"Thanks." Another minute elapsed.

"Hello?" I instantly recognized his voice.

"Anthony...hey this is Kyle."

"Who?"

"You know, Kyle Allendale?"

"Uh...I'm not..."

"From lifeguarding class, you know?" Another pause. "Um...with Will, Sara, and..."

"Oh yeah! Kyle! Hey...how are you doin'?"

"Okay. I wanted to see how you were."

"Oh, pretty good. You know...work and stuff."

"Yeah, oh...how's Jill?"

"She's great. We hang out all the time."

"Did you and her ever go out, you know, that...um..." I swallowed deeply, "Saturday night?"

"Oh yeah! We are totally, you know, dating and stuff." I smiled.

"Awesome. That's really cool."

"Yeah. Hey listen Kyle, I've gotta run, you know, time to show some other's how to save a life as good as you and Will! It was really good hearing from you man."

"Wait. Anthony?"

"Yeah?"

"How's Ernie?" He paused.

"Real good." His voice softened.

"That's cool." I smiled. "Anthony?"

"Yeah Kyle?"

"Can I come and get him?" The line was silent for a few seconds.

"Sure Kyle. When do you want to...whenever is good for you."

"How about...this Thursday?"

"Okay. I'll have him all ready." He paused, "he'll be glad to see you."

"Thanks, Anthony...I really need, I mean...thanks."

"It's okay, Kyle. I hear ya. See you soon." He hung up.

I sat at the phone, for a minute, staring down at the handset before I reset it on to the receiver. I was going back, but knew that it wasn't going to be the same.

"Mom?"

"What's up?" She was sitting at the kitchen table, reading the newspaper.

"I need to, I mean, would it be okay…"

"What?" She looked up.

"If I went down, you know back to, down to the Keys to pick up something."

"Uh…I dunno, Kyle." She took a sip of her coffee. "Are you going to fly?"

"Oh…no, I'll just drive the wagon."

"Kyle, that's really far."

"I know, Mom."

"Are you going to do it in one day?"

"I guess." I hadn't really thought about that.

"Well, Kyle, that's like a seven hour trip. One way."

I thought for a second. "Oh, well, I'll just spend the night there."

"I don't know." She shook her head.

"Mom?"

"Yeah?"

"I left something down there."

"What are you talking about?"

"Something I need to get." I looked down at my feet. She didn't say anything.

"Kyle…" She paused, "okay."

"Thanks, Mom." I smiled, and climbed back upstairs to my room.

Chapter Twenty-Nine

The two days dragged on, but I was finally leaving, and couldn't get out of town fast enough.

I tossed my repacked duffle bag into the back seat of the old white station wagon, and threw the map onto the front passenger seat. Although far from perfect, it was a good break from Lakeland, and at least I would see Anthony, and grab Ernie, which was my real goal.

My mom was right, it was a really long drive…about 350 miles worth. I never realized how big Florida was until I cut south of Bartow and past Sebring. I mean, even *my* impression of Florida, and I lived here, was beaches, palm trees, Disney World, and old people.

I never wanted to stop, but bathroom breaks and fill ups reminded me that 350 miles of back roads was easily an all day affair. It wasn't that it was hard, after all, especially when my mind would wander to her, and Dad. I wondered where she was, hopefully looking for me, or at least safely sitting in a university library somewhere, studying, while heavy rain kept her inside.

Dad, on the other hand, I imagined, well hoped, that he was stuck on some cool "mission" someplace where there were absolutely no phone lines for hundreds of miles. Or, just maybe, he disappeared into the middle of nowhere with a beautiful woman from Pripyat. But, well there's just no telling, and I started to fear the worst.

I passed big Lake Okeechobee off to my left, and made my way briskly through orange groves and sugar fields. "Please don't break down," I would say to the old wagon, every time we drove past some dilapidated farm house or broken down tractor on the side of the road.

I should have left earlier. The 150 miles between Frostproof and the outskirts of the monstrous Broward County took way too long.

Had my radio gotten better reception, it may have gone by quicker, but no matter how you sliced it, my mother was dead on.

I had finally reached Miami, and I was home free, or so I thought, having a mere 140 miles, or so, left between me and the familiar cafeteria, dorms, gravel driveways, and picnic tables. It was slow going, on the clogged highways weaving into, and through the big city.

Exits after exits, to business districts, neighborhoods, schools, fire stations, and beaches, forked off the interstate. Then, I spotted it, the exit for Miami International Airport.

For a moment, I contemplated pulling off, but there was obviously nothing there for me now. I could have walked through the concourse, eaten a slice of mushroom, olive, jalapeno and green pepper pizza, and talked my way into the airline club, but that would just remind me of how I had abandoned her, on the floor, at the gate while I boarded the plane. My eyes swelled up as I passed the exit, mentally kicking myself for trying so hard to make the "right" decision. The world would probably be a little better if more people made decisions like I *should* have that night. She definitely was, you know, really cute and sweet.

The congested highway eventually gave way, to the south, the traffic thinning out. I glanced down at the map, confirming that nothing but bridges lay between me, and a brief reprieve, from my recent onset of hopelessness.

It had only been a month and a half since I had passed the old gas stations, and tourist traps, but it had felt like years. I had time, now, to take in more of the sites, having to pay attention to where I was, and the surrounding traffic, so maybe I was just a little more aware. Still, I hoped that this drive would not displace my memory of the first bus ride down here from Miami, catching the first sight of cocky Will as he boarded the bus at the airport.

I stopped for gas in some old place, hopefully for the last time, grabbed a Sprite from the fountain, no ice, and rejoined the other vehicles moving south west down the Oversea Highway.

More and more dive shops and small restaurants dotted the thin stretch of land between the highway and the water. The smell of the ocean filled the air, tempting me to roll down the windows, letting in the warm salty breeze. I was getting closer.

I passed the little airport at Marathon, which was the last outpost and quick air connection back to the mainland. Two big DC-3s sat on the tarmac, one warming up its engines, prepping for their attack on a mosquito stronghold on some distant muddy pocket of land out in the gulf. I had less than twenty miles to go.

Isla completely invaded my thoughts, as she tended to do every day, especially in the late afternoon. Wishing for her, or for time reversal, was futile, but that didn't stop her memory from its torment. It picked away at my brain, before either I shook it off and cranked up the radio, or I sank in my seat, my eyes slowly watering up. The first sounded much easier than it was.

I had reached the side street, and my turn to the south. But off ahead, toward the west, that was reserved for her.

Arriving at my destination was not as I expected, probably because the only other time I was here was by bus, or returning in the van distracted by Isla. It was okay, I guess.

I parked and walked over the familiar gravel and shell covered driveway, near the sailboat launch area, and off toward the cafeteria. My brain was having trouble processing the timeline, briefly confused by the same feeling I had a month and a half earlier, walking over and past the same structures and sights.

It was sunny out, not a cloud in the sky to obscure the blue-green color bouncing off the tropical sea. As I headed toward the cafeteria, I heard laughter and activity to my right, at the swim area where we had undertaken our lifeguard training. I walked over, onto the wooden planks and, off in the corner, was Anthony.

"Anthony!" I shouted, causing him to turn around.

"Hey, Kyle!" He waved, motioning me over, "you made it!" He grinned.

"Yep." This felt pretty good, as long as I didn't think too much about her.

"We're almost done, so…you want to wait here and watch?"

"Yeah. Sure." I sat down on the edge of the wooden dock, dangling my feet over the swim area, while Anthony instructed the few people that were in the water. Sitting here caused me to remember hanging out with Sara, Kristen and Will while we watched the flickering dive lights beneath the water. I smiled.

The class wrapped up, and Anthony grabbed his baseball hat and towel.

"You hungry?" He patted me on the back.

"Yeah."

We walked the familiar surfaces back down the dock, and toward the cafeteria, passing the dorms and picnic tables to our left. We were about to pass the scuba shack. Not good.

"Kyle?"

"Yeah?" I swallowed the boulder building in my throat.

"How've you been?"

I paused. "Good."

"Really?"

"Um, I guess." I looked down, while we walked a few more paces.

"Kyle?"

"Huh?"

"Why did you come back?" Come on…don't do this to me.

"Uh…I dunno."

"I mean, was it really for Ernie?"

"Yeah."

"I mean…no offense, but you could have gotten a cat anywhere." He patted me on the back.

"I know." My voice lowered, while my throat closed up. I glanced over at the harbor and scuba shack, and stopped.

"She's gone."

"Who?"

"*You* know." He shook his head.

"Sara?"

"No, not Sara." I couldn't contain the swelling and redness, which was forming again, in my eyes. I didn't say anything, but just stared at the docks of the harbor.

"Oh, buddy…" he put his arm around my shoulder. "I'm sorry."

I shook my head, and rubbed my nose with the back of my wrist. He slowly guided me toward the shack and docks, presumably to get me away from being seen by others.

"I can't get her out of my mind," I shakily spoke.

"I know." He let go, and stared out toward the water.

"I can't." I tried to collect my dignity, but couldn't. "I really…"

"It's okay."

"No. I really…" It was no use; my emotions weren't letting go. "I really miss her." He deeply sighed, not knowing what to do about my obvious confession.

"I know." He looked down.

"God damn it." I wiped my eyes, trying to recompose my situation, but it was no use. We stood there, looking out over the boats and harbor for a few minutes without speaking.

"Not that this is going to help…" He broke the silence. "But you were the only thing that made her happy." I looked down toward my shoes, and locked my fingers behind my head.

"I mean…you were it." He added, knowing that it wasn't helping my situation, but he felt obligated to let me know.

"Do you know?" he paused, contemplating the rest of what he needed to say, "that she left that Friday night before, just so she would be at the airport when you got there?" We started walking again toward the vending machines and bench.

"After she told me and Jill what Ernie likes to eat, she told us that she found out that you lived in Lakeland, and that Orlando was the closest airport…" he paused, "and that she had to get to the airport that night, so that she could check all the departing flights to Orlando the next day." I couldn't talk.

He continued, "she figured that, well, that maybe she could convince you not to leave." This was torture.

"She left around nine that night, and said she was going to hitch a ride, or something." I dropped down into the bench, and buried my face into my hands. The thought of her on some lonely highway, alone, was killing me.

"Only Jill and I knew where she was going."

"Did she say where she was…you know, eventually heading?" My voice trembled.

"No. We never saw her again." A few moments passed, before he added, "Later that night, you know…" he stopped.

"What."

"Well, never mind."

"No…what?" I sniffled.

"Well, Jill said that she had never seen someone so determined."

"More determined for what?"

"She told me that Isla *had* to see you."

"How did she know that?"

"Jill told me that she could easily tell that Isla was falling in love with you. I mean, she said that Isla didn't care about anything else." That was all it took. I reburied my face deep into my hands and quietly tried to contain my sporadic breathing.

Eventually the seagulls dove around enough for the required distraction that moved us into the cafeteria. Most of the others had already eaten, so it was easy finding a table with Jill, who was eating alone.

"Hey, Kyle."

"Hey." She could tell.

"You came to get Ernie?"

"Yeah."

"He's really cute."

"And loves to eat!" Anthony added.

"You're cool with me, you know taking him back?"

"Oh yeah. He would like to live with you," she comforted.

I slowly ate, not having anywhere more important to go, and ultimately only the three of us remained in the dining hall.

"Where are you staying tonight?" Jill gathered her plate and cup.

"Uh…I haven't really thought about that."

"Well, there are a couple of extra rooms over near us."

We finished up, and exited back outside. "Hey…I need to go look at something," I added.

"No problem, just come back to Jill's room on the second floor when you're ready." Anthony smiled, as they walked away.

I turned toward the marina and the vending machines, and around to the side entrance to the office and conference room, where Isla and I had sat that one evening. I slowly opened the door, hoping that no one would be occupying the table, and entered.

Fortunately, for my sanity, or maybe unfortunately, the room was empty. I pulled out a chair, hopefully the one I had sat in that evening in June, and stared toward the window and position Isla had sat.

Closing my eyes, I attempted to recall her image sitting just feet away, with the sound of the tapping of rain on the shells outside and the palm leaves brushing against the window. I was in the exact same place, and no matter how hard I concentrated, I couldn't go back to June.

I remained, for a while, hoping that the door would be opened by her. It wouldn't take that much of a change in physics...I mean, I was already in the room, the chairs were already arranged, the sun was setting, no rain, but that's okay. All that needed to happen was for her to materialize and simply walk into the room. That's it...the future would then take care of its self. Simple.

"Please come back," I whispered, slowly shaking my head.

I few moments later, I rose from my chair and slowly exited the room to the outside. I headed past the dorms and maintenance building, and down the dirt path that I had remembered.

I made my way up the stairs and into Jill's room.

"Hey there!" she called, and there was Ernie, stretching on the bed, as she leaned down and petted him.

"Okay, here's his bag of food, and...oh, you'll need his litter pan." She pointed toward the corner.

"Got it." I stared at Ernie.

"And...well, I guess, that's it."

"Oh, and there is one room up here, and four downstairs that are empty tonight," Anthony reminded.

"Okay, thanks." I smiled.

I scooped up Ernie, and opened the door. "I'll put him in a room, then come back to get the rest of the stuff."

I held Ernie, and walked downstairs, and over to room number three. I stared at the door, for a moment, interrupted by Ernie squirming in my arm.

I reached out and twisted the knob, swinging the door open. It was empty.

There were no sheets on the bed, but a pillow was already incased. The same old chair and side table, with clean white sheets and towels folded neatly on top, and two Styrofoam bowls in the corner near the bathroom, one having some old crumbs and the other having a slight film where water had been, at the bottom.

I put Ernie on the floor, shut the door, and walked back upstairs to Jill and Anthony.

"Hey...has anyone stayed in that room since...you know?"

"Nope," Jill comforted, as she handed me the cat food and litter pan.

I thanked them again, and went back downstairs, into *her* room.

Ernie was picking the crumbs out of the bowl, so I added some cat food, and water. I then grabbed the sheets, and made the bed, while watching Ernie get reacquainted with his old surroundings.

When I finished, I dropped down, on to the side of the bed and blankly stared at the floor. This was cruel.

I tried to feel her presence. I concentrated with all of my might, and winced my eyes tightly shut, trying to make her magically reappear, but simply grew lightheaded. I tried again, and again. I wiped my eyes, and stared at the floor where we had sat fifty something days earlier. It had only been a few weeks.

An hour, or so passed, and I reached up to turn out the light, sinking my body back into the mattress. I stared at the ceiling, and then slowly shut my eyes, concentrating and hoping to catch the scent of her hair from the pillow. She was all I dreamed about.

The next day, I unmade the bed, packed our stuff, as well as the little Styrofoam bowls, and went back for one last time, to grab Ernie.

I reentered the room, and sat down on the bed, once more. I looked down at the pillow, and swept my hand over and underneath it. Feeling something that didn't belong, I retrieved my hand from beneath the pillow and brought the thin filament into the light. It was a strand of her chocolate brown hair. I gazed at it for a minute then dug it deep into my pocket.

As I closed the door, for the last time, the image of her, on the bed haunted me. I could feel her; I could almost smell her hair. I was sure it was only my mind, screwing with me, but I remained for a few moments more, not wanting to leave until her image faded.

Ernie and I drove down the winding side street and back out to the main road, and made our typical right turn. He sat comfortably in the right seat, licking, spotting moving vans, and pawing at the dangling seatbelt buckle if it caught the light just right.

I wasn't sure if I felt any better, but I sought comfort knowing that I had, at least, Ernie.

We stopped a couple of times for gas, once to eat, twice for Ernie to play and eat some grass, oh, and stalk birds. He was really sweet, not surprising considering his first adopted mother.

The long drive continued, but at least I had my little orange tabby friend. We passed back by the Miami International Airport exit, which shot a shock wave through my heart, and on northward.

We stopped one more time, Ernie frustrated that he couldn't pee in the litter pan while the car was moving. This gave me another chance to check the map and our progress…we were almost there.

An hour or so, later, we arrived back to the house in Lakeland.

"Hey, mom." I walked inside, through the garage, and dropped my bag in the laundry room, so that I could later sort the few items I had worn.

"Who's this?"

"Ernie."

"Okay…I guess…" She looked down and reluctantly pat him on the head.

"I know," I replied.

He settled in to his new home, while I unpacked the cat food, litter pan, and placed the old Styrofoam bowls in the corner, near my bed. At least I had Ernie, I thought, as I drifted off to sleep.

Chapter Thirty

That night I awoke, in the middle of the night, as I often did since leaving her, obsessing over only one thing. Mainly, replaying that night in the airport, over and over again, the time in the airline club, and the short walk to my departing flight. This night was a little different however, but still left me staring blankly at my slowly revolving ceiling fan, only to "awake" the next day, fully drained and exhausted.

This night was more about Miami. Not my drive through it, or past the airport exit, but more of our dialogue in the conference room back in June. Where was it that she lived in Miami? I was wishing I had the answer, because I could at least attempt to track down her mother and then locate Isla. It wouldn't have been too hard, well, at least had I known where her mother was, I mean, but…Miami is kind of a big place.

That night, while I lay awake, I tried to think about the first order of business to attempt my search. Probably think about where Cubans would tend to rent apartments. Shit…like that was going to be easy. Maybe my mother would have some suggestions, and actually make herself useful in my monumental endeavor.

I remember going to some similar place like Isla described where her mother worked, with my own mother, while her hair was cut. After all, my mom was the type of woman Isla's mother cut hair for, and although somewhat overbearing, Mom did have knack for "networking" and somehow was able to start with a pair of deuces and end with twenty-one. But, I was also pretty sure that my confidence in her abilities would most likely fall short this time, and this wasn't like her winning every time at Monopoly or usually beating Vegas casinos at Blackjack.

Still, the scenes Isla described seemed real to me. I hoped that it wasn't a bad synapse improperly firing in my brain causing me to mis-remember events that may have not actually happened, triggered by my delirium for Isla and the now well known fact that I hung on her every word she merely thought about speaking.

My mother usually had to be up around five, so I was going to catch her as she got ready for work. I walked downstairs and sat at the kitchen table, passing out from sleep deprivation some time later.

"Honey?" I heard something.

"Kyle." She rubbed my shoulder.

"Isla?" I was still groggy.

"Who?" I opened my eyes and strained to see my mother in the dimly lit kitchen.

"Oh…uh, nothing." I scratched my head, and leaned back in the chair.

"What are you doing up so early?" She opened a drawer and grabbed a spoon to stir the creamer into her coffee.

I thought for a second, trying to figure out why I was sleeping at the kitchen table.

"Mom?"

"Kyle?" She smiled, half teasing me.

"Mom…do you remember much about Miami?" She halted her stirring for a second.

"Why, sweetie?" She turned toward me, setting her mug on the counter.

"Um, well, how long were we there for?" She grew concerned, most likely because she thought I was going to ask some more about her breakup with my dad.

"After your father…uh, well *after* we divorced?"

"I guess." She was a little relieved that I wasn't going down that road, and walked over to the table and pulled up a chair.

"I think about two years. You know, until the firm finally transferred me back here."

"Yeah." I looked down at the table, trying to figure out what I needed to ask next.

"Hey, Mom?"

"Huh?" She smiled, and was probably glad to have some time alone with her "sweetie" albeit at five in the morning.

"Where did you get your hair cut, you know, down there?"

She leaned back in her chair and furrowed her eyebrows.

"Why Kyle, what's the problem?"

"Come on, do you remember, or…?"

"Kyle…." She crossed her legs, and calmly placed her hands on her knee like she was about to initiate some big contract negotiation, or something. I looked around the room, trying to gather what thought process I wasn't too exhausted to formulate.

"Mom?"

"Yes?" She smiled again, but now with a more slightly frustrated tone.

"Do you remember who cut your hair, or not?"

"You don't remember? You used to go there with me."

"Uh…kind of." Again, I vaguely remembered, but I more remembered Isla telling me of her memory of *her* time with her mother in a salon.

"It was Raul. Remember, he would try to teach you Spanish?" I think I recalled the name, but that was about it.

"Oh, so it wasn't a woman?" This was a total long shot, thinking that it could have possibly been the same place where Isla would wait for her mother.

"No…it was a man, and his name was Raul." She chuckled.

"Oh." I paused. "Hey…did I go there, you know, a lot with you?"

"I wouldn't say a whole lot, but…yes, you went a good bit, you know late afternoons, up until the summer."

"How many times, you know, do you think I went with you?" She looked up, trying to use her practically perfect memory, which may have at least lent itself to landing the bigger clients at her firm, well, and most likely counting cards.

"Uh…you probably went about every two weeks, or so. Why?"

"I really don't know, something…I just want to know, I guess." We stared at each other for a few seconds. "Mom?"

"Yeah?"

"Do you remember a girl there?" I exhaled, not on purpose, but loud enough so that she could tell something was really bothering me. She sat back again, and tapped her fingers on top of the table, most likely attempting to recall, taking a few moments to contemplate the questions presented.

"Uh, yeah…like a little Latin girl, or something." I leaned up toward the table and put my hands on top.

"What!"

"What's wrong, is that bad?" She cocked her head to the side, confused, while I composed myself.

"Oh, uh no. How…how old was she?"

"Probably your age, or maybe like a year or two older. I really don't remember. Why Kyle?" She was growing concerned.

"Do you remember her name?"

"I don't think I ever heard her say it, I mean, you should know, you were the only one sitting with her every time we'd go." I tried to remember even sitting with someone, which my memory tried to re-establish, but I couldn't differentiate between my visualization of Isla's experience or if I was remembering it properly, or anything about it at all.

She laughed. "It was really cute, because you would save lollypops from the bank for her, and also fortune cookies from this Chinese restaurant you, your sister, and I would go to."

"Yeah." I think I was starting to remember.

"And you'd get all excited when you'd get to give her whatever you saved. It was really sweet. That's why you're my sweetie!" She laughed.

"Can you remember anything else, you know, about her, or whatever?"

She wrinkled her forehead again, straining to recall any additional details. A few moments later, she straightened up in her chair and smiled because it was coming back to her, and that she felt like she was actually going to be my hero that morning. "Yeah…I think so."

"Well…what? I mean, what else?"

"She and you would sit together for hours on the couch, mostly alone in the waiting room, while my hair and nails were done. You were always ready to go to the salon, which I thought was kind of weird, until I figured out you had a little friend there."

I paused, trying to understand this revealed situation. "Did her mother work there?"

"Yeah…I think so. You remember pretty well."

"I guess."

"That little girl was really quiet with everyone else, but you and she would chatter away there on the couch." I didn't speak, and hoped she would continue with her recollection.

"She had beautiful hair, and was very sweet, but...I dunno, kind of special."

"What do you mean?"

"It's probably the language barrier, but she was a little strange. You know, not normal for a little girl." She continued on, "You know, like...well not mentally underdeveloped or autistic or anything, but more...just a little weird I guess, but very delightful and pleasant."

"Oh and it was really cute, the way you and she would look at magazines and books together. Mainly fashion magazines, but you didn't seem to mind, as long as you were sitting next to your little friend."

"Did she and I go to school together too?"

"No, I got the impression that she didn't go to school, or that she was home schooled or something." She smiled again, presumably remembering me in my "sweeter" years.

"Oh."

"Then one time, in May, she left."

"Huh?"

"You know, that was it. One day she was just, well, gone."

"What happened?" I think I remember something about not seeing someone who I really wanted to see, but my memory of that age was fuzzy, to say the least.

"Well, let me think..." She took a couple of seconds to recollect. "You had asked for a stuffed animal for your birthday, a stuffed kitten, I think, which was odd for an eight year old boy, and especially since you were bugging the hell out of me all spring for a big fighter jet toy that you didn't get for Christmas."

"Yeah. I think I remember."

"And when I got you that stuffed kitten, I had never seen you more happy. Well, until a week or so later when we were driving to my hair appointment with kitty in tow. You know, I was still laughing 'cause I couldn't figure out what you were wanting with a stuffed animal."

"Oh." I think I knew, but needed to hear it from her.

"Yeah, well I figured it out pretty quickly why you wanted it."

"Yeah." I looked down at the table, my old friend "the lump" forming in my throat.

"She wasn't there, then, or any time after that. I mean, you went with me three more times, with the stuffed kitten, until I couldn't take it anymore."

"You didn't let me go back."

"Well, yeah, but wait. Let me tell you why." She leaned in toward the table.

"I felt so bad for you, and I wanted to find out where she went. You know, maybe arrange a time or something where me and her mother could get you two together, to play, or just look at magazines."

"Oh." My nose started to tingle, which was not good, usually signaling my eyes to water next.

"I talked to her mother, who at first didn't want to say anything, but when I showed her the kitten you were going to give to her little girl...I mean, that's why you asked for it, right?"

"Yeah."

"She gazed at the kitten, and told me that she knew why you got it for her." She sighed, probably now most likely realizing why this bothered me.

"She said that her daughter wanted a real kitten, but she told her that they couldn't afford one, and also really had no place to keep it. She said that all she talked about was a kitten, well that, and you."

"Oh, boy," I whispered, the lump growing larger in my throat.

"I asked where the little girl had gone, and she told me that she had to go back with her father, back to Russia." She looked at me, trying to see if any of this was making sense.

"I think I remember." I rubbed my eyes with my fingers.

"You were devastated. I mean, you wanted to keep going back to the salon, but eventually I had to stop bringing you. That was right before..."

"What...before, what?"

"You had that ear infection."

"Oh, yeah...that."

"Do you remember how bad it was?"

"No." My eyes were glazing over.

"You couldn't go to school that fall, and so you became my little partner, and on the days you felt well enough, you would follow me to work, meetings, errands; we became pretty close. You were a very sweet little boy, but would get a little sad from time to time."

"Yeah."

"I felt really bad for her mother too. And, well, it was all kind of tragic."

"What…'cause she had to go with her father back to Russia?"

"Well, yeah, but, I mean, I was back down there for a deposition, I dunno like four years ago and saw Raul again, for old time sake. Got my hair and nails done."

"Yeah?"

"I remembered the girl's mother and asked Raul how she was and if her daughter ever came back." She paused, took another sip of her coffee, then looked back up and stared into my eyes, "He said that her mother had died."

"Huh?"

"Yeah, Raul said that she had gotten a horrible phone call that night, around closing time, something about her daughter missing out in some desert somewhere, and that she was presumed dead." She paused again, "and he said that she was hysterical, but didn't know anything more. That night, she died in a traffic accident."

I stared at the table for a minute, or two, and attempted to gather my thoughts and emotions, thinking that this had sounded familiar. And, as if my emotional begging and attachment for Isla could not have been any stronger, the connection now being uncovered made me practically wish that I had been in that accident with her mother.

"Mom?"

"Hmm?"

"That stuffed kitten."

"Yeah?"

"I gave it to Dad, didn't I?"

"Yeah, you sure did."

I stood up, and slowly pushed in the chair, then quickly walked upstairs and climbed back into bed. I sat on the edge of the bed, thinking that maybe there was such a thing as fate, and that it was working overtime down there in the Keys, and that it had given up on me for leaving Isla there at the airport, crying on the floor in front of my gate, begging for me not to go. Fate had given me all the chances it was going to, and now it was just me.

Curling up on my side, pulling my legs up as tight as they would go, I strained…wishing I could have been on that cargo plane, four years ago. Wishing I could go back ten years and tell her to just hold on, and that I'd always be there for her. Again thinking over and over, pleading, that I could go back to the airport and walk with her out into the rain and parking lots. All I would have had to do was just not get on that plane.

Chapter Thirty-One

About a week or so later, a letter arrived. It was from Sara, and contained some photographs that she had taken.

Dear Kyle,
My summer has been really busy!
But, it's almost over. Ugh! How is yours going?
I talk to Kristen almost every other day, boy she's crazy!
I just wanted to tell you how much fun I had with you
down there in Florida. You are a sweet guy, and I hope
we stay in touch and stay close forever. I know that
things happen, and I wish I would have told you how cool
I thought you were, but hey, I guess I just did! Don't
get your hopes up ☺, but it looks like my soccer team
is heading to Disney World for an exhibition game! It's
not until winter break, but isn't that cool?! I'll call you
as it gets closer, but I know I talk to you often anyway
so I don't really know what I'm saying! Haha!
I put some pictures of stuff in the envelope, so make
sure you don't accidently throw them away. There are
four of them, just so you know. I have more, but
haven't gotten the other film developed, so I'll send
you some more when I do.
Okay, well that's about it! I miss you and I'll talk
to you again real soon!

Love ya!
-Sara

Enclosed were the four photos she had referred to. One was kind of blurry, of me and Will screwing around trying to sink the other's boat. The next one was of just Sara that I had taken with her camera, while she and I sat on the catamaran. The third photo was of Kristen and Will, with her holding the bunny ears over his head. The last one was of the four of us, taken by Cindy.

They made me smile, as I showed Ernie. None were of her, but the last one was taken right before Will, Kristen, Sara and I were separated for that first dive trip where I was buddied with Isla. I breathed in deeply then repacked them gently back into the envelope, putting it in the small drawer of my nightstand, next to another envelope which contained the strand of Isla's hair.

Chapter Thirty-Two

My final year of school was well underway. Not tending to prior friendships pushed me toward better grades, and continued obsessions of Isla. It was eating me alive, and all I had to show for it was a couple of failed dates, my fault of course, and a perfect 4.0 average, not to mention all the other extra-curricular crap, and some lost pounds.

The fall progressed, slowly, and so did my application process to colleges. Sara was going to Texas A&M, which would have been the logical choice considering my new respect for something called "studying", and the fact that she was basically one of my only friends. We still talked, on the phone, every other week, like clockwork, which always reminded me of my purgatory from Isla.

Will and Kristen fully embraced fate, and their full-on attraction toward each other, selecting NYU, and sealing their history once and for all. Don't ask me how Will got in there, but I think his step-dad being some rich oil tycoon had something to do with it.

Winter break arrived, Christmas holidays, setting up the stupid tree, going here and there with family that I'd rather not be around, getting insignificant presents that I never wanted, and trying to fake happiness so that I didn't get sent to one of my mother's shrinks. My reprieve with Sara was just around the corner.

I only had another week left before the final semester of school would begin, and I was leaving the next morning for my Disney World reunification.

"Kyle?" My mother came into my bedroom, that night.

"Huh?"

"Can you take your sister with you tomorrow?"

"No."

"Kyle!" She was shocked, because normally I was pretty submissive.

"I'm not doing it."

"Why not?" Her eyes were wide in disbelief.

"Because she's not coming."

"Kyle...let's talk about,"

"No," I interrupted.

"Hear me out."

"I ain't doing it." I folded my arms, while I leaned back against the headboard of my bed.

"Kyle, is this girl...your little girlfriend from the Keys last summer?"

"No."

"Come on...I can tell, it's okay." She sat down on the side of the bed.

"She's a friend, and, yes, she is a girl, and yes I met her in the Keys, and yes she is from last summer. But, no, she is not my girlfriend."

"Hmm." She looked down.

"Sorry, Mom, I'm just not bringing anyone."

She paused for a moment, "Okay, Kyle." She got up from the bed, and left the room.

The next day, I made the short drive to "The Magic Kingdom". Meeting up with Sara, early, in front of the train station at Main Street, and saying "hi" to her teammates.

"Okay...see ya'll later!" Sara took hold of my hand, and guided me away from the others. I had forgotten how pretty she was, but holding her hand felt like I was cheating on someone else.

Had it not been for my self-induced torture, the morning would have been a lot more fun. It was just the two of us, which was really nice, she being the most likely candidate for my best friend in the entire world. She made me laugh, somewhat distracting me from other thoughts, and reminding me of last summer before fate and biochemistry collided me into Isla.

We rode some rides, ate, and drank way too much Mountain Dew, causing some sort of sugar and caffeine induced intoxication. She had turned eighteen, and that coupled with her genuine affection, surely made it look like we were a recently married couple enjoying our honeymoon. However, it was more saccharine than sweet.

There was no doubt that it was fun, and the potential was most certainly there where I could have set inertia in motion landing me firmly at Texas A&M that fall. But, the voodoo that was cast upon me would never release its grip. It, most likely, would have ended soon after it started, leaving a saddened and confused Sara in its wake.

I tried to enjoy the moment. The afternoon marched on, and the winter sun was making its final contribution to the orange sky, as we neared the last section of the park.

We rode Space Mountain, raced the cars together, raced them again and again, ran over to 20,000 Leagues Under the Sea, then back to Space Mountain for the second time. The lines were very short, which added to the relative coolness factor, and our desire for an early dinner.

A hamburger each later, we rode a couple more rides in Tomorrow Land, me silently wishing for a "Back Last Summer Land." We had one attraction left to ride.

"Oh…" Sara pulled a thick envelope out of her pocket. "Here, let's sit down, over there." She pointed toward some benches near a section that was under renovation.

She scooted closer, and handed me a stack of photographs.

"Remember that one?" She laughed at a picture of Will with a shocked look on his face, after Kristen had whispered something in his ear.

"Oh, and this one!" The four of us standing by the cafeteria. We filed through a few more.

"This one is my favorite." It was of her and me sitting on the edge of a sailboat, after getting back from the bay one afternoon. We looked through a few more, before only one remained.

"I don't really remember…I guess you took this one," she added. It was a photo of her, Kristen and Will standing in front of the docks. She looked at it closer, as did I.

"This was the last one on the roll." She strained, trying to recall. The three of them, with the sun above and off to the left, the docks in the background, and a slightly blurred image of Isla off in the distance, to the right. My chest grew tight while I stared for another second.

"Well, these are for you!" She put them back into the envelope and handed them over; me securely placing them into my right front pocket.

We entered the "Dream Flight" ride, and got in line. It was weird, in a freaky sort of way, the lobby depicting a loose interpretation of an airport terminal, which had the obvious result of quieting my laughter, and abolishing my smile.

The line was a little longer than the other rides had been, most likely due to guests trying to get in the last ride of the evening. Sara, leaning against one of the rails, recognized something was different, now, from the rest of the day.

"What's up?" She smiled.

"Huh?" I turned toward her.

"I dunno, it's just, you look a little sad, or something."

"Oh...no it's not...I'm fine, really." I cracked a brief grin. We didn't say anything for a few seconds.

"Hey, Kyle?" She swept her dirty blonde hair from her eyes.

"Yeah?"

"You know...I mean, if you want..." She paused. "You could come to school with me in the fall." She pleasantly blinked, awaiting my response.

"Oh. Uh, I...man." I stared back, not wanting to be put on the spot.

"Well, I guess, I mean, you could...I know you'd get in."

"Yeah."

"We'd have lots of fun." She was probably right, I guess.

"I know." I looked down, then back up at her pretty blue-green eyes.

"Kyle?" It was happening.

"Huh?" I took a deep breath, while she stayed silent for a couple of seconds.

"I don't know what to..." she continued, "you know...say."

"About what?"

"You."

"Oh."

"I'm sorry, Kyle." She reached out and touched the back of my hand.

"I really am."

"For…" I was going to ask what she was talking about, but it was pointless.

"I know, Kyle."

"About what."

"Her." I swallowed.

"Oh."

"It's okay." She leaned in closer.

"No."

"It's gonna be okay."

"No, it's not."

"Trust me."

"No."

"Please trust me." She positioned her feet to where they were touching mine.

"I can't…" My eyes were starting to water.

"You have to believe me, Kyle." There was a brief pause.

"I can't handle it."

"I know. You were, her…only friend in the world." She wrapped her arms around me, firmly hugging.

We stood there, for a couple more seconds before the line picked up its pace, and we neared the boarding section. I didn't say anything, nor did she.

We carefully progressed onto the moving rubber floor, and stepped into our plastic shell, taking us away into the dark tunnel. She reached her arm around me, placing her head on my shoulder.

We silently passed through the ride, displaying distant port-of-calls, and happy tourists arriving, shopping and sightseeing. Sara was wonderful, but I was totally incapable of re-establishing any prior thoughts I had about her from the early summer. She kept her head firmly planted on my shoulder, probably sensing our inevitable and most likely permanent, separation in little over an hour.

The ride was finished, and we climbed out of the car on to the moving walkway, propelling us along toward the amber lights of the terminal lobby. As we stepped off the rubber floor, and on to the carpet, she pulled me aside into a dark corner.

"Kyle."

"Yeah."

"It's over." She softly shook her head.

"No." I lightly shook my head.

"She's gone."

"No, she can't…"

"She's gone."

"No." I sank to the floor, leaning against the grey, carpeted wall, and stared at the floor in front of me. Sara knelt down next to me, her hand on my shoulder.

"I'm sorry, Kyle," she gently whispered.

"I can't live without her." I buried my head into my crossed forearms so that she wouldn't see the tears swelling up in my eyes.

"I know."

"I can't."

"It'll get better."

"No it won't." My voice was practically inaudible.

"Trust me."

"It won't."

"I know it will." She fumbled with her father's ring, hanging on the necklace.

"No."

She sat with me, for some time, us being miraculously left alone, most likely because we were basically out of view, and around a dark corner.

We eventually left the terminal, Tomorrow Land, and rallied back at the front of the park where we had met many hours before.

We didn't say much, as the rest of her friends gathered. She leaned in for one last hug. "See ya around," she whispered, before letting go.

Chapter Thirty-Three

As the spring semester started, and after no real deliberation, I had picked my school, and a month and a half later, I was accepted. It wasn't a far drive, and I needed to rent an apartment nearby because we couldn't have pets in the dorms, but the University of Miami was as close as I could get to all the memories that really mattered.

That summer, I went back down to the Keys, a counselor this time. The weather was beautiful, clear, sunny and hot. The DC-3s continued their patrol, the sponge war's waged on, and room number three was now occupied by someone else, despite my insistent and repeated requests for swapping.

I hung out mostly with Cindy, who turned out to be pretty cool, with nothing materializing, entirely because of me. Jill and Anthony were a total item now; he and I becoming good friends. It was my new home, sort of.

The fleeting memories of last summer were fading; being replaced by new ones of the three months I had spent there.

Time passed by, I turned nineteen, and college started that fall. It had been well over a year, but she still visited while I dreamed, just enough to remind me that she still had my soul deeply tucked into her pocket next to the glossy shell. I had picked my major, and never reconsidered. Astronomy…it was the only thing that made sense. At least the stars above us were the same, wherever she was.

I tried to remember where she had told me she saw the flyer on the bulletin board, leading her to the Keys, but I soon realized that there were so many hallways and bulletin boards that I couldn't even begin to guess. I took some comfort in knowing that I was at a college where she had wandered some of the halls, and in a city where she had once lived. It wasn't a lot of comfort, but there was nowhere else I felt like I really belonged, as far as college went.

Occasionally, I would try to remember way back to the conversation I had with my mother early that August morning, and what transpired in that salon many years ago. Somehow, these feelings of emotional isolation from…well, the feelings were strangely familiar. I quickly attempted to dispatch the analysis from my brain, so that I could maybe feel a little less completely defeated, but I was starting to think that the ear infection might have been something entirely different.

Ernie, from who knows what, developed something the veterinarian called renal insufficiency. I didn't really understand too much about it, other than it was something with his little kidneys and he needed to get I.V. fluids every week, or so, and sadly it grew worse and worse as the months progressed. It sucked because, my grades, and Ernie, were all I had. That, and the air mattress I dreamed on every night…having to refill the air every other morning. I heard from Sara less and less, she had stopped writing, and we only talked a couple of times a year.

Chapter Thirty-Four

I was twenty, and another school year was well underway. I still thought about her, hoped, wished, and begged as the only image that was left of her in my head, was of the blurred, faded photo that I carried around, carefully folded in my wallet.

Terry, previously tracking down my new phone number, ultimately left me alone. He probably figured that I really didn't know anything about her father and if I had any inclination of his location I would have already told him. His last phone call left me a little disturbed, and he reminded me that if I only told him that fucking guy's whereabouts, he would make it worth my while, whatever the hell that was supposed to mean.

Annoyingly, I would often wake up, in the middle of the night, no matter how tired I was. Sometimes it was just a dream that woke me, or poor sickly Ernie attempting to get comfortable, but mostly it was my subconscious reminding me that I was going to be alone for the rest of my life, no matter who was around. Often struggling to fall back asleep, the only successful method being to concentrate on Isla's room and lying next to her on the narrow bed, back in room three.

I had no meaningful relationships. All quickly ending before any got started as a direct result of my depression, and the inevitable comparison. Sadly, she was only occasionally occupying my dreams now; the only one remaining was a faint feeling of us sitting alone together on the beach, staring out at the distant storm.

Months passed, and the spring semester was now drawing to an end, with finals fast approaching. People always said that time healed wounds, but this case was different. It actually grew worse; the more time went by. At least in the beginning, the images of her soft skin, beautiful coconut scented hair, hypnotic eyes, cosmic beauty and wonderful mind were still fresh in my conscience and the odds of being reunited were greater. But now, the harder I tried to hold on, the more blurred the images became, and the more creased the photo of her befell. It was going on three years now, and I still prayed every night that she would return my soul.

During the middle of April, things took an even deeper turn south. Time for Ernie had finally elapsed, and after extensive protest, the veterinarian finally convinced me to put sweet Ernie to sleep. Just when I thought that life had thrown me all the curve balls it could, it decided to whack me square between the eyes.

It was a shitty day, driving Ernie to the vet, giving me flashbacks of the time I picked him up and drove him back from the Keys. I contemplated turning around, and heading back to my apartment many, many times, but there was nothing that anyone could do anymore for his little kidneys.

Arriving at the veterinarian office, and being escorted into an exam room by one of the technicians was complete torture.

"I'm really sorry about Ernie," she said, attempting to console.

"You have no idea."

I gently pet and groomed Ernie for a few minutes, while I waited for the veterinarian to come render the final blow to whatever I still had connecting me to Isla, not to mention taking away my only real pal with whom I shared many sad and lonely nights.

As I softly held Ernie, the doctor first injected him with a powerful sedative, remarking, "he won't feel a thing, he's just going to fall asleep. Then, and only then, will I give the other injection."

I picked up Ernie and sat down in the chair in the corner of the exam room, while the doctor left to allow enough time for Ernie to fall deeply asleep. I leaned back in the chair and laid him on my chest and stomach, holding him tight, but not so much where I made his last few moments uncomfortable.

His little green eyes lost their alertness, and his eyelids became heavy. His breathing calmed, and he continued to stare up into my eyes. He knew that he was leaving me, all alone, and it was like he was telling me that he was sorry.

As he drifted deeper toward unconsciousness, I made sure I told him one final thing.

"I'm gonna miss you Ernie, and I'm really sorry. Tell my dad I'm sorry we never got to go on that trip," I paused and took a deep breath. "And *please*, if you ever see her, tell Isla that I love her." My eyes blurred, probably like his did.

He was completely asleep, and his body was like a limp stuffed animal. It took every ounce of my sanity to stay focused and not mentally break down, and I really only could hold on for a few more minutes, which would hopefully be just long enough for me to make it outside, and into my car.

The doctor reentered, and without saying a word, injected Ernie with the life-stealing fluid, while he lay on my chest. The doctor stood back up, patted me on the shoulder and left the room.

Ernie's breathing slowly halted, and I could hear the last exhale he would ever make coming from his little wet nose. It was over. I buried my head into his, and began to cry.

"I'm sorry, Ernie."

I thought I was being quiet, muffled by my nose deep in Ernie's lifeless orange, striped fur, but again, I was wrong. The technician re-entered the room, saying again that she was sorry and they'd be in touch regarding the bill and his little body, then gently scooped Ernie up, leaving me all alone.

I stared at the linoleum floor for a few moments, in complete shock and defeat, while covering my nose and mouth with both of my hands, again, in an attempt to mask my deep sobs.

"Ernie." I mumbled, as I stood up, opened the door and walked down the hall, and exited the office.

Chapter Thirty-Five

One evening, the phone rang as I was staring out of my apartment's small window at an approaching storm.

"Hello?"

"Kyle?" A familiar voice, excited on the other end.

"Hey, Will!"

"What's up man?" I hadn't talked to him in over 6 months.

"Not much."

"Well, a little birdy told me that it was your birthday!" It was May first, and I was twenty-one.

"Yeah? Who?"

"You're little blonde friend."

"Sara?"

"Yup!"

"I talked to her an hour ago!" I responded, laughing.

"I know, she called to remind me."

"You suck!"

"I know, but I'm a dude, and we're not supposed to remember that shit." He laughed. "Well…what's going on Kyle?"

"Just school, you know."

"Yeah…me too."

"How's that going for you?"

"School sucks, but Kristen…well, you know."

"No? What?"

"Ah…so, Sara didn't tell you?"

"No? Tell me what?"

"I asked her to marry me." I was silent for a second.

"You're shitting me!"

"Nope!"

"What did she say?"

"Fuck you, Kyle!" We both chuckled. "What the hell do you think she said?"

"Congratulations, stud muffin."

"Thanks bro...don't worry you'll get an invite, and it won't be for a while."

"What...I mean, how did you, you know, ask?"

"Yeah...check this out," he was fired up, "so she had somehow convinced the manager of the lingerie store where she works part time..."

"Okay?"

"Well, basically she had me come over, after the store was closed..."

"Yeah?"

"And, was my little sexy model the whole night." He laughed.

"Oh my god...she's freaking crazy!"

"Yeah...so, early the next morning, I mean, we didn't sleep so..." he paused, "we were at some little coffee shop down near Central Park, really tired, and still horny."

"Okay...you can spare me the details." I laughed.

"Yeah right! Anyway, I popped the question right there."

"Man, that's really awesome."

"Yeah...she's really cool." We didn't speak for a couple of seconds.

"So...how are things?" he calmly asked.

"Good...real good."

"Really?"

I paused for a second. "Yeah." My voice lowered.

"Oh." Another silent pause, "well, that's good."

"Yeah." I pulled the handset away from my face, and wiped my nose.

"Kyle?" I couldn't respond.

"Hey, Kyle?"

"Huh?" My voice trembled, a little.

"What's wrong man?"

"I dunno." I sighed.

"It's okay, Kyle."

I took a deep breath. "No Will. This fucking sucks."

He paused. "I know man."

"God damn it, Will. I can't deal with this shit." I wiped my nose again, with my sleeve. He was quiet.

"I can't."

"Kyle."

"I just can't deal with this."

"Kyle."

"No, Will! Listen man! I cannot deal with this shit anymore." I swallowed. "I'm fucking done."

"Come on Kyle…please?" I couldn't respond, "Kyle?" Seconds passed.

"Kyle?" I didn't say anything.

"Kyle?" I dropped my head to the little desk next to the narrow window, the handset resting on its side.

"Kyle!" His voice shouted through the earpiece, "I'm coming down there!"

"I'm fucking coming down there! We'll deal with this together!"

"Come on, Kyle. Come on! I'll be there…I'm getting on the first plane tomorrow morning."

"No." I spoke toward the mouthpiece, "Don't come."

"Kyle?"

"Don't come, Will." I leaned my head in closer.

"I'm sorry Kyle. I really am."

"I know," I whispered. We didn't talk for well over twenty seconds, or so.

"Kyle?"

"Yeah."

"Please call me…you know…if you need something."

"Okay."

"Please, don't…I mean, just call me. Call me tomorrow."

"Okay."

"Promise, okay?" He paused. "Take it easy, Kyle."

"Yeah."

"Good bye, buddy." I couldn't answer, and a second later, he hung up the phone.

I stared again out of the window for well over an hour, wiping my nose over and over again. But, it was getting late, and I needed to get to the library to check out some books for a research paper that had to be done by the end of the semester.

Although practically completed, I was getting to be an expert at diverting my obsessiveness toward class, grades and research papers. I walked the mile or so, toward the larger buildings of campus, as it started to rain.

I was jogging, dodging puddles and ducking under awnings and buildings' ledges, before finally making my way into the campus library. It was a Saturday night, and the library closed in a couple of hours, at midnight.

It was practically vacant, not surprising in that parties, dates, pizza and movies were well underway. I cornered around pillars, bookshelves, desks, and ultimately collected the two books I needed, one being some advanced telescopic imagery of distant galaxies, nebulae and stars.

I found a quiet corner table, next to a large picture window and glass door, which probably hadn't been opened in years, where the rain was now firmly pelting. I slowly opened the astronomy book, and placed some blank paper on top of the other book off to the side.

A couple of hours passed, as the rain continued. I stopped for a moment, got up and stretched. It was getting late, and I was kind of groggy, but really wanted to completely finish the last bit of research, so that I could finally be done writing it tomorrow. I sat back down and set the alarm, on the watch Terry had given me, for 11:35pm, which would give me just enough time to replace the two books, hit the restroom, and exit the library.

I read on for a little while longer, as I grew more and more drowsy. I felt my head drooping toward the table surface, and the book, and quickly snapped it back upright. I checked my watch, 11:20.

My head hit the open astronomy book, landing on the side of my face. The twilight of my consciousness faded, drifting me deeper and deeper away into steady breathing and flickering eyelids.

The light from the table lamp was fading into darkness. I took one last deep breath, before an image of Isla with her arms and hands raised, twisting them together in some sort of ancient ritual reinforcing and wrapping her fingers deeper around my conscience, appearing as I transitioned deeper toward sleep. The clouds hovering over the path in front of her, cast aside by the spell she directed with her hands, skyward.

She was walking toward something that I had built over and over again in my mind thousands of times, for the past few years, so that she would have a warm, dry place to sleep. I had painfully, mentally, assembled the giant structure stone by stone, slab by slab, brick by brick, painting by painting; hand blown every piece of glass, carved out every piece of ivory, sculpted every artifact, and welded every flake of gold. It was her palace, on the banks of the Yamura River there in India, where she was finally entering.

The images faded to us walking through the women's restroom in the airline club, where she tightly held my hand, guiding me back to the shower stall. As perfectly as before, we passed by the flickering lone light, and on to the furthest stall door to the right. She smoothly opened the door, pulling me into the individual changing area, while I dropped my bag at the door she latched it behind us. She gently placed her backpack on top of my duffel bag.

She pushed the curtain to the side, and reached in and turned on the shower.

"Kyle?" She turns around.

"Yeah?"

"This is my first time." This isn't happening, I'm dreaming.

"Isla?"

"Kyle?" She pulls back, not hearing me.

"I'm really scared, Isla."

"You are mine."

"No, please." Tears forming in my eyes.

"This means more than it would to others."

"I know, Isla…please don't." Again, she can't hear me.

"It will only be us, forever. Okay?"

"Wait!"

"No one else will ever matter again. Do you understand?"

"Yes, but please! Please don't."

"There can be no one else, *ever*," she continues, not diverting.

I try to settle my breathing, she's not able to hear a word I'm saying.

"Once this happens."

"Please, no. I can't do this; you can't do this! No one else matters to me! I'm all alone now."

"Our thoughts will never leave orbit from each other."

"No, you can't! Since the night I left, not a day has passed that I haven't suffered! I know now…I can't live without you…I won't go on. You can't do this to me." My voice now trembling.

"You can never go back."

I briefly pause. "God damn it! I was wrong! I can't handle the pain…I can't go through life anymore without you!"

"Are you really sure?" she whispers, her eyes starting to narrow, again, not hearing my shouts.

"I am so in love with you! Do you understand? You have to hear me!"

"You have to be absolutely sure." Her eyes calmly stare, glossy with tears.

"I didn't know it was gonna be like this!" My voice completely shaken.

"It's happening, Kyle."

"I love you, Isla…Can you hear me!"

"It's happening."

"*I love you!*"

"Our souls are connecting." She sniffles one last time, and closes her eyes, the steam now filling the air.

A loud annoying beeping fills the air. It's my watch. I open my eyes, and sit up, now looking down, 11:35pm. I collect my books, and paper with the sketches of arrows pointing at hearts, and stand up.

I take one last look at the table where I was just sitting, a few drops of my own tears the only thing left, and I stared for what seemed like almost half an hour, completely still yet unfortunately completely awake. I then turn around, walking away.

A stiff breeze roars from behind, knocking the paper out of my hand, scattering them about. I pause for a second, in absolute defeat, and lean down to retrieve them.

I hear an old, familiar, double monotone beep of a watch marking the top of the hour. I stand up, turn around and drop the astronomy and ancient history of India books to the ground. I couldn't move.

"Kyle." She walks toward me, soaking wet, me having no ability to speak.

"I found you."

She walks closer, across the scattered papers. From her old white sneakers, with broken laces, to her smooth tan legs, to her ripped fingernails and wrist watch, to the green backpack which contains the tattered purple towel, up to her beautifully perfect mouth and lips, her little scar, nose, hypnotic eyes, and all the way to her dark brown hair; the wind blowing the scent of coconuts into my nose.

"Please." My voice shakes.

"I won't leave you." She moves closer.

"You can't."

"I can't."

"I love you, Kyle. With every part of my soul."

She approaches, and is now standing inches away. She grasps onto my hands, and pulls herself in closer. She rises up on her toes, and closes her eyes as she leans into me, moving her hands up to my face. One last time, she opens her eyes, to check her aim, and softly touches her lips to mine, diving the rest of her body into me, and welding our souls back together…and this time its forever.

We stood there in complete euphoria, inseparably connected until reminded that the library was closing. Releasing, but she still firmly hanging on my shoulder, and with my arm around her waist, we slowly exited the library.

I couldn't believe where I was. I really couldn't believe any of my senses, and it was going to take some time for me to get used to the fact that she was here. But it was true, and I was touching her, hearing her breathe, and smelling the soft scent of coconuts.

The rain had stopped and the clouds gave way to the dark open sky, but we didn't stop holding each other.

"How did you…" I asked.

"I am so sorry. I tried to call you, I never got any notes from you. I was sad, I tried to call you but could never get through. I tried over and over again." She looked down, at our hands grasped together. It obviously upset her.

"I tried too. I kept getting all my letters returned." I said, while her lower lip began to quiver in sadness, recalling the almost three years which we were separated.

"How did you find me?" I started to smile, and so did she.

"Oh. Terry." She softly replied in the wonderful accent that I longed to hear again.

"Really?"

"He asked me where my father was every six months. And I did not know," she paused. "But one day I heard from my father. He called because he was sick in hospital. He wanted me to come see him."

"Did you?"

"No. But I had Terry's phone number, and said that I would tell him on one con-dition."

"I think I know," I smiled, and so did she.

"Yes. I told him I needed to know where *you* were. At first he said he did not know, but I told him that I knew he was lying."

"How did you know that?"

"I did not know, I, uh...bluffed him."

We walked on, toward the apartment; me feeling compelled to inform her about Ernie, but not wanting to ruin the perfect setting.

"Isla?"

"Yes?" She grinned.

"Um, Ernie, he..."

"Yes?" She stopped and faced me.

"He was very sick, and um..."

"It is okay."

"I had to put him to sleep." I looked down at her hands, which were firmly holding mine. She took a few moments to process the situation that I threw at her.

"It is okay, Kyle." She broke a slight, compassionate smile so that I knew she didn't hold me somehow responsible.

"I'm sorry."

"It is okay, I know that you were a good person to him." She leaned into me, and gave me a warm, wonderful hug.

"Yeah. But, I wanted to take care of him, for you."

"You did. He is in a good place."

We just stared at each other. Her eyes shifted back and forth, slowly looking at each of my eyes. Suddenly, a huge smile grew on her face.

"Kyle?"

"Huh?"

"There is a supernova tonight." She nodded her head, excited.

"Really? I didn't hear anything about that?" I was excited too at the prospect that something so rare could be happening tonight, of all nights. However, I normally paid close attention to that sort of thing, but never heard a thing regarding it.

"Yes. It is happening right now, really far away." She happily said, and slowly turned around, pointing up and off toward the northwest.

"We will not see it for a while," she continued, "but that is okay."

She turned back around, and firmly grabbed me between her arms, burying her head deep into my neck and chest, and happily exhaled. From that night forward, we never spent another apart.

About the Author

Christopher Chapman is a visual writer. When you read his work, you will feel like you are there, inside the story. You will experience the sights and sounds, and all the feelings of a moment. The conversations are dynamic, real, and within a few pages, you will truly begin to know the characters.

Christopher Chapman is a licensed attorney in Florida, where he has lived on and off his entire life. He fondly writes of the quirkier, and less known parts of the state, having the reader feel like a local when they dive into his work. He desires the reader to "feel" the humidity of the tropical air, and visit with characters not often met in fiction.

Be on the lookout for upcoming books from Christopher Chapman, including *Thunderbird*, which is a story about a military security contractor who falls in love with a middle-eastern woman who he was hired to protect.